Merely W9-AYI-528

Colin McElreath, Viscount Grantham, has sold his soul to the devil—a devil of an irate English father. For cash. Colin is about to become a very wealthy man—a very wealthy *married* man . . .

The powerful Baron Davies urgently requires a respectable husband for Gillian, his disgraced daughter, and he sees Colin as the perfect candidate. When Colin balks, Davies isn't above using his daughter's large dowry as an incentive—or applying a bit of blackmail. He threatens to expose the undercover work the Free Fellows do for the government, and as a charter member of the Free Fellows League, Colin has sworn to protect the League at all cost. Also someone has been masquerading as Colin, which indirectly landed Gillian in her predicament, so Colin is faced with no choice.

He doesn't know whether to laugh or to cry at the irony. After a lifetime of avoiding society misses, he is about to marry one.

Miss Gillian Davies is about to become a blushing bride.

And Colin McElreath is merely the groom . . .

"Rebecca Hagan Lee taps into every woman's fantasy."
—Christina Dodd

Don't miss her first novel of the Free Fellows League

Barely a Bride

or her other delightful novels . . .

The Marquess of Templeston's Heirs Trilogy

Once a Mistress
Ever a Princess
Always a Lady

Turn the page for more acclaim for Rebecca Hagan Lee . . .

Barely a Bride

"Magical."
—Huntress Reviews

"Combines sexual tension with deep angst . . . Superb."
—Midwest Book Reviews

PRAISE FOR
THE MARQUESS OF TEMPLESTON'S HEIRS TRILOGY

Once a Mistress

"Sparkling romance and passion that sizzles . . . Lee taps into every woman's fantasy."
—New York Times bestselling author Christina Dodd

"An emotional, sensual tale . . . *Once A Mistress* is one book you want to take off of the shelf quickly before they are all gone."
—Romance Reviews Today

Ever a Princess

"The battle of wits between a princess in disguise and a self-made American produces some spirited and entertaining results in Lee's latest historical, the second in her series involving the heirs of George Ramsey, and a delectable treat for those who enjoy witty historicals served up with a generous measure of danger."
—Booklist

Always a Lady

"The third in Lee's Marquess of Templeston's Heirs series is a charmingly clever romance deftly seasoned with wit and graced with some delightfully unforgettable characters."
—Booklist

"An engaging historical romance starring two charmingly delightful lead protagonists . . . an enchanting early Victorian love story."
—Midwest Book Review

Merely the Groom

Rebecca Hagan Lee

B

BERKLEY SENSATION, NEW YORK

MERELY THE GROOM

A Berkley Sensation Book / published by arrangement with the author

PRINTING HISTORY
Berkley Sensation edition / April 2004

Copyright © 2004 by Rebecca Hagan Lee.
Excerpt from *Hardly a Husband* copyright © 2004 by Rebecca Hagan Lee.
Cover design by Lesley Worrell.
Cover art by Leslie Peck.

ISBN: 0-425-19525-2

BERKLEY SENSATION™
Berkley Sensation Books are published by The Berkley Publishing Group,
a division of Penguin Group (USA) Inc.,
375 Hudson Street, New York, New York 10014.
BERKLEY SENSATION and the "B" design
are trademarks belonging to Penguin Group (USA) Inc.

PRINTED IN THE UNITED STATES OF AMERICA

10 9 8 7 6 5 4 3 2 1

It's always nice to know that somewhere far away, there are people who think of you and wish you well. It's especially nice when the people who want the best for you are family as well as friends. I know that in faraway Georgetown, Texas, two very special friends and family members want the best for me. This book is dedicated to my Texas connections: my cousin, Cheryl Lee Wilkinson, and her father, my uncle, Lamar Lee. With love and gratitude for reading every book and letting me know when I've done a good job, and for always being my cheerleaders extraordinaire.

Prologue

> *"If we are marked to die, we are enough*
> *To do our country loss; and if to live,*
> *The fewer men, the greater share of honor."*
> —WILLIAM SHAKESPEARE, 1564–1616
>
> KING HENRY V

DERBYSHIRE, ENGLAND, 1793
The Knightsguild School for Gentlemen

"Don't look down," Jarrod Shepherdston, twenty-second Earl of Westmore, ordered as he and Griffin Abernathy, seventeenth Viscount Abernathy, gave Colin McElreath, twenty-seventh Viscount Grantham, a leg up onto the outer wall of the bell tower that stood watch over the quadrangle in the center of the Knightsguild property. "There's nothing to fear. Just keep your mind on what you're doing and you'll be fine."

"And whatever you do, Colin, don't look down." Griffin gave Colin one last boost up the wall, then stepped away and stood shoulder to shoulder with Jarrod to watch as their fellow Free Fellow began the Herculean task of overcoming his fear of heights by climbing the Knightsguild bell tower.

Don't look down. There's nothing to fear. Just keep your mind on what you're doing and you'll be fine.

Colin pressed his face against the moss growing between the crevices in the mortar in the old stone wall, and reached up, feeling for a handhold as he inched his way up the tower. He clenched his teeth, jammed the toe of his boot into a crevice, and slowly crept skyward.

Don't look down.

Easy for them to say. Jarrod and Griffin had their feet firmly planted on English soil. They weren't climbing the outside of a bell tower in the middle of the night in order to conquer their aversion to heights. But then his cohorts, the two other Free Fellows, didn't fear a bit of altitude. They were destined to become England and Scotland's greatest heroes, and heroes were above such foibles.

And he would be, too. After tonight. Colin took a deep breath, closed his eyes, and fought the fear. It was well after midnight, but it wasn't completely dark. The pale sliver of moonlight was enough to illuminate his way. Colin didn't know whether that made the journey easier or harder. It was a long way to the quadrangle below.

Don't look down.

Grunting with the effort, Colin felt for the next handhold. He gripped the stone with his hands and planted his right foot into a foothold, pulling with his arms while pushing with his feet, propelling himself forward toward his goal. Left hand, right foot. Right hand, left foot. Pulling and pushing. Pushing and pulling in rhythm as he moved higher and higher. Until the bit of mortar providing a foothold in the stone beneath his right foot tumbled to the quadrangle.

Colin tightened his grip, clinging to the wall, fighting the terror threatening to overtake him. Perspiration beaded his upper lip and his heart pounded against his chest as he scrambled to regain his foothold and keep from falling.

"Thunderation!" Griffin swore, ducking as bits of stone and mortar rained down on the courtyard. "He missed a foothold. He's slipping."

Jarrod looked up, shielding his eyes with his hand as he squinted into the night sky, mentally gauging Colin's progress. "He's hit that tricky bit. But he's made it halfway and I'll wager he hasn't wasted a single thought on anything except reaching the top of the tower," he replied with the greater wisdom of his advanced age of ten years and six months. "He'll be all right."

"If the fall doesn't kill him," Griffin replied.

"I don't think he's far enough off the ground for the fall to kill him," Jarrod said. "The most he'll do is break an arm or a leg. And injure his stubborn Scots pride."

"Then he'll make it," Griff predicted. "He knows we're watching, and he's far too proud to allow us to see him fail."

Jarrod nodded. "Especially since his disappointment over Esme Kelverton is the reason for all of this."

Jarrod was right. The climbing of the Knightsguild bell tower had become a graduation rite of passage in recent years—like scaling the bridges while punting down the river Cam was one of the old and venerable ways of celebrating graduation from Cambridge, but graduation from Knightsguild was two years away and Colin wasn't climbing it in celebration. He was climbing it to test his mettle. To prove that Lord Kelverton had made a huge mistake in doubting his worthiness as a future bridegroom for his daughter.

"Colin wasn't to blame. He couldn't help the fact that Esme Kelverton's father broke Colin and Esme's marriage contract because Lord McElreath can't gamble worth spit." Griffin shrugged his shoulders.

"That's true," Jarrod said. "But you thought of it because of *him*." He nodded toward Colin. "Because he went and got his hopes dashed and his heart trampled by a *girl*."

"The League was my idea, but we all want to be heroes. We all embraced the idea and we all agreed to it." Griffin stared at Jarrod. "Besides, I thought it would take his mind off his problems. And a broken heart is as good a reason to form a secret League as any."

"That's true." Jarrod nodded his head. "And suggesting

we perform feats of bravery and daring seemed a perfectly acceptable way to prove our worthiness to be Free Fellows." He turned to Griffin. "But I didn't expect Colin would choose to scale the bell tower so soon."

"Why not?" Griffin retorted. "Tall places are the things he fears most."

Everyone knew true heroes were born to accomplish acts of extraordinary courage and bravery and climbing the bell tower was the perfect way to start. It was a feat only the most athletic and determined boys could accomplish. Jarrod and Griffin had done it twice. On two consecutive nights. In complete secrecy. Their goal hadn't been to prove their athletic prowess or test their mettle, but to help Colin overcome his fear and forget his heartbreak over his broken betrothal.

After picking the lock on the outer door of the structure, and reaching the bell tower by way of the interior stairs, Jarrod and Griffin had used ropes to lower themselves down the outer wall in order to painstakingly craft the dozen or so additional hand and foot holds needed to make the climb easier for Colin. Jarrod and Griffin had gladly forfeited two nights of sleep, and risked discovery and a public caning in order to come to the aid of their compatriot.

Now, all they could do was stand below and keep watch as Colin struggled to prove himself the hero they knew him to be.

High above them, Colin squeezed his eyes shut, gritted his teeth, ignored the bile rising in his throat, and reached for a foothold. Keeping his gaze focused on his goal, Colin toed the moss-covered stone until he found a crack in the wall. He wedged the toe of his boot into the crevice and pushed toward the top.

Three more feet or so and he'd make it. Colin inhaled deeply, then slowly expelled the breath and took another. *Don't think about it. Don't look down. Breathe.* Push. Pull. Climb until there was nothing else to climb.

Colin swallowed his bile once again and stared into the opening of the bell tower. A rush of satisfaction raced through him. He'd done it! He'd climbed the tower! And survived!

He had conquered his fear and proved himself worthy of the honor of being a founding member of the secret league he and Griffin and Jarrod had founded. Colin had always known he had what it took to be a true hero despite the fact that he'd had a foolish fear of tall places and a father with a penchant for gambling away his inheritance.

He didn't have the money Jarrod and Griffin had or the pure English bloodlines, but he had an ancient and honorable title and the blood of Scottish kings flowing through his veins. And Colin was loyal and true. He would never fail or betray his friends or cause them to doubt his devotion. Just as he would never have failed Esme or given her reason to doubt his fidelity or his worth.

Esme. Colin sighed. Esme Kelverton was the impetus behind the Free Fellows League. If Lord Kelverton hadn't broken the betrothal agreement between Colin and Esme, there wouldn't be a Free Fellows Charter or League. And Colin wouldn't have felt compelled to prove his worth to his schoolmates by climbing the bell tower and conquering his fear.

The business they were about was serious, and their dreams of becoming England's greatest heroes were not to be taken lightly. Heroism required dedication—dedication to honor and to one's country—and dedication required sacrifice. The heroes they read about and dreamed of becoming were dashing figures willing to forgo the comforts of family and home, of wives and of children, in order to fulfill their destinies. True heroes remained free of encumbrances in order to make the ultimate sacrifice. Griffin, Colin, and Jarrod prepared to do likewise.

There would be no more long, tearful nights filled with empty longing for the familiar comforts of home and hearth. No more waiting in vain for letters from loved ones. No more tender hearts thoughtlessly trampled by ignorant females who looked down their noses at lesser titles and dwindling fortunes. Females whose fathers blamed a son for his father's shortcomings and who thought more of the title than of the boy.

Colin exhaled, remembering his emotional exchange with his two compatriots the day he had learned his future father-in-law had broken the betrothal agreement between Colin and his daughter. The day Jarrod had discovered Colin sniveling like a baby and commented upon it. Moments later, Colin had punched Jarrod in the nose. Jarrod had retaliated by blackening Colin's eye, and Griffin had gotten a split lip when he attempted to separate the two of them.

As a result, the three boys had been sent to Norworthy. They had been punished for brawling and had received a caning before the whole assembly. A friendship forged in blood and pain began that day, and later that night, the Free Fellows League was born.

"I canna blame Sir Preston," Colin had confided in a Scots burr thick with emotion when the three of them had slipped out of their dormitories and headed to the kitchens to draw up the rules of the Free Fellows League, "for wanting the best for his daughter. And there's no doubt that with my father's ill fortune at the card tables, my prospects have dimmed. The only thing I'll inherit is a title and a mountain of debts." He took a deep breath and fought to keep from crying. "But I canna help but feel bad about Esme. We've been betrothed from the cradle. I thought she cared more about me than about my prospects."

Jarrod had let out a contemptuous snort. "You do better to learn it now. Nobody cares about *us*. We're eldest sons. We're supposed to stay alive because as long as we're breathing the family line is safe. We're supposed to breathe, but we're not supposed to live. The only thing anyone cares about when it comes to eldest sons is their titles and prospects," Jarrod pronounced, staring at Colin and Griffin as he imparted the wisdom his extra year of life and his higher rank had afforded him. "And there's no use sniveling about it because, you see, *girls* are the very worst sort of snobs. They have no choice. They have to marry a man with good prospects. To do anything less is to disappoint the family." He drew himself up to his full height. "Better to do as we've decided and swear off girls altogether."

"That's right," Griffin had chimed in. "Who needs them?"

"Not us." Jarrod reached around Griff and gave Colin a keep-your-chin-up punch in the arm. "We're going to be the three greatest heroes England has ever known! And no girl is going to stop us!"

And no girl had! Colin grinned down at his friends from the top of the tower. He had done it! He had conquered his greatest fear and scaled the wall of the tallest building on the Knightsguild grounds.

Jarrod and Griffin smiled up at him and gestured for him to come down. Colin turned toward the interior stairs, but Jarrod shook his head.

"Not that way!" Jarrod called.

Colin took a deep breath and swung his leg back over the side of the bell tower. He might have known Jarrod wouldn't let him take the easy way down. No stairs. The only way down for him was the same way he'd come up. The hard way.

Feeling for his first foothold, Colin began the arduous journey from tower top to ground. A quarter of an hour later, he'd made it.

Expecting congratulations from his friends, Colin was met with a brusque greeting and an order from Jarrod.

"Now," Jarrod said, as soon as Colin's feet touched terra firma, "do it again. Only faster this time. We haven't got all night."

"Yeah," Griffin chimed. "If we're late for morning assembly, there will be canings all around."

Colin climbed. Up and down two more times before Jarrod was satisfied. And when they left the quadrangle and hour or so before the breakfast bells rang, the bonds between them had become unbreakable bonds forged from fear and pain and imbued with the sweet thrill of victory.

Three nights ago, Griffin, Colin, and Jarrod had formed a secret society guaranteed to protect them from further pain wrought in the name of love and family and had fashioned a charter to govern it. They called it the "Official Charter of the Free Fellows League," and as they pricked their thumbs with the paring knife and eagerly signed their names to the paper in blood, the three had sworn to honor the agreement as long as they lived.

And tonight the members of the Free Fellows League had triumphed in their maiden mission. They had overcome their initial obstacle in their journey to becoming England and Scotland's greatest heroes.

The work of the League had begun.

Chapter 1

"Many a good hanging prevents a bad marriage."
—WILLIAM SHAKESPEARE, 1564–1616
TWELFTH NIGHT

LONDON
Early spring, 1812

"*What do you mean you don't know where she is?*" The first Baron Davies was rapidly losing patience with the Bow Street runner he had hired to investigate the disappearance of his daughter.

"I mean, my lord, that we cannot find her." He cleared his throat, straightened his scarlet waistcoat, and pulled himself up to his full height. "We have found no trace of her in London, sir. Your daughter has disappeared."

Lord Davies thumped his fist on the top of his oak desk. "Tell me something I don't know. No one has seen my daughter in a week, not since she and her mother became separated at Lady Weatherby's musicale. I know Gillian has disappeared. What I don't know is why. Or why a man of my wealth and stature has yet to receive a request for ransom."

The runner cleared his throat once again, shifted his weight from one foot to another, then discreetly tugged at the hem of his jacket. "We don't believe your daughter was kidnapped, my lord."

Baron Davies shot to his feet. "Then, blast it, man! Where is she?"

"We believe your daughter eloped, sir."

"Eloped?" Baron Davies's face turned an alarming shade of crimson, and his voice rose. "Eloped?" He shook his head. "Impossible!"

"I'm afraid it's highly possible, sir," the Bow Street runner replied. "Indeed, it is highly probable that your daughter eloped with a gentleman to Scotland."

"What gentleman? Who?" Baron Davies demanded. "What *gentleman* would do such an ungentlemanly thing as to run off with a *true* gentleman's daughter?"

The Bow Street investigator bit the inside of his cheek to keep from smiling. It was well known in society and in London's merchant class that the regent had only recently elevated Lord Davies to the rank of baron and of gentleman, but that Carter Davies, a wealthy, self-made silk merchant, had always considered himself the equal of any peer. "We believe he may be a confidence man—a rogue gentleman—who preys upon the innocent daughters of peers and upon wealthy widows, offering the promise of marriage and the romance and excitement of elopement to Gretna Green and other Scottish border towns."

"My daughter would never demonstrate such poor judgment as to elope with a rogue," Baron Davies insisted. *"Gentleman* or otherwise. Gillian is above such foolishness."

"Perhaps not."

Both men turned at the sound of the softly spoken contradiction.

Lord Davies raised an eyebrow when he recognized the voice as that of his wife. He reached out a hand to her. "Do you know something we should know, my dear?" he asked in a voice that was uncharacteristically gentle.

"I think I might," she answered.

Lord Davies nodded thoughtfully. "Our Gilly has been

missing for a week. Why haven't you said something before now?"

Lady Davies took a hesitant step forward.

The investigator bowed over the baroness's hand. He had never met Lady Davies before now, but he understood why the baron treated her with gentleness and admiration. Although she was reed thin and gave every appearance of fragility, there was an underlying strength in her that shone like a beacon in the night. She was calm and soft-spoken, and she exuded an air of strength and serenity. "My name is Wickham, my lady. I am employed at Bow Street."

"Yes," Lady Davies said. "I know what you are. I recognized your scarlet waistcoat."

Wickham smiled. Bow Street runners were oftentimes called robin redbreasts because they all wore distinctive scarlet waistcoats as part of their uniforms. "We appreciate any light you might shed on your daughter's disappearance."

Lady Davies took a deep breath and fought to keep from giving way to her rising sense of panic. "There was a huge crush at Lady Weatherby's musicale. Gillian and I were separated. During the first intermission, one of Lady Weatherby's maids brought me a note from Gillian. She wrote to say that she had a headache and was returning home. I stayed at Lady Weatherby's until the end of the program. When I returned home, I assumed Gillian was here." She looked at her husband and then at the Bow Street investigator. "Our daughter has never lied to us. I had no reason not to believe her. I didn't know she wasn't in her room until the following morning, when her maid informed me that Gillian hadn't returned home and that her bed had not been slept in.

"My husband is a very wealthy man, Mr. Wickham, and when he said he believed Gillian must have been kidnapped, I agreed. I thought that must be what happened to my daughter until I heard your explanation." She turned to her husband. "And recalled Gillian's keen infatuation with a particular young man who seemed to turn up wherever and whenever we ventured out."

"Were you ever introduced to that particular young man?" Mr. Wickham asked.

Lady Davies nodded. "He said his name was Mr. Fox. Mr. Colin Fox."

Mr. Wickham frowned. "Can you describe him?"

"He was young, tall, well-dressed, and quite handsome. His hair was light-colored. Light brown or brownish blond."

"What about his eyes? What color were they?" Wickham asked.

"Blue," Lady Davies answered. "A nice shade of blue."

The investigator groaned.

"Do you know him?" Lord Davies asked.

"No, sir," Mr. Wickham said. "But I am well acquainted with young men like him. Their method of operation is a dedicated pursuit of their chosen young lady during the little season, followed by an elopement during the height of the real season when the possibility of disgrace usually engenders silence and a monetary payment for that silence." Mr. Wickham didn't disclose the fact that these unscrupulous men often married these young ladies under an assumed name, then abandoned them before returning to London and eloping with someone else.

"Could he have abducted our Gillian against her will?" Lord Davies asked.

"It's possible," Wickham said. "But it's much more likely that he romanced her and that she was a willing partner."

"But she would never . . ." the baron stuttered.

"She might," Lady Davies reminded him. "If she fancied herself in love with a man of whom you would not approve." She looked up at her husband. "Our most sensible and levelheaded daughter is young and in love for the first time in her life."

"But to *elope?*" Lord Davies still couldn't comprehend it. "With a plain mister when her father is a baron and she is a member of the peerage?"

"Begging your pardon, sir, but it wouldn't be the first time," Wickham volunteered. "Lord Chemsford's, Lord Barfield's, and Lord Exeter's youngest daughters all eloped to Gretna Green with young men who were not members of the peerage."

Lord Davies whistled beneath his breath. "What of the scandal? Once we locate our daughter, how do we protect her good name and prevent scandal? How is it possible that I haven't heard so much as a whisper of gossip about the young ladies whose names you mentioned?"

"It's simple, my lord," Wickham answered. "You do as the other gentlemen did. Either embrace your daughter's choice of a husband or, if the marriage is legitimate, arrange a swift annulment. Or a legitimate marriage to someone of your choosing."

"Annulment?" The baron looked puzzled. "But it's been a week. Surely he and she . . ." he stuttered. "By the time we locate her, she could be increasing."

Wickham nodded in agreement. "By your own admission, you're a very wealthy man, my lord. Do as Lord Exeter did and marry your daughter off to a gentleman in need of cash as soon as it can be arranged."

Lord Davies snorted. "Bribe some unsuspecting gentleman to marry my daughter?"

"Indeed, sir," the Bow Street runner said. "A gentleman of an old, respectable family is generally best."

Lord Davies clenched his fists while a muscle worked in his jaw. "First things first," he replied. "First find my daughter, then find out if her judgment proved faulty." He looked to his wife. "There's no need to bribe anyone unless it's necessary. No need to do anything until we know the truth."

Chapter 2

"'Neither maid, widow, nor wife."
—WILLIAM SHAKESPEARE, 1564–1616
MEASURE FOR MEASURE

EDINBURGH, SCOTLAND
Two days later

*C*olin *McElreath felt the short hairs at the*
back of his neck stand up in alarm as he made his way
through the narrow rabbit's warren of the close behind the
ancient stone buildings clustered at the mouth of the Firth
of Forth. He paused beside the steps that led to the back
door of the Blue Bottle Inn, drew his dirk, and glanced
over his shoulder to see if the presence he sensed had followed him out in the cold predawn light and decided to set
upon him.

There was no one in sight, but Colin was sure someone
was watching. The prickling warning along his spine and
the back of his neck was never wrong. He always paid it
heed, because it had kept him alive more times than he
cared to count. His chosen profession and Edinburgh's
back alleyways were dangerous. Much too dangerous for
him to discount.

Flipping his heavy black cloak out of the way of his
sword arm, Colin glanced around once again and caught

sight of a woman peering through the lace curtains of a second-floor window at the back of the Blue Bottle.

He exhaled the breath he'd been holding and relaxed as his nerve endings returned to normal. He *was* being followed. But by a gaze this time, rather than by an assailant. And that gaze was female.

Colin turned slightly and stole another glance at the window. She was still there. Watching. He pressed his lips together to keep from giving voice to his frustration. Having females watch him was nothing new. The ladies had always had an eye for him. His looks guaranteed admiring glances from the fairer sex wherever he went. The only thing out of the ordinary about having a woman peer at him through the lace curtains of a window was that this window belonged to the Blue Bottle Inn.

Colin frowned. He would have preferred to remain undetected, but the waves in the thick glass windowpanes that kept him from seeing her clearly also made it impossible for her to distinguish his features. Colin wagered that she wouldn't recognize him if she met him face-to-face on the street.

And the same could be said of him. He had the impression of youth, but in truth, the mass of thick, dark hair framing her pale, oval face was the only feature Colin could truly discern, and for all he knew, her hair might be liberally streaked with gray.

He sheathed his dirk. He was safe. She might be looking out the window every few minutes, but she wasn't looking at him. She was looking for someone else. Eagerly anticipating someone else's arrival.

His presence in the alley had been a disappointment.

Her presence at the Blue Bottle Inn was a surprise.

The Blue Bottle was a waterfront establishment that generally catered to seafarers, smugglers, spies, and a collection of other unsavory fellows who met to engage in illegal pursuits and to discuss a bit of treason. It was where

men like Colin went to plant false information and to ferret
out the truth. It was not an establishment that catered to
women. Other than an occasional serving girl and the
innkeeper's wife, Colin had never seen any women inside
the Blue Bottle. And never any ladies. Although he couldn't
say why or how he knew, Colin was certain that the woman
peering at him through the lace was a lady of quality. He
was equally certain that she—whoever she was—posed no
threat to him.

She had her own worries.

He lifted the latch on the kitchen door and quietly
slipped inside the inn, hoping to make his way to his room
with no one the wiser, but the murmur of voices, the sound
of footsteps scraping across the stone floor, and the flicker
of light from the massive hearth warned him that there
were others about.

Colin frowned. He'd spent over half the night slipping
in and out of the cobweb of narrow alleys and closes that
made up Edinburgh's inner city, trailing two well-dressed
French agents as they made the rounds of every alehouse
and brothel in Old Town along the way from the Blue
Bottle to the castle at the top of the Royal Mile. He had
left one of the French agents snoring heavily, sleeping the
sleep of the thoroughly debauched in an upstairs room in
the White Lily Tavern at the end of Queen's Close, then
followed the other to the harbor and watched as he was
ferried out to a merchant ship anchored in the firth.

The merchant ship was familiar to him. Less than a fortnight ago, Colin had sailed into the Firth of Forth aboard
an identical ship. But the ship from which Colin had dis-
embarked had sailed under a British flag and been named
The Lady Dee. The ship docked in the firth tonight bore
Dutch colors and was called *The Diamond Princess*. Colin
wondered at that. Why would a ship of the same line bear
Dutch colors while docked in Edinburgh? It seemed an odd
thing to do, but Colin was in no condition to worry with the

puzzle. He was bone weary and eager for a warm bed and a couple of hours of dreamless sleep.

The Frenchman at the White Lily was no threat. He was under constant surveillance—sharing a bed with one of Colin's most trusted informants. He wasn't going anywhere, and the Frenchman on *The Diamond Princess* would sail with the tide. The only thing left for Colin to do was make it to his bed unseen before the rest of the inn's occupants began stirring.

Unfortunately, that was harder done than said. He pressed his back against the kitchen wall, blending into the darkness, concealing his face in the shadows, remaining hidden as he eavesdropped on a conversation that had begun in the corridor and continued into the kitchen.

It was Douglas, the innkeeper, and his wife.

"What are we goin' to do about the young lassie?" the innkeeper asked.

"Send her packing," Mrs. Douglas answered.

"We canna turn her out," Douglas protested. "We told the man we'd keep her. Besides, she hasna coin to go elsewhere."

"Then he should have paid more. If she has no coin, she cannot stay here."

"Och, Tillie . . ." The innkeeper sighed.

"Well, she cannot," Tillie protested. "So dinna start feeling sorry for the lassie."

Colin clamped his jaw shut against the sudden urge to join the innkeeper as he championed the young woman's cause. He pressed his back closer against the wall, willing himself to become a part of it and remain undetected. He didn't much care for the innkeeper's wife, but she had taken a fancy to him. And since Colin had been sent to Edinburgh for a reason, he wouldn't jeopardize his mission by alienating her.

Passengers from *The Diamond Princess* and *The Lady Dee* and the other ships in the firth, routinely sought bed

and board at the Blue Bottle, and someone frequenting the
Blue Bottle was in league with Bonaparte and his network
of spies. Colin's mission was to find out who that someone
was and stop the flow of information from England, through
Scotland, and back to France. He had been tracking the
source of the information for nearly a year, posing as a busi-
nessman with special interests—smuggling interests—in
France. It had taken him months to become a familiar face
and earn a measure of trust from the men who frequented
the Blue Bottle and who worked along the Edinburgh waterfront.

Colin needed to stay on good terms with the innkeeper
and his wife. He couldn't risk losing his room at this particular inn. Because the Blue Bottle Inn was conveniently
located beside the docks, served hot food, whisky, wine,
and ale, and was fairly clean, it was the favorite meeting
place of the men he shadowed, and Colin knew from experience that it was easier to track his quarry if he slept where
they slept, ate where they ate, drank where they drank.

But Colin was rapidly losing patience with the
innkeeper's wife. He could never abide hard-hearted
women who nagged at their husbands and children and rel-
ished pointing fingers at their shortcomings. Unfortunately, Mistress Douglas was proving herself to be that sort
of woman, and that did not bode well for Colin's future
stays in Edinburgh. Or the job he'd been sent to do.

"I canna help feeling sorry for the lassie," Douglas argued. "She's alone and frightened and far away from everything that's familiar. Anyone with half an eye can see that
she's accustomed to far better than what we have to offer."

"She's lucky to have a roof over her head." Tillie gave a
derisive snort. "Any roof. Even one that's not as fine as the
one she was accustomed to. She's lucky I agreed to keep
her here at such a low price. The rotter who left her won't
likely be returning any time soon. Not after getting what he
came for."

"Aye," Douglas murmured. "That appears to be the way of it."

"It's always the way of it," Tillie told him. "Any whore on the street can tell you that."

"Her eyes are always red and swollen. No doubt her puir heart is broken." The innkeeper made a sympathetic clucking sound.

"You've always had a kind heart," his wife told him. "That's why we never have enough coin to keep us in a comfortable old age. You're always taking in strays and giving our hard-earned gold away."

Douglas bristled. "The stray cats I took in earned their keep. And *I* won't be comfortable in my old age knowing we took tainted gold from a man we knew was up to no good."

"I only took the gold because I feared he'd smother her in her sleep and leave her body here and us to answer for the killing." She looked at her husband.

"We'll be lucky if he doesna come back and smother all of us in our sleep. You took his money, Tillie, and promised to watch the girl. You made us his accomplices. He no doubt thinks he paid you enough to make certain the girl stayed put. And what's more, he probably thinks he purchased our loyalty."

"My loyalty costs a lot more than he was willing to pay," she said. "I ain't going to smother her. But I don't intend to keep her on charity, either. If she stays here, the young lass will have to earn her keep," his wife pronounced. "And we've plenty of dishes she can wash and floors she can scrub."

"You've grown hard, Matilda," Douglas replied. "The Bible says that we should help the needy."

"That's all well and good so long as ye don't fall for every hard-luck story that comes along."

"I never gave a brass farthing to anyone who didn't need it worse than we did." The innkeeper sighed. "I think she knows he's not coming back for her, but she waits at the window just the same. Every time I take her tray, she asks if her husband has returned. It breaks my heart. She's such a pretty thing. What if the young lady were our little lassie?"

"If she were our little lassie, she would've known better than to run away with a pretty fellow who'd abandon her to the mercy of strangers."

"Weel," Douglas drawled. "Since she's already been abandoned to the mercy of strangers, the least we can do is show her some."

"You be merciful," Tillie told him. "I'll make certain she earns her bed and board."

And I'll make certain she doesn't have to, Colin vowed, suddenly fiercely determined to thwart the innkeeper's wife and rush to the aid of the unknown lass who waited at the window, watching for the return of her errant spouse.

He smiled a satisfied smile as he formulated a plan of action. He'd have to be a bit more frugal with his remaining coin and provide a full accounting of where it went to Jarrod when he returned to London, but it was a small price to pay to save a lady from the humiliation of having to perform manual labor in order to appease the innkeeper's wife. It would be a noble sacrifice, and noble sacrifices appealed to Colin's sense of chivalry.

He was, after all, a hero—albeit a shadowy, anonymous one. But a hero just the same, and every hero understood that doing his duty involved sacrificing his comfort for the good of someone else. Especially when that someone else was a damsel in distress.

Colin remained concealed until the sound of their voices grew less distinct, signaling the fact that the innkeeper and his wife had left the kitchen and moved to the inn's common room. He couldn't see what they were doing, but the rattle of pewter and cutlery against wood, the scraping of iron over stone, told Colin that Douglas and

Mistress Douglas were busy attending to their morning chores: stacking pewter plates on the sideboard, laying out the mugs and utensils in preparation for breakfast, and stirring the coals banked in the massive hearth, coaxing them into a roaring flame.

He released the breath he'd been holding and quietly eased out of his hiding place. In order to reach the stairway that led to the upstairs sleeping rooms and the comfort of his rented bed, Colin would have to pass through the common room, and he hadn't a prayer of crossing it without Douglas or Mistress Douglas seeing him. Unless he entered the Blue Bottle in the same manner in which he'd exited without being detected last evening.

Heaving a weary, inaudible sigh, Colin retraced his steps. Carefully unlatching the kitchen door, he slipped over the threshold and into the morning mist.

The air was heavier than it had been when he entered. Colin used the fog to his advantage, hugging the stone outer wall of the inn as he made his way from the back entrance to the Blue Bottle to the small laundry that adjoined it.

Colin had learned on one of his previous stays at the Blue Bottle that the window of his bedchamber overlooked the roof of the laundry. He'd decided upon first glance that the roof and the inn's narrow ledge could be used as something more than a roosting spot for pigeons. They provided an ideal means of coming and going undetected, provided one was agile or foolhardy enough to pull oneself onto the laundry roof and then up onto the narrow stone window ledge in the dark of night.

Colin was agile enough, having first gained the necessary skill and stealth at Knightsguild, and having subsequently added years of practice in pursuit of pleasure and in the service of his country.

When Jarrod had recruited Colin for this particular line of work, he had reminded him that sneaking in and out of windows in the dead of night was one of his specialties—as a good many society ladies could attest.

Jarrod was right. Sneak thief work *was* one of the things he did best, but that didn't mean he found it palatable. Climbing through windows had never been Colin's preferred mode of entrance. Years of practice had made it possible for him to conquer his fear of heights, but with age came wisdom and the healthy sense of fear with which he'd been born.

In the past few months he'd begun to realize that skulking about dark alleys, frequenting unsavory establishments, climbing in and out of upper-floor windows had lost a great deal of its allure. And climbing in and out of the window of the Blue Bottle Inn was no exception. It was a long way from the second floor window to the cobblestones below, and Colin had suddenly realized that he was in no hurry to meet his maker or test the flames of hell.

All things considered, he'd rather have taken the stairs.

But he'd lost that option when he'd lingered a bit too long in the alley, staring up at the woman in the window. He wondered how she'd feel if he slipped into her bedchamber instead of his own and offered to watch over her and keep her warm for the night, wondered suddenly if she would watch for him at the window when *he* left, the way she watched for her errant husband.

For there was no question that Colin would leave. He always left. His life was one long, dangerous mission after another. He left on assignments and never looked back, never wondered what it would be like to stay. Never wondered what he was missing. Never wondered if anyone regretted his leaving.

His work didn't allow for such luxuries, and Colin hadn't allowed himself to dwell upon it. Not since that long-ago day when he'd discovered his betrothal contract had been broken, and Esme Kelverton was lost to him forever. If any of the women he'd left behind had ever watched for him the way the woman in window watched for her loved one, Colin wasn't aware of it. And if the truth were known, he'd always liked it that way. He was, after all, a Free Fellow, and Free Fellows didn't give any thought to sentimentality. Until now . . .

Chapter 3

"O what may man within him hide, though angel on the outward side!"
—WILLIAM SHAKESPEARE, 1564–1616
MEASURE FOR MEASURE

Gillian stood at the window, shivering in the cold and damp long after the man in the black cloak moved out of her line of view. She leaned closer, staring down at the street below, wondering suddenly where the man in the black cloak had gone.

He'd been there one minute, then vanished into the fog the next. Gillian almost doubted she'd seen him at all. But the quickening of her pulse when she'd caught sight of the tall figure in the morning mist told her there was no reason to doubt her vision. He had been there. She hadn't imagined him. She hadn't been jumping at shadows.

Gillian exhaled, and her breath frosted the thick glass, obscuring her vision even more. Pulling her shawl tighter around her shoulders, she swiped the end of it against the windowpane in the vain attempt to bring the alley below into sharper focus.

But for what purpose?

She had been staring out of this window for days. Waiting and watching in vain.

Her pulse might have raced at the sight of him, but the man in the alley wasn't the man she'd hoped to see. Because the man in the alley wasn't her husband.

Her husband. Gillian straightened her shoulders, lifted her chin a notch higher, and sighed. She, who had never done an impulsive thing in her life, had eloped with a dashing stranger—a hero—a spy—one of the brave, shadowy figures who slipped in and out of France and the Peninsula in order to help England win the war against Bonaparte. She still wasn't quite able to believe it.

She was married. Frowning, Gillian glanced down at the third finger of her left hand. Where there should have been a ring, there was nothing. Her finger was bare. Her husband hadn't sealed their vows with a ring. In his haste to whisk her off to Scotland, he'd forgotten the ring. He'd assured her that he had a gold band for her and a family betrothal ring to go with it, but she would have to wait until they returned to England to take possession of it. He'd assured her that the absence of a wedding band didn't change the fact that she was married. Or the fact that she was no longer the innocent Miss Gillian Davies.

The marriage bed and the intimate acts that went on beneath the covers of it were no longer a mystery. They had proven to be more than a bit disappointing, but they were no longer a mystery. Gillian shuddered at the memory. Her loss of innocence had been embarrassing, messy, and painful. But mercifully brief.

It had also been incredibly *lonely*. She had thought that the act would be one of sharing, when the two would become one. But she'd experienced none of the closeness, none of the sharing she'd expected. After the embarrassingly intimate act, she'd felt alone, lonely and ill used, and she'd lain wide awake battling tears of frustration and disappointment as she listened to him sleep. If she were completely honest with herself, she had to admit that although she'd loved the romance and the stolen kisses she and Colin had shared during their secret trysts in London, the intimate acts of the marriage bed had been a colossal disappointment. But she supposed that was the way of it for married women. And she was Mrs. Colin Fox. She had been for over a week.

She'd been married nine days, six of which she had spent alone. Her husband—her bridegroom—the man who had swept her off her feet and romanced her all the way to Gretna Green, had left her *alone* in a cold, cramped room in a less-than-reputable inn, far from the border on the Edinburgh waterfront, and although Gillian was relieved that she hadn't had to endure a repeat of the marriage bed, she was very much afraid of being left alone, and she was very much afraid that he wasn't coming back.

Biting her bottom lip to keep her teeth from chattering, Gillian leaned her head against the windowpane and sighed, watching as her breath coated the glass once again. She hadn't liked the things he'd done to her beneath the bed covers, but she had liked him. Even loved him. He had been quite dashing and a wonderfully romantic companion— right up until he'd relieved her of her maidenhead.

She wasn't sure if her misgivings about the marriage had begun at that very moment, but sometime between her romantic elopement and the loss of her maidenhead, Gillian had begun to have severe doubts about Colin and reservations about their future.

She discovered, upon losing her virginity, that she was married to a stranger. Colin changed so much in that brief time that Gillian barely recognized him. It was almost as if, having succeeded in marrying her, he no longer wanted her. It was almost as if he didn't care about her at all. Gillian glimpsed it in his eyes, heard it in his voice, and she began to worry.

She told herself that she had imagined the change. She told herself that Colin loved her. She told herself there was any number of reasons for the way he looked at her and the way he spoke to her. She could tell he was disappointed. But he was her husband, for better or for worse, and Gillian did her best to please him.

But she'd only had three days in which to prove her devotion. He had left, and now she feared for his safety as much as for her own. She knew his work was dangerous, knew he could be captured—perhaps even wounded or killed—and she'd tried to be brave and strong and patient, but it was hard to be brave and strong and patient when she was plagued by hunger and cold and loneliness and the constant nagging fear that somehow everything had gone terribly wrong.

If only he'd left her with some money or her jewelry or something of value to trade for coal and food. If only he hadn't needed it all. Gillian bit her bottom lip a little harder, hoping the pain in her lip would distract her from the empty rumbling of her belly and the cold. She had never thought of herself as a particularly selfish person and would have willingly given her husband the cash and coin she kept tucked away in the hidden pocket of her reticule for emergencies, if he'd only said he needed it.

But Colin hadn't mentioned needing her emergency money to finance his journey. He'd simply taken it, along with her grandmother's pearl earrings and the gold locket her parents had given her to mark her fourteenth natal day.

Three days after their marriage, Colin had taken everything she had, slipped silently out of their room, and disappeared. And she didn't know if he was coming back for her.

During the past few days, Gillian had suddenly become aware of the precariousness of her situation. She'd been so busy worrying about her husband and the state of her marriage that she hadn't given a moment's thought to herself. But then she realized she had no money to pay for the coal for the fireplace or for the little luxuries she'd always taken for granted, like food and hot water and clean clothes, a bed to sleep in, and a roof over her head. Gillian supposed it was cowardly to admit it, but she was a stranger in a strange land, and she'd suddenly become very aware that any day now, she could find herself at the mercy of innkeepers she could not pay.

She couldn't go back home. Edinburgh was a long way from London and without money her best option had been to go down to the docks and obtain passage on her father's ship, *The Lady Dee*. Gillian calculated that it should still be anchored in the firth, but her room faced the close instead of the waterfront. Unfortunately, her only access to windows that faced the waterfront was the inn's taproom, and her first foray into that territory had proved disastrous. After being rudely and roughly accosted by several of the inn's drunken patrons, Gillian had been forced to call the innkeeper for help. He'd escorted her to her room and strongly suggested that she remain there where she was safe.

But later that day, Gillian had tried again. She avoided the taproom on her second attempt to find out if *The Lady Dee* was still in port by slipping out of her room and down the back stairs. She'd gotten as far as the laundry before the sudden appearance of a gang of sailors sent her ducking into a storeroom. She'd pressed her back against the wall of the storeroom, barely breathing as the sailors lurched past her. She thought briefly about presenting herself to them, of throwing herself on their mercy and begging to be taken to the captain of *The Lady Dee*, but her sense of self-preservation prevailed. These men were common sailors. Drunken sailors. Gillian could smell the rum and grog they'd consumed and she could tell from their conversation that they'd been months at sea and were currently on the prowl for loose women. She was a woman alone. Appealing to their sense chivalry was risky at best and useless at worst.

Praying for courage, Gillian fought to maintain control of her shaking limbs as she waited for the group of men to stagger past.

"Are you looking to get yourself raped?"

Gillian turned to find the innkeeper's wife standing beside her. "N-no."

"Then what are you doing here?" Mistress Douglas demanded.

"I wanted to see the ships in the harbor."

The innkeeper's wife narrowed her gaze. "Why?"

"I heard *The Lady Dee* was in port," Gillian answered.

"She was," the innkeeper's wife answered. "But she's gone. Sailed on the morning tide."

"Are you sure?"

"Very." The innkeeper's wife stared at Gillian, studying her reaction. "If you were looking to book passage on her, you're out of luck. Course, you'd have been out of luck anyway. She was fully loaded. There wasn't any room for passengers. And there's the matter of your bed and board at the inn. I don't hold with folks—even quality folks—skipping out on a bill," she warned. "If you try that again, I'll call the constable. Unless you've a mind to pay your bill in full tonight . . ."

Gillian shook her head.

"Then you'd better get back to your room, before I rent it to someone else."

Gillian had returned to the Blue Bottle and she hadn't left her room since. There was no reason to leave. Where would she go? And how would she get there? Nor could she guarantee any sort of welcome should she manage to make it home to London.

The best that she could hope for was that her husband would return or that he had posted the note she had written to her parents, informing them of her elopement to Gretna Green as he'd promised to do once they reached Scotland. Gillian had wanted to leave the letter to her parents on her bed, but Colin had insisted that they'd needed a few days' head start to Scotland in the event that her father decided to pursue them. Colin had reminded Gillian that her father was much more likely to accept their marriage if it was a fait accompli when the baron learned of it. And Gillian had agreed because it had sounded so romantic when Colin suggested it. They were two lovers marrying in secret like Romeo and Juliet. Gillian scoffed at her foolishly romantic heart. She should have known better than to be swept off her feet. She should have known better than to accept the first romantic proposal or succumb to the lure of the flattery and the first romantic kiss she'd ever received.

She'd been a fool. A stupid, romantic, innocent fool. And he'd been an exceptionally convincing lover. Gillian had been convinced he loved her right up until the moment he took her virginity and stole her cash. Now, she was equally convinced that she was a gullible idiot.

She only hoped that if she did manage to return to London, Papa and Mama would be so glad to see her and be so relieved to find her unharmed that they would welcome her with open arms. She would beg their forgiveness and pray it would be forthcoming. Someday. Papa would be hurt and angry with her for behaving in a disgraceful manner and for leaving his bed and board and eloping with Colin, but she had followed her heart, and Papa would forgive her eventually. Papa would forgive her for anything except causing a scandal.

That was unforgivable. Especially now that Papa had realized his lifelong dream and become the first Baron Davies. He had worked long and hard to get his title and his letters patent and be accepted among the peerage, and he wouldn't look kindly on having his only daughter dishonor his name.

And Gillian didn't blame him.

She was his pride and joy and his hope for the future. Papa had had high hopes for a matrimonial alliance between the house of Davies and one of the premier families of the peerage. Papa would never understand or forgive her marrying beneath her. He would never understand her succumbing to the lure of romance in order to become plain

Mrs. Colin Fox when she might have become a baroness or a viscountess or even a countess.

Gillian shook her head. She didn't question her father's love. She knew he loved her and that he would forgive her almost anything, but she also understood that some things were beyond his realm of forgiveness. And causing scandal was one of them. It would break his heart, but Papa would never forgive his only child for besmirching his name and reputation or for ruining their chances to advance themselves.

Gillian fought the rush of tears. Only the weak wallowed in self-pity, and she'd never thought of herself as weak, but she was scared, and she didn't know where to turn. She had no money and no way of leaving the inn. And no one except her missing husband and the innkeepers knew she was there.

So Gillian did the only thing she could do to occupy the time. She waited at the window until she grew too tired or too cold to continue. When she could no longer bear to keep vigil by the window, Gillian retreated to the bed, where she slept for as long as she could. And when she awakened, she began the cycle all over again.

Day after day, night after night, Gillian bided her time, waiting and watching, counting the figures passing beneath her window. She had seen *him* twice more since that morning—the stranger in the long black cape—moving stealthily through the morning fog and again amid the evening shadows. She watched as he came into view, then vanished out of sight, and wondered what had brought him to Edinburgh. What secret business sent him creeping through the city's back alleys? Was he a well-dressed young gentleman sampling Edinburgh's stewpots? Was he a physician called out at all hours to tend his patients? Or a surgeon engaged in the nefarious business of corpse snatching? Or a sorcerer who appeared and disappeared at will? Might he be a soldier stationed with his regiment in the castle at the top of the hill? A ship's captain making the rounds of the nightly entertainments? Or a city watchman hired to patrol the narrow streets after dark?

Gillian whiled away the hours by imagining who the people passing beneath her window were and what they did to earn a living. She recognized some. The greengrocers, the milkman, the laundresses, and the street vendors who traveled back and forth through the close to the market square in the center of town.

But the mysterious gentleman who appeared in the wee hours before dawn and late at night after darkness had fallen captured her attention most of all. She wondered if he knew she was there. Wondered if he knew she watched him. She pretended to be a princess trapped in her ivory tower and wondered what, in heaven's name, would become of her if her prince didn't ride to her rescue?

What, in heaven's name, was he doing? Colin cursed beneath his breath as he stepped up onto an overturned laundry tub. The tub shifted beneath his weight, and Colin's left foot landed in a puddle that smelled of laundry soap, soaking his boot and splashing his trouser leg. Cursing once again, he heaved himself onto the wooden tub, then pulled himself up and onto the roof of the laundry that stood in the narrow close behind the Blue Bottle Inn.

Bloody hell, but that hurt! The pain in his side increased tenfold as he moved silently over the roof, then reached up and pulled himself over the wall and onto the window ledge. Colin glanced toward his window, gauging the distance, and prayed he could make it. If there was ever a time he wished he could brazen it out and walk in through the front door of the Blue Bottle, tonight was the night. But he'd left the inn's taproom wearing the clothes of a smuggler and carrying a knapsack. He couldn't return to his room wearing the formal evening clothes he'd donned in order to gain entrance to the reception at the home of a Scots patriot who had ties to America and to France.

The footpad who had set upon Colin as he left Lord MacMurray's Prince Street mansion hadn't been a footpad at all but a paid assassin. Fortunately for Colin, he hadn't been a very good assassin.

The blade meant to penetrate Colin's heart had scraped across his ribs. The wound hurt like the very devil, but he had suffered worse. Still, Colin couldn't rid himself of the sick feeling in the pit of his stomach. He had killed a man tonight. Colin hadn't known his name, but he had recognized the look on his face and known him for what he was.

But who had paid him? The French agents he'd been following? Or someone else? He knew the agents, and they knew him. They were in the same business: the spying business. And they'd dogged each other off and on for months and infiltrated rival groups of smugglers. Colin had tracked them from Paris to Edinburgh, all the way to the Blue Bottle Inn on several occasions. During their previous encounters, they had played a comfortable game of cat and mouse, but something had happened tonight to change the equation. Tonight, someone had hired an assassin to take Colin out of the game. And Colin had killed him.

He was tired and bloodied, and he had no choice but to climb back in through the window. Changing back into his smuggler's clothes was impossible, and returning to the tunnels was equally impossible. Colin couldn't risk another foray through the maze of smugglers' tunnels running beneath the waterfront where he'd spent the major portion of the evening helping his band of smuggling compatriots unload casks of French wines and bolts of brocades and lace.

Colin had slipped away from the smugglers in order to dress for Lord MacMurray's midnight reception. He'd thought he'd slipped away undetected, but someone had seen him. Someone had paid an assassin to lie in wait for him, and that meant the other man had either followed him or had known where he was going and why.

All in all, it had been one hell of an evening. The night was still young, and he was lucky to be alive. He hoped he could say the same come sunrise.

Colin inched his way along the ledge, past the first window and on to the second. He was almost there when he heard movement inside his room and realized someone was searching it. Pressing his back to the wall, Colin retraced his steps until he reached the first window.

This morning, he'd wondered how the lady inside that room would feel if he slipped inside her window instead of his own.

Now he'd have the chance to find out.

Retrieving his dirk from beneath his coat, Colin slipped the tip of the blade between the lock and the window casement and carefully eased the window open. He knew he was taking an enormous risk, but he meant the lady no harm. All he wanted was safe shelter from the cold. Colin had cheated death once tonight, and he didn't fancy a confrontation with the men ransacking his room or a tumble from the ledge to the cobblestones below.

The room was pitch black. Colin thought there would be some light from the fireplace, but if there had been a fire in the grate earlier in the day, it had long since burned itself out. The room was almost as cold as the air outside. Colin crawled over the windowsill and closed and locked the window behind him. Biting his bottom lip to keep his teeth from chattering, Colin made his way across the room to the bed, praying all the while that the lady was alone.

Colin briefly considered spending the night in the chair by the window, but he was freezing, and there was no point in suffering the cold any more than he had to. He glanced at the woman on the bed, decided she wasn't faring much better, and quickly eased himself onto the bed beside her.

She lay curled in a tight ball with her back to the door and the bed coverings pulled tightly around her. Colin relayed cautiously and sent a prayer of thanks heavenward that she was alone. With luck she would sleep until morning, and he'd be gone before she knew he was there.

But good fortune deserted him.

The woman stirred in her sleep, moving closer, seeking warmth as she pressed her back to Colin's front.

Colin's body responded immediately. He was fully clothed, down to this tall leather boots, and he lay atop the covers rather than between them, but he felt her through the layers of fabric and instantly regretted his impulsive decision to share his warmth.

"Colin? Is that you?"

Colin nearly leaped from the bed as she called him by name. He knew she couldn't see his face in the darkness, but she had him at a complete disadvantage. She knew his name. And he hadn't a clue about hers. Who the devil was she? And how in Hades had she come to know his name?

He breathed in the scent of her. The fresh, lemony fragrance emanating from her hair and her skin seemed woefully out of place at the Blue Bottle Inn. The light, delicate scent teased his nostrils and filled his senses, urging him to recall the face of the woman who wore it, but the only impression he had—of a pale, oval face framed by thick, dark hair—came from the glimpse he'd caught of her standing at the window and failed to produce any names or mental images, or memories of intimate moments.

"Colin?" she queried once again.

"Hmm?"

"I didn't hear you come in."

"You were sleeping." He spoke in a hushed whisper. "I didn't want to wake you."

"You sound different," she mumbled sleepily.

Colin cleared his throat and told as much of the truth as he dared. "I've caught a chill." He didn't like lying to her, but until he knew who she was, Colin couldn't do otherwise.

"Move closer," she urged, inhaling his scent. "I'll keep you warm." He smelled of sandalwood and something else . . . something she couldn't put a name to. Something strangely reassuring.

"I don't think that's a good idea," he answered honestly, moving away. "I'll stir the fire and add some more coal."

"Don't bother," she replied. "The fire's been out all day, and I haven't any coal to add."

No wonder the room was like ice. "Why hasn't the innkeeper brought coal for the fire?"

"Because I couldn't pay for it," she whispered. "I have no money."

"I'm sorry," he said.

"It doesn't matter," she told him. "What matters is that you've come back."

Colin took a deep breath and then blew it out. "I haven't come back to stay."

She took a moment to digest this information, and when she spoke, Colin heard the disappointment and the resignation in her voice. "When do you leave?"

"I'll be gone by the time you awake."

"I see."

He breathed in the scent of her. "No, I'm afraid you don't. But at the moment, there's no other way."

She recognized a note of what sounded like genuine regret in his voice and swallowed her pride in order to ask, "Can you take me with you? Away from this place?"

She couldn't see him, but she felt the movement when he shook his head. "I wish I could."

She sighed. "Will you do something for me before you go?"

"If I can," he said carefully.

"Don't leave without saying good-bye."

It wasn't very much to ask, and Colin found himself agreeing. "I won't."

"Thank you."

"You're welcome . . ." Colin searched his memory for a name to fit the voice and the scent. But no name came to mind, and he was left with a vague sense of loss. "Anything else I can do for you?"

"Hold me," she whispered. "Until I fall asleep."

The room was still shrouded in darkness when Colin awoke with the young lady in his arms. Her head was pillowed on his chest, and the stab wound he'd suffered earlier in the evening ached like the very devil. Colin didn't know for sure, but he thought the ache must have awakened him.

He rolled to his side, shifted her weight from his shoulder to the pillow, and left the bed. Leaning down, Colin gently tucked the covers around her shoulders. His breath fanned her cheek moments before he impulsively covered her lips with his.

He meant the kiss to be a mere brush of his lips on hers, but his intent could not contain his sudden urgent need to make it more. Colin ran his tongue over her plump bottom lip, savoring the taste and texture of it, teasing her, testing her, seeking permission, asking her to grant him entrance.

She yielded, parting her lips and acquiescing to his silent request. Their breaths mingled as he deepened the kiss, moving his lips on hers, kissing her harder, then softer, then harder once more, testing her response, slipping his tongue past her teeth, exploring the sweet, hot interior of her mouth with practiced finesse.

Colin caressed the interior of her mouth, using his tongue in a provocative imitation of the mating dance. And she followed his lead, returning his kiss with an urgency and hunger that thrilled him as much as it surprised him. He made love to her mouth, and the jolt of pleasure he felt shook him down to his boots. Blood pounded in his head, and his arms trembled from the strain of holding himself above her while every nerve in his body urged him to lower himself to the bed and bury himself in her softness.

Resisting the temptation to wait until dawn in order to get a look at her, Colin pulled his mouth away from hers and pressed a kiss against her hair. "Good-bye," he murmured, and left.

Sitting in the chair by the window the next morning, Gillian wondered if it had all been a dream. She wondered if the man who had held her in his arms last night had been her husband or a figment of her imagination. And she couldn't recall Colin feeling or sounding the way he'd sounded last night. He was different from the way she remembered—more thoughtful and gentle. And his kiss . . . She sighed. His kiss had to be a figment of her imagination, because it was so much better than she remembered. Colin had never kissed her like that before. He had never kissed her with such tenderness or such passion. And although he'd left her once again, there had been nothing hurried or perfunctory about the way his mouth claimed hers. If she hadn't seen the spot of blood on her nightgown this morning, she would have thought that he was a dream, but there was no doubt that he'd been real.

She started at the sound of a knock on the door. Rubbing her eyes with the back of her hands, Gillian scrubbed away all evidence of sleep before answering. "Who is it?"

"Mistress Douglas," the innkeeper's wife answered. "I've brought your breakfast."

"I didn't order breakfast," Gillian answered, trying hard

to ignore the insistent rumbling of her stomach at the mention of food.

"I brought it anyway," Mistress Douglas explained.

Gillian frowned. "I cannot pay you for it," she admitted reluctantly in a voice tight with pride.

"No need," the innkeeper's wife answered. "Meals are included with your bed and board."

Meals hadn't been included at supper last night or yesterday's nooning hour, or at breakfast when Gillian had waited in vain for a meal, hoping the innkeeper or his wife would take pity on her.

"Unless you've a mind to go without, I'd open the door," Mistress Douglas told her. "This tray is heavy, and I've customers waiting downstairs."

Gillian didn't need further prompting. She unlatched the door and swung it wide, stepping back to allow the innkeeper's wife to enter. The aroma of eggs and kippers, fresh-baked bread slathered in butter, accompanied by a pot of steaming tea, filled the room. Gillian came close to swooning as she watched Mistress Douglas set the wooden tray on a table near the fireplace. "It smells heavenly."

Mistress Douglas gave Gillian a dismissive snort, then turned on her on her heel and headed for the door. "Mr. Douglas will bring you a bucket of coal for the fire once we're done with breakfast."

Undaunted by the other woman's rudeness, Gillian tried again. "I don't know how to thank you for your kindness."

"It ain't kindness," Mistress Douglas said at last. "And there's no need to thank me. I was only doing what he paid me to do."

"What my husband paid you to do?" Gillian asked.

Mistress Douglas shook her head.

"Then whom?"

"The smuggler."

"I don't know any smugglers."

The innkeeper's wife shrugged. "Don't matter," she

replied. "So long as he knows you." She nodded toward the wooden tray. "There's an envelope. He left it for you."

Gillian waited until the innkeeper's wife left, then closed the door behind her and secured the latch. She hurried over to her breakfast tray and picked up her fork.

An envelope of cream-colored vellum lay on the tray exactly where Mistress Douglas said it was. Gillian stared at it as she poured a cup of tea. She managed to keep her curiosity about her mysterious benefactor at bay until she'd satisfied her overwhelming hunger, but once she'd finished her eggs and kippers, Gillian lifted the envelope from the tray.

Her fingers trembled as she lifted the heavy cream vellum and turned it over to study the seal. The green wax puddle over the folded edge of the envelope bore the impression of a mounted knight.

Gillian ran the pad of her finger over the impression, intrigued by the choice. The vellum wasn't the sort of stationery one would expect a smuggler to use; neither was the wax seal.

Seals were personal representations. Before he'd been awarded his title and coat of arms, her father had used gold wax pressed with the symbol of a lion. He'd selected the lion because it reaffirmed what everyone already knew: Carter Davies was the acknowledged king of the silk merchants. So, why would a smuggler choose to use green wax and the figure of a mounted knight? Why not a boat? Or a Jolly Roger? Or a cutlass? Or were those symbols a bit too obvious?

Gillian broke the seal and pulled out a folded sheet of paper. She unfolded the sheet of paper and was astonished to find a fifty-pound banknote issued by the Bank of England and three gold sovereigns.

A sheen of unshed tears burned her eyes as Gillian read the note and realized her prayers had been answered:

Madam,

I have taken the liberty of presenting the innkeepers with full payment for your complete room and board until the end of the month.

It is my way of thanking you for allowing me to intrude upon your privacy while I sought shelter from the cold. You gave me refuge when I needed it most, and I'm grateful.

I have also taken the liberty of securing a coach and hiring a driver to take you wherever you wish to go. Please do not hesitate to avail yourself of his services as soon as possible.

I enclose additional funds should you require them for the journey.

The Blue Bottle Inn is no place for a lady.

You needn't stand watch at the window any longer. The way home is yours.

I am,
Your servant,
Galahad

Gillian's breath caught in her throat. He wasn't a figment of her imagination. Nor was he her husband. She had shared a bed and an intimate kiss with a stranger. A smuggler. A smuggler who knew she waited at the window and watched. A smuggler who knew she had seen him in the early morning fog and the nighttime shadows. Gillian folded the sheet of paper and returned it to its envelope.

She should be shocked, perhaps, even ashamed. But she was not. She was grateful. She was deeply, profoundly grateful to her mysterious benefactor for coming to her rescue. Gillian hadn't been alone after all, because the man who called himself Galahad had known she was there.

The original Galahad had been renowned for his purity and virtue. Gillian tucked the envelope and the fifty-pound banknote in the lining of her bodice. She couldn't vouch for this Galahad's purity, but Gillian had to commend him on his virtue for, like all true chivalrous knights, he had come to the aid of a damsel in distress. And he kissed like a dream. . . .

She scooped up the gold sovereigns and hid one between the lining and the sole of her right shoe, then removed a stocking from the small traveling case she'd packed in preparation for her elopement and dropped the remaining sovereigns in the stocking, fashioning a knot between each one to keep them from clinking together. Once the coins were secure inside the stocking, Gillian lifted her skirts and tied the stocking around her waist.

He may not have meant to, but her husband had taught her a valuable lesson when he'd taken her jewelry and her emergency cash. Now Gillian knew better than to be so trusting and careless with the things she valued. She knew better than to be swept off her feet by a handsome face and a charming manner. She knew better than to give her heart and her self away to a man who would leave her behind without so much as a note or a kiss.

Gillian was going home to London where she belonged. She was going to take her mysterious Galahad's advice and find a way to make amends to her parents. And if that failed and her father refused to take her in, the money Galahad had given her would allow her to find suitable lodging until she could locate her errant husband and demand explanations for the many questions he'd left unanswered.

Chapter 4

"The very life-blood of our enterprise."
—WILLIAM SHAKESPEARE, 1564–1616
KING HENRY IV, PART I

LONDON
A fortnight later

"*Y*ou're late." *Jarrod, the fifth Marquess of* Shepherdston and founding member of the Free Fellows, spoke without preamble when the doors opened and Colin entered the room.

"As you can see, I came as quickly as I could." Colin's hair was still damp from his quick bath when he walked into the private meeting room to find Griffin, Duke of Avon; Daniel, Duke of Sussex; and Jarrod conversing over glasses of Scotch whisky while they waited for him to arrive. Colin had only arrived in London a little over an hour earlier, having landed in Dover the previous afternoon following a brief journey to Paris. He had traveled straight through to London, stopping only long enough to change horses and barely had time to pop into the suite of rooms he kept at Jarrod's London town house to bathe and change before Henderson, Jarrod's butler, had delivered several messages, including one from the marquess requesting Viscount Grantham's presence at White's. The marquess had, Henderson said, called an emergency meeting of the League in their customary private rooms at White's.

"I'm sure we're all pleased that you bathed and changed out of your travel clothes, but time is of the essence here."

"I'm pleased to see you, too, Jarrod," Colin retorted, meeting Jarrod's unwavering gaze. "Henderson didn't relay your message until after I'd begun my bath. And for your information, I needed a bath because I rode like bloody hell to get here."

"When did you get in?" Griffin asked, deflecting a bit of the verbal sparring.

"A little over an hour ago," Colin answered.

"From where?"

"Paris by way of Dover."

Griffin gave a low whistle of admiration. He pulled out a chair and pushed it in Colin's direction. "Sit down before you fall down."

Colin sank down onto the chair and stretched his legs.

"Pour the man a whisky." Griffin nodded toward Sussex. "And you—" He stared pointedly at Jarrod. "Ease off and give the man a chance to catch his breath before we begin."

Accepting the whisky Sussex proffered, Colin sent Griffin a grateful smile before he downed a swallow of the warm, soothing liquor. Jarrod had always been the leader of the Free Fellows League. A year older than Colin and Griffin, he'd been a natural leader at ten and the one they had always admired and to whom they had looked for answers. Jarrod was older and richer, and as a marquess, he had been the highest-ranking Free Fellow. But Griffin had returned from the Peninsula as the hero of Fuentes de Oñoro, and the Prince Regent had elevated him from a viscount to a duke.

Now that he was the Duke of Avon, Griffin outranked Jarrod, and he enjoyed using his new status as leverage on occasion. But Griffin was careful not to abuse his newly acquired power. He didn't have any intentions of taking over Jarrod's position as leader of the Free Fellows League. He simply enjoyed lording it over Jarrod once in a while. It made up for all the years Jarrod had lorded it over him and Colin.

The Duke of Sussex was another matter. Technically, Daniel, Duke of Sussex, took precedence over all the other Free Fellows because his title was older and because he'd been born the son of a duke. But Daniel wasn't an original member of the Free Fellows League. He hadn't attended the Knightsguild School with Jarrod, Colin, and Griffin. Daniel had been educated at Eton. He had only learned about the secret Free Fellows League through happenstance and his cousin, Manners, who also attended Knightsguild and had occupied the cot next to Jarrod's.

Sussex had only gained entry to their secret league because Jarrod and Colin had persuaded Griffin to allow him in on a probationary basis when Griffin returned from the Peninsula because the young duke had proven himself useful, loyal, eager, free, and readily available while Griffin was away serving with his cavalry regiment in Spain and Portugal.

Jarrod watched as Colin savored his whisky and exchanged a knowing look with the new Duke of Avon. "All rested and comfy now?" he asked, continuing the familiar verbal skirmishing he and Colin had established over the years.

"Quite, thanks," Colin replied, taking another sip of his whisky.

"Then you won't mind if we return to the purpose of this meeting and begin the briefing. I believe you'll want to hear this, Colin," Jarrod confided, "especially since you're the primary topic." Jarrod frowned, then glanced at each of the other Free Fellows to emphasize his point and the importance of the information he had to impart. "We've a problem with the current operation."

"Go on," Sussex prompted.

"Colonel Grant received information from one of his confidential sources that a prominent Bow Street runner has been investigating the movements of a gentleman known as Colin Fox."

"What?" Colin sat up in his chair.

"You've attracted the attention of Bow Street," Jarrod replied.

"Are you certain?" Sussex asked.

"Colonel Grant's sources are extremely reliable," Jarrod reminded them. "And I confirmed the information earlier today."

"Is there any way to put them off Colin's scent?" Griffin asked.

Jarrod shrugged. "This particular runner has a reputation for unimpeachable tenacity, and he's being paid a handsome sum to investigate a very personal matter involving Colin Fox and a young woman of good family."

Although they'd originally begun as a secret group of schoolboys, the Free Fellows League had grown and changed as its members had grown and changed. The members had put their secret league to work against Bonaparte, working very closely with the Foreign Office and the War Department. The covert work that Colin and Jarrod and Sussex did came under the auspices of a staff of graduates of the Royal Military College and Lieutenant Colonel Colquhoun Grant. While Grant gathered battlefield information on the Peninsula, Jarrod, Colin, and Sussex gathered information on a much larger field of battle, and all of it was analyzed, enciphered, deciphered, and included in the constant flow of military dispatches overseen by Griffin's father, the Earl of Weymouth.

While Griffin's role as a cavalry officer and a national hero had become public, the Free Fellows League and each member's connection to it remained secret to all but a handful of close associates.

The Free Fellows used code names, aliases, and secret personas, and all the Free Fellows knew that Colin Fox and Colin McElreath, Viscount Grantham, were one and the same. As Viscount Grantham, Colin McElreath lived the life of a London gentleman, but he moved within the underbelly of London and traveled the width and breadth of England and Scotland as Colin Fox. He did the same in France, using his French mother's family connections to move within French society as Viscomte Grantham, and assuming the persona of Colin Reynard in the seamier waterfront districts and in the French countryside.

Having Bow Street runners nosing around investigating one of their own was cause for alarm. Bow Street runners were investigators organized in 1750 by novelist Henry Fielding and his brother John to patrol the streets of London and keep the city safe. The runners' office was located on Bow Street in London, but the investigators didn't confine their activities to London. They worked for fees and rewards and were often hired by businessmen and members of the peerage to investigate private matters.

"Impossible!" Colin reached across the table and helped himself to the whisky decanter. After pouring two fingers of whisky into his glass and offering to refill Griff's and Sussex's glasses, Colin turned his attention back to Jarrod. "I haven't been with a woman in over a month. Not since *our* last visit to Madame Theodora's." The color rose in Colin's cheeks, and he gave Jarrod a meaningful look, reminding his friend and colleague that the last time he'd spent an evening with a female, Jarrod had accompanied him to the exclusive Portman Square town house Madame Theodora and her girls occupied. "Since that time, I certainly haven't had the time, energy, or inclination to become involved in a *very personal matter* with a young woman of *good family*, whomever she might be."

His curiosity piqued, the Duke of Sussex smiled at Colin's reply and asked, "Have you any idea who the young woman is rumored to be or what Grantham was supposed to have done?"

"Colonel Grant didn't reveal her name to me," Jarrod said. "But my own sources suggest that she's a member of the ton. At the moment, I don't know who the young woman is."

"Who hired the runner?" Griffin joined the discussion.

"The girl's father," Jarrod answered. "But I don't know which girl or which father. Apparently, there's been a spate of elopements to Scotland recently. All involving daughters of minor peers."

Scotland. The memory of the face at the window of the Blue Bottle Inn in Edinburgh flashed through Colin's mind as he listened to Jarrod speak. *Apparently, there's been a spate of elopements to Scotland recently.* Colin sighed. His instincts hadn't failed him. He hadn't been mistaken. The woman standing at the window had been a lady. A lady in need. A damsel in distress. Some unfortunate young woman had eloped to Scotland and been abandoned by some pinchbeck gentleman, by the man she trusted and married. Colin had done the right thing in leaving the note and the money. "Damnation!"

"What?" Jarrod demanded.

Colin slapped his forehead with the heel of his hand. "I thought it unusual at the time," he said. "Because I had never seen one there before. And now, it makes sense."

"What makes sense?" Jarrod prompted.

"There was a lady at the Blue Bottle Inn."

"So?" Griffin prompted.

"The Blue Bottle is not the sort of establishment that caters to ladies. Certainly not the sort of establishment to which a gentleman would bring a lady. And yet, there was one. I saw her through the window." Colin didn't see the point in confiding that he'd also spent the night holding that same lady in his arms or that he could still remember her scent and the taste of her lips. "I had never seen any women at the Blue Bottle other than the innkeeper's wife, the serving girls, or the waterfront whores who keep company with the sailors and smugglers who frequent the place. And I overheard the innkeeper and his wife discussing the fact that she was a lady whose husband had left her in their dubious care."

"Have you any idea who she was?" Griffin asked.

"No," Colin said. "But I know she was English." He wiped his hand over his face. "Bloody hell! But I should have paid closer attention when I signed the register. It might have given me a clue."

Jarrod shook his head. "To what? She could have used any number of names to sign the register. Or the man who accompanied her, if a man did accompany her, could have used any number of names." He looked at Colin. "And it's possible that she was some gentleman's wife or mistress. Reputable or not, the Blue Bottle is a waterfront inn. Ships dock in the firth every day. She might have sailed into Edinburgh. Or journeyed there in order to sail out. What clue could you have found when you were unaware that someone was eloping with young women and using your alias to do it? There was no way for you to know anything was amiss."

But he *had* known something was amiss. He had known it the moment he saw her staring out the window. And his suspicions had been confirmed when she'd called him by name. Colin nearly choked on his whisky as a horrible thought took root. "That spate of elopements you mentioned . . . Did they all involve the same man?"

Jarrod shrugged his shoulders in an eloquent but uncharacteristic gesture. "We don't know if it's the same man. We do know that he only used your name in one elopement."

"The question is whether he is using *my* alias," Colin said. "Or whether I'm using *his* name."

"Or whether it's simply a coincidence," Jarrod replied.

Colin didn't believe in coincidences. As far as he was concerned, everything happened for a reason. And everything that happened occurred naturally or was manufactured. "Is that a possibility?"

Jarrod looked to Sussex and Griffin for answers.

"It's possible," Sussex told them. "But not likely."

Griffin agreed. "I don't think it's a coincidence. Sussex and I checked parish registers, government rolls, militia, regular army, and navy enlistment rolls, and court records when we decided to use it as Colin's alias. We checked everything we could think of. We found the surname connected with men named Charles, Edward, James, George, Paul, Matthew, Christopher, Michael, Stephen, Tristan, David, Daniel, William, Harry, Robert, and a half a dozen others. But we didn't find a single living adult male named *Colin* Fox in London proper or any of its surrounding areas."

Griffin and Sussex had used their positions as dukes to gain access not only to public records but also to records that were part of the military and the government. The two of them, along with a handful of trusted staff members, had spent countless hours personally checking those rolls. Griffin and Sussex were nothing if not thorough. And Jarrod knew that they were very aware of the danger Colin faced.

Now that Griff had become a national hero and had retired from active duty in his cavalry regiment at the Prince Regent's and the prime minister's request, Colin had become the Free Fellow most at risk.

Because Griffin and Jarrod and Sussex occupied higher positions in society and were subject to more social obligations and more scrutiny than Colin, they were limited, in many ways, to planning, arranging, and financing the clandestine war against Bonaparte. The others engaged in the occasional secret smuggling holiday, but Colin, as a relatively unimportant and poor viscount, was the primary foot soldier in the field.

The duty of protecting him and his secret identity fell to Jarrod, Griffin, and Sussex, and they took the duty very seriously.

"Griff and Sussex didn't find any other man named Colin Fox in London or any of its environs, and now we suddenly have two Colin Foxes operating in the same territory," Jarrod said, finally reaching for his glass of whisky. "That's too provident—even for coincidence."

"I agree," Colin said. "But there was that incident in London before I left for France and another, at the Dover docks upon my return."

"What?" Griffin leaned forward on his chair.

Colin looked at Jarrod. "Remember the statement we received from Scofield's Haberdashery for a suit of clothes billed to Colin Fox?"

Jarrod nodded and began to explain the circuitous route he used in order to protect the source of the income used to pay the Free Fellows League bills. "We thought it odd at the time. When he's working, Colin almost always pays in cash." He looked at Sussex and Griffin. "Except when carrying large amounts of cash would be imprudent. Any charges he makes are routed through a series of clerks and factors in half a dozen different businesses. All charges eventually make their way to me. Colin and I review the charges, and my private secretary sends payment through the same series of clerks and factors that we change quarterly."

"But in this case," Colin continued. "The man wasn't my tailor, and I hadn't ordered a suit of clothing from him."

"Did you investigate?" Griffin asked.

"Yes," Jarrod answered. "Unfortunately, the tailor was the same tailor Lord McElreath uses, and we thought it possible that Colin's father might have some knowledge of his alias and used it in order to . . ." Jarrod broke off to avoid causing Colin any embarrassment. Everyone knew Lord McElreath was a source of embarrassment to his son, and the Free Fellows did their best to avoid causing Colin grief about it. After all, one couldn't choose one's sire or prevent him from indulging in embarrassing behavior.

But Colin would have none of it and quietly resumed Jarrod's explanation. "Avoid incurring more debt in his name."

"In which case, it was better to pay the bill and keep things quiet until Colin had a chance to speak with his sire and see if our suspicions were correct," Jarrod concluded.

"Unfortunately, I haven't had an opportunity to speak with my father about it."

"And the other incident?" Sussex prompted. "Did it involve your father as well?"

"No," Colin answered. "It happened as I exited the ship in Dover. I was one of the last to leave the ship, and as I came down the gangplank, I heard a gentleman ask if Colin Fox was aboard. The crewman pointed to me and said, 'There's Colin Fox.' The man looked at me, then shook his head and said, 'Can't be. Wrong eyes.' That was two days ago."

"Could it have been the Bow Street runner?" Griff asked.

Colin took another sip of his whisky before answering. "It could have been, but if it was, he was without his scarlet waistcoat. And I didn't recognize him."

"Anything else happen on this trip to raise your suspicions?" Sussex wanted to know.

"Someone tried to kill me."

Chapter 5

"The attempt and not the deed confounds us."
—WILLIAM SHAKESPEARE, 1564–1616
MACBETH

"Were you hurt? What happened?"

Colin recognized the note of alarm in Jarrod's voice. "I was set upon as I left Lord MacMurray's reception in Edinburgh. At first I thought a footpad had attacked me, but he turned out to be a hired assassin. His blade glanced off my ribs. It hurt, and it bled like the very devil, but it did little damage beyond slicing my waistcoat and shirt." He frowned. "The blade must have glanced off one of the buttons on my waistcoat."

"What happened to the assassin?" Griff asked.

"He should be paying his respects to Lucifer about now," Colin answered.

Jarrod pursed his lips in thought. "You're quite certain he was an assassin and not an agent for the French or the Spanish government?"

Colin snorted. "I don't know, Jarrod. He could have been an agent for someone's government, but quite frankly, I didn't have time to ask. He tried to skewer me in the heart. At the time, I thought it more important to dispatch him as quickly as possible rather than keep him alive so that you might have a chance to interrogate him."

Jarrod glared at the man he loved like a brother. "Jesus, Colin, you know what I meant!"

"If you're asking if I recognized him as an agent, the answer is no," Colin replied. "I've been playing cat and mouse with the French and the Spanish for months. I'd never seen this man. And he wasn't carrying any papers, any money, or any personal items that might aid in identifying him. He was hired for the purpose of killing someone—either the impostor or me. I don't know which." Colin paused, trying to sort out the pieces of the puzzle.

"You think the impostor Colin Fox might have been the target instead of you?" Jarrod asked.

Colin shook his head. "I didn't know there was an impostor until I came here. But I believe someone has been to the Blue Bottle and that he's used my alias."

"What makes you so sure?" Sussex asked.

"The presence of the lady and the fact that someone tried to kill me." Colin looked up and found three pairs of eyes focused on him. *And the fact that the lady called me by name and assumed I was her husband.* "We've been playing a game of cat and mouse for months, and no one has ever attempted any violence. But someone meant to kill me in Edinburgh."

"Or him," Griff pointed out.

"Or him," Colin agreed. "But the impostor had good reason to kill me if he thought there was a possibility that I might discover he was committing crimes using my alias. . . ."

"And there was every reason to believe you would discover it if someone at the Blue Bottle Inn realized there were two Colin Foxes," Jarrod picked up where Colin left off.

"Especially if one of the Colin Foxes had a bride who might question the presence of another Colin Fox," Griffin added.

"And there's always the possibility that you might have discovered he'd eloped with other young ladies. . . ." Sussex said. "All of whom remain mysteries."

"Unfortunately," Griff said. "And unfortunately, there's an equally good chance that none of these incidents are related. It may all be coincidental."

"You think so?" Colin asked.

Griff shook his head. "No, I don't think so. But we won't know for sure until we learn who hired the runner."

Jarrod raked his fingers through his hair. "We've got at least two Colin Foxes—one we know and another we don't know who eloped to Scotland with one or more unidentified young ladies of good family. We have a mysterious lady in an inn in Edinburgh and an unidentified dead assassin who may or may not be the Colin Fox we don't know and at least one father and a Bow Street runner trying to figure it all out."

"It should make for a very interesting investigation," Sussex said. "For Bow Street and us."

Jarrod nodded. "I agree. And even if it is a coincidence, it's much too close for comfort or safety."

"So is that Bow Street runner," Colin reminded them. "I have enough trouble with the French and the Spanish. I can't have robin redbreasts following my every move. How are we going to manage them?"

"We're going to manage them by getting to the bottom of this little mystery. We need to find out who hired our tenacious runner and how much he or she knows before the runner finds you," Jarrod replied.

"When do we begin?"

"Tonight," Jarrod replied. "And we begin with the heavy artillery."

The other three Free Fellows groaned.

"That's right, my friends." Jarrod smiled. "This mission calls for evening wear and a night on the town." He glanced over at the clock on the mantel. "Time to vote. I know you've all received invitations for tonight. So, what's it to be? Lady Harralson's? Lady Compton's? Or Almack's?"

To anyone else in London society, the obvious answer was Almack's Assembly Rooms. But Lady Harralson and Lady Compton were two of the ton's leading hostesses. They were universally liked and openly generous with their invitations, including men and women whose family connections involved trade or commerce—the men and women who would never receive the coveted vouchers to Almack's.

Lady Harralson was a popular choice of the young ladies who were unable to gain admission to Almack's, and her parties were well attended. The food was good and the libations adequate. Lady Harralson loved to dance and always hired the best orchestras, but she disliked gambling and rarely allowed her male guests to escape the dancing in order to while away the hours with cards and liquor.

Lady Compton, on the other hand, was an inveterate gambler. She limited the dancing and devoted a great many rooms to all sorts of gaming. She liked what men liked and put on the best spread in London. Her wines and liquors were the best vintages and the highest quality. Gentlemen flocked to her gatherings because she made them feel comfortable and at home. Unfortunately, the only women who truly enjoyed Lady Compton's were gamblers, older widows, and the hunting set.

Of the three, Almack's was *the* best place to learn the latest gossip, but Free Fellows generally avoided Almack's like the plague.

Almack's was the place where every ambitious, marriage-minded young woman and her mother wanted to be. It was the place where young ladies of good families went to find husbands and young bucks went looking for brides and fortunes. Griffin, the only married Free Fellow, had found his bride there. Everyone who was anyone in society sought the coveted vouchers that granted admission, but only a select few actually received them.

The Free Fellows were among the select few. All of them possessed vouchers guaranteeing admission, although none of them used them unless absolutely necessary. The Free Fellows despised the place. It was hot, overcrowded, and the refreshments were cheap and uninspiring. Almack's was the last place any of them would ever choose to go—including Griffin, who was beyond the reach of the marriage-market mamas and their marriageable daughters because he had been happily married to his duchess, Alyssa, for nearly two years—but it was also the place most likely to yield the information they needed.

"Lady Compton's," came the unanimous reply.

"We can't all appear at Lady Compton's," Jarrod told them as he walked over to the bell pull and rang for a waiter. "The fairest way to settle this is to cut cards. High card goes to Almack's. The next highest card goes to Lady Harralson's. The next highest card goes to Lady Compton's. Agreed?"

Griffin nodded an affirmative, and the others followed suit.

"Good," Jarrod pronounced.

After the servant delivered the sealed deck and exited the room, Jarrod broke the seal and shuffled the cards. He offered the first cut to Griffin, then to Colin and Sussex, taking the last cut for himself.

"All right," he said when they'd finished, "Show them."

All four men flipped over their cards.

"King," Griffin said.

"Six," Colin replied.

Sussex smiled. "Two."

"And six for me. It's settled." Jarrod lifted the whisky decanter and refilled their glasses. Raising his, he offered a toast to the Free Fellows League before bringing the meeting to a close. "Colin and I will put in appearances at Lady Harralson's."

"Fine," Sussex replied amicably. "And be sure to wear comfortable shoes. The last time I attended one of Lady Harralson's parties, she had me partner every woman in the place. I thought the dancing would never end."

Colin grimaced. He liked dancing but he didn't like being on display or having members of the ton judge him by the cut of his coat and the quality of the fabric. It made him uncomfortable to have strangers openly speculate on the weight of his purse or whether or not he was going to be the final ruination or the salvation of the McElreath family. Colin hated knowing that so many people were privy to the fact that his father was a reckless gambler who owed nearly everyone in London and Edinburgh and paid no heed to how his wife and children endured constant shame, humiliation, and deprivation.

He liked the dancing but the crush of curious spectators and the thought of seeing his hostess filled him with an odd sense of trepidation. But he wasn't going alone, and he'd rather attend Lady Harralson's evening of dance than appear at Almack's, where the scrutiny and speculation was tenfold. Or find himself at Lady Compton's, where his father often sat down to cards. As far as Colin was concerned, he couldn't have cut a better card.

"Sussex is attending Lady Compton's evening, so that means it is knee breeches and buckles for you, Your Grace." Jarrod nodded toward Griffin. "And diamonds for your duchess."

Griffin arched one eyebrow. "She's not going to be happy about this."

Jarrod grinned. Alyssa, Duchess of Avon, hated Almack's almost as much as they did. "I know. But you'll need her to help you identify the newest crop of eligible young ladies."

Griff rolled his eyes at Jarrod's logic. "If that's the case,

I'd do better to escort my mother-in-law. Alyssa pays less attention to Debrett's than any woman I know, and she'd much rather stay home."

"Persuade her," Jarrod urged. "Tell her the League will make it worth her while."

"*I'll* make it worth her while," Griff said. "The League doesn't have anything Alyssa wants."

"I don't know," Sussex teased. "I seem to remember your duchess inquiring rather pointedly about my mother's latest hothouse creations. . . ."

"Name your price." Griff laughed. Two years earlier, Alyssa had rejected Sussex and his magnificent gardens, and married Griff, not only for love but also in part for the challenge Griffin's neglected country house, Abernathy Manor, had offered. "Because identifying a bevy of eligible young ladies isn't the only reason I want my wife by my side." Griff was under no illusions about his progress since he'd returned home from the battlefield. He still had nightmares, and it was no secret to any of the Free Fellows that Griff had returned from battle on the Peninsula with an intense dislike of large crowds and loud noises. Griff would never appear at Almack's without his wife, and everyone knew it. Not only because Griff loved his duchess, but also because Alyssa's presence provided the sense of calm and security he needed in order to complete his mission in Almack's uncomfortable environment.

"*Gratis,*" Sussex answered.

"I'm obliged." Griffin nodded, knowing that Sussex made the offer of a plant for Alyssa, rather than risk insulting him by offering to take his place at Almack's. He also understood that no matter how much they dreaded darkening Almack's Assembly Room doors, his friends knew he dreaded it more and would offer to take his place without hesitation. But fair was fair. They had agreed on a cut of the cards, and Griff had no intention of allowing his friends to take on the task he'd drawn.

The Free Fellows weren't venturing into the ton for purposes of entertainment or to answer their social obligations but as a means to an end to shield Colin. And they all understood that it was as important to note the young ladies missing from tonight's most fashionable gatherings as it was to note the names of the young ladies who were present.

Because the social engagements to which they were invited were restricted to members of the ton, a Bow Street runner would most likely never gain entrance. At the moment, that slight advantage was the only advantage the Free Fellows had. They intended to make full use of it, appearing at all the evening's social engagements in the hopes they could identify the young woman in question and locate the impostor before he posed a real threat to the League and the work in which they were engaged.

Chapter 6

"*I* don't know how we're going to manage, Colin."

Colin stood beside his mother and sister, watching as she wrung her hands and marveling at the fact that after all these years, his mother could doubt her ability to manage whatever life threw her way.

Colette Hepburn McElreath had been born in France of Scottish expatriate parents. Her grandparents, Malcolm and Marianne Hepburn, had fled to France following the defeat of the Young Pretender, Bonnie Prince Charlie, in '45. Colette had grown up in France but had been sent back to Edinburgh at the age of eighteen to marry Donald, Earl of McElreath.

The young Earl of McElreath had possessed an ancient birthright, a title, and a respectable fortune when they wed, but over the years, most of it had gone to pay gambling debts. Colette had managed to survive the ordeal of childbirth in order to produce five living children: an heir, two other sons, and two daughters. She had weathered constant worry and hunger and nearly thirty years of marriage to a charming but spendthrift gambler whom she apparently adored.

Colin wished he could feel the same, but the truth was that he felt only duty-bound to love the man who had sired him despite the fact that he had little regard for the weaknesses and lack of character his father often exhibited. But Colin truly loved his mother and held her in the highest esteem. And while it seemed highly improbable that the prospect of paying for a London season could upset her after all she had endured through the years, it had upset her. Terribly. Colette was a much better mother than Donald had been a father, constantly struggling to make life better for her children. "Don't worry, Maman." Reaching down, Colin placed his hand over hers. "I'll take care of it."

"I don't like leaving your father on his own so much," she continued. "You know how he gets. . . . But Liana must make her debut, and someone has to chaperone her. And then there's the burden of the house, the staff, the clothes, the jewels, the presentation, the parties. . . ." Lady McElreath threw up her hands in a classic Gallic expression. "They're so hideously expensive. . . . Still, your papa gambles and gambles . . . and the debts . . ."

"Sssh, Maman. Don't fret. I'll see to it that Liana has her season with all the trimmings."

"How can you?" His mother wrinkled her brow. "You have no fortune. Nothing but a title."

"I've put away a few pounds. . . ."

"A few pounds?" Lady McElreath shook her head in dismay, and Liana looked stricken. "My son, we need a few *thousand* pounds."

Colin smiled down at his mother and sister. "I've got enough."

"Truly?" Liana spoke up for the first time, and the look of hope in her eyes tugged at Colin's heart. "Because we can make over some of Maman's gowns. I don't mind. I understand finances, and I can make do with what I've got."

"You've made do long enough," Colin told her. "This is your chance, Liana. You deserve it, and it's time you had a new wardrobe." It was long past time that his sister had a new wardrobe and his mother, too, for that matter. Colin wasn't entirely certain that Liana had ever owned a new dress made just for her. It seemed that everything she owned had previously belonged to someone else and been made over to fit her. And while his mother and sisters were skillful and frugal seamstresses, there was no disguising worn fabric or frayed laces and trims. Colin knew from experience that life among the ton was often a vicious and precarious place for those whose purses were chronically lean. As long as he was able to prevent it, his sister needn't suffer petty slights and painful insults from those with more money than compassion and manners. Colin glanced at his mother. "Order whatever you and Liana want or need. I'll see that the bills are paid. On time."

His sister beamed up at him, but Lady McElreath was more guarded. "Are you certain you have enough, Colin? Because everything costs so much. . . ."

"Maman," Colin said gently, "I'm sure. Besides . . ." He winked at her. "What's the cost of a new wardrobe compared to seeing my beautiful sister turn the ton upside down?"

Liana was practically bursting with excitement, and Lady McElreath was almost as thrilled as her daughter. They were so excited that they had spent the past hour talking of nothing but fashion and fabrics, comparing styles, and compiling a mental list of available seamstresses. Colin listened with half an ear as he scanned the room, looking for anything or anyone that seemed out of the ordinary. He had hoped to glean a bit of ton gossip from his mother and sister, but apparently, there was very little to gossip about—other than who had purchased what from which dressmaker.

The number of people on the dance floor swelled to crushing proportions, but Colin noticed that Jarrod was not among them. At least for the moment. But that situation appeared likely to change. Colin watched as a pretty redhead made her way through the crowd to where Jarrod stood near the refreshment tables. Less than a moment later, Jarrod and the young lady were in deep conversation, and it became quite apparent that Jarrod was destined for the dance floor. The mighty Marquess of Shepherdston was about to succumb to the lure of the music and a pretty girl.

And that was music to Colin's ears, because the Free Fellows had a longstanding wager of two hundred pounds in the betting books at White's as to who would be the next man to fall prey to the leg shackles of marriage. Watching Jarrod with the pretty redhead, Colin could almost hear the silver coins jingling in his purse.

"Good evening, Lord Grantham. Lady McElreath. Lady Liana."

Colin looked around and found his hostess, Lady Harralson, standing at his elbow. He'd been so intent on watching Jarrod that he'd failed to see the danger stealing up beside him. Silently cursing the heat rising up his neck, Colin swallowed hard and replied. "Good evening, Lady Harralson."

"Are you enjoying yourself?" She spoke not to Colin but to his mother and sister.

"Very much," Liana replied breathlessly. "Thank you for inviting us, Lady Harralson."

"My pleasure," she replied. "It was the least I could do for such old and dear friends. After all, if things had worked out differently, I might have been a part of your family."

"But then, you wouldn't have been Lady Harralson," Colin replied. "Or able to be such a successful society hostess."

"That's true," Lady Harralson answered. "But I'll always remember that I was yours before I became Lady Harralson."

"That was a very long time ago, Lady Harralson," Colin reminded her. "We were children."

Lady Harralson ignored his interruption and continued on her favorite theme. "Being Lady Harralson doesn't change the fact that your family will always be welcomed here and will always occupy a special place in my heart." Although she smiled at Liana and at Lady McElreath, this time Lady Harralson's words were meant for Colin.

Lady McElreath exchanged glances with her son.

Colin flushed.

Lady Harralson placed her gloved hand on his arm. "Aren't you dancing, Lord Grantham?"

"Not yet."

Lady Harralson laughed as she pinned him with a knowing look. "Not *ever* if you can help it."

Colin's ears turned a deeper shade of red. "I see my reputation precedes me."

"It does indeed, my lord," she confirmed. "My sources in the ton assure me that Lord Grantham seldom dances—especially when there are members of the ton present to witness it."

"Your sources are correct, my lady."

She shook her blond curls. "That's surprising to me, because I remember how much you once enjoyed dancing and being the center of attention."

"You remember the boy, Lady Harralson, not the man."

She pursed her lips in thought. "I suppose that's true, but I'm afraid I wouldn't be true to my reputation if I didn't make it clear that no one attends one of my parties in order to avoid dancing."

Colin inhaled deeply and then slowly released his breath. "Will you not make an exception?"

Lady Harralson shook her head. "No exceptions," she said.

"Not even for a weary man?" He wasn't above attempting to play upon her sympathy.

"You don't look weary, Lord Grantham."

"A tribute to Shepherdston's valet," he assured her. "For I'm dead on my feet."

"Too dead on your feet to dance?" she asked.

"With you?"

She held up her dance card, opening it for him to see. "My dance card is already full, Lord Grantham. But there's a certain young lady who hasn't danced all evening, and I wouldn't be much of a hostess if I didn't try to remedy the situation."

Colin groaned. Any young lady who had failed to find a dancing partner in this crush was certain to be awkward and shy, have two left feet, possess the face of a gargoyle, and carry the approximate tonnage of a frigate. He held up his hand to ward off the possibility.

"Give in, Colin," she cajoled, "for you know you can't refuse me."

He relented with an inner groan. No, he couldn't refuse her. He'd never been able to refuse her. Lady Harralson had always had a way of getting around his slightest bit of resistance and of getting her way. She was three years older than he, and Colin had been betrothed to her from his cradle. The only time he had ever known Mary Esme Kelverton to fail to achieve her heart's desire was when she failed to persuade her father to abide by the betrothal agreement Lord McElreath and Lord Kelverton had drawn up years earlier in order to settle a gambling debt. Lord Kelverton had hated breaking his word, but marriage was serious business. And Lord Kelverton couldn't take a chance tying his only daughter to a bad risk. Lord McElreath had gambled his fortune away, and his heir would inherit nothing except a title and debts—debts even the Kelverton fortune would not be able to settle should McElreath's heir prove the adage: like father, like son.

Esme had been twelve at the time and Colin only nine, when Lord Kelverton broke the marriage contract that had bound them together.

Five years later, Esme was sent to London to marry Lord Harralson. She seemed happy with her much older husband, but Colin had never quite gotten over the loss of his betrothed. From that day forward, Colin had been acutely aware of the fact that despite his impeccable breeding and his ancient title, Lord Kelverton had found him lacking. Colin McElreath, Viscount Grantham, hadn't been good enough or rich enough to be Esme Kelverton's husband.

He closed his eyes, blocking out the sight of Esme's persuasive face. He shrugged his shoulders.

Lady Harralson took that as a sign of obvious capitulation and reached for his elbow. "Come, I'll introduce you."

Gillian crumpled her dance card in her hand and methodically added another corner of it to the growing pile of bits and pieces hidden within the folds of her gown.

It was, she decided, no great loss, since the elegant, fan-shaped, cream-colored card was blank.

So far, she hadn't had a single opportunity to make use of her favorite dancing slippers because no one—not one single eligible gentleman—had signed her dance card.

Oh, she had had several offers, but her mother had actively discouraged the gentlemen making those offers. Still, Gillian had to admit that they'd been an interesting lot of fortune hunters, rogues, rakes, and lechers. Gillian frowned and ripped another piece from her dance card. She didn't blame her mother for discouraging those so-called gentlemen. That was a chaperone and a mother's duty.

And if the truth were known, Gillian would have discouraged them herself, if her mother hadn't done so. She wasn't interested in being seen with any of them anyway, because none of the men who approached her tonight would have dared approach her—or any other young lady of unblemished reputation—a month ago. No matter how attractive or wealthy or well connected she was.

Gillian sighed. That could only mean one thing: Word of her elopement had reached the ears of the members of the ton. She was disgraced. Her reputation ruined. And she had no one to blame but herself.

Oh, how the mighty had fallen. Gillian firmed her lips and gritted her teeth to keep from succumbing to the tears burning her eyes and her throat. She knew she wasn't considered a great beauty. Her eyes were too big. Her face was too small. Her chin too pointed, and her dark, curly hair too unruly to fit the classical ideal of beauty, but she was attractive enough to have garnered her fair share of suitors and attention, regardless of her father's massive fortune. Or so she believed.

Now, it seemed that the opposite was true.

But who could blame these would-be suitors for attempting to take advantage of her situation? There were plenty of marriageable girls with unblemished reputations and respectable dowries. Only the most desperate suitor would consider a girl with a tarnished reputation, and those suitors necessarily looked first to her fortune and then to her character.

Although Lady Harralson had gone out of her way to welcome her and to dispel rumors, Gillian knew that accepting the invitation and coming here tonight had proved to be a huge embarrassment and an even bigger mistake. One of the biggest of her life. One of the biggest in a growing list of regrettable decisions. She should have refused the invitation and stayed at home. But she had been home over a week, and Papa had insisted she resume her place in society. Gillian had reluctantly agreed in an effort to please her father and mother and to make amends for the distress her foolish indiscretion had caused.

"It doesn't look as if anyone believes the story that I

spent a fortnight in the country visiting relatives." Gillian glanced at her mother and managed a wan smile.

Lady Davies reached over and gently patted Gillian's hand. "It doesn't matter whether they believe it or not, Gilly. What matters is that you aren't hiding in shame. What matters is that you're here and can hold your head up high."

"I would rather be home hiding in shame."

Lady Davies smiled. "No doubt you would. But you are made of sterner stuff than that. And besides, you did nothing wrong."

Gillian glanced around and lowered her voice to the barest whisper. "Of course, I did, Mama. I eloped."

Gillian made it sound as if what she had done was a crime, but her mother knew better. "You trusted the wrong young man," Lady Davies replied. "But that's over and now it's best we carry on as if nothing unusual has occurred. Besides, even Shakespeare wrote of the foolish things love makes us do. Especially when one is young and impulsive. Your only crime was in following your heart."

"All the way to Scotland," Gillian answered, bitterly. "I had never done an impulsive thing in my life until that night. And I should have kept it that way. I should have listened to Papa and let him arrange an advantageous match for me instead of allowing an attractive man to romance me with moonlight and kisses and tempt me into running away. I should have insisted he ask Papa for my hand. Then I would have discovered whether or not he truly loved me."

"Oh, Gillian." Her daughter's obvious self-recriminations nearly broke Lady Davies's heart. "I doubt it would have changed anything if you *had* insisted. You may not believe it, my darling, but you are a born romantic. And what born romantic would choose to believe her papa when a handsome young man is flattering her at every turn, and telling her everything she desperately wants to hear? How could you not be swept off your feet? How could you not believe yourself in love with the first man you kissed?" She patted Gillian's hand. "You blame yourself but that young man wanted you for his own selfish purpose and I believe he would have done whatever he needed to do to get you."

Swallowing her pride, admitting her humiliation, and telling her parents the truth about her elopement had been the hardest thing Gillian had ever done. Harder even than leaving London without saying good-bye. But seeing the pain and the worry lines on her parents' faces and knowing she had been the one to put them there—knowing she had caused them needless distress—lay heavy on her mind and on her heart.

She had gone from being a daughter who had never caused her mother and father a moment of concern to a young woman who had brought their family name and reputation to the brink of ruination in one gloriously romantic and selfish act.

Gillian looked at her mother. "Do you really believe that?"

Her mother nodded. "I'm convinced of it."

"Did you believe yourself in love with the first man you kissed?"

Lady Davies nodded her head. "Of course."

"Was it Papa?"

"No," Lady Davies answered. "The first man who kissed me was the handsome younger son of a lord who was desperately in need of my dowry. I thought I was madly in love with him."

"What happened?" Gillian leaned closer to her mother.

"I lost him." Lady Davies gave her daughter a wistful smile. "My father refused his offer, and he married someone with a bigger dowry. At the time I thought my life was over and that my heart would break. I thought my father was cruel and unfeeling. But he only wanted the best for me, and he was right."

"How can you know for sure?" Gillian asked, tearing another chunk from her dance card and hiding it among the folds of her skirt.

"That's easy," Lady Davies answered. "I fell in love with your father. And now, when I see my beau from long ago around town, I'm always amazed that I ever thought myself in love with him."

"You see him?"

"On occasion," Lady Davies confided. "At social engagements like these. You see, his older brother died some years later, and he inherited the title."

"You have no regrets?"

"Why should I?" Lady Davies met her daughter's gaze. "The point is that I only thought I loved him. I was madly in love with the idea of being in love. The truth is that I didn't really understand what love was until I married your father."

"I truly believed he loved me," Gillian said.

"Perhaps he does in his own way."

"He left without so much as a note. He didn't bother to say good-bye." Gillian had told her mother and father nearly everything that had happened to her since she'd eloped with the elusive Colin Fox, but she had been too ashamed to admit that her husband had taken her cash and her jewelry and sneaked away, abandoning her to the mercy of the owners of the Blue Bottle Inn. She'd made no mention of Edinburgh. The shame that the memories and the revelations of Edinburgh brought did not bear repeating.

As far as her mama and papa were concerned, the extent of her trip to Scotland began and ended at the inn in Gretna Green. And although she carried his note tucked inside the secret pocket in her chemise, Gillian hadn't breathed a word about her mysterious Galahad or the money he had given her. Galahad was her secret, and Gillian intended to keep him that way.

Lady Davies looked her daughter in the eye. "There's no

doubt that you love us, Gillian, but you didn't leave your papa and me a note when you left with your young man."

Gillian shook her head. "But I did, Mama. I wrote you a letter explaining our decision to elope to Scotland because Colin was afraid Papa wouldn't accept him as a suitor because he didn't possess a title."

"We never received your letter," Lady Davies said.

"I know," Gillian admitted. "And I'm so sorry. You didn't get my letter because I gave it to Colin. He promised to post it once we reached Scotland."

"Then he misled you on several accounts." Lady Davies narrowed her gaze. "And the suggestion that your papa wouldn't accept your young man as a suitor because he didn't possess a title is ridiculous! Your papa has the greatest admiration for men who make their own way in the world. Why shouldn't he? He's been in trade all his life."

"But once he became a baron, he made no secret of the fact that he wanted a loftier title for me," Gillian protested.

"Of course he did," Lady Davies replied. "In our society, a title is everything. With a title, the world is your oyster. It can open doors, that money alone cannot budge. Your father understands that. Nevertheless," her mother continued, "your papa would have accepted whomever you loved so long as it was clear that the man loved you in return." She frowned at Gillian. "And you should have trusted your papa enough to know to know that."

Her mother was right. Gillian should have trusted her father and her mother enough to confide her attraction to Colin Fox. If she had, she wouldn't have ended up abandoned at the mercy of the innkeepers of the Blue Bottle Inn. Her reputation wouldn't have been hanging by a very thin thread and she wouldn't have had to hear the harsh truth about her marriage or to remember the look of disdain on Mistress Douglas's face the morning Gillian left the inn and boarded the coach that would take her home to London. "He comes here a lot—sometimes by ship and sometimes by land, either through Gretna Green or Berwick," the innkeeper's wife had whispered. "There were others, you know. I overheard him boasting in the taproom about how he earns a handsome living at it."

Surprised by Mistress Douglas's revelations that her absent husband had been boasting about his business in the taproom of a busy inn, Gillian took the older woman's bait. "At what?"

"Eloping with well-to-do young ladies. He left one in Selkirk two months ago and another at the Dalkeith Inn last month. You aren't the first young bride he's wedded, bedded, and bid farewell to in Scotland."

Reaching into her coat pocket, Gillian crumpled the letter she'd written to her husband—the letter she'd been about to entrust to the innkeeper's wife. "I see." She had held her head high, swallowed the painful lump in her throat, and stifled her tears. "Thank you for telling me, Mistress Douglas."

"Well," the innkeeper's wife had looked uncomfortable, "I thought you should know."

Mistress Douglas's words had completed her humiliation. The hot rush of love Gillian had felt for her dashing young husband died a quick, crushing death. She couldn't love him anymore, but she couldn't hate him, either. She couldn't feel anything for him at all. Or for anyone else. She was numb and quite suddenly past all caring.

"But what I believe doesn't matter," Lady Davies was saying. "What matters is what you believe. Are you still in love with him? Think about it," her mother urged. "Ask yourself if you would want to face him if he walked into this room tonight."

Gillian straightened on her chair and quickly scanned the room, looking for any sign of him. She didn't love him. But that didn't mean she was ready to come face-to-face with him. "Has he?"

"No," Lady Davies told her. "At least, not that I've seen. But you need to prepare yourself for whatever answers you find."

Gillian bit her bottom lip. A sure sign that she was worrying.

"Do you still want answers, or have you changed your mind?"

"I haven't changed my mind," Gillian said. "I still want answers."

"I hope so," Lady Davies breathed. "Because your father has hired a Bow Street runner to find him."

Gillian inhaled sharply.

"No need for you to worry, my dear," Lady Davies said. "Mr. Wickham understands the damage this could do to your reputation and our family name. He's entirely trustworthy and discreet."

Gillian wasn't concerned by her mother's revelation, but by the sight of a tall man moving through the crowd toward them. Her heart pounded in her chest, and she had trouble breathing, before she realized that the man moving past her bore little resemblance to the man she had married except in the width of the shoulders. And yet . . .

She wasn't as numb as she thought. Or quite past all caring.

"Gillian?"

"I'm fine. For a moment, I thought that he"—she pointed her fan in his direction—"was headed this way."

"Viscount Grantham?" Lady Davies inquired, following her daughter's gaze toward the row of chairs on either side of her along the wall of Lady Harralson's grand ballroom to where Viscount Grantham stood visiting with his mother. "You know him?"

Gillian shook her head. "No, but he . . . for a brief moment, he reminded me of . . . someone else."

"He reminded you of *him*," her mother guessed quickly. "But as far as I can tell, the only likeness Lord Grantham has to your young man is his height, the breadth of his shoulders, and his Christian name."

"You know Lord Grantham?"

"I know his mother." Gillian's mother nodded toward Lady McElreath and her eldest child. "We both serve on the Greater London Orphans Relief Fund Committee and the War Veterans Relief Fund Committee. I know his baptismal name is Colin, and I recognize Grantham when I see him, not only because Lady McElreath introduced us once at one of her drawing rooms, but because Grantham and his oldest sister greatly favor their mother. Anyone looking at them can tell that that's a mother and her two children."

Gillian glanced down the row of chairs. "There is definitely a family resemblance. The mother and the daughter are quite lovely."

"The girl is Lady Liana. She's making her curtsy at the next royal drawing room." Lady Davies frowned. "She's here so the gentleman can get their first look at her. But she isn't officially out, so she won't be allowed to dance with anyone but her father or brother until she's presented." She looked at Gillian. "And there's Lady Dunbridge and her niece. They aren't dancing, either."

Her mother told the truth. Gillian wasn't the only lady who wasn't dancing. She wasn't even the only *young* lady who wasn't dancing. But she was the only young lady not dancing who had been presented to society and who wasn't chaperoning someone else, acting as a companion to one of the elderly matrons, or rumored to be increasing.

Gillian gave a little self-deprecating laugh. She hadn't heard all the pertinent rumors circulating the ballroom, so she had no way of knowing for certain, but she hoped that wasn't the rumor about her. *Or the truth*. But she knew Papa was afraid she might be. Not that her parents wouldn't welcome a grandchild, but Gillian knew that they would prefer to meet her husband before they met his heir. She hadn't told her father about Colin's other wives, but she knew the only reason her papa hadn't secured an annulment of her marriage was because he was waiting to see if she was increasing.

A month had passed since her elopement, and Gillian wasn't able to enlighten her father about her condition because she simply didn't know. Her monthlies had never been regular. She never knew when they would appear or how long they would last. And now that she desperately needed the information, there was no way to know for sure if she had missed them.

Gillian shifted on the hard seat and tore another bit off the edge of her dance card. She felt like such a hypocrite. She no longer belonged in the society she inhabited. She wasn't a husband-hunting innocent and she had no business pretending to be one. It didn't matter that, in their circles, marriage was little more than a binding legal agreement. What mattered was that she had followed her heart and trusted a man who betrayed her. What mattered was that Gillian knew how it felt to put her faith and her hopes and her dreams for the future in the hands of a man who had dashed them. What mattered was that she didn't want to be a guilty accomplice in doing the same to any man who was foolish enough or desperate enough to pay court to her.

Her father might think it vitally important for her to resume her place among her peers and salvage what was left of her reputation, but Gillian knew in her heart that she had no right to do so. She was a fraud. A counterfeit virgin. The only husband she was interested in finding was the one she'd married—the one who had left her alone in Edinburgh. The one who had abandoned her and disappeared without a trace. Until she knew what had become of him, until she knew why he had chosen her, there was no point in pretending to lead a normal life. She sighed. Still, it would have been nice to forget her troubles and dance. . . .

As if reading her thoughts, Gillian's mother leaned closer and whispered, "Don't worry, Gilly-flower, the dancing won't last much longer."

Her mother's use of her pet name brought Gillian's tears to the surface. She took a deep breath. "Oh, Mama, how could I have been such a fool?"

"Sssh, Gilly." Lady Davies gave Gillian's fingers a gentle squeeze. "We're all fools at one time or another. You made an error in judgment. A mistake. That's all."

"You and Papa have been so wonderful to me and so forgiving."

"You're our daughter," Lady Davies told her. "Your father and I are sorry that you felt the need to elope, but in the vast scheme of things, an elopement is nothing. We were afraid you'd been kidnapped and taken against your will. We feared for your life. And now that you've returned to us safe and sound, we want you to be happy."

"Kidnapped?" Her mother's words gave Gillian pause. The idea had never entered her mind until now. . . . Was it possible? Had he romanced her and convinced her to elope to Gretna Green in order to conceal a kidnapping? And if so, why hadn't he demanded a ransom after stealing all her jewelry and coin? Unless he'd needed her jewelry in order to prove he had her . . .

"We never got the letter you just described, Gillyflower," Lady Davies confided, "but we did receive a packet containing your gold locket and a note requesting fifty thousand pounds to cover your living expenses."

"What?" Gillian's face lost all color. "When?" She turned to her mother. "Oh, Mama, I'm so sorry for the trouble and the pain I caused you." Her tears brimmed over and slowly rolled down her cheeks. She looked down at her lap, at her mother's hand covering her own. "I can't believe it! Fifty thousand pounds."

"Sssh, now. Don't cry. We didn't pay it," Lady Davies rushed to reassure her daughter. "We would have, of course, if we had thought you sent the note or if you needed the money. But since the note arrived the morning of the day you returned home, we knew you hadn't sent the request." She smiled at Gillian. "No more tears. We can't have everyone thinking the rumors are true."

"Even if they are." Gillian looked up at her mother. "Mama, I've made such a mess of things. What am I going to do?"

"You're going to muddle through as best you can, Gillian. And before you know it, everything will be all right. You're not alone. Your father and I are here, and we're going to support you in every way we can." Lady Davies removed a delicate handkerchief from her evening bag and pressed it into Gillian's hand. "Dry your eyes and smile," she said. "I see Lady Harralson and it looks as if our hostess is as good as her word."

Gillian dried her tears, then looked up and met her mother's gaze, a glimmer of hope mixed with disbelief sparkling in her eyes.

"That's right, my dear," Lady Davies continued. "She promised us an evening of dancing, and she's escorting a gentleman of whom I could definitely approve."

"She is?"

Lady Davies nodded. "A viscount, no less."

Chapter 7

"This is the night
That either makes me or fordoes me quite."
—WILLIAM SHAKESPEARE, 1564–1616
OTHELLO

"Lady Davies, may I have the honor of dancing with your daughter?" The viscount's warm, rich voice, deeply reminiscent of his native Scotland, sent shivers of awareness up and down Gillian's spine as Lord Grantham took her mother's hand in his and bowed.

Gillian cast a sidelong glance at him from beneath the cover of her lashes as their hostess, Lady Harralson, tapped the viscount on the arm with her fan and admonished, "Lord Grantham, you cannot ask for such a favor until you've been properly introduced."

"I have already made Lady Davies's acquaintance," Grantham explained. "We met several months ago at one of my mother's 'at homes.'" He smiled at his hostess.

Having met her obligations as hostess, Lady Harralson took the opportunity to withdraw. "I'm pleased to know it." She nodded to Lady Davies and to Gillian. "Lady Davies, Miss Davies, I shall leave Lord Grantham in your charming company and see to my other guests."

Viscount Grantham thanked his hostess, then turned his attention to Gillian's mother. "If I am not mistaken, Lady

Davies, you and my esteemed mother serve on the same charitable committees."

Lady Davies blushed as he released her hand. "That's correct, Lord Grantham. How kind of you to recall."

"I rarely forget so charming a meeting," Colin replied. The truth was that he rarely forgot any face or meeting. His memory for people and places was one of the talents that had kept him alive, but neither one of the ladies present needed to know that. He smiled at Lady Davies once again. "Unfortunately, I haven't had the pleasure of meeting your daughter."

Lady Davies took the hint. "Lord Grantham, may I present my daughter, Miss Gillian Davies?"

Colin studied the young lady sitting before him. His curiosity was piqued. Miss Davies was beautiful. She had thick, dark hair and big, blue eyes surrounded by dark lashes, which dominated a rather small oval face with a slim nose, determined chin, and plump, red lips. Her eyes were red-rimmed and slightly swollen, but that didn't detract from her looks. She didn't appear to be awkward and shy or have two left feet, and her face was as far removed from the image of a gargoyle as it was possible to be. And as for having the approximate tonnage of a frigate . . . As far as Colin could tell, she was sleek and slim and curved in all the right places. She wasn't beautiful in the conventional sense of the word, but she was beautiful nonetheless. It seemed impossible to him that all the other men present failed to notice.

Colin smiled down at her.

Gillian offered him her hand, and Colin pressed his lips against the soft fabric of her glove. "A pleasure, Miss Davies."

She told herself that his actions were smooth and practiced and his words, requisite good manners, but Gillian warmed to them in much the same way as her mother. When he smiled, Lord Grantham came dangerously close to being irresistible.

Lady Davies turned to Gillian and continued the introductions. "Gillian, may I present Lord Grantham?"

Gillian looked up and stared into his eyes. "Delighted, Lord Grantham."

She expected him to release her hand, but he surprised her by keeping a firm grip upon it as he straightened to his full height and gently tugged Gillian to her feet.

Bits of ivory-colored paper fluttered to the floor like delicate blossoms on a windy day, coming to rest on the top of Colin's shiny black leather shoes.

Gillian blushed red with embarrassment.

Colin ignored the scraps of paper littering the floor around them. He reached for the silver cord looped around Gillian's wrist and took hold of the tiny pencil hanging beside the remains of her mangled dance card. "May I?"

Gillian lifted her chin a notch and looked him in the eye. "Be my guest."

Colin scribbled his name on what was left of her dance card. "I am in your debt, Miss Davies," he told her, offering her his elbow as the orchestra began tuning up for the next set.

"Are you?" Gillian replied, placing her gloved hand in the crook of his arm.

"Aye," Colin answered, his voice a soft, rumbling burr.

"In what way?" Gillian curtsied as Lord Grantham bowed and the first strains of an old-fashioned minuet began.

"You spared my feelings by removing the names of all the other gentlemen who have signed your dance card." He caught a whiff of a delicately tantalizing fragrance, and then lost it amid the stronger, overpowering scents of heavy perfumes and profusely perspiring bodies surrounding them on the dance floor.

Gillian looked up at him from beneath the cover of her lashes. His eyes were green, she realized. A crisp, gray green that sparkled with wit and humor and that challenged her to respond in kind. Gillian smiled her first genuine smile of the evening. "You undoubtedly know better than that, my lord."

Colin arched his eyebrow in eloquent query.

"If other gentlemen had signed their names to my dance card, you and I wouldn't be dancing now."

"How so?" Colin asked the question, not because he didn't understand but simply because he was curious to hear her answer. And satisfying curiosity was what a mission of discovery was all about.

"There would have been no need for Lady Harralson to prevail upon you to rescue me by asking me to dance."

"I didn't rescue you, Miss Davies," Colin replied gallantly. "You rescued me—from a deadly dull evening."

Gillian couldn't contain her spontaneous burst of laughter. "How is that possible? Lady Harralson's evenings are never deadly dull for those who love to dance."

Colin grimaced.

Gillian laughed once again. He danced like a dream, flawlessly executing the intricate steps with aplomb. Yet he clearly pretended to despise it. "I vow that you're a fraud, Lord Grantham. If you've no fondness for dancing, why have you come to Lady Harralson's?"

Colin never missed a step. "I received invitations to Almack's, Lady Compton's, and here." He shrugged his shoulders. "This seemed the best choice." He had learned long ago that his best course of action was always to tell as much of the truth as possible whenever possible.

Unfortunately, his partner didn't believe him. "Better than Lady Compton's?" She feigned shock. "Now, I know you're a fraud. Or the most virtuous gentleman in all of London."

He arched an eyebrow in query, eloquently encouraging her to elaborate.

"I've yet to meet a man who would rather dance than gamble or pass up the best evening repast in town," Gillian continued.

Colin grinned. "You appear to be most fortunate in your acquaintances, Miss Davies."

"Indeed?" She arched her brow and did her best to mimic his expression and his tone of voice.

"Indeed," he confirmed. "For an evening at Lady Compton's is generally expensive, and my purse is not so fat that I would risk losing it on games of hazard against men with greater resources than I am able to muster. I only wager with friends who have always generously offered me the opportunity to recoup my losses."

"Wise as well as gallant," Gillian murmured, as the dance brought them face-to-face and palm-to-palm.

"Prudent," he protested, fighting a sudden, aching need to feel her lips against his. "Not necessarily wise."

The look on his face was mesmerizing. Gillian focused her gaze on his mouth, astonished to find herself wondering how it would feel pressed against her bare flesh. "One would guess that a gallant and prudent man is a rare, if not extinct breed. I doubt that there are many other men who would make that claim."

He frowned at her unflattering assessment of English gentlemen. "Of course there are," he assured her. "I've no doubt that there are a great many men like me—all equally prudent and gallant." Colin thought of his Free Fellows League brethren and legions of brave soldiers who had died in the battles against Bonaparte.

"You believe in honor and nobility and chivalry and—"

"You don't?" he guessed.

Gillian smiled a sad smile. "When one reads Sir Thomas Malory and the writings of Queen Eleanor, one is tempted to believe every man possesses such virtues or aspires to possess them—" She broke off when she recognized the look of wonder on Colin's face. "What is it, my lord?"

"You surprise me," he answered.

"In what way?"

"By engaging in philosophical discussion of Malory and the poetry of Eleanor of Aquitaine." He met her gaze. "I expected . . ."

"More?" she asked.

"Less," he said.

"Oh, well . . ." She blushed. "Sorry to disappoint you, Lord Grantham, but I *am* a learned woman and as such, I am quite capable of forming and expressing intelligent opinions—"

"Who said I was disappointed?" The light in his green eyes burned hotter.

"Aren't you?"

"Not at all."

She blushed even redder, glanced down at her feet, and resumed the threads of their abandoned discussion. "I believe in the *ideals* of honor, nobility, and chivalry. I just don't believe they exist in pure, incorruptible form."

"You can be assured that they do," Colin said softly.

"It would be nice to think so," Gillian mused, curtsying once again as the music faded away and the dance came to an end. "But—"

"But someone hurt you—" Colin interrupted.

"But I gave up believing in chivalry and fairy tales long ago. My experience has led me to conclude that you are unique among your peers. No one else could possibly be the sort of gentleman you appear to be."

Colin knew she was mistaken, but in the case of one impostor, he prayed she was right.

"Why didn't you ask her to dance?"

Jarrod turned at the sound of the softly spoken question and discovered a pretty, brown-eyed redhead looking up at him. "Whom?"

"Gillian," she answered. "Gillian Davies, the woman

dancing with Lord Grantham. The woman at whom you've been staring for the better part of a quarter hour."

"Davies?" Jarrod frowned in concentration. "Any relation to—"

The young woman nodded. "Baron Davies is her father. And despite the fact that her father is richer than Croesus, Gillian is quite nice. Unfortunately, she seems to be in disgrace."

Jarrod lifted his eyebrow. "Oh?"

"Yes," she answered, lowering her voice to make certain no one could overhear. "The story is that she's been visiting relatives in the country for the past month. But there's a nasty rumor circulating around town that she wasn't in the country at all, but that she eloped to Scotland with a bounder who left her there."

"Do you believe the story or the rumor?" he asked, staring at Gillian Davies once again. Was it possible? Could she be the one?

She hesitated, chewing her bottom lip for a moment. "I find it difficult to believe that Gillian would ever do anything to disgrace her family. But then again, no one goes to visit relatives in the country at the beginning of the season." She looked up at him. "I'm sure it's just a rumor. I'm sure Gillian's reputation is beyond reproach." Her voice quavered. "She'll make you a wonderful marchioness."

Jarrod whipped around, focusing his full attention on the young woman standing at his side. "What makes you think I'm interested in making Miss Davies my marchioness?"

"Because you're the Marquess of Shepherdston, and because you've been staring at her most of the evening."

"I only noticed her because she wasn't dancing," Jarrod answered honestly.

"And you were trying to summon the courage to ask her to dance with you. . . ."

"Not at all," he argued.

She arched one pale reddish blonde brow in disbelief. "Then you're staring at Gillian because she's beautiful."

Jarrod frowned. He wasn't accustomed to being contradicted, and his blue eyes flashed fire as he turned his gaze on her. "Not true."

"Gillian *isn't* beautiful?" she asked hopefully.

Jarrod shook his head. "She's quite beautiful, but so are a great many other ladies here tonight. I noticed Miss Davies because I found it strange that she wasn't dancing."

"Lucky Gillian," the young woman muttered. "Because *I* haven't been dancing, Jarrod, and you didn't pay me the slightest bit of attention until I spoke to you."

She'd broken the rules of etiquette by speaking to him and by daring to call him by his given name. And that daring finally captured his full attention.

"Are we acquainted?" he asked.

She presented him with a mysterious smile. "I'm well acquainted with you, my lord. But apparently, you are unable to say the same." She looked him up and down and then gave him a dismissive glance. "I apologize for interrupting your search for a marchioness, Jays. And when you dance with her, please, give my best to Gillian."

Jarrod frowned as she turned to walk away. Only one person in the world had ever had the temerity called him Jays. And she had been a scrawny, knock-kneed, flame-haired, precocious five-year-old girl named Sarah Eckersley. "Sarah? Is it you?"

She turned on her heels and beamed at him. "All grown up and in the flesh."

Jarrod eyed the creamy expanse of flesh displayed above the fashionably squared neck of her evening gown. The shockingly bright orange-colored hair she'd despaired of as a child had darkened over the years, mellowing into the soft, rich color of burnished copper, and the freckles that dotted her pale skin had all but disappeared, leaving a scant few paler freckles to decorate the bridge of her nose.

Only her eyes were the same. He should have recognized them if nothing else, for Sarah Eckersley's big, almond-shaped eyes had always been more gold than brown and had always seemed much too large for her face. Years ago, she had been a funny little kitten with full-grown cat eyes. But now, it seemed, the kitten had filled out and grown into a breathtakingly lovely queen. "How long has it been?"

"Long enough for you to forget about me and look for someone else."

His breath caught in his throat. "Sarah, I'm not—"

"Looking?" Her eyes sparkled with mischief. "I beg to differ, Jays."

It took a moment for Jarrod to recover his speech. "It's not what you suppose. I'm not interested in dancing with Gillian Davies or in making her my marchioness."

"Why not?" she demanded.

"I don't happen to be in the market for a wife," he answered.

"Then what are you doing here?"

He shrugged. "Would you believe I came to dance?"

She didn't believe it for a moment. "You don't appear to be dancing."

Jarrod grinned at her. "Only because you haven't asked me to."

<hr />

"What kept you?" Jarrod inquired once Colin managed to make his way through the crush of people surrounding the refreshment table.

"Nothing kept me," Colin told him. "I've been here well over two hours." He watched Jarrod deposit two soiled buffet plates and two empty punch cups on a large tray near the refreshment table for removal to the kitchen.

"I didn't see you arrive," Jarrod admitted.

"I was here when you got here," Colin explained. "Over

there—" He nodded toward the far end of the ballroom, where chaperones sat on a row of chairs keeping close watch on their charges. "Talking with my mother."

"Your mother is here?"

Colin nodded once again. "Chaperoning my younger sister."

"It doesn't seem possible that little Liana's ready to come out."

"She's seventeen," Colin confirmed. "And looking forward to her first real season." The rounds of parties heralding the little season had begun several weeks ago, but the real season didn't start until parliament began its session in May.

"Why aren't they at Almack's?"

"They haven't received vouchers. And frankly, my mother was relieved, because she didn't know how she was going to finance Liana's debut. Especially when everyone knows my father has gambled everything away." A flush of color rose from Colin's neck to the tips of his ears, and he glanced down at the floor. "She needs my help."

Jarrod sighed. Lady McElreath routinely needed Colin's help with the day-to-day expenses of running a home and rearing his siblings. "Seasons are damnably expensive," Jarrod reminded him. "Do you have that kind of blunt?"

Colin looked up from his perusal of the polished leather top of his right shoe. "I've got some capital put away. It should cover the cost of a full season. It won't leave me with much, but Liana's a good lass. She deserves the chance to make a good match, and a full London season with all the trimmings is the best way to accomplish that."

"I could—" Jarrod began.

"No," Colin said firmly. "Thank you, but no. You do plenty." He smiled. "I already owe you the roof over my head and a great many of the clothes on my back. I can't accept more."

"You don't owe me anything," Jarrod protested. "And I have plenty of money. There's no need for you to spend all of your capital on Liana's coming out when I can easily afford to finance it."

Colin managed a self-deprecating laugh. "I know you can. Hell, everybody in London knows you can." His voice deepened to a low, rough burr. "I deeply appreciate your most generous offer. And, believe me, I'm very tempted to take you up on it, but I've managed to make a bit of money off the investments I've made for you and Griff. It's not a big fortune, but it's a tidy sum, and it will be put to good use in launching Liana into society."

"Launching?" Jarrod smiled. "Unleashing is more like it." Colin's younger sister was a true beauty with a mind and a will of her own.

Colin grinned. "Aye, our Liana will cut a wide swathe among London society. And we'll get to enjoy watching her winnow out the lesser men and boys."

Jarrod sobered. "We'll have to be on our guard. We've a charlatan in our midst, preying on the hearts and purses of young girls and their families."

Colin studied the expression on his friend's face. "Was that the case with her?" He nodded toward the dance floor. "Did our impostor prey on her?"

"On whom?" Jarrod asked.

"The young lady you were partnering on the dance floor," Colin replied.

Jarrod smiled. "No," he answered. "Sarah is relatively safe from the likes of that charlatan."

"Sarah?" Colin had never heard Jarrod mention a Sarah, and Jarrod seemed to be well acquainted with this one.

"Sarah Eckersley," Jarrod answered. "Her father is the rector of the church in the village of Helford Green near my childhood home. Although Helford Green comes with an adequate living, Sarah would be of little interest to our impostor, for she has no fortune, and her only family is her father and her maternal aunt."

"Then Liana should be safe from the impostor as well," Colin said. "For it's no secret that we've no fortune of which to boast."

"Unfortunately, the same cannot be said of the young lady you were partnering," Jarrod said.

Colin didn't respond.

"I wasn't the only one dancing," Jarrod reminded him with a twinkle in his eye. "I see Lady Harralson persuaded you to rescue Miss Davies."

"Rescue?" Colin was genuinely puzzled. "From whom?"

"From the passel of jackals who've surrounded her all evening and from the ignominy of being ignored by the other gentlemen present." Jarrod glanced at Colin and then turned toward the dance floor. "With one notable exception—of course."

Colin followed Jarrod's gaze to where Miss Davies was dancing with young Lord Courtland. "It appears I'm no longer an exception."

"No," Jarrod agreed with a knowing smile. "You seem to have broken the ice."

"That's what Lady Harralson hoped would happen when she asked me to partner Miss Davies."

"Lady Harralson certainly chose the right champion." Jarrod struggled to keep from grinning at the irony. "Let's hope Lord Davies is more impressed by your valiant rescue of his daughter from social humiliation than he is by your supposed elopement with her to Gretna Green."

"What?" Colin was astonished.

"Unless I miss my guess, you just danced with the daughter of the man who hired Bow Street to find you."

"Great Caesar's ghost!"

"And then some," Jarrod laughed.

"Are you certain she's the one?"

Jarrod shook his head. "Not entirely. The story is that Gillian Davies just returned from a month spent visiting relatives in the country, but the gossip is that she eloped to Gretna Green with a mysterious gentleman."

Colin ran his hand through his hair and frowned. "And marriageable daughters don't normally leave London at the beginning of the season in order to visit relatives in the country. No matter how devoted. Especially when their fathers have just been elevated to the rank of baron." He looked at Jarrod. "What say we arrange a meeting with the baron tomorrow afternoon?"

Jarrod nodded. "For your protection and the protection of the League, it would be best if the request for a meeting comes from the War Office."

"Will Colonel Grant's staff agree to it?" Colin asked.

"The information you supply to us in your work as Colin Fox is invaluable," Jarrod reminded him. "Colonel Grant's staff is very much aware of that and wishes to get to the bottom of this mystery as badly as we do. I've no doubt they'll approve of a meeting with the Bow Street investigator and the baron in order to find out what they know. The question is whether you want to meet with them or whether you prefer someone else to do it?"

"I'm the man whose movements his Bow Street runner is tracking," Colin said. "You arrange the meeting. I'll attend it."

Jarrod raised an eyebrow. "We don't know who the impostor is. We don't actually have proof that an impostor exists. All we know is that someone eloped with a young woman using your alias. If that young woman turns out to be Gillian Davies, her father may hold you responsible, despite our best efforts to prove otherwise."

"She may have eloped with someone using the same

name, but Miss Davies knows she didn't elope with *me*."

"That may not matter to her father," Jarrod warned. "Baron Davies is a man of considerable wealth and influence. If he's determined to salvage his daughter's damaged reputation, he may not care whether you were the man responsible for damaging it or not."

"I'm aware of that," Colin said. "And I'll do whatever I have to do in order to protect our mission."

"Then, *bon chance, mon ami*," Jarrod said. "I've dealt with the man, and I know firsthand that you're going to need it."

Chapter 8

"We were not born to sue, but to command."
—WILLIAM SHAKESPEARE, 1564–1616
RICHARD II

Baron Davies faced the Bow Street runner from across the vast expanse of a heavy mahogany desk. "What do you mean, my daughter's marriage isn't legal?"

"Exactly what I said, sir." Wickham took a deep breath, mentally counted to ten, and explained his latest findings in greater detail. "I'm sorry to be the man responsible for relaying this information to you, Lord Davies, but I'm afraid your daughter's marriage cannot be legal."

"She told me she eloped to Scotland, stood before a magistrate, and repeated her vows before witnesses," Lord Davies related the facts he'd gleaned from Gillian. "Once she crossed the border into Scotland, she no longer required my permission to wed. Under the law, her marriage was perfectly valid."

"That's true, sir," Mr. Wickham agreed. "And had it not been for the fact that the man she wed has two other wives, her marriage would be quite valid—providing he signed his true name. Unfortunately, your daughter's bridegroom has two other wives he married, under different names, before he wed your daughter."

"So, he's a bigamist?" Lord Davies's face turned a dark shade of scarlet.

"It would seem so." Wickham nodded. "He married the other two women and your daughter within three months of one another. And all at the same anvil in Gretna Green." He paused a moment in order to frame his next words. "It seems the magistrate—and I use that term loosely—who married him was equally unscrupulous and quite amiable to well-placed bribes of coin and jewelry. He swears that the man who married your daughter also married two other women—under different names, of course. According to the magistrate, your daughter's husband wed three women in or- der to—" The Bow Street investigator cleared his throat. "In order to—well, I'm sure you can imagine why a scoundrel would pretend to marry an innocent young woman."

"To seduce her?" Lord Davies banged his fist down on his desk. "That bounder married my daughter with full knowledge of the fact that he had already married two other women in order to seduce her?"

"Well, yes," Wickham admitted. "And to relieve her of her coin and her valuables before sending her home in dis- grace, where he would then continue to blackmail her for more cash in return for his silence."

The baron was livid. "How dare he make my daughter his third wife? If he was going to become a bigamist, he should have made her his first wife. How dare he consider Gillian his third choice?"

Mr. Wickham thought the baron's display of temper was misplaced. It seemed to him that Lord Davies's concern should be for his daughter's emotional state of mind and the physical complications that might arise from her brief encounter with a scoundrel. As far as Wickham was con- cerned, a bigamist was a bigamist, and the order of any marriages, beyond the first legal one, was of no impor- tance. But the rich were different from ordinary folk, and Wickham had had enough dealings with the rich to know that the best way to handle Lord Davies's display of temper was to wait until it passed before he continued. "This cannot, in any way, be construed as an insult to your daughter, sir. In fact, our Mr. Fox would consider his choosing your daughter a compliment. He found her worthy of his attention."

"Of course she's worthy of his attention! He's a scoundrel, a criminal, and a bigamist, while she is a lady, a beauty, and a considerable heiress!"

"That goes without saying, sir," Wickham attempted to soothe the baron's wounded pride. "And it is quite possible that Mr. Fox's fondness for your daughter outstrips any affection he feels for the other two. He may even have genuinely desired a legal marriage with your daughter. But the fact that he married your daughter after he'd married the other two women makes your daughter's elopement and marriage null and void."

"What of her reputation?" Lord Davies demanded. "My daughter made a mistake by eloping with a bounder, but she married him in good faith."

"Yes, she did," Mr. Wickham, agreed. "And I believe your daughter is an honorable young woman. Unfortunately, she ran afoul of a man who uses a number of different names and to whom honor means little."

Mr. Wickham's diplomatic turn of phrase went a long way to mollifying Lord Davies. During their association, the Bow Street runner had quickly learned that Lord Davies tended to be very prickly wherever he perceived an insult or slight to his rank or his name. And the idea that a scoundrel would marry two other women before he married a baron's daughter was abhorrent to him.

"Have you any idea where to find the rogue?" Lord Davies asked.

The Bow Street runner did have an idea where to find the rogue, but only because he'd found a note from Lieutenant Colonel Colquhoun Grant of the War Department

awaiting him as soon as he arrived in his office this morning. The note from Colonel Grant requested an afternoon
meeting between Viscount Grantham and Baron Davies to
discuss the runner's current search for Mr. Colin Fox.

Wickham related the details of the note, then followed
by saying, "I took the liberty of issuing an invitation to
Viscount Grantham to meet with us this afternoon in order
to discuss information Viscount Grantham claims to have
about the identity and the possible whereabouts of our
elusive Mr. Fox."

"Grantham?" Baron Davies cocked his head. "What has
he to do with this?"

"Mr. Fox has lived up to his name. He's been almost impossible to follow," Wickham admitted reluctantly. "And
every trail I've managed to uncover has led, in some way,
to the War Office. Lord Grantham is attached to the War
Office. I haven't been apprised of the nature of his connection or the extent of his involvement in the department." He
frowned. "That part is rather murky. But the fact remains
that the colonel sent word that Viscount Grantham had information to impart about the man we seek but would only
do so in a private meeting with you."

Baron Davies gave a thoughtful nod. "My daughter told
me her husband was attached to the War Office and was
acting as a clandestine agent for our government against
Bonaparte and the French."

Wickham sighed. He hoped Miss Davies's information
was correct and her erstwhile spouse was exactly what he
pretended to be. But declaring oneself an agent for the
government had become the latest fashion among young
thieves and confidence men. It sounded heroic, romantic,
and exciting, and young ladies flocked to heroes in droves.
And the idea that a young man was a clandestine agent
working for the good of his country appeared to give license to all sorts of behavior, on the part of all involved
that would otherwise be considered quite beyond the pale.

According to Bow Street's most recent estimates, approximately one in every six young men of a certain age and background in London claimed to be acting on behalf of the British government or on behalf of one of its allies. "I'm afraid your daughter may be mistaken, sir."

The runner didn't need to elaborate.

Baron Davies understood that his daughter had trusted a man who lied to her, married her under false pretenses, and abandoned her in a foreign land, leaving her to make her way home as best she could. If he lied about marrying her, then he'd most likely lied about everything else. "When is the meeting to take place?"

The Bow Street runner glanced up at the clock on the mantelshelf. "Lord Grantham should arrive any moment."

"Good," Baron Davies pronounced. "I'll be interested to hear what the young viscount has to say."

Colin entered Lord Davies's study some ten minutes later. He extended his hand to the baron as Lord Davies's butler announced him. "Good afternoon, Lord Davies." Colin greeted the baron and then shook hands with the Bow Street runner. "Mr. Wickham. I'm Grantham. And before we begin, I must inform you that anything that's discussed in this room must remain entirely confidential. We three"— Colin cast a sideways glance at the butler—"are the only participants, and if word of this meeting or any of the subjects we discuss leaves this room, I shall hold you entirely responsible."

"Of course." Lord Davies wasted no time on pleasantries. "Your warning is well taken and your threat quite unnecessary. I assure you that neither Mr. Wickham nor I wish to have the contents of this meeting divulged. We are all gentlemen and shall be held to the highest standard of behavior."

Colin nodded his assent.

Davies motioned the younger man into the study before dismissing the butler. "That will be all, Saunders. I'll ring if there's anything we require. Otherwise, we are not to be disturbed for any reason." Lord Davies waited until the butler withdrew from the study before turning his attention back to Colin. "So tell me, Lord Grantham, what do you and the War Office know about the man known as Colin Fox?"

Colin narrowed his gaze at the baron as the older man quickly dispensed with polite formalities and began demanding answers. Colin recognized a formidable opponent when he saw one. Baron Davies didn't mince words.

But Colin wasn't easily quelled. "I've come to ask you and your Bow Street detective the same questions."

Lord Davies was momentarily taken aback. "Why would you ask us about the man we've been hunting?"

"I ask because you've been hunting the wrong man," Colin answered.

"Impossible!" The Bow Street runner exclaimed. "I've been on Colin Fox's trail from the moment Lord Davies's daughter returned from Scotland."

Colin felt a sinking sensation in the pit of his stomach. He ground his teeth together to keep from giving voice to his sudden, acute disappointment. He hadn't realized until that moment how much he had wanted Jarrod's information to be incorrect. But Jarrod's sources of information were impeccable, as always.

Colin didn't believe in coincidence, and even if he did, he'd be hard pressed to believe that the reason for this meeting and Gillian Davies's return from Scotland were unrelated. "You have been on the trail of one Colin Fox," Colin informed the Bow Street runner. "Unfortunately, you've been on the trail of the wrong Colin Fox."

Wickham looked skeptical. "Are you telling us there's more than one?"

"That's exactly what I'm telling you," Colin said.

"How do you know?" Lord Davies demanded.

His hopes of surviving the meeting with Baron Davies and the Bow Street runner with his secret identity intact were dwindling, but Colin followed Colonel Grant's orders and did his best to stanch Lord Davies's quest for information. "My position in the War Office makes me privy to information about Colin Fox of which ordinary citizens are unaware." Colin paused before elaborating. "Of which you are unaware."

"I am aware that the man is an unscrupulous criminal who should make his home in Old Bailey or aboard a transport ship," the baron replied. "And I'm not going to rest until I see that he does."

Colin inhaled. "And I'm here to ask that you suspend your search and allow the War Office to handle this matter."

"I will do no such thing!" Lord Davies exclaimed. "That bounder eloped to Gretna Green with my daughter and abandoned her at a coaching inn after relieving her of her virtue." The baron's voice shook from the force of his anger. "He ruined my daughter, and I intend to see that he pays for it."

"Your daughter must have been a willing participant in her elopement," Colin said, playing devil's advocate and baiting the hook to see if the baron would bite. "Eloping to Scotland is scandalous behavior, but it's not insurmountable so long as your daughter's paramour had the clergy or the authorities bless the union before he relieved her of her virtue. It may take a while, but marriage tends to soften attitudes, and your daughter should be able to recover her position in society."

"That might be true if my daughter was legally wed," Lord Davies snapped, "but the fact that the scoundrel with whom she eloped already had two wives makes her marriage redundant. If it becomes known that my daughter married a bigamist, I'm afraid it will cause a scandal from which she may never recover."

"Does she know her marriage isn't valid?" Colin asked suddenly.

"Of course not! We just discovered it ourselves." Lord

Davies raked his hand through his thinning hair. "And to think I sent her back into the ton last night to try to quash the rumors. If word of this gets out . . ." The baron glared at Colin. "If you or the War Office are protecting or harboring this scoundrel, I demand to know why!"

The knot in Colin's stomach grew tighter as he recalled the look of betrayal on Gillian Davies's face when they'd talked of honor and chivalry. Colin took a deep breath before carefully choosing his words. "The War Office is not protecting the man with whom your daughter eloped."

"But it is protecting someone," Mr. Wickham guessed, looking Colin in the eye. "Or you wouldn't be here."

"I came to find out how much you knew."

"About Colin Fox?" Wickham queried.

"About the man you are hunting," Colin corrected.

"We know enough," Lord Davies interrupted. "My daughter told me that the man she married was attached to the War Office and was acting as a clandestine agent for our government against Bonaparte and the French."

"Miss Davies claimed her husband was a government agent?" That was news to Colin. Unpleasant news. Dangerous news. Jarrod wasn't going to be happy about it at all.

"Yes," Lord Davies answered. "And now the War Office has sent you to keep us from bringing one of your spies to justice."

"One of *my* spies?" Colin managed to sound incredulous. "I'm afraid you overestimate my importance to the War Office." He looked first at the baron and then at the runner. "I have no spies."

"You are attached to the War Office," Wickham reminded him. "And while the nature of your involvement is shrouded in secrecy, those of us at Bow Street are aware of Colonel Grant's role in recruiting and training covert agents to act on behalf of His Majesty's government."

Colin didn't attempt to dispute Wickham's word. When he replied, his answer was truthful. "I was unaware that the man you are seeking claimed to be an agent of His Majesty's government."

"Every trail I followed led to the War Office," Wickham said.

"Only because you've been following the wrong trail," Colin insisted.

"Then how is it that you are involved, Lord Grantham? How did you know we were hunting anyone?" The baron finally asked the most obvious questions. "Especially, a man who shares your Christian name? Unless you are the man we seek? Unless you and Colin Fox are one and the same?"

Chapter 9

"The devil can cite Scripture for his purpose."
—WILLIAM SHAKESPEARE, 1564–1616
THE MERCHANT OF VENICE

"*I am not the man you seek,*" Colin denied calmly.

"But you *are* Colin Fox," Wickham stated, pinning Colin with a knowing look as understanding finally dawned.

Colin met his gaze. "Colin Fox is a name I've had occasion to use."

"Did you use it when you eloped with my daughter to Gretna Green?" Lord Davies accused.

"I've never been to Gretna Green," Colin said.

"I suppose you're going to deny an acquaintance with my daughter as well," Lord Davies sneered.

"Not at all," Colin retorted. "I met your daughter for the first time last night at Lady Harralson's soiree. I partnered her in a dance. I didn't elope with her."

"But Colin Fox did," Wickham said. "And shortly thereafter, Lord Davies hired me to find him."

"Exactly," Colin said. "And every trail you investigated led to the wrong Colin Fox."

"My investigation has made the War Office uncomfortable," Wickham surmised.

Colin nodded once again. "The work I do is vital," he said. "We cannot afford to have anyone inquiring about Colin Fox."

"Especially when the Colin Fox I've been seeking has no connection with the War Office," Wickham added.

"Now you understand my dilemma," Colin told him.

"I don't care about your dilemma." Lord Davies crossed his arms over his chest and glared at Colin and at Wickham. "I care about my daughter's disgrace."

"I had nothing to do with your daughter's disgrace."

"That's of little consequence to me," Lord Davies informed him. "I hired Bow Street to find Colin Fox, and Mr. Wickham has accomplished that task."

"Lord Grantham has green eyes. According to Lady Davies, the other Colin Fox's eyes are a nice shade of blue. Since Lord Grantham cannot change the color of his eyes, he cannot be the only Colin Fox," Wickham reminded the baron.

"Unless my wife and daughter are mistaken about the color of the rogue's eyes being a nice shade of blue," the baron said, "instead of a nice shade of leaf green."

"Women don't usually mistake that sort of thing," Wickham disagreed. "Lord Grantham isn't the Fox we seek."

"But he's the one we have."

Colin didn't like the sound of that. "Lord Davies—" he began.

But the baron cut him off. "Do you know where the blue-eyed Colin Fox is?"

"No," Colin admitted.

"Can you prove there is a blue-eyed Colin Fox?" Lord Davies asked.

"Not at the moment," Colin admitted. "But I don't have to. Your daughter can prove there's another one. She eloped with *someone,* sir. Someone who married her using the name I sometimes use."

"And you've no idea who that someone is," Lord Davies concluded.

"None. But I'll wager his decision to use that particular name wasn't a coincidence."

"Is it possible that he's using his real name?" Wickham asked.

Colin shook his head. "According to our information, there should only have been one Colin Fox in greater London and its environs."

"And now you've got two," Wickham said.

"Of which we're aware."

Wickham pursed his lips in thought, then began to pace the width of the room. "I agree with you, Lord Grantham. That's not coincidence."

"Coincidence or not, it's going to be fortuitous for my daughter," Baron Davies announced. "Because I intend to see that something good comes of this disaster." He gave Colin a speculative look. "You're a viscount, Lord Grantham, from an old and respectable family. Gillian could do far worse."

Lord Davies's suggestion stunned Colin. "You can't mean to imply that I should assume responsibility for another man's actions—"

"What other man?" The baron was all innocence. "As far as I know, you're the only man."

"Your daughter knows otherwise," Colin reminded him.

"My daughter desperately needs a way out of the mess," Lord Davies replied. "And I mean to do the best I can for her and the child she may be carrying by providing it." He looked Colin up and down. "You may not be the scoundrel who seduced and abandoned her, but you've admitted to using the same name. As far as I'm concerned, you and Colin Fox are one and the same."

"We are *not* one and the same," Colin corrected.

But Baron Davies wasn't listening. "She married Colin Fox in good faith, and that's the same as marrying you."

"It is *not* the same," Colin's Scottish burr grew more pronounced as his voice took on determined edge. "I did not marry your daughter. And she did not marry me."

Baron Davies looked Colin in the eye. "But you will," he said. "And so will she."

"Oh, no . . ." Colin held up his hand as if to stop the words and the idea he knew would follow. For once the baron gave voice to the idea, there would be no going back.

"It would be an ideal solution," Wickham added, suddenly realizing the advantages of Lord Davies's proposition.

"For whom?" Colin demanded.

"For everyone involved." Lord Davies grinned. "My family, His Majesty's government, Colonel Grant and those who work within the War Office and keep its secrets, Bow Street and Mr. Wickham, the other Colin Fox—if he exists—and you, Lord Grantham."

Colin arched an eyebrow at Lord Davies. "You know I had nothing to do with your daughter's unfortunate elopement, yet you expect me to pay for it. Tell me, Lord Davies, how that solution benefits me?"

"You get to marry my daughter." Lord Davies reached over and clapped Colin on the back. "And you get to continue your vital work for His Majesty's government; otherwise I'll continue my investigation, and I won't stop until I uncover every scrap of information there is about Colin Fox and his position in the War Office."

Jarrod had warned him, but still, Colin was stunned at the baron's apparent ruthlessness. "You would endanger the lives of the brave men fighting for their country just to secure a husband for your daughter?"

"I'll do whatever's necessary to secure *you* as husband for my daughter, because your position doesn't allow for scandal any more than hers does."

"No offense, sir, but I'm not inclined to marry, and your daughter may feel likewise."

"My daughter is disgraced," the baron said. "If she

marries you, she gets a husband, a respected name and title for herself and the child she may be carrying, and protection from blackmail and scandal."

"Protection, a respected name, and title would be all she'd get," Colin said bluntly. "As you are no doubt aware, I'm in no position to take a wife or accept a legal heir. My line of work doesn't afford me that luxury. And neither does my bank balance." He frowned. He might have been able to afford a wife yesterday, before he'd promised to pay for Liana's season. But today, it was out of the question. "And if I did consent to marry her, I wouldn't have a place to put her or a child who would become my legal responsibility." He looked at the baron. "I occupy a suite of rooms in the Marquess of Shepherdston's town house across the park. I don't have a home of my own in which to take her."

"You marry my daughter, and you'll be able to afford anything your heart desires," Lord Davies told him cheerfully. "I'm a very wealthy man, and as my only child, my daughter stands to inherit a vast fortune. Her dowry is quite handsome."

Colin had always known he would have to offer himself up as a sacrifice on the altar of matrimony one day. He had always understood that marrying money was the only practical solution to his problem. He couldn't maintain his place in society and support his mother and siblings without a considerable income, and although his financial investments were turning a profit, Colin couldn't make enough money to pay his father's gambling debts and support them all.

Bloody hell, but the baron's solution was tempting! More tempting than he wanted to admit. Colin had never dreamed he'd be faced with a moral dilemma. He'd never imagined that he would find the idea of selling himself to a rich prospective father-in-law objectionable, but that was before a rich prospective father-in-law had made an offer.

Now, the idea seemed sordid somehow, like trafficking in slaves and sugar in the West Indies or seducing and stealing from unsuspecting virgins. "It's tempting, Lord Davies, but I'm not for sale."

"Everyone's for sale at some price." Lord Davies studied the expression on Colin's face. "And I mean to buy my daughter a respectable husband, *whatever* the price. Surely, that comes as no surprise to you, Lord Grantham. It's the way in which the world works and the way in which most unions are fashioned—especially among the peerage. You're a poor viscount. You must have realized that you would have to secure a wealthy heiress as wife someday."

"I've been a dedicated bachelor since I was but nine years of age because I'm a poor viscount with little chance to inherit even the most moderate of incomes," Colin informed him. "I've always known I would have to marry well in order to support my family in the manner my name and title demands. I didn't know I would find the proposition so distasteful."

"I, for one, am delighted to hear it!" Baron Davies threw back his head and laughed. "Because I've already had one request for fifty thousand pounds for her upkeep from her first husband and I'd find it distasteful to have *another* fortune hunter marry my daughter. The fact that you find the idea of marrying her for my money repugnant sets my mind at ease. I hate to disappoint you, Lord Grantham, but you're no matrimonial mercenary. And that's all the more reason you should marry her."

"I don't follow," Colin said.

"It's simple," Lord Davies explained. "I prefer you to a true fortune hunter. You have more to offer than you know. In the course of performing your vital work for His Majesty's government, you will be able to find the man masquerading as Colin Fox and bring him to justice without risking my daughter's reputation. Who better to see justice done for a lady betrayed than her father and her new husband?"

"That's blackmail."

"Of course it is," the baron agreed.

"I'll be sacrificing my freedom."

"Yes, you will," Lord Davies replied. "But you'll be amply rewarded for doing so, and you'll have the satisfaction of knowing that you sacrificed your freedom to protect a young woman's reputation and your country's secrets."

Chapter 10

"The first thing we do, let's kill all the lawyers."
—WILLIAM SHAKESPEARE, 1564–1616
KING HENRY VI, PART 2

*H*e had sold his soul to the devil. *An* English devil. A ruthless *merchant* devil. Life, as he knew it, was over.

Colin McElreath, twenty-seventh Viscount Grantham, stared down at his signature on the smooth vellum paper as he pressed his signet ring into the puddle of melted red wax on the document. It was done. He was about to become a very wealthy man. And his new solvency had only cost him his good name, his title, his future, his freedom, and fifteen hundred pounds sterling.

Colin was relinquishing his Free Fellow status, sealing his fate for cash because duty required it. Because his first loyalty was to the Free Fellows League and the work they did. The work they had sworn to do. But Colin had an equally large obligation to his family. Because his father, the ninth Earl of McElreath, had squandered what had remained of the family fortune and because the man standing before him—the newly created Baron Davies—was a rich silk merchant who urgently required a respectable son-in-law for his disgraced daughter and had ruthlessly set in motion the means to make it happen . . .

"Welcome to the family," the baron said. "It's been a pleasure doing business with you, my lord."

Colin grunted in reply, wincing at the baron's choice of words. *Pleasure? What pleasure?* Colin's wince became a frown. A few bold strokes of his pen had forced him into the ultimate sacrifice. He'd sold himself for a few million pieces of silver, sentenced himself to a lifetime of *marriage* to a girl who had foolishly entrusted her heart and her virtue to a scoundrel who had eloped with her, then abandoned her at an inn in Edinburgh. A scoundrel impersonating a government agent. A scoundrel impersonating him.

Colin didn't know whether to laugh or to cry at the irony. After a lifetime of avoiding society misses, he was about to marry one. His betrothed was damaged goods, but her good name and her place in society were safe.

Miss Gillian Davies was about to become a blushing bride.

He was merely the groom.

Baron Davies took the marriage contract Colin had just signed, scrawled his name at the bottom, and set his seal beside his signature. When he was done, he blotted the ink and passed the paper along to Wickham and to Mr. Hayes, the solicitor, who had delivered the marriage contract a half hour earlier and who had stayed to witness the signing of it.

After verifying the signatures, the solicitor returned the document to Lord Davies.

Lord Davies barely allowed the ink to dry before he carefully folded the contract, slipped it into a sheepskin folder, and locked the contract in the top drawer of his desk. He pocketed the desk key, then rubbed his palms together. "I believe this calls for a celebration."

Colin didn't know if the situation called for a celebration, but he made no objection as Lord Davies walked over to the drinks table and began pulling out bottles.

He didn't need the ceremony, but he certainly needed the drink.

"Brandy, Madeira, claret, or whisky?" The baron asked, looking first to his future son-in-law, then to his solicitor and the Bow Street detective.

"Whisky," Colin answered.

"Claret for me, sir," Wickham replied.

"Brandy, if you will, sir," Mr. Hayes responded.

"And whisky for me." Lord Davies couldn't keep the note of glee from his voice. He poured the drinks and handed the glasses around before lifting his in toast. "Here's to a long and successful union."

"Hear, hear," Wickham and the solicitor echoed.

"To Lady Grantham," Colin murmured softly, briefly clinking his glass against Lord Davies's before taking a hefty swallow of the bracing whisky.

"I'll have Hayes draw up another copy of the agreement," Lord Davies offered, "and have it sent around to your solicitor for review. We can negotiate the points you deem less than advantageous once your solicitor has had an opportunity to read it."

Colin nodded. "I've no complaints with the generous dowry or the general terms of the contract, Lord Davies. I find it quite favorable."

"Mr. Hayes and I decided any marriage contract we devised must offer a few more incentives once my daughter returned from Scotland without her groom. Her purity can no longer be guaranteed, and we thought it prudent to make allowances for that fact. Mr. Hayes suggested that we treat her as if she were a new widow and proceed accordingly."

Colin bit his tongue to keep from pointing out that a new widow wouldn't need to worry about protecting her good name and would, most likely, have inherited at least a widow's portion of her husband's estate, whereas the illegal wife of a bigamist might be haunted by the specter of scandal and gossip for years. But the solicitor's suggestions explained the modest amount of the pin money he was to provide while he lived and the generous and extremely favorable terms regarding the jointure and children's portions after his death.

The marriage contract Lord Davies and his solicitor had
crafted minimized the bridegroom's expenses and maximized the gain. In this marriage document, the husband
benefited from the alliance to a much greater degree than
the bride. He gained a fortune and the prospect of an heir.
She gained safe haven and protection from those who
would sully her name. Lord Davies had waived a number
of the customary safeguards generally included to protect
his female offspring and ordered a contract drawn up that
virtually guaranteed that his daughter's intended would
have no reason to cry off at the last minute. While Colin
didn't object to benefiting financially, he greatly objected
to the idea that Gillian Davies might suffer financially.
"I've signed the existing contract," Colin reminded him,
"but I'd consider it a personal favor if you would have your
solicitor include a larger separate estate for your daughter's
protection." He looked Lord Davies in the eye. "My father
is an inveterate gambler. I'll not have it said that I entered
into an agreement that left my bride-to-be vulnerable. As
an heiress, she should be protected from financial ruin in
the event I develop a similar propensity for losing vast
quantities of my wife's fortune."

Lord Davies bit back a smile. "I don't foresee that happening."

"I'm sure my maternal grandfather didn't foresee that
happening to my mother, either," Colin pointed out. "And
as a consequence of losing her fortune, my mother and my
siblings are dependent upon my generosity and the generosity of strangers in order to survive. I would not have a
similar situation thrust upon your daughter or upon my
heir, should God see fit to grace me with one. I insist upon
that modification of the contract." He glanced at Mr.
Hayes. "I admit that I can be bought, but that particular
issue is not negotiable."

"Agreed." Lord Davies was wise enough to realize that the young viscount was smarting from the impending loss of his bachelor status and the manner in which it had come about. Grantham was a good negotiator, but an older, more experienced and ruthless one had bested him. In large part, because the young viscount was more far more honorable than he believed himself to be.

After witnessing that exchange between Lord Davies and Viscount Grantham, the Bow Street runner drained his glass and set it on the drinks table. Lord Davies's solicitor immediately followed suit. "We should be going, sir," Wickham said.

"Yes, of course." Lord Davies pulled an envelope from his jacket pocket and handed it to the detective. "Thank you, Mr. Wickham. I appreciate the work you've done on my daughter's behalf."

Wickham took the envelope and tucked into his pocket. "I'm pleased everything has worked out to your satisfaction, my lords."

Saunders knocked on the study door.

Lord Davies opened it. "Mr. Wickham and Mr. Hayes are leaving," he told the butler. "Please see them out."

"Very good, sir." Saunders bowed and allowed the detective and the solicitor to precede him before he withdrew from the study and closed the door behind them.

Lord Davies waited until the others had left the room before he turned to Colin and asked, "Is there anything else you'd like?"

Colin placed his empty whisky glass on the drinks table. "A reprieve."

The baron laughed. "After all the trouble I went to in order to force your hand? Not bloody likely."

"The blackmail of an innocent man is troubling business," Colin retorted. "But you were quite up to the task."

"Only because you made it possible," Lord Davies answered. "You allowed it. Had you not agreed to meet with me this afternoon, I would still be engaged in the hunt for the other, more elusive Colin Fox."

"Unfortunately for us, you were much more likely to damage my work and bring harm to my colleagues with your persistent probing than locate the impostor and put an end to his nefarious ways." Colin exhaled. "I took a calculated risk that I could prevail upon you to end your search, and I failed."

"You failed because I have as much to protect as you," Lord Davies said. "And equal justification for doing so. I can't allow your *impostor* to continue to victimize my daughter or other young ladies of good family. You understand the risks and the rules of the games you play. The young ladies your impostor preys upon did not. Don't they deserve the same measure of protection and secrecy you and your colleagues enjoy?"

"Yes," Colin replied. "And I entered into a personal contract with you in order to insure they have it."

Lord Davies smiled. "Doesn't the fact that I'm willing to guarantee you profit handsomely from our personal contract mean anything?"

"Of course it does," Colin answered. "It means I'm going to profit handsomely from blackmail."

"Take heart, my boy," Lord Davies encouraged. "You're being blackmailed, you aren't committing it."

"I might as well be," Colin said. "Because I'm profiting from it just the same."

"Think of the advantages, not the disadvantages," the baron advised.

"I have," Colin told him. "The advantage is that I'll be wealthy enough to insure my family no longer has to suffer the consequences of my father's misdeeds." He looked the baron in the eye. "The disadvantage is that now, your daughter will have no recourse but to continue to suffer the consequences of hers. She made an error in judgment, Davies. And forcing her to marry a man she doesn't love so she can hold her head up in society won't necessarily correct that error or make for a long and happy union. It would be far better for the both of us if we were permitted to choose."

"She chose her first husband," Lord Davies said. "That's how we found ourselves in this predicament. My choice is the better one."

"You can't know whether it is or not."

"I'll stake my life on it."

"Easy for you to say." Colin snorted. "You don't have to live with me." He turned and measured his steps back to the window overlooking the immaculate garden. "You've only to look at my sire to see that I'm not exactly cut from quality husband cloth. So tell me, Lord Davies, are you willing to stake your daughter's life on whether you've made the better bargain, or shall we call the whole thing off?"

"I know I've made the better bargain," Lord Davies said. "You've shown more concern for Gillian in an hour's meeting with her father than that bounder did after three days of marriage to her." He walked over and clapped Colin on the shoulder. "Be patient, my boy, and love will come in time."

Colin snorted once again. *Love will come in time. Would it? And if so, for whom?* Gillian Davies had already demonstrated her love for someone else. And Colin had sworn not to love at all. If love decided to make an appearance, it would spell heartache for both of them. "When do you propose the wedding take place?"

"Tomorrow morning," Lord Davies answered. "Have you a special license or should I procure one?"

Colin pinched the bridge of his nose. "I have one." He had purchased a special license to marry when he'd begun working in the War Office. Not because Colin wanted to marry—Free Fellows avoided the parson's mousetrap at all costs—but because Colonel Grant had suggested it. A special license enabled the bearer to marry any place and at any time, and clandestine operatives never knew when it might be handy to have one. Colin hadn't expected to use it for years. He certainly hadn't expected to use it on the morrow. But it appeared that his luck had run out.

"Then we're all set," Lord Davies pronounced. "I'll notify the vicar and have the household prepare a breakfast."

"What about your daughter?"

"What about her?" The baron asked.

"Do you intend to notify her before the wedding?" Colin's pointed question gave Lord Davies pause. "Or do you intend that it should be a surprise?"

The baron flushed bright red. "I confess to taking the coward's way out and thinking it might be best to break the news before breakfast tomorrow morning."

Colin studied the man who would become his father-in-law on the morrow. "If it's all the same to you, Lord Davies, I'd appreciate the opportunity to speak with her today." He gave the baron an ironic smile. "If your daughter objects to the idea, I'd prefer to know it before we're asked to plight our troth."

Chapter 11

*"So every bondsman in his own hand bears
The power to cancel his captivity."*

—WILLIAM SHAKESPEARE, 1564–1616

JULIUS CAESAR

"Papa?" Gillian opened the door to her father's study and stepped inside. "Saunders said you wanted to see me?"

Lord Davies gave his daughter a welcoming smile. "Yes, Gillian, please come in and join us."

Gillian arched an eyebrow in silent query. She had seen two gentlemen leave the house by way of the front door as she made her way down the stairs. She hadn't realized her father had another guest until she noticed the broad-shouldered gentleman staring out the window overlooking the west lawn.

Colin turned to face her. "Good afternoon, Miss Davies."

Gillian's breath caught in her throat. Viscount Grantham was every bit as handsome in the daylight as he was in the evening.

He stared at her, taking in every detail of her appearance from the top of her curly black hair to the tips of her pale blue slippers and everything in between. Her soft lemony fragrance surrounded him, awakening his senses and confirming his worst suspicions. He had smelled that scent

before. Not last night at Lady Harralson's, but weeks earlier in a dark room in the Blue Bottle Inn in Edinburgh. He
had held the woman wearing that scent in his arms all
night, and the fragrance of lemons had clung to his jacket
and haunted him for days afterward. Colin reacted to it
now with a powerful hunger that caught him unawares, like
a hard fist in the stomach. "A pleasure to see you again."

Gillian blushed in spite of herself. "Likewise, Lord
Grantham."

Lord Davies studied his daughter. "It seems you and his
lordship are already acquainted."

Gillian wrinkled her brow. "We are," she answered.
"Lady Harralson introduced us at her party last night. Lord
Grantham and I danced a minuet."

Lord Davies was genuinely surprised. "A minuet, eh?"

Gillian's eyes sparkled as she looked at her father.
"Lord Grantham is a wonderful dancer." She glanced at
Colin from beneath the shadow of her lashes. "And surpris-
ingly light on his feet for so big a man."

Her compliment surprised him. Colin gave her a warm
smile. "I'm a man of hidden talents."

"You do the fair maidens of London a great disservice by
keeping your talents on the dance floor hidden, my lord."
She returned his smile. "Especially during the height of the
season. I'm sure you realize that we suffer from such a
dearth of willing dance partners that hostesses all over town
are pressed into service making introductions in a valiant effort to supply enough to meet the overwhelming demand."

Colin laughed. "Touché. But I beg to differ with you on
one point, Miss Davies."

"Oh?" Her voice rose a bit. "And what point might that
be?"

"Our first meeting," he said. "Our hostess, Lady Harralson, presented me for an introduction, but your mother,
Lady Davies, introduced us."

"That's right," Gillian agreed. "Mama did introduce us."

She turned to her father. "She and Lord Grantham's mother serve on the same ladies' charities. Mama met Lord Grantham at his mother's house."

"Satisfied?" Colin demanded of Lord Davies.

"Entirely," the baron replied.

Gillian frowned. "Papa, I don't understand. What is this about?" She looked at her father as if she suspected he and Grantham were in league.

Colin looked at Gillian. "Your father thought I might be someone I am not."

The blood drained from her face, and her eyes widened in alarm. Unshed tears burned her eyes as she battled to maintain control. "You think . . ." She looked from her father to the viscount and back again. "He came to call and . . . Oh, Papa, you told him, didn't you?" Her voice broke, and Gillian colored as the hot rush of embarrassment reached her face.

Lord Davies nodded.

"You shouldn't have." Gillian wished the floor would open up and swallow her. "Lord Grantham didn't . . . I only met him last night. He had nothing to do with"— she paused—"what happened to me."

Colin cleared his throat. "I'm afraid your father had no choice but to tell me after his investigator followed a trail that led to my door."

"It's your Christian name," Gillian said. "You share the same Christian name, but Papa's investigator made a mistake. You are not the man Papa meant to find."

"He's exactly the man I wanted to find," Lord Davies contradicted.

Gillian's resolve seemed to desert her, and she abruptly dropped onto the big leather ottoman in front of the massive wing chair. She wanted to apologize to the viscount, but she didn't have the words to express what she was feeling.

"I travel the length and breadth of England and Scotland on business," Colin explained. "Colin Fox is a name

I've often had occasion to use. That's why your father's investigator found me."

"Why would you travel the width and breadth of England and Scotland using another man's name?" Gillian asked.

"I'm a viscount," he stated in the firm, confident tone the other higher-ranking Free Fellows often used. "It's common practice for those in my position to travel incognito in order to avoid attracting unwanted attention from highwaymen, bandits, and ne'er-do-wells." He shrugged his shoulders. "And as far as I know, I'm not using another man's name," Colin answered. "He's using mine."

"I could be mistaken," Gillian admitted, "but I was given to understand your family name is McElreath."

"It is."

Gillian sighed. "As we seemed to be at sixes and sevens over whose name belongs to whom, perhaps it's best if you explain yourself."

"All right." Colin admired her forthright approach. "The man you knew as Colin Fox and I are sharing more than a Christian name. We appear to be sharing an identity."

"You can't be . . ." Gillian began. "Colin Fox is an agent with His Majesty's government." She glanced up at Viscount Grantham's face and faltered. "Isn't he?"

The look in her big, blue eyes was devastating. The hurt she had suffered and the doubt she felt shimmered in their depths.

"It's possible." Colin looked at Lord Davies and dared him to contradict him. "Or all of this may be a big misunderstanding, but since he married you using a name I also use—" He broke off as Gillian blanched.

"I'm married to both of you?" She guessed.

"No," Colin said softly.

Gillian breathed a sigh of relief.

"You're not legally married to either of us."

Gillian buried her face in her hands. "I was afraid of that," she murmured.

Colin would have sworn she was innocent of the deception, but her answer begged the question. "You knew the man with whom you eloped was using a false name?"

Gillian shook her head. "I had no idea. I believed he was who he said he was." She uncovered her eyes, but she kept one hand over her mouth almost as if she meant to keep her admission inside. "I believed everything he told me."

"When did you stop believing?" Colin's voice was little more than a gruff whisper.

Gillian looked down at her hands. At the third finger of her left hand where a ring should have been. "When she told me I wasn't the only one."

"Who told you?" Colin asked.

"The innkeeper's wife."

"The innkeeper at the inn in Gretna Green?" Lord Davies asked.

Gillian didn't answer, and Colin had a vivid memory of a woman's face at the window of the Blue Bottle Inn. And Colin had an equally vivid memory of the spite in the words of the innkeeper's wife when she had spoken of the lady upstairs.

"Why didn't you say anything?" Lord Davies asked.

"I didn't want to cause a bigger scandal than I already had," she said sadly. "You were trying so hard to keep everyone in the ton from learning I'd eloped. I didn't want to make it worse by telling you that I was foolish enough to elope with a man who had already married two other women." She met her father's penetrating gaze. "I thought that if I did as you asked, Papa, and played along, you would forget about finding him, and the gossip would fade away. I thought I might get a second chance to make things right." Tears rolled down Gillian's face, but she was oblivious to them.

"You *are* getting a second chance." Colin leaned down and tilted her face up, lifting her chin with the tip of his index finger so he could look into her extraordinary blue eyes. "If you want one. For, you see, Miss Davies, I didn't come to call upon you, I came to ask you to marry me."

"You want to marry me?" Gillian wasn't sure she heard him correctly.

"I do," Colin answered.

"Why?" she asked bluntly, reeling from shock.

"What difference does it make?" Lord Davies interrupted. "The viscount wants to marry you. Smile prettily and accept the man's proposal."

"I can't just smile prettily and accept the man's proposal, Papa. No matter how much I would like to." She looked at Colin. "Papa confided my predicament to you, but was he completely forthcoming? Did he explain that I'm no longer a . . . ?" She blushed and tried again. "You understand that I'm ruined and could be carrying another man's child?"

Colin was gallantry personified as he looked Gillian in the eye. "Society's definition of ruined and my definition of ruined differ widely. Once we're wed, any child you carry will be ours. Yours and mine." Colin surprised himself with his honest declaration. "And while we're confessing, you might as well know that if you decide to wed me, some in the ton will delight in accusing me of fortune hunting."

"Is it true?" she asked.

"Well," Colin gave her a lopsided grin, "I'll be the first to admit that a fortune would come in handy, for I've nothing to offer you but my name and title." Colin wiped his palms down the sides of his buff-colored trousers.

"And a ruined society miss is ripe for the picking," she replied bitterly.

"Unfortunately," he said. "But that was never my intent in coming to meet with your father."

"Until Papa, no doubt, offered you a very large dowry."

"Which I did not seek," Colin told her, his Scottish burr thickening with every word. "But would be a very great fool to refuse."

Her blue eyes flashed fire. "And you're no fool, are you, Lord Grantham?"

"That remains to be seen, doesn't it, Miss Davies?" he answered in kind.

"Be reasonable, Gillian. That's the way these things are done. You know it as well as I, and there's no reason the man shouldn't get something in return," Lord Davies intervened. "Especially when he's risking his reputation and his good name in order to save yours."

"To save my good name, Papa? Or yours?" She demanded.

"What difference does it make?" Lord Davies asked. "You're my daughter. They're one and the same."

"It makes a great difference to me, Papa. I should like to know if the man you selected for me to marry wants your fortune more than he wants me."

"If you had asked that question of the man *you* selected to marry, you wouldn't be in this position now, Gillian."

"Papa!"

"It's true," her father declared.

"I thought he loved me," Gillian murmured. "I thought he wanted to marry me."

"He lied," her father pointed out. "He *told* you he loved you and married you *after* he married two other equally unfortunate young women. Lord Grantham, to his credit and to his detriment, told you the truth. He didn't come to me seeking a fortune or a bride. He came to discuss my investigator's findings and explain the situation." Lord Davies looked at his daughter. "I chose to hold him responsible and to force his hand into accepting a marriage he did not want."

"But Papa, he's innocent. . . ." Gillian protested.

"So were you, Miss Davies," Colin answered gently, "when someone used my assumed name in order to prey upon you. I don't believe that was a coincidence, and I intend to see that the wrong he did you in my name is corrected."

"At what cost to your personal life?"

Colin grinned. "I have no personal life."

"At all?" She was curious in spite of herself. "No young lady pining for you?"

"If there is a young lady pining for me, I am not aware of it," he said. "I have a mother and father and younger siblings. I even have a few friends, but I have no romantic entanglements." He shrugged. "I can't afford them."

"Then how can you afford a wife?" she asked.

"I can't," he said, simply. "My wife will have to afford me."

Gillian was thoughtful. "What will you ask in exchange?"

"Courtesy," Colin answered. "And discretion. For my family and my friends."

Gillian arched an eyebrow. "That goes without saying. What do you expect for yourself?"

"Nothing. For myself, I expect nothing beyond what you are willing to give."

"Not even courtesy and discretion?"

"If you feel I've earned your courtesy and discretion, you'll grant it. Otherwise, I shall have to live without those things. I hope that as my viscountess, you'll extend me the courtesy and discretion the title warrants so long as we are in public. But I shan't expect you to do the same in private if that's not your inclination."

"Can I expect the same from you?" Gillian asked. "Forgive me for being wary, Lord Grantham, if you seem to be the answer to a prayer. You say all the right things, and I want to believe you, but my judgment is suspect when it comes to selecting husbands."

"My judgment is not," he answered. "I'll be a husband of whom you can be proud, Miss Davies. I won't disappoint you or give you cause to regret your decision." Colin narrowed his gaze at the baron.

Gillian smiled at him, a genuine, beautiful smile that gave Colin a tantalizing glimpse of the woman she had been before she'd met the impostor Colin Fox. "Since I've need of a husband," she said. "I would prefer one who appreciates what I bring into the marriage."

Colin gave her a sweeping bow, the sort of bow cavaliers had once bestowed on ladies of the court. "At your service, my lady."

Chapter 12

"This happy breed of men, this little world."
—WILLIAM SHAKESPEARE, 1564–1616
RICHARD II

*T*he Free Fellows League gathered to compare notes in their customary room at White's before dinner that evening.

Griff and Sussex were already there when Colin entered the oak-paneled room and handed his hat and coat to the butler. "Good evening, Griff. Sussex."

Griff looked up from the leather sofa. "Jarrod's on his way. He had a last-minute meeting with two of the cryptographers charged with enciphering the information to be sent to Scovell and Grant on the Peninsula."

"How goes the cryptography work today?" The Duke of Sussex folded the newspaper he'd been reading and placed it on a mahogany side table. He lifted his feet from the leather ottoman, set them on the Turkish rug beside the fire, and then reached for the glass of French brandy he had been nursing for the past three-quarters of an hour.

"The ciphering or the deciphering?" Colin glanced around the room, then poured himself a whisky from the tray of decanters on the drinks table and sat down in the leather chair opposite Sussex's.

"Both," Sussex answered.

Colin shrugged. "The good news is that our code appears to be unbroken."

"The bad news," Jarrod interrupted, from his place just inside the doorway, after entering the room in time to hear Sussex's question and Colin's answer, "is that according to dispatches I received from Major Scovell and Colonel Grant, so does theirs." Jarrod tossed his hat and coat onto a chair, then walked over and joined Griff on the leather sofa.

"Drink?" Sussex offered.

Jarrod nodded toward the silver pot warming on a tray sitting on a butler's table. "Coffee."

Sussex poured a cup and handed it to Jarrod.

"Thank you." Jarrod took a sip of coffee, then set it aside and rubbed his palms together and began the meeting without preamble. "What did we learn from our excursion into the ton last night?"

"That an evening at Almack's is not to be borne unless one is already married," Griff chuckled.

"That's not news," Jarrod told him. *"We,"* he nodded to include Colin and Sussex, "haven't been to Almack's since we accompanied you on your bride-seeking mission. We know to avoid the place like the plague. That's why we're still single."

"You're fortunate you cut lower cards." Griff looked at the others. "Because Almack's was crowded with young ladies seeking husbands last night."

"Any clues to the identity of the young lady?" Jarrod asked.

Griffin took a deep breath. "Grant's sources were correct. There have been a spate of elopements to Scotland this season, but none—at least at Almack's last evening— that were unaccounted for. Alyssa and I made discrete inquiries and turned up several minor peers, and one member of the royal family with daughters who eloped to Scotland this season, but as far as we could tell, all of them have either accepted the marriages or secured other, more suitable husbands for their wayward daughters."

Sussex leaned forward in his chair. "Just out of curiosity, have you the name of the families to whom those wayward daughters belong?"

"Lord Chemsford and Lord Barfield are barons. Lord Wensley is a viscount, and Exeter's an earl. And the rumor, though unsubstantiated, is that the daughter of the royal family member belongs to the Princess Royal."

"Good work, Your Grace," Jarrod grinned. "I'm impressed that you and your duchess were able to learn so much in so little time."

Griff gave his friend a mockingly regal nod. "We had help."

"Your parents?" Jarrod guessed. "Or Lord and Lady Tressingham?"

"You know better than that." Griff laughed. "My father only dons knee breeches and buckles for appearances before the king, the regent, and on state occasions. Almack's must survive without him. And as for Lord Tressingham . . ." He rolled his eyes heavenward. "Alyssa's father would never cross Almack's threshold unless the patronesses suddenly allowed horses and hounds on the premises. And although my mother-in-law rarely declines any invitation she thinks her daughter, the new duchess, might accept, Lady Tressingham did not accompany us last evening." Griff stared at Sussex. "Lady Miranda St. Germaine did."

"Miranda made an appearance at Almack's?" Jarrod was stunned. It was well known in their circles that Lady Miranda St. Germaine avoided Almack's as often as the Free Fellows did.

"She did, indeed," Griff repeated. "And she was almost as beautiful as Alyssa."

"Miranda at Almack's," Sussex murmured. The fact that she'd accompanied her close friend, Alyssa, Duchess of

Avon, to Almack's explained why Miranda hadn't put in an appearance at Lady Compton's last evening after Sussex had sent a note around to her town house inviting her and her mother to meet him there. He had hoped her presence would enliven the conversation. Although Lady Compton spread the best buffet table in town, the time spent waiting for it could be long and tedious, especially if one tired of gambling. And Miranda St. Germaine was intelligent, well read, possessed a biting wit, and played chess extraordinarily well. As far as Sussex was concerned, Miranda was the ideal female companion, so long as her sharp tongue and quick wit were directed at someone else. He'd been looking forward to sharing a companionable evening at Lady Compton's with her, and Sussex had been more than a bit perturbed when Miranda sent a note back around to his house, declining his invitation in favor of a previous invitation.

He'd spent a deadly dull evening with his mind only half engaged in the turn of the cards wondering with whom Miranda had spent the evening. "Miranda at Almack's," he echoed. "I don't believe it."

"Believe it," Griff said. "She wore a blue evening gown that matched her eyes, and with that figure . . ." He broke off to allow Sussex's imagination to take over. "Suffice it to say, Miranda looked magnificent. I'll wager she fended off a dozen would-be suitors the first ten minutes we were there."

"What suitors?" Sussex demanded, scowling at Griffin.

"What difference does it make?" Jarrod intervened. "Miranda doesn't have to marry anyone. She's a peeress in her own right."

"What suitors?" Sussex repeated.

Griff bit the inside of his cheek to keep from grinning from ear to ear. Alyssa was right. Sussex was interested in her best friend. "I didn't know all of them. But I saw Linton, Carville, Nash, and an Austrian archduke."

"Fortune hunters," Sussex spat contemptuously.

"Linton and Nash, perhaps," Griff said. "But Carville's well set, and the Austrian archduke is . . . well . . . a young, handsome, very rich Austrian archduke."

"He might be young, handsome, and very rich, but the Austrian archduke is wasting his time. Miranda is English clear down to the bone. She would never consider an Austrian," Sussex scoffed.

"That's your opinion. Miranda may feel differently. She is, after all, a marchioness in her own right with far too few single prospects who outrank her. And I hear she's tiring of her role as everyone's favorite bridesmaid. She may feel an archduke is quite a catch." Griff shifted his weight on the sofa, then reached down to massage his right thigh in an effort to relieve the ache from the saber wound he'd suffered during the Battle of Fuentes de Oñoro. The wound still pained him, especially when he stood for long periods of time, and he'd spent much of last night and much of today on his feet.

"Here." Colin slid his leather ottoman toward the sofa. "Prop your leg up."

"Thanks." Griff propped his leg on the ottoman and accepted the glass of whisky Jarrod got up to fetch for him. "And now that I've told you what I learned at Almack's and about Lady St. Germaine, why don't you tell us what you learned at Lady Compton's, Your Grace?"

Sussex narrowed his gaze at Griff as the other duke tossed him the gauntlet. Sussex knew that his past history with the Duke of Avon and his duchess made for continued friendly competition and relegated his status as a Free Fellow to that of a probationer. It wouldn't always be that way, but Sussex knew he still needed to prove himself. Unfortunately, Lady Compton's hadn't been the place to do it. "I discovered her chef is superb and that most of the people who attend Lady Compton's soirees are there to feast and gamble. Gossip and marriageable young ladies were scarce."

"What about angry papas?" Jarrod asked.

Sussex frowned. "There were plenty of those." He focused his attention on Colin. "Including yours. But, for the most part, their anger was directed at Lady Luck and the turn of the cards. I heard a great deal about gambling debts and where to find the most understanding moneylenders. I didn't hear so much as a whisper about anyone's daughter's elopement. What about you?" Sussex asked. "Did you learn anything from your foray into Lady Harrelson's world of dance?"

Jarrod nodded. "We heard quite a bit of gossip about a particular young lady who spent much of the evening beside the dance floor rather than on it." Jarrod lifted his cup and saucer and took another drink of his coffee. "She didn't dance at all until our hostess persuaded Colin to partner her."

"She wasn't the only young lady who spent much of the evening beside the dance floor rather than on it," Colin surprised Jarrod and the other two Free Fellows by leaping to Gillian's defense. "The young lady you partnered didn't dance with anyone before she danced with you," Colin reminded Jarrod.

"You danced?" Griff teased. "Don't tell Alyssa. She'll be distraught at the idea." He pinned Jarrod with a look. Colin liked to dance, although he seldom took the opportunity to do so. But Jarrod . . . In all the years he had known him, Griff had never seen Jarrod dance with anyone except Alyssa. He hadn't realized Jarrod *could* dance until he'd partnered Alyssa for the first time while Griff was unable to. "Is the world as we know it coming to an end? I can't believe you partnered an unmarried young lady. Her mother must have been overjoyed."

"Her aunt," Jarrod corrected. "Sarah's mother died when she was a child."

"Sarah?" Sussex struggled to recall all the Sarahs in his acquaintance.

"You don't know her," Jarrod assured him. "Her father is rector in the village at my childhood home. Sarah's an old friend with no fortune. She's of no interest to our impostor."

But she appeared to be of interest to the Marquess of Shepherdston, and everyone in the room knew it.

"Now," Jarrod continued, "the young lady with whom Colin danced is an entirely different story."

"Oh?" Griff leaned forward.

"Yes," Jarrod affirmed. "Colin's partner is quite a considerable heiress who was rumored to have spent a month in the country visiting relatives at the start of the season."

"What about her father?" Sussex asked. "Is he suspect?"

Jarrod nodded. "Enough so that I arranged a meeting between Baron Davies and Colin this afternoon."

"Baron *Carter* Davies?" Griff asked.

"The same," Jarrod affirmed. "I suspected, from the gossip I gleaned at Lady Harralson's that Miss Davies might be the young lady for whom we were looking. So Colin and I decided a meeting with the baron was in order to see if the rumors would bear fruit."

Griff whistled in admiration. "Davies has got enough blunt to pay Bow Street to investigate anyone connected to the War Office—or anyone *rumored* to be connected to the War Office —for as long as it takes to find the impostor or until he gets what he wants. He could raise myriad questions about, and cause no end of trouble for, the Free Fellows. Damnation! What a tangle!"

"Don't keep us in suspense, Grantham." Sussex turned to Colin, barely able to contain his curiosity. "Tell us how your meeting with Lord Davies went."

Chapter 13

"The world must be peopled. When I said I would die a bachelor, I did not think I should live till I were married."

—WILLIAM SHAKESPEARE, 1564–1616
MUCH ADO ABOUT NOTHING

"*I'm marrying his daughter in the morning.*" Colin didn't mince words.

"What?" The Duke of Sussex choked, spewing brandy across his chair and his fine evening trousers. He brushed the droplets of wine from his clothing and gave Colin his full attention. "You're joking, aren't you?"

"No, I'm not." Colin looked at Jarrod. "If you'll be so kind as to open your safe, I'll deliver on my wager. I believe I owe each of you five hundred pounds."

Jarrod got up from his seat on the sofa, walked over to the safe concealed behind a tasteful landscape, and spun the dial. He removed a heavy metal cash box and handed it to Colin.

Colin unlocked the cash box and began counting out the fifteen hundred pounds needed to cover the wager.

Sussex set his brandy glass aside and shook his head. "Damn the wager, Grantham," the duke said. "You don't owe me anything. I'm not an original Free Fellow. I wasn't one of you when you made that wager."

"You're one of us now," Colin said. "And, unlike my father, I always pay my debts. Take the money."

"All right." Sussex held up his hand. "But I reserve the right to repay the wager at a later date." Sussex wasn't trying to be insulting, but he was very much aware that Viscount Grantham's resources were not as large as those of the other Free Fellows.

Colin frowned. "Unless you're getting married on the morrow, too, there's no need to repay me at a later date. According to the terms of the marriage contract I signed this afternoon, making good on my wager isn't going to beggar me." He acknowledged the other two Free Fellows. "Neither will financing a season for my sister." He handed a bundle of pound notes to Jarrod and another to Griff, then locked the cash box and put it back in the safe.

"Remarkable." Jarrod closed the door of the safe, spun the dial, and swung the landscape back into place before returning to his seat on the leather sofa. Reaching over the back of the sofa, he opened the lid of the intricately carved teakwood box on the table and selected a cigar. Jarrod snipped the end off the cigar, struck a match to light it, and inhaled a lungful of aromatic smoke, then blew it out. "You danced one dance with Miss Davies last night and signed a contract to wed her this afternoon." He narrowed his gaze at Colin. "Did I miss the love at first sight? Or did you make such an impression on the baron that he immediately chose you to become his son-in-law? Satisfy our rampant curiosity and tell us how your impending nuptials came about," Jarrod prodded.

"It appeared to be either the foregone conclusion or the natural progression of the meeting," Colin replied sharply.

"Bloody hell!" Jarrod exploded. "Damnation! It went that badly, eh?"

"If we'd been fighting with swords, I'd be severely wounded or worse." Colin managed a self-deprecating smile. "As it was, I managed to survive the verbal encounter with a bit of dignity and a small measure of my pride intact."

Sussex shifted in his chair. "There's no doubt that Miss Davies is the young lady who eloped to Scotland, then?"

"No," Colin said. "There's no doubt that she eloped with someone using the name of Colin Fox or that her father hired a very good Bow Street runner to locate him. Unfortunately, I was the first Colin Fox they found."

"Happenstance?" Jarrod asked.

"Not bloody likely," Colin replied. "But the other Colin Fox has proved more elusive than I. It's as if he's disappeared from the face of the earth."

The Duke of Sussex inhaled deeply, then slowly released the breath. "It's likely he has, for a while." He looked Colin in the eye. "He's probably gone to ground. Quite possibly for all eternity. You did kill the man who attempted to kill you. And it's possible that the man you killed was the impostor Colin Fox."

Colin took time to frame his reply. "The man I killed was a hired assassin. He had brown eyes. He couldn't have been the impostor Colin Fox."

"He couldn't have been the impostor because his eyes were brown," Jarrod said, "and the impostor's eyes are green like yours—"

"Blue," Colin corrected. "According to Lady Davies, the impostor's eyes are a nice shade of blue."

"Then why are you marrying the baron's daughter?" Sussex demanded.

"Because he chooses to believe that his wife and daughter might be mistaken," Colin answered. "He chooses to believe that the impostor's eyes might be a nice shade of grayish green. Like mine."

"The baron intends that someone shall redeem his daughter's virtue, and better the viscount he has than the rogue he doesn't," Griff summed up the situation.

"Exactly," Colin confirmed.

Sussex frowned. "And now that the other Fox has disap-peared, you've no way of proving he existed or that he eloped with Lord Davies's daughter."

Colin shot the duke a nasty look. "That's right. But I don't intend to prove he existed or that he eloped with Miss Davies. Attempting to prove it would put Miss Davies's reputation at risk and endanger our mission. And that's what we're trying to avoid."

"Point taken, Lord Grantham." Sussex gave Colin a mock salute. "But it's a pity that you're assuming responsi-bility for someone else's actions."

"Isn't that what life's about?" Colin asked. "Isn't that what we do nearly every day of our lives?" He shrugged his shoulders. "Bonaparte wreaks havoc on the Continent. We assume responsibility for protecting this little corner of the earth. My father gambles. When he doesn't pay his credi-tors, I assume responsibility and make good on his debts. At some point in his life, nearly every man assumes responsi-bility for someone else's actions."

"And now you're accepting responsibility for the ac-tions of an impostor who used your alias in order to prey on an unsuspecting young lady," Sussex said.

Colin took a deep breath. "I did what I had to do in or-der to squash Lord Davies's investigation of Colin Fox." He lifted his whisky glass and took a hefty swallow, savor-ing the fiery liquid as it made its way from his throat to the pit of his belly. "He's not the sort of man to give up. And our confrontation wasn't the sort of meeting I care to re-peat any time soon."

"Neither is tomorrow's meeting, I'll wager," Sussex added.

Jarrod made a wry face. "I warned you that the baron would be a formidable opponent."

"You were correct," Colin affirmed.

"How much does he know?" Sussex asked.

"Very little about the impostor," Colin answered, "but

more than I would like about my movements during the past month."

"Enough to endanger our mission?" Jarrod asked.

"Lord Davies and his investigator knew enough to endanger not only our mission and the Free Fellows League but every War Office operative under Colonel Grant's command. Nothing I said would dissuade him from pursuing his investigation. He was willing to do whatever he had to do in order to find the man responsible for his daughter's disgrace." Colin raked his fingers through his hair. "Since I'm not able to produce another Colin Fox or explain why he assumed my identity in order to commit this crime against Miss Davies, it seemed that the best course of action was for me to simply accept responsibility for his actions."

"Damnation!" Sussex exclaimed.

"My thoughts exactly," Colin agreed.

"You're innocent," Griffin protested. "You had nothing to do with it. We can prove that."

"At what cost?" Colin asked. "Exposing the Free Fellows League and the work we do? We can't take that risk. Gillian—"

"Gillian?" Jarrod queried. "When did she become Gillian?"

"When he agreed to marry her," Sussex retorted. "That generally entitles him to call her by name."

"The point," Colin continued, ignoring the interruption, "is that Miss Davies told her father that the man she married—one Colin Fox—was a clandestine agent working for our government against Bonaparte."

"And Fox's trail led to Colonel Grant's door, because what he'd told her was the absolute truth." Jarrod slapped his forehead with the heel of his hand. "Have we been so careless a charlatan can follow in our footsteps?"

"No," Sussex and Colin answered in unison.

"We haven't been careless. If we had, I wouldn't be

here today. I'd be lying in an Edinburgh close with any number of unpleasant puncture wounds and my throat sliced from ear to ear for good measure, and he'd be working to accomplish his mission."

"Which is?" Jarrod demanded.

Colin frowned. "I don't know. Yet. But I mean to find out." *And somehow Gillian is the key.*

Sussex lifted the brandy decanter and offered some to Jarrod and Colin before refilling his glass. "Of all the names in England from which to choose, he chose the one he knew you had assumed. That tells me that he meant to make you responsible. He meant to lay all of his crimes at your door."

"He meant to *use* me by laying all of his crimes at my door," Colin said. "Because that was one way to slow my progress and prevent me from discovering what he was really about. I don't intend to let that happen. I mean to uncover his mission."

"Was eloping with Miss Davies simply a diversion?"

Colin glared at Jarrod. "No," he answered. "It was part of the plan. I don't know whose plan. But she was a pawn in someone else's game. And the game isn't over." He stood up and began to pace.

"He's right," Griff said. "And just because our impostor is lying low doesn't mean his work is done. There is more here than meets the eye. This isn't about taking advantage of unsuspecting young ladies for monetary gain. There's a more ambitious plan afoot. And we must discover what it is."

"But sacrificing yourself to protect the members of the League is going above and beyond the call of duty, Colin." Jarrod was awed and repelled by the idea.

"You would do the same if the impostor had used your alias instead of mine." It was the truth, and Jarrod knew it, but he didn't like having Colin remind him of it.

"What about your Free Fellows vows?" Sussex asked.

"We shall give our first loyalty and our undying friendship to England and our brothers and fellow members of the

Free Fellows League," Colin quoted the tenth item in the Free Fellows league charter. "I'm doing what I think is best in an effort to fulfill that vow."

"So, you're marrying the baron's daughter."

"That's the sum of it, Jarrod. I'm marrying the baron's daughter tomorrow morning. And because I've not yet reached my thirtieth year, I owed each of you five hundred pounds."

"Which you've paid in full." Jarrod shook his head. "Still, I can't help thinking there must be another way out of this quandary."

"This is the best way out of this quandary," Colin said. "I'll sacrifice a little personal freedom, but I'm gaining more than I'm losing."

Griff managed a smile. "If I know Lord Davies, you're gaining a fortune along with your lovely bride."

"That's correct," Colin said. "I've been a poor viscount all my life. I'm prepared to give being a rich viscount a try. I believe it will suit me much better." He gave the other Free Fellows a lopsided grin. "And it's not as if I have much of a personal life, anyway. I accepted Lord Davies's blackmail because it would solve a great many problems for all of us. Believe me, this is the best way. For her. For me. For our families and for the Free Fellows."

"When will the wedding take place?" Griff asked.

"Tomorrow morning at ten at Lord Davies's town house. The announcement will appear in tomorrow's edition of the *Morning Chronicle* and the *Times*. A wedding breakfast will follow."

"Have you told Lord and Lady McElreath?" Griff asked.

"Not yet," Colin replied. "I plan to tell them later this evening when I go to collect the Grantham jewelry."

Jarrod, Sussex, and Griff exchanged meaningful glances. There had been some disturbing rumors over the past few months regarding the disposition of the McElreath and Grantham family jewels. Colin hadn't said anything, but he had to have heard that his father had been pawning the most impressive pieces of the collections.

Colin intercepted the exchange. "I'm aware of the rumors. And the truth is that I don't know if my mother still has the Grantham jewelry. Unfortunately, the only way to find out, at this late date, is to ask her."

"Do you think they'll attend the ceremony?" Jarrod asked, suddenly worried that Colin would have no one to stand up for him or represent his side of the family at the wedding. Members of the Free Fellows League eschewed weddings as a general principle and custom dictated that the close bachelor friends of the groom avoid them in practice.

"My mother will," Colin answered. "My father's presence at my nuptials is less certain."

Griff stood up and reached out his hand to Colin. "Alyssa and I would be honored to stand up for you and Miss Davies."

Colin was stunned. "Free Fellows don't—"

Griff laughed. "I know the Free Fellows unwritten tenet is that we don't attend weddings, but I broke that rule by attending my own." He looked Colin in the eye. "Allow me to ease the way for you and your bride and to represent the other Fellows by standing up for you at your wedding."

Jarrod walked over to Colin. "Listen to him," he urged. "Now is not the time to be stubborn. Griff's a duke and a war hero. His august presence at your wedding will go a long way in shielding your bride from the nasty rumors and innuendo that are sure to surface as a result of this hasty marriage. And having Alyssa there will insure that Miss Davies is accepted and welcomed at all the best places."

"Shepherdston's right." Sussex rose from his chair to join the others. "There are a great many advantages to having a duke and his duchess attend your wedding. If I were married, I'd offer to do the same."

"Thank you," Colin answered, taking hold of Griff's hand. "I'll be honored and grateful to have you and Alyssa there."

Griff clapped Colin on the back. "That's what friends are for."

Chapter 14

*"And oftentimes excusing of a fault
Doth make the fault the worser by th' excuse."*
—WILLIAM SHAKESPEARE, 1564–1616
KING JOHN

Gillian was about to become a bride. Again.
And the nervous fluttering in her stomach increased in direct proportion to the ticking of the clock on the mantel and the flurry of wedding preparations currently under way in her parents' London town house.

At ten o'clock in the morning, Gillian would promise to love, honor, cherish, and obey for the second time in as many months. And for the second time in as many months, she was marrying a man who was very nearly a stranger. The difference this time was that she was marrying her father's choice of a stranger instead of her own.

And she wasn't traveling the length of England in order to do it. This time, she need only make it out of her bedroom, down the stairs, and into the drawing room. Racing to Scotland might prove easier.

Gillian closed her eyes and murmured another in a series of fervent prayers. She prayed her father would be a much better judge of bridegroom than she had turned out to be, and she gave thanks that the wedding ceremony was going to be held in the drawing room of her parents' home instead of the church sanctuary where she'd been baptized and that only a handful of people would be present to witness it. There was less chance of God striking her dead when she repeated her vows in a drawing room. The church sanctuary was altogether too risky.

When she'd eloped with Colin Fox, she believed in the vows she'd repeated with all her heart. It didn't matter that she'd repeated them before the anvil in a blacksmithing shop without benefit of clergy. The blacksmith reading the words of the ceremony, a stable full of horses, two witnesses, and Colin were all she'd needed to feel like a bride.

Tomorrow's ceremony would feature a rector, a special license, her parents, and a bridegroom—another Colin—one who carried the title of viscount and who hadn't eloped with three women within months of one another. Tomorrow's wedding would be perfectly legal—in the eyes of God and in the eyes of the law—but Gillian felt like a fraud.

"Stop fretting, Gilly-flower," her mother spoke from the doorway of Gillian's bedchamber. She had come to help Gillian select a dress for the wedding and could tell, with one look, that her assistance was needed in other ways as well.

Gillian drew herself up to her full height, straightened her shoulders, looked her mother in the eyes, and attempted a bluff. "Who's fretting?"

"You are," Lady Davies said. "And there's no need. Everything will be all right."

"Will it?" Gillian asked sadly. "He's only met me twice. And he's only marrying me because Papa's paying him handsomely and forcing him to accept damaged goods."

Lady Davies canted her head to one side and watched as Gillian twisted a delicate lace handkerchief into a tight little knot. "I've only met him twice myself, but Lord Grantham didn't appear to be particularly weak in character or resolve. Did he appear that way to you?"

"No, he did not," Gillian admitted.

"Then, perhaps it's time you realized that men of true character are rarely forced to do things they do not wish to do." Lady Davies walked over to Gillian and rescued the scrap of knotted lace from Gillian's hands. "Lord Grantham may have reasons for agreeing to marry you of which you are unaware, but I'll wager they are good and honorable reasons that have very little to do with the handsome sum your father is paying him." She looked her daughter in the eye. "If it were only about the money, my dear, he would be marrying an heiress whose reputation isn't hanging by a very thin thread."

Gillian was thoughtful. "If it isn't about the money, then why choose me?"

"Perhaps he likes what he sees," Lady Davies said. "Perhaps he thinks you've a good head on your shoulders and will be a good companion and an asset to his name."

Gillian gave a very unladylike snort of sarcastic disbelief. "I can see how my most recent demonstration of intelligence and sensibility led Lord Grantham to draw that conclusion."

Lady Davies ignored Gillian's sarcasm. "Then it's up to you to change his opinion." She smiled at her daughter.

Gillian looked at her mother as if Lady Davies had said something extraordinarily profound. "Lord Grantham told me that our wedding could be a second chance for me if I wanted one."

"Do you want a second chance, Gillian? Or do you want to continue to punish yourself for the rest of your life for being fooled by a man who took advantage of your generous heart and your romantic nature?"

"I want a second chance," Gillian said. "But I can't help thinking that Viscount Grantham deserves better." Gillian admitted her fears aloud. Men like Viscount Grantham deserved women with untarnished reputations. They deserved—he deserved—the best. And she wasn't the best. Not anymore. Still, it was nice to think that he might have chosen her. . . . Gillian bit back a wistful sigh and ruthlessly suppressed the hundred unnamed, restless yearnings plaguing her. *Don't think about it,* she admonished herself, *just do what you have to do.* "I can't help thinking that he deserves an undamaged bride—someone who hasn't made a foolish mistake. Someone who would make him a much better viscountess."

Lady Davies took a deep breath. "The contracts have already been signed, my love. I think Lord Grantham has made his decision, and he's picked you."

"But, Mama—"

"Gillian," Lady Davies's voice was firm. "He's a grown man. You cannot protect him from himself. He's made his decision. You're going to become Viscountess Grantham tomorrow morning. Lord Grantham is giving you a second chance. Why don't you give him one as well?"

"I wish I could believe he felt something for me," Gillian said wistfully.

"Believe it, Gilly-flower, because he wouldn't be marrying you if he didn't." Her mother leaned over and kissed Gillian on the cheek, then took her daughter by the hand and led her over to the armoire. "Now, we'd better get busy. We've a trousseau to assemble and a wedding dress to select."

❧

The hired butler announced Colin when he arrived at his mother and father's rented London town house.

The town house, situated several blocks off the park on the edge of Berkeley Square, provided its residents with a fashionably acceptable address, and its distance from the park made it slightly more affordable than other closer mansions. But Colin still wondered how his father managed to afford it.

Waiting for the last quarter hour for his mother to appear had given Colin plenty of time to study the details of his surroundings, and he'd concluded that although the drawing room was adequately furnished, the furnishings were not of the same quality as those found in Jarrod's or Griff's London homes, and it couldn't begin to compare with the Duke of Sussex's Park Lane mansion.

He was reevaluating the wood carving in the mantel when his mother entered the room.

"Colin, what a pleasant surprise!" His mother rushed to embrace him.

He bent to kiss her cheek. "Evening, Maman."

Lady McElreath accepted his greeting, then moved to a damask-covered sofa and perched on the edge of the seat. She lifted a silver coffeepot from the tray on the table that Nelson, the butler, delivered to the drawing room. Lady McElreath filled a delicate bone china cup with hot coffee, set it on the matching saucer, and offered it to Colin. "Come sit down and tell me what brings you here tonight."

Colin accepted the cup of coffee and sat down on a wing chair angled near the sofa. "I came to invite you to a wedding."

"Really?" Lady McElreath poured herself a cup of coffee. "Whose wedding?"

"Mine," Colin answered.

His mother's cup rattled against the thin bone china saucer, and several drops of the hot liquid splashed her hand. "You're getting married?"

Colin nodded. "Tomorrow morning at ten. At Number Seven Park Lane. The announcement will appear in the morning papers. I thought it best I inform you before you read it in the papers."

"Thank you for telling me. That was considerate of you," Lady McElreath replied, her voice laden with sarcasm and displeasure.

"I didn't come here just to tell you about the wedding." Colin frowned. "I came to invite you. You'll receive an engraved invitation in the morning, but I came in person because I thought you and Father and the children might want to attend."

"Of course I would," Lady McElreath said strongly. "And now that you've issued the invitation, might I know the name of the lucky young lady who is about to become my daughter-in-law and the newest member of our family?"

"Miss Gillian Davies."

Lady McElreath sighed. "Oh, Colin, are you sure?"

"Quite sure," he answered firmly. "Why?"

His mother took a deep breath. "There have been recent rumors about—"

Colin cut her off, unwilling to hear uncomplimentary comments about his bride-to-be from the mother he loved and admired. "Maman, you know there are rumors about everyone in the ton. And you, of all people, should know better than to lend them any credence."

"Yes, well, I'm not the only one likely to have heard them," she told him. "Or to have given them credence— especially in light of this rather sudden wedding." She looked over at her son. "I wasn't aware that you were acquainted with Miss Davies until you danced with her last evening."

"I met Miss Davies a fortnight ago while she was visiting relatives in the border country," Colin replied, relating the story he had spent the last quarter hour concocting. "The wedding may seem hasty to you, but it won't come as a very great surprise to the members of the ton who read tomorrow's announcement and remember that I danced with three ladies last evening: you, Liana, and Gillian."

"But, Colin, you're a viscount, and your father and I had high hopes that you'd make an excellent match," she said.

"I believe Gillian and I *are* well matched."

"Her father is new money. You are old money. Lord Davies just acquired the title of baron," Lady McElreath reminded him. "Your title predates Macbeth."

Colin looked his mother in the eye. "Unfortunately, our fortune hasn't exhibited the same longevity."

She sent him a sharp look. "I'll not hear a word of blame against your father for that."

Colin had always found it rather ironic that while his mother could voice her concerns and frustrations about his father's gambling to her eldest son, she wouldn't allow any of her children to do so. "I'm not blaming Father for losing the family fortune," Colin said. "That decline began long before he inherited. I blame Father for continuing the decline, for not meeting his obligations to his family or to his creditors."

"He's a good man. A loving man. He would do anything for me or for his children."

"Except stay away from the gaming tables," Colin muttered.

"The gambling is a sickness he cannot control."

"I know that, Maman," Colin said wearily.

"He loves you," his mother said. "He wants only the best for you, his son and heir. He wants a lady from a great family and fortune."

"I've no doubt that Gillian's parents want a husband of great family and fortune for her," Colin pointed out.

"We are a great family," Lady McElreath insisted. "The McElreaths are one of the oldest families in Scotland and England, and my family, the Hepburns, are equally ancient and well-connected in Scotland and France."

Colin took a deep breath and slowly exhaled it. "Then consider my marriage to Gillian Davies an excellent bargain. I am heir to the great and ancient name and titles, and Gillian is heir to the great and modern fortune." He gave his mother a firm look that brooked no argument. "Father was your choice. Gillian is mine. And despite what you've heard or choose to believe, she *is* a lady of family and fortune and should be welcomed as Viscountess Grantham and treated with the respect her title and her place as my wife affords her—especially since her money will permit our *great* family to continue to live the life we've never been able to fully afford."

Lady McElreath inhaled sharply at her son's tactful reprimand. "I would never make your bride feel unwelcome or treat her with anything less than the respect to which she's entitled as your wife."

"I never thought that you would, Maman." Colin soothed his mother's ruffled feathers. "I simply wanted to make my position perfectly clear. Just as you will not hear a bad word against Father, neither will I tolerate an unkind word or remark directed at Gillian."

"You may rest assured that she will never hear one from me or from anyone around me," Lady McElreath replied.

Colin nodded. "I knew I could count on you, Maman. Thank you." He finished his coffee and set the cup back down on its saucer. "There is one other detail that demands my attention before the wedding." He looked at his mother. "I require the Grantham betrothal ring and wedding set and the rest of the Grantham jewels. I wish to present the betrothal ring to Gillian before our wedding and present her with the other Grantham jewels during the wedding breakfast."

Lady McElreath rang for the butler and instructed him to ask her lady's maid to bring her jewel boxes. The maid delivered the jewel cases ten minutes later. After unlocking the leather cases, Lady McElreath dismissed her lady's maid and sent her back upstairs to bed. She handed the blue leather case to Colin. "The red case is for the McElreath jewels and the blue one contains the Grantham jewels."

Colin lifted the lid on the blue leather case and stared at the top tray. The Grantham betrothal ring and wedding band were missing, and all the other rings in the case were set with cut glass. He lifted two additional trays to look at the necklaces, bracelets, earrings, and diadems stored for safekeeping, then looked over at his mother. "These are all cut glass and paste."

"Yes." She nodded. "I know."

"What happened to the real ones?" Colin asked.

"They were sold."

The only person who could have sold them was the Earl of McElreath: his father, his grandfather, his great-grandfather, or one of his earlier ancestors. Colin suspected he knew all too well who had pawned the jewelry, but he asked the question nonetheless. "By whom? And how long ago?"

"He meant to retrieve them," Lady McElreath said quietly.

"When? And from whom?" Colin demanded.

Lady McElreath took a deep breath. "It began years ago while you were away at school. Your father pawned a few of the lesser pieces of the Grantham jewelry to pay debts. He meant to retrieve them. He promised that as soon as his luck changed, he'd buy the pieces back from the pawnbroker, but . . ."

"His luck never changed," Colin concluded bitterly.

"You were a little boy away at school," Lady McElreath repeated. "He thought he'd have plenty of time to replace the pieces he'd lost before you reached your majority."

"Maman," Colin reminded his mother. "It's been nearly eight years since I attained my majority."

"I know," she answered, nodding her head and staring down at the red leather case she held in her lap.

"Has he pawned the McElreath jewels and replaced them with paste, too?"

"No," Lady McElreath replied. "He hasn't touched mine."

Colin clenched his teeth so tightly his jaw ached. Of course his father hadn't pawned the jewels his mother would wear in public and replaced those with paste. The

Earl of McElreath had a position to uphold. He was an inveterate gambler and a gentleman. Gambling away his son's inheritance was unfortunate, but losing the jewelry that belonged to the Countess of McElreath was unthinkable. Replacing that jewelry with paste would upset and embarrass his wife, cause speculation, and ultimately require some sort of explanation among the ton. It might also lead people to think that Lord McElreath couldn't afford his expensive gambling habits. And a man in his position could do without that sort of speculation and grief. Far better to pay his creditors and fuel further trips to the gaming tables with the jewels meant for his son's bride. "Of course not," Colin agreed. "It was far more sensible to lose the courtesy title's family stones."

"Don't be so hard on him, Colin," his mother admonished. "You're nine and twenty, and until now, you've shown no interest in taking a bride."

"Part of the reason I've shown no interest in taking a bride is because I knew I had nothing to offer a young lady of quality." The other part of the reason was the vow Colin had taken when he and his two friends had created the Free Fellows League. But the League was their secret, and his mother didn't need to know about that.

"That's nonsense!" Lady McElreath scoffed. "You have a great deal to offer any young lady of quality."

"Do I, Maman?" he queried. "Because Lord Kelverton made it quite clear that I had nothing to offer Esme."

"Oh, good heavens, Colin, that was years ago! You were a little boy. Esme was a young girl."

"We were betrothed from the cradle. Lord Kelverton knew Father's predilection for gaming, but that never lessened his desire to join our families by having me marry his daughter until . . ." Colin stopped and turned his focused stare on his mother. "That's it, isn't it?"

"What's it?" She pretended not to understand, but Lady

McElreath had never been any good at pretending, and Colin knew it.

"The reason Lord Kelverton broke the marriage contract. Father's gambling didn't concern Lord Kelverton until he discovered that Father had gambled away Esme's future inheritance."

"They weren't Esme's future inheritance, they were yours," Lady McElreath said.

"Yes," Colin agreed. "The jewelry belongs to our family, but the heir doesn't wear it, his wife does. How long would it be before some sharp-eyed member of the ton humiliated Esme by pointing out that her wedding gift was a collection of worthless paste?" Colin scooped a handful of jewelry, held it up, and then let it slip through his fingers back into the blue leather case. He closed the case and handed it to his mother. "Here, Maman, you keep these. They're of no use to me."

"What will you do for a betrothal ring?"

Colin shrugged. "I don't know. But you needn't concern yourself about it, Maman. I'll take care of it." Colin stood up, walked over to his mother, bent, and kissed her on the cheek. "Good night, Maman."

Lady McElreath stopped him before he reached the drawing room door. "Colin! Wait!"

He turned to find his mother tugging at her betrothal ring and gold wedding band.

"Use these," she said. "They're real."

"No, Maman," Colin shook his head. "Thank you, but no. I won't ask my bride to seal her wedding vows with borrowed rings."

"She need never know these aren't the Grantham jewels," Lady McElreath said, holding out the emerald and diamond betrothal ring and her gold wedding band, urging her son to take them.

"I'll know, Maman," Colin said quietly.

Lady McElreath bit her lip and nodded.

"Sleep well, Maman. I'll see you in the morning."

"Colin . . ."

She made another attempt to stop him, but Colin ignored the pleading note in her tone of voice. He had a great deal to accomplish before his wedding and only a few more hours in which to do it.

Chapter 15

"In thy face I see
The map of honor, truth, and loyalty."
—WILLIAM SHAKESPEARE, 1564–1616
KING HENRY VI, PART 2

If anyone had questioned his bravery in the moments before Gillian entered the drawing room of her parents' town house, Colin could not have found offense or been tempted to issue a challenge to defend his honor. He would have had no reason. He couldn't argue fact, and the fact was that although he had never fancied himself a coward, every instinct for self-preservation he'd ever possessed was urging him to make a break for the front door.

Colin's heart pounded in his chest, and he could almost smell his own fear and feel the color leeching from his face as he fought to come up with some graceful way to make his exit. For the first time in his life, Colin thought he might faint or run screaming out the door in sheer terror. And Griff must have sensed it as well, for he placed his hand on Colin's arm and murmured beneath his breath, "Steady on, Colin. The panic will pass."

Colin disagreed. The panic was rising. And his rising panic declared that he was a lifelong Free Fellow, and a Free Fellow didn't stand before a clergyman and promise to love, honor, and cherish a woman he barely knew. Except Griff. But the situation had been different when Griff's father ordered his son to marry.

Colin glanced over at his friend. How in Hades had Griff survived it?

"Breathe deeply," Griff advised, reading his mind once again. "And keep breathing. It will be over before you know it."

Would it? Colin knew he'd only been standing before the rector and the assembled guests for a few minutes, but it felt like an eternity. And he didn't know how much longer he could continue to stand on legs that wobbled from the strain of standing still or that threatened to give way at any moment. Colin shifted his weight from one leg to the other and back again. He'd felt less fear facing down assassins. Leaning toward Griff, Colin whispered, "I can't—"

"Yes, you can," Griff whispered back. "Look." He nodded toward the doorway. "Here's your bride."

Colin followed Griff's lead and turned toward the doorway as Gillian entered the room on her father's arm.

His panic died a quick death at the sight of her, replaced by a much more powerful emotion. "*Bon Dieu,* but she's breathtaking!"

"She is that," Griff agreed. "Almost as breathtaking as my Alyssa."

That was Griff's opinion. As far as Colin was concerned, no woman had ever been or could ever be as breathtakingly beautiful as Gillian Davies was at that moment. He couldn't see her face clearly through the lace of her bridal veil, but he gave what he hoped was a warm and welcoming smile instead of the wolfish grin he was fighting hard to control. And though her veil obscured it, Colin thought she returned his smile with a rather shy smile of her own.

He drew another deep breath and slowly expelled it, surprised to find that he was suddenly calm and completely

certain that exchanging vows with Gillian was what he'd
been born to do. Who would have guessed that that tanta-
lizingly soft fragrance of lemons and musk would fill him
with as much resolute determination to have her as his wife
as the image of her in her wedding dress?

And what a wedding dress it was! Colin shook his head
as if to clear it. The silk layers clung to her figure, molding
to her body in all the right places. The dress skimmed over
her trim waist and hips, brushing her thighs as she moved,
and the bodice beneath the squared neckline created a delicate cradle for the gentle swell of bosom visible through
her veil. His mouth went dry as she moved forward, and
Colin fought to follow Griff's advice and breathe.

If he had had to choose a color for her to wear, Colin
would have chosen a bright robin's egg blue to accentuate
the color of her eyes. He'd never much cared for the pale
confections of muslin, ribbons, and lace currently in
vogue. He appreciated the daring styles, but the insipid
colors did nothing for most of the blond, blue-eyed, fair-
skinned young ladies of his acquaintance. And he expected
something brighter and bolder from his bride. Something
to match her personality. But Gillian had just changed his
mind about fashion. He would never have guessed a dress
of pale, almost translucent pink the color of delicate rose
petals would become her ivory complexion. But it did.

The sight of her in that dress stole the air from his lungs,
and the lump in his throat threatened to keep him from repeating the vows that would bind him to her for all eternity
and grant him permission to see what lay beneath the tantalizing panels of delicate rose-colored silk and lace.

Colin waited until Gillian's father moved away before
he stepped closer.

The rector lifted his prayer book and nodded toward
Colin. "If you will, Lord Grantham, take hold of your
bride's left hand."

Gillian handed her nosegay of flowers from the garden

to the Duchess of Avon, who was acting as her matron of honor, as Colin reached for her hand. She hadn't carried any flowers at her first wedding, and she hadn't had anyone to attend her. The blacksmith had provided the required two witnesses. She smiled at the duchess and received a warm smile in return. Gillian still couldn't quite believe that England's newest hero and his wife had not only graced them with their presence at her wedding to Viscount Grantham but had offered to stand up for them. And what was even more surprising was that the Duke and Duchess of Avon were genuinely honored to do it.

Gillian cast a sideways glance at her groom. If one could judge a man by the company he kept, Colin McElreath was an exceptional man, highly regarded by his august friends. And he was about to become her husband.

The clergyman cleared his throat and began the service. "Dearly beloved, we are gathered together here in the sight of God, and in the face of these witnesses, to join together this man and this woman in Holy Matrimony. . . ."

He looked at Gillian and then turned to look at Colin. "I require and charge you both as you will answer at the dreadful day of judgment, when the secrets of all hearts shall be disclosed, that if either of you know any impediment why you may not be lawfully joined together in Matrimony, ye do now confess it."

A half hour ago, Colin would have willingly listed any number of impediments to matrimony; now all he wanted was to seal the deal and, in the vernacular of his father, let the chips fall where they may.

He narrowed his focus until all he could see was Gillian's gloved hand in his. All he could hear was the steady beat of his heart, the rector's words, and Gillian's soft breathing. All he could smell was the scent of the orange blossoms wound around the circlet of her veil mingling with the lemon fragrance she wore.

"Colin McElreath, twenty-seventh Viscount Grantham,

wilt thou have this woman to thy wedded wife, to live together after God's ordinance in the holy estate of Matrimony? Wilt thou love her, comfort her, honor and keep her in sickness and in health; and forsaking all others, keep thee only unto her, so long as ye both shall live?"

"I will," Colin replied in a voice that resonated with willingness to take his vows to heart and to honor them.

Gillian looked up at him and recognized the firm resolve in his clear green eyes. *He means it,* she realized. With the exception of promising to love her, Colin McElreath meant every word he'd just repeated.

Gillian smiled. Theirs was a hastily thrown together wedding, but Colin repeated his vows as if it had been planned for months or even years. He may not have wanted to marry her, but he made certain that everyone within earshot thought otherwise. He was saving her from her own romantic foolishness, offering himself up as husband to replace the one who had played her false and then abandoned her, but no one listening to him promise to love, honor, and cherish her would ever have reason to doubt him.

She moistened her lips with the tip of her tongue. Lord Grantham was giving himself over to her, and Gillian vowed that he wouldn't regret his decision. She didn't know how or when, but she promised herself that one day, she would earn his respect and his admiration—if not his heart.

"Gillian Davies, wilt thou have this man to thy wedded husband, to live together after God's ordinance in the holy estate of Matrimony? Wilt thou obey him, serve him, love, honor, and keep him in sickness and in health; and forsaking all others, keep thee only unto him, so long as ye both shall live?"

"I will."

The rector had them repeat more vows and make more promises until at last, he paused and asked for the ring.

"Here." Griff handed Colin a gold wedding band.

Colin stared at the gold band as he waited for Alyssa, Griff's duchess, to help Gillian unbutton and remove her gloves. He and Griff had purchased the wedding band and the betrothal ring at Dalrymple's Jewelers earlier that morning.

Colin had still been reeling from the discovery that his father had gambled away the Grantham titular jewels when he made his way to Griff's Park Lane mansion shortly after dawn.

He hadn't worried about waking Griff or Alyssa. Griff rarely slept through the night since his return from the Peninsula, and his duchess was known to be an early riser.

They were having coffee in the morning room when Colin rang the front doorbell. Griff and Alyssa invited him to join them, and then listened as Colin relayed the details of his interview with his mother and the fact that the jewelry he'd intended to give to his bride was a collection of paste made from cut glass and base metal.

The revelation came as no surprise. But what was done couldn't be undone. And no amount of recrimination could change that. Colin needed help. Alyssa and Griff had looked at one another and spoken one word in unison. "Dalrymple's."

"Dalrymple's?" Colin echoed.

"Dalrymple's Jewelers on Bond Street," Griff answered as Alyssa held out her left hand so Colin could admire the jeweler's work.

The Duchess of Avon's betrothal ring was a delicate confection comprised of a large purple center stone surrounded by a circle of smaller green stones, accented by several diamonds, and set in a gold setting. It looked like a purple flower blooming in the midst of a group of bright green leaves sparkling with droplets of rain or dew.

"It's lovely," Colin said. "But I doubt I'll be able to marshal the finances needed to purchase anything quite as lovely."

"But the girl you're marrying is a very wealthy young lady," Alyssa said.

Colin nodded. "She is. But I'm not. And I refuse to use any portion of her dowry to purchase her betrothal ring. She shouldn't have to buy her own ring—in whatever fashion. Unfortunately, a betrothal ring equal in value to the one my father gambled away is beyond my current means." Colin raked his fingers through his hair in a show of frustration. "Where am I going to find a betrothal ring I can afford at this late date?"

"We'd give you the bird's egg if we could," Alyssa offered, describing the betrothal ring with the huge canary yellow diamond that Griff had refused to present to her. "But it's an Abernathy family heirloom, and it's so horribly big and gaudy no one with taste wants to wear it." She looked at Colin. "I'm the second or third Abernathy bride to prefer something smaller. The only person we know who loves it is the Prince Regent."

"And your mother," Griff added. "And not because it's beautiful but because it's worth a bloody fortune." He paused for a moment, then turned to Colin. "Don't worry. Everything is going to be fine."

"How can I help but worry?" Colin asked. "I'm getting married at ten, and the jewelers on Bond Street—including your favorite, Dalrymple's—don't open until nine, and I've no betrothal or wedding ring to offer."

Griff laughed. "It's times like these when it pays to be a very good customer."

"I'm not a good customer," Colin replied. "I'm not any kind of customer."

"I am."

"Are you planning to write me a letter of introduction?" Colin asked.

"No." Griff shook his head. "I intend to do better than that. I'm your best man, and since you've no experience in the purchase of fine jewelry, I intend to go with you and see that you purchase a ring worthy of your viscountess."

"What do I use as capital?" Colin asked. "I don't have a king's ransom to spend on a betrothal ring."

"You won't need it. Not with Dalrymple. His work is original and quite beyond the pale. He uses the highest quality stones and settings, and he'll create companion pieces to match anything you choose as a betrothal ring." Griff looked at Colin. "He's the best, and it just so happens that he's been itching to get a close look at the bird's egg to see if there is any way to tastefully reset it without cutting the diamond. I'll wager we can work out an arrangement to make your purchases more affordable."

"Griff . . ." Colin started to protest, but Griff wouldn't hear of it.

"I'll stand good for any pieces you choose until you're able to pay for them."

"I can't ask you to do that," Colin said.

"You aren't asking," Griff said. "We're offering."

"But . . ." Colin began again.

Griff held up his hand to forestall the argument he knew Colin was about to make. "This is one time you shouldn't allow your pride to stand in your way."

"I have no pride," Colin retorted. "Or I wouldn't have laid this problem at your door."

Griff laughed. "You're the proudest, most stubborn Scot I've ever met. And the finest." He reached over and placed his hand on Colin's arm. "Don't worry, Colin, after nearly twenty years of friendship, I know enough of your character to know you'll repay any amount I advance you or die trying."

Colin frowned.

"What now?"

"I keep thinking about Shakespeare."

"Shakespeare? You?"

"Aye," Colin answered. "I keep worrying about Polonius's speech to Laertes in *Hamlet*. 'Neither a borrower or a lender be for a loan oft loses both itself and friend and borrowing dulls the edge of husbandry.' "

Griff laughed once again. "Aren't you the fellow who once scoffed at Shakespeare's grasp of human nature?"

"I am," Colin admitted. "But this is different."

"I vow it is," Griff agreed. " 'Tis a world gone mad when Viscount Grantham purchases jewelry, gets engaged, and quotes Shakespeare in the same day."

"Griff . . ."

"One more word," Griff warned, "and I'll make you a gift of the money." Griff lifted the coffeepot from its resting place in the center of the table. "Here. Have some more coffee while I get dressed, and then we'll go roust Dalrymple out of bed."

Griff was as good as his word.

A quarter of an hour later, Colin had stood before the jeweler's impressive display of original designs. After studying everything the jeweler had to offer, Colin had finally selected a large oval pink sapphire surrounded by a dozen matched round diamonds in a delicate gold setting.

He had purchased the simple gold wedding band he held in his hand because it complemented the betrothal ring Gillian had just unbuttoned her glove to reveal.

As he stared down at her hand, Colin was enormously pleased with his choice. Although he'd debated over the purchase of the blue sapphire or the pink one, Colin realized that the unique setting and the pink sapphires suited Gillian's delicate hand and coloring much better than the more common blue sapphires.

He took her hand in his once again, held the gold band at the tip of the ring finger on her left hand. Colin's gaze never left her face as he repeated his final vows. "With this ring, I thee wed, with my body I thee worship, and with all my worldly goods I thee endow: in the Name of the Father, and of the Son, and of the Holy Ghost. Amen." He removed her betrothal ring, slipped the slim gold band onto her ring finger, and then placed the pink sapphire ring behind it.

The pink sapphire betrothal ring was the most beautiful ring Gillian had ever seen. The elegant design of the setting and the color, cut, and arrangement of the stones reminded her of the graceful dance costumes worn by the ballerinas at the Royal Ballet. And the sparkle of the gems added to the illusion of movement and dance. The beauty enchanted her. And the plain gold wedding band matched it to perfection. The rings fit her hand as if they'd been made just for her, and Gillian couldn't help but admire the way they sparkled.

Gillian had not dared hope that Lord Grantham would think to send a betrothal ring on the morning of the wedding—especially after such a brief engagement. After all, Colin Fox had planned his elopement with her for weeks, and he hadn't remembered to provide rings for the ceremony. And Lord Grantham had only had one evening in which to prepare. Gillian sighed. She was aware that in aristocratic families, betrothal rings oftentimes were heirlooms passed from one generation to the next. Gillian was grateful that this particular ring was part of Lord Grantham's family treasury. And she was particularly glad that he'd been able to persuade his mother to part with it. As she bowed her head and closed her eyes for another prayer, Gillian selfishly prayed Lady McElreath wouldn't want it back, because she would be loathe to return it.

"I now pronounce you husband and wife."

They didn't budge.

"Lord Grantham?" The rector spoke.

"Yes?" Colin looked at him.

"That concludes the ceremony. You may kiss your bride if you want to do so."

"May I?" Colin focused his attention on Gillian's mouth and the way she bit her bottom lip to stop its tremor as he turned to ask permission.

Gillian stared down at the nosegay of flowers and nodded. Colin lifted her chin with the tip of his index finger.

Gillian tilted her head to one side and looked at him from beneath her veil in a move that would have seemed coy on another woman but was completely natural for her. She watched as Colin lifted her wedding veil off her face, then closed her eyes as he leaned toward her and gently brushed his lips over hers. She expected a different sort of contact, but Colin's kiss, made up of equal measures of tenderness and reverence, affected her far more deeply than she thought possible. It was almost as if he'd touched her soul instead of her lips. And although she didn't remember closing them, Gillian opened her eyes and met Colin's intensely poignant green-eyed gaze. "Thank you," she whispered.

"My pleasure."

"I meant for the beautiful ring," Gillian clarified. "I didn't get a chance to thank you for remembering to procure one for the occasion."

Colin smiled. "I meant for the kiss."

Gillian blushed.

"But I'm delighted to know you like the ring."

She glanced back down at her hand. "It's incredible. I've never seen anything so beautiful."

"I have." Colin stared down at her.

The husky tone in his voice caught her attention, and Gillian looked up at him once again. "You have?"

He nodded. "A few minutes ago," he replied, softly. "When you walked in the door. And I'm very grateful that this particular occasion called for that dress and a kiss."

"Oh." She swallowed hard, barely managing the one syllable as her body sizzled with awareness at the look in Colin's eyes. "You like my dress?"

His voice was barely recognizable. "Very much."

Gillian beamed at him. "I was going to wear blue, but this one matched my betrothal ring."

"Thank God for pink sapphires," he breathed.

The rector cleared his throat. "The ceremony is over, my lord, except for the signing of the register." He nodded toward the far end of the drawing room where the parish register lay open to the proper page, waiting for the bride and groom and the witnesses to record the wedding.

Colin offered her his elbow. "Shall we?"

Gillian nodded.

"All right," Colin said, tucking her hand in the crook of his arm and making his way through the small gathering of friends and family to the parish register.

Colin signed the register and handed the pen to Gillian. "Your turn, Lady Grantham."

Gillian blinked at the use of his title in relation to her, then carefully penned her second new name in as many months. *Gillian McElreath, Viscountess Grantham.*

Chapter 16

"Wisely and slow; they stumble that run fast."
—WILLIAM SHAKESPEARE, 1564–1616
ROMEO AND JULIET

"May I offer our most sincere felicitations on your wedding, Lady Grantham?"

Gillian looked up as the Duke of Avon bowed over her hand. "Thank you for coming, Your Grace. I'm honored that you and Her Grace stood up for us."

Gillian greeted guests in the huge dining room of her parents' town house as they arrived for the wedding breakfast. When they'd entered the dining room and begun welcoming guests, Colin had been right beside her, but now he stood a few feet away, surrounded by late arrivals. Although the wedding party was quite small and the guests limited to immediate family and friends, the baron and Lady Davies had issued a greater number of invitations to the wedding breakfast. And it seemed that everyone who had been invited had decided to attend.

The dining table, large enough to seat thirty people, had been moved from the center of the room to one wall, draped in yards of white satin and lace, and loaded with a buffet of fine foods—from thick juicy roasts to delicate seafood. Smaller tables had been set up in the center of the dining room for the bride and groom, their families, and members of the wedding party.

Gillian nervously fidgeted with the skirts of her wedding dress and readjusted her veil. She shifted her weight from one foot to the other and waited impatiently for the trial by fire to begin. She glanced at her new husband, wishing she appeared as relaxed as he did. Although she told herself everything would be fine, Gillian dreaded the scrutiny and the comments of the guests. The staff had worked long and hard in order to arrange such an impressive breakfast on incredibly short notice, and they had managed beautifully, but rumors about her still abounded, and her sudden marriage to Lord Grantham was certain to add a bit of fuel to that flame. It was only a matter of time before one of the wedding guests forgot their manners long enough to mention it.

Fortunately, marriage to Lord Grantham came with a few bonuses—none the least of which was the fact that the Duke and Duchess of Avon had not only attended the wedding but had participated, serving as best man and matron of honor for the bride and groom. The duke and duchess's parents had also accepted invitations to the wedding breakfast, and now, Gillian's father—a baron who had previously only dreamed of moving in such imposing circles—was playing host to the Duke and Duchess of Avon, the Dowager Duchess of Sussex, the Marchioness of St. Germaine and the Dowager Marchioness of St. Germaine, the Earl and Countess of McElreath, the Earl and Countess of Weymouth, the Earl and Countess of Tressingham, as well as Viscount and Lady Harralson and a half-dozen other prominent London hostesses and businessmen who had all come at Lord Grantham's invitation. She didn't know quite how he had managed it or why they had chosen to do it, but the cream of London society had just closed ranks around her and her family, accepting them into their midst. Gillian still couldn't believe it.

"The honor was ours." The Duchess of Avon moved to stand close to her husband's side. "May I?" She reached for Gillian's left hand. "I've been dying to get a closer look at your ring." She studied the flawless pink sapphire. "It's stunning!" She glanced at her husband.

"Don't look at me." Griff held up his hand. "I didn't select it. Colin did."

"Then you owe him an apology," Alyssa commented. "For Colin has excellent taste in jewelry." She turned Gillian's hand so the sapphires and diamonds sparkled in the light, then leaned close and confided to Gillian, "And take it from me, that's a wonderful quality in a husband. Mr. Dalrymple outdid himself on this one."

"Mr. Dalrymple?" Gillian queried. "The jeweler on Bond Street?"

Alyssa nodded. "Yes."

"But when?" She paused. "We only agreed to marry yesterday. . . . How did he manage?" Gillian asked, glancing over to where Colin stood talking with a man who bore such a resemblance that he could only be his father. "Are you certain this ring didn't come from a Grantham family collection? That he didn't borrow it from Lady McElreath?"

Alyssa bit her bottom lip, wondering if she'd just put her foot in her mouth. "No," she answered honestly. "The Grantham family betrothal ring wasn't half as fine as this one. . . ." She looked to Griff.

"Go on," Griff urged, "you've told her this much, you might as well tell her the rest."

Alyssa took a deep breath. "Colin purchased this magnificent ring from Mr. Dalrymple this morning, especially for you."

Gillian was stunned. "He bought it this morning?"

Griff nodded. "Colin woke Dalrymple up a little after dawn and stayed over two hours reviewing everything the jeweler had until he found the perfect ring. I know, because I accompanied him."

"And you still managed to make it on time for the ceremony." Gillian was impressed by the effort Colin had made on her behalf.

"We wouldn't have missed it for the world," Alyssa assured her. "And we're so very pleased to welcome you to our family."

"Your family, Your Grace? I didn't realize you and Lord—" She stumbled over his formal title and caught herself in time. "I mean, Colin, are related."

"Call me Alyssa." The duchess laughed, then nodded toward her husband. "And my husband is Griffin—or Griff, for short. And we aren't Colin's blood relations. It only feels that way, doesn't it, Griffin?"

"It does indeed," the duke answered. "And actually, we are blood relations." He held out his right palm so his wife and Gillian could see the thin, barely detectable white scar bisecting it. The three original Free Fellows had pricked their thumbs in order to sign the Free Fellows League Charter in blood, but they had completed the ritual afterward by raking the knifepoint across their right palms, creating thin ribbons of blood that merged as the boys shook hands with one another and became blood brothers for the rest of their lives. "Colin and I met at school when we were boys. We've different parents, but he is my brother. We mingled our blood and made it so."

Alyssa looked at Gillian and gave a mock shudder. "Little boys are the only creatures on earth who mark their friendships by drawing blood."

Griff arched an eyebrow at his wife and in a voice heavy with innuendo, replied, "I disagree."

"Little girls don't—"

"Perhaps not," he admitted, "But you and I have become the closest of friends since I drew blood from you."

"Griffin Abernathy!" His blatant sexual intimation in Gillian's presence surprised his wife. "I'm shocked that you would say such a thing with Colin's bride in earshot!"

"No, you're not," he said. "Surprised, perhaps, but not shocked." He looked at his wife. "I've done far more shocking things in your presence—and you know it."

Alyssa giggled at the memory of some of the more shocking things he'd done in her presence. "You're right," she told him. "I'm surprised that you would say such a thing in Gillian's presence and—"

"And . . ." he prompted.

"I'm surprised you have scars of which I've been unaware." She took her husband's right hand and kissed his palm. "I thought I knew them all intimately."

"I keep a few in reserve," Griff teased, "just to keep you guessing, because you seem to enjoy searching for them."

"You enjoy the search every bit as much as I do," Alyssa reminded him.

Gillian blushed at the easy intimacy between the duke and duchess. It was clearly apparent that theirs was a love match, and Gillian couldn't suppress a twinge of envy. They shared the sort of companionship she always hoped she would have with the man she married. Unfortunately, that sort of camaraderie had been impossible with the first man she'd married. But now that she'd been given a second chance, Gillian prayed she might one day share the same sort of loving relationship with Colin McElreath.

"Now, see what you've done," Alyssa pretended to admonish her husband. "You've made Gillian blush again."

"Brides are supposed to blush." Griff's eyes twinkled when he turned to look at Gillian. "That's why they call them blushing brides."

"But I'm the man who is supposed to make this one blush," Colin interrupted, coming to stand beside the bride in question.

"Then we shall leave you to it," Griff said, glancing around the room, gauging the number of people present. "While Alyssa and I say hello to our parents and seek a less congested corner of the room."

"We'll be back shortly," Alyssa promised. "But we've monopolized the bride long enough. There are loads of people you need to speak to, and well . . ."

"My mother-in-law is beckoning." Griff lifted Gillian's hand once again and brushed her knuckles with his lips.

Alyssa sighed. "She's my mother and I love her dearly, but she still insists on showing Griffin off as if he were her own personal trophy."

"At least she likes you," Colin teased.

Griff laughed. "Now that I've become a duke, Lady Tressingham thinks I walk on water. Amazing what an elevation in title can do. I remember when she despised the sight of me." He shrugged his shoulders. "A word to the wise: You don't just marry a person, you know, you marry the family as well."

"Don't scare her off," Colin warned. "For I'm about to introduce Gillian to mine."

"Just smile," Alyssa told her. "And you'll do fine. Lady McElreath is very nice, and Lord McElreath is . . ." She thought for a moment. "*Engrossed* in cards, but at least he offers useful advice. All my parents ever talk about is—"

"Breeding," Griff replied.

"Pedigrees," Alyssa countered. "Those listed in Debrett's and those listed in the annals of horses and hounds. And I don't know which is more boring."

"Come along," Griff urged, "before we become equally boring." He reached for Alyssa's hand. "Many happy returns, Lady Grantham," Griff said to Gillian before he pulled Alyssa into his arms and kissed her soundly.

"Thank you, Griff," Gillian answered, smiling as a blushing Alyssa tucked her hand in the crook of Griff's arm and steered him toward a waving Lady Tressingham.

Gillian sighed.

"They've been married two years," Colin explained, "but they still act like newlyweds."

"I don't mind," Gillian said. "I think it's very nice. And very encouraging."

Colin gave his bride a warm smile. "I'm glad to hear it."

Gillian leaned against him, shifting her weight from one

foot to the other, and Colin automatically placed his hand at the small of her back to steady her.

"Tired?" Colin asked.

"A little," she admitted. "Everything has happened so fast, and it's all been a bit of an ordeal." Realizing what she'd said, Gillian looked up at Colin to see if she'd accidentally insulted him. "I'm sorry. I didn't mean marrying you has been an ordeal," she added hastily. "Just that everything leading up to it has been."

"No need to apologize," Colin told her. "I understand. Yesterday I was a sworn bachelor, and today I'm a married man." He turned to Gillian. "Not that I'm complaining. It's just that I don't know quite what to expect next." He wasn't complaining. He was being completely honest with himself and with her. When he'd come to this house to meet with her father yesterday afternoon, Colin hadn't expected his way of life to change. Oh, he admitted there were times when he longed for a real home, a wife and children—perhaps a spaniel or a wolfhound to sleep beside the hearth—but deep down, he had known that that sort of life was impossible for a man in his position, for a poor viscount who relied on the largesse of his friends and colleagues and who excelled in the secret art of war.

Colin took a deep breath. The scent of Gillian's perfume filled his nostrils—a warm and compelling scent of lemons and orange blossoms and musk—that drew him. Much like Gillian seemed to do. Gillian. His wife.

Colin smiled. He hadn't thought about marriage in relation to himself since Lord Kelverton had put Esme out of reach. If he longed for someone to love, someone to come home to, and someone to call his own, Colin never acted upon those longings. He had simply put them aside and refused to question why. He had the Free Fellows League and his work, and that was enough. Until fate—in the form of an unknown impostor—had placed Gillian Davies in his path.

The impostor had assumed Colin's secret identity and *pretended* to marry Gillian, but Colin had done him one better. He *had* married her, and the knowledge gave Colin a particularly warm feeling inside. It filled the place in his soul that had been empty for so very long. . . . For the first time in years, Colin believed he might have a future beyond the war with Bonaparte, that he might have a reason to stay alive.

"I wish I could promise that this will all be over soon." He nodded toward the crush of people still waiting to speak to the bride and groom. "But I don't know how long it will last. Or what comes next. My friend, Shepherdston, has offered us his country house for a honeymoon, if that's agreeable to you. As for the rest of it . . ." He shrugged his shoulders. "I don't own a home in which to take you or a threshold over which to carry you."

Gillian studied Colin's face—the way his blond brows framed his mesmerizing green eyes, his perfect nose, his mouth and the pout of his bottom lip. Gillian stared at his mouth. Colin McElreath was her husband now. Less than an hour ago, he had stood beside her and solemnly promised to love, honor, and cherish her. Then he kissed her so tenderly she thought her heart might break.

She smiled shyly at the memory of his kiss. What would it be like to have him love, honor, and cherish her with his body? Gillian blushed at her thoughts. A fortnight ago, she'd hoped she was done with that part of married life. She had hoped she would never have to endure the pain and the mess and the embarrassment that came with the marriage bed again. And now she was contemplating a honeymoon with a man who, although legally her husband, was little more than a stranger. Gillian wondered suddenly how she could think of sharing Colin McElreath's bed on the basis of their brief acquaintance and one sweet kiss.

But she was. And the idea was as appealing as it was alarming. "Perhaps it would be best if we concentrated on taking one step at the time," she suggested. "And not look too far ahead."

He had hoped for more, but Colin recognized the wisdom of taking things slowly. Colin stared down at his bride. Her face was so guileless and her thoughts so apparent. A few short weeks ago, Gillian Davies had fallen in love. She'd had romantic dreams of love and marriage and had risked everything by eloping and sharing a honeymoon with another man. She had no way of knowing that the man with whom she eloped was a charlatan or that he'd married at least two other women in as many months. Now she was facing the reality of marriage to him. And the possibility of sharing a marriage bed with a near stranger. It didn't matter that her marriage to him was legal. Colin was a stranger, and he knew that being married to him would take a little getting used to, especially since she gave every indication of being in love with someone else. Colin sighed. He wasn't a normally patient man, but he would try.

"Fair enough." Reaching down, he took Gillian's hand in his. "And the first step I need to take is to introduce my bride to my mother, father, and brothers and sisters, so they can welcome you into the family. Ready, Lady Grantham?"

Gillian took a deep breath, followed the Duchess of Avon's advice, and smiled.

Chapter 17

"And then to breakfast with
What appetite you have."

—WILLIAM SHAKESPEARE, 1564–1616

KING HENRY VIII

Gillian smiled as Colin introduced her to his mother and father. "Maman, Father, may I present my bride, Gillian?"

Gillian curtsied to the earl and countess. "It's a pleasure to meet you both."

"The pleasure is ours, my dear." The earl lifted Gillian's hand and brought it to his lips.

Her father-in-law had once been as handsome as his eldest son, but years of hard living had left their marks. The earl's skin was pasty white, his face and jaw bore signs of acute dissipation, and his eyes were bloodshot and drooping. He had dressed for the wedding in a well-tailored tailcoat and striped trousers, but the careful tailoring couldn't hide the paunch that too many late nights, too much rich food, and too little physical exercise had caused. Now, the Earl of McElreath stank of brandy and tobacco and bore only a passing resemblance to his handsome son. "Welcome to the family."

"Thank you, sir," Gillian answered, smiling at Lady McElreath. "I'm honored to be a part of the McElreath family."

"We are honored to have you," Lady McElreath added. "May I present my daughters, Liana and Caroline?"

The girls curtsied. "Lady Grantham."

"Please, call me Gillian."

"Gillian," they replied in unison.

"Oh, Maman, look at her betrothal ring!" Liana, the oldest daughter, nudged her younger sister in the arm and pointed to Gillian's left hand. "Isn't it beautiful?"

Gillian held out her hand, offering Liana, Caroline, and Lady McElreath a better look at the pink sapphire surrounded by the perfectly matched diamonds.

Lord McElreath leaned forward and studied the ring. "That beauty must have cost a pretty penny." He threw his son an accusing glance.

"The price is of no concern," Colin replied coolly. "It was a wedding gift for my bride." He glanced at Gillian. "A token of my affection and esteem."

"The price is of great concern," Lord McElreath contradicted, "when you spend a fortune on your bride's ring but refuse to help your father with his debts."

"She was well worth the cost," Colin reminded his father. "Especially when I've so little else to offer."

"You just gave her an old and honorable title as the Viscountess Grantham," Lord McElreath pointed out.

"The title is an honorable one," Colin agreed, looking his father in the eye. "Unfortunately, it's attached to a mountain of family debts I didn't incur."

"There's no call to be rude to your father," Lord McElreath admonished.

"And there was no call for you to be rude to my bride on her wedding day." Colin dismissed his father and leaned forward to kiss his mother on the cheek. "Thank you for coming, Maman." He nodded toward his sisters. "And for bringing the family."

Lady McElreath turned to Gillian. "Please excuse Lord McElreath. He's not at his best. He had a very late night last night and was not prepared to attend a wedding this early in the morning—else he wouldn't have acquired an aching head."

"I'm sorry about Father's aching head," Colin said, "but an aching head doesn't give him the right to behave like a cad in the presence of his new daughter-in-law."

"Your father is no cad," Lady McElreath said softly. "He's a gentleman."

"Then he should remember to behave like one." Colin glared at his father before turning his attention back to his mother. "If you will excuse us, Gillian and I have other duties to attend to."

"I understand," Lady McElreath said. "And I wish you much happiness on your wedding day and every day, Colin and Gillian."

"Thank you, Lady McElreath," Gillian replied.

"Yes, thank you, Maman." Placing a hand at the small of Gillian's back, Colin steered her away from his parents and over to their table.

"A pleasure meeting you," Gillian called over her shoulder.

"That went rather well, don't you think?" Colin said as they reached the relative quiet of their table.

Gillian surprised him by giggling at his dry attempt at levity. "Your father disliked me on sight. Your mother is reserving her judgment as to what sort of wife I'll be. My betrothal ring sparked an argument with your father but made a good impression on your sisters—so I think, on the whole, it did go rather well." She paused. "Better than I expected."

"I find it hard to believe that your expectations are so low," Colin said. "Tell me, Lady Grantham, is that generally the case? Or did you make an exception for the meeting with my parents?"

Gillian laughed once again. "I made an exception for your parents."

"Really?" Colin arched an eyebrow in mock disbelief. "And why did you believe that was necessary?"

"I assumed that your parents, like most parents, wanted only the best for their son and heir." She looked up at Colin. "And that they would naturally be disappointed to learn he had settled for less."

Colin frowned. "My parents believe I married for reasons of infatuation, if not for love."

"How?" Gillian began. "We only met two days past."

"Infatuation only takes a moment's glance," Colin said. "But I told my mother I met you weeks ago while you were visiting relatives in the border country."

"But your father . . ."

Colin seemed to read her mind. "My father's behavior had very little to do with you or with our wedding. He was rude because he's ashamed."

"For appearing foxed at our wedding?" Gillian asked.

"For having to appear anywhere when he's not at his best." Colin sighed. "And he must save his best for the gaming hells, because we've not seen it since Gregory was born."

"Gregory?"

"My youngest brother."

She looked up at Colin. "How many brothers have you?"

"Two." Colin told her. "Malcolm and Gregory. There are five McElreath children. Three males and two females, of which I am the eldest."

"Why didn't I meet your brothers?" Gillian asked. "Didn't they come?"

"Oh, the young hellions are here somewhere," Colin warned. "I saw them swarming around Griff earlier. But . . ." He glanced over at the floor-to-ceiling windows where Griff and Alyssa stood.

"Are you as rich as Papa says?" a small voice demanded.

"Speak of the devil." Colin looked down to find his youngest brother, eight-year-old Gregory, tugging on the end of Gillian's veil. "Rudeness must run in the family to-day," Colin said by way of explanation. "Lady Grantham, may I present my youngest brother, Master Gregory McElreath?"

"Gregory." Gillian held out her hand.

"Gregory, it's customary to bow in the presence of a lady, and this lady is your sister-in-law, Gillian, Lady Grantham."

Gregory bowed. "Well? Is it true? Are you?" He asked again, returning to the subject he found most intriguing.

"I don't know," Gillian answered. "How rich does your papa think I am?"

"Papa says you're rich enough to cover all his chits with coin to spare."

"Nobody's that rich!" Ten-year-old Malcolm said in a weary voice wise beyond his years.

Colin bit back a smile. "Lady Grantham, may I present my other brother, Master Malcolm McElreath?"

She nodded, and Colin continued his introduction, "Malcolm, may I present my wife, Gillian, Lady Grantham?"

"How do you do, Lady Grantham?" Malcolm bowed politely.

"Very well, thank you," Gillian replied.

"Are you rich enough to cover all of Papa's chits?" Gregory persisted.

Gillian turned to Colin. "What are chits?"

"Gaming debts," Colin answered.

"Doesn't your papa have chits to cover?" Gregory asked.

Gillian shook her head. "My papa doesn't gamble."

Gregory's eyes grew big as saucers. "At all?"

"No."

"Then what does he do when he goes to his club?"

"My papa doesn't belong to a club," Gillian answered.

"How does he spend his time?" Malcolm asked.

"He goes to his office at Davies Silk and Linen Importers."

Malcolm was shocked. "He's in *trade?*"

"He's a silk and linen merchant," Gillian said. "He has a fleet of ships that sail the trade routes to China and the Orient, the East Indies, Africa, even the Americas."

"I thought he was a baron," Malcolm said.

"He is," she replied.

"Then he cannot be a silk and linen merchant," Malcolm recited. "Gentlemen do not engage in trade."

"My father made his fortune as a merchant *before* he was granted the title of baron," Gillian answered proudly. "He's the first Baron Davies."

"Oh." Gregory gave a disdainful sniff. "Who made a merchant a baron?"

"The Prince Regent," Colin said.

"Did he save Prinny's life or something?" Gregory demanded.

"In a manner of speaking." Colin's reply was extremely diplomatic.

"How?"

"Baron Davies provided a service to his country by repaying a series of loans the Prince Regent owed to a foreign bank."

Malcolm rolled his eyes skyward. "So her papa bought his title by paying off Prinny's chits."

"Exactly," Colin said. "Baron Davies gained his title in exactly the same manner our ancestor gained his title many years ago. The difference is that our ancestor helped ransom James the First of Scotland from the English. Baron Davies provides a great service to his country by importing silks and linens. None of us would have anything to wear if it weren't for men like the baron. And his fleet of ships and his business contacts have made him one of England's wealthiest men and given him entrée to society."

"There's another difference as well," Malcolm added.

"What's that?" Colin asked.

"The baron hasn't gambled his fortune away."

"No, he hasn't," Colin agreed. "And we're very fortunate that he trusted us enough to allow his daughter to marry into a family where gambling is a way of life."

"Why shouldn't he trust you?" Malcolm asked. "Gaming isn't your way of life. Or Maman's. Only Papa's."

Colin shook his head. "Not just Father. Like most men, I wager upon occasion."

"Are you like Papa? Or do you win more than you lose?" Gregory asked.

"I win more than I lose," Colin said, reaching out to ruffle his young brother's hair. "The secret to gaming is never to wager more than you're willing to lose."

Gregory tugged on Colin's tailcoat.

Colin leaned down. "What is it?"

"Would you please tell Papa the secret to gaming so he won't lose anymore? Then Maman won't have to worry about keeping us fed and clothed. And we won't have to go to bed hungry."

The idea that a child born of the peerage went to bed hungry appalled Gillian. "You'll never have to worry about going to bed hungry again," she promised. "Because I'll wager that your brother Colin and I *are* rich enough to pay all your Papa's chits with coin to spare."

"Truly?" This time Malcolm was impressed. "From money earned in trade?"

"Yes, indeed," Gillian answered, looking up at Colin. "Aren't we?"

Colin nodded. "I'll wager her dowry alone is enough to redeem Father's chits. And send you both to Eton and provide dowries for your sisters."

"You got rich just by marrying a *girl?*" Gregory asked.

"No." Colin smiled at his bride. "I got rich by marrying a very special girl."

Malcolm looked Gillian up and down. "Have you any sisters?"

"I'm afraid not," Gillian told him.

Malcolm shrugged. "That's all right, I'm marrying Lady Miranda St. Germaine anyway." He glanced over at the statuesque, auburn-haired Lady Miranda. "Just as soon as I grow up."

Chapter 18

"I do desire we may be better strangers."
—WILLIAM SHAKESPEARE, 1564–1616
AS YOU LIKE IT

She had smiled so long her face hurt, and Gillian was certain Colin felt the same way. And there were still formalities to be observed.

Alyssa and Griffin, Lord and Lady Davies, and Lord and Lady McElreath joined Gillian and Colin at the main table to begin the toasts and the distribution of presents to their guests and to the Davies household staff.

Griff presented the first toast to the bride and groom. "Here's to Colin and Gillian, Lord and Lady Grantham! May God bless you with health, wealth, a houseful of happy, healthy children, and a deep and abiding love for one another which never dims and from which you never wish to recover. Amen."

"Hear! Hear!"

"To Lord and Lady Grantham!"

Gillian's father waited until the resounding chorus of cheers faded before he presented his toast and his wedding gift to the bride and groom. "My dear old friends and my dear new friends, please raise your glasses to my beloved daughter, Gillian, and her bridegroom, Lord Grantham, the truest of gentlemen and the best man any father could hope to have wed his only daughter." He looked to Colin. "To-day, my daughter will leave my home and begin a new life with her husband. Lady Davies and I hate to see her leave. This big, old house will be empty without her, but our loss is Lord Grantham's gain. Gillian has brightened our lives from the moment she came into the world. When we bought this house, her presence in it made it a home. And we have no doubt that she will do the same for you, Lord Grantham." Gillian's father removed a thick vellum enve-lope from inside his coat pocket and handed it to Colin. "Colin, my son." The baron glanced over at the Earl of McElreath. "Your father and mother and Lady Davies and I would deem it a very great honor if you will accept this as our wedding gift."

Colin glanced at Gillian and at his parents and realized they were as surprised by the baron's gesture as he was. Colin understood that his mother and father hadn't been part of the process, but he deeply appreciated the baron's generosity in including his father and mother in the giving of the gift.

"Don't keep us in suspense," someone called. "Open it!"

"May I?" Colin asked.

Lord Davies nodded.

Colin opened the envelope and withdrew a pair of heavy brass door keys and the deed for Number Twenty-one Park Lane.

"What is it?" Gillian asked, leaning close to peer over Colin's arm.

Colin opened his palm to reveal the keys. "A house," he answered, stunned. "Door keys and a deed for Number Twenty-one Park Lane."

"Twenty-one Park Lane!" Alyssa exclaimed. "We're practically neighbors! It's a lovely house with a fine, old-fashioned formal garden that could be magnificent with a bit of attention."

Number Twenty-one Park Lane was the former home of

the late Lord Herrin who had died without wife or issue. It was a beautiful home just down the lane from the Duke of Sussex's residence, around the corner from Griff and Alyssa's town house, a block from Shepherdston's house, and two and a half blocks away from the Davies town house.

Colin stared at the deed and then shook his head as if to clear it. If he had had any doubts about the lengths to which Davies would go to see his daughter well settled, Colin laid them to rest. The baron had bought him a house. His name was inscribed on the legal document in big, bold letters. Colin McElreath, Lord Grantham. If he accepted the house Gillian's parents offered, two of the original Free Fellows and their wives would be the newest Free Fellow's neighbors. He and Griff and Sussex could labor to decipher French ciphers over coffee in the gardens where the corners of their properties converged. Colin couldn't decide if Fortune had decided to shine upon him or if Fate was simply showing her hand.

"We know it was presumptuous, but we took the liberty of having it cleaned and made ready," Lord Davies said. "In the event you decided to honeymoon there."

Colin looked up from the deed. "My friend, the Marquess of Shepherdston, has made his country house in Bedfordshire available for our use."

Lord Davies nodded. "The house is ready should you wish to use it tonight." He smiled at Gillian. "The staff is temporary, though. Your mother and I thought it best that we not overstep our bounds by hiring a permanent one. As mistress of the house, you should be allowed to hire your own staff."

"But, sir—" Colin began.

"No, it's not part of the marriage settlement." Lord Davies anticipated Colin's protest. "It's a gift."

"I don't know what to say to such a generous gift." Colin's pride warred with his gratitude. Pride won. "It's too much."

"That all depends on your point of view." Lord Davies laughed. "Every bridegroom needs a threshold over which to carry his bride. Or would you rather begin your married life living with your in-laws? Or your parents?"

Colin smiled. "I see your point, sir. And I thank you for your generous gift, Lord Davies."

Lord Davies clapped his new son-in-law on the shoulder. "Wise decision, lad."

Gillian threw her arms around her father's neck and hugged him tightly. "Oh, thank you, Papa."

Lord Davies shrugged his shoulders. "I cannot take complete credit for the idea," he admitted, looking over his daughter's shoulder to where his wife stood with tears shimmering in her eyes. "I selfishly wanted to keep you close. I wanted to refurbish the fourth-floor apartments and the nurseries for your use, but your mother thought the two of you needed a greater degree of privacy. A home of your own seemed the ideal solution."

Gillian met her mother's gaze and then walked over and embraced her. "Thank you, Mama, for understanding."

"Your father and I lived with his mother and father when we first married." She smiled at the memory. "We loved them dearly, but living in their home wasn't the best way to start a marriage."

Lord Davies chuckled. "Your mama threatened to leave me on numerous occasions. And I remember thinking that if I had to choose between my wife and my mother once more, *I* would leave."

"We didn't truly become husband and wife until we left his parents' bed and board. And if we hadn't managed to find a cottage of our own, you would never have made an entrance into the world," Lady Davies told her.

Lord Davies agreed. "Twenty-one Park Lane can't compare to Plum Cottage but—"

"Plum Cottage?" It was the first time Gillian had ever heard the name.

"A tiny cottage outside London proper," Lady Davies said. "There were plum trees in the garden. They bloomed shortly after we moved in. We named the cottage after the trees. Plum Cottage." She smiled at her husband. "We left Plum Cottage and moved into this house just before your fourth birthday, but we still own the cottage. We couldn't bear to part with it."

"I've never heard you speak of it," Gillian said.

"Some memories should only be shared on special occasions," her mother said. "Today is a special occasion, and Plum Cottage is one of those memories."

"Thank you for sharing it, Mama."

"You're welcome, Gilly-flower. Now," her mother whispered, "go home with your young man and make a few special memories of your own."

When all the toasts to the health of the bride and groom had been offered and accepted, and Gillian and Colin had presented their gifts to the members of the wedding party and to the household staff, Gillian turned to Colin, "I should go upstairs now and change into a traveling dress." She smoothed her hands down the front of her dress in a gesture Colin was beginning to associate with nerves.

"You look beautiful." Colin stared at her, taking in every nuance of her appearance as he attempted to inscribe her image on his memory. Gillian was every man's dream in that dress. What healthy male would want her to change out of it? Unless he was the man granted the good fortune to watch or to help as she removed it? "I had hoped you might keep that dress on."

His obvious disappointment at her decision to change into a more suitable traveling dress surprised as well as pleased her. "I don't have to change," she told him. "It is my wedding day. And this is my wedding gown. I can wear it if you'd like."

"I'd like," he murmured in the low, husky burr she was beginning to recognize.

Gillian rewarded him with a smile before she turned to say good-bye to her mother and father. Colin placed a hand at the base of Gillian's spine and escorted her to the door. Lord and Lady Davies walked with them and stood watching as the young unmarried ladies gathered on the circle of lawn surrounding the front steps.

Standing by his side, Gillian tucked her left hand in Colin's and tossed her wedding bouquet toward the cluster of young ladies. She smiled as her new sister-in-law, Liana, jumped to catch it.

Colin frowned as Liana came away with the nosegay and waved it at him.

"Don't worry," Gillian said. "She hasn't made her curtsy to the regent yet, and she can't get married until she does."

"Unless she decides to elope," Colin replied without thinking.

"That's always a possibility," Gillian answered in a small voice. "But Liana seems the sensible sort. I doubt she'll make the same mistake I made."

Colin looked at his bride. "I didn't mean to—"

"No matter," she said. "It's over and done with."

"No regrets," he said.

Gillian managed a smile. "I wish it were that easy," she said. "But I've plenty of regrets. And my biggest regret is that I met *him* before I met you."

Swallowing the lump in his throat, Colin brought Gillian's hand to his lips and planted a gentle kiss on the fleshy part of her palm. He didn't speak. He couldn't. For he knew, even if she did not, that he was a sworn Free Fellow, and if Gillian had met him first, she wouldn't be standing beside him today wearing his ring and sharing his name.

Chapter 19

"Your heart's desires be with you!"
—WILLIAM SHAKESPEARE, 1564–1616
As You Like It

Curiosity and pride of ownership got the better of them in the end as Number Twenty-one Park Lane beckoned them like a lover to bed.

Colin placed his hand beneath Gillian's elbow and handed her into the coach that would take them on their honeymoon. Gillian settled on the padded seat, closed her eyes, and heaved a sigh of relief at being able to relax and to drop the smile she'd worn throughout the morning.

She felt the sway of the coach and automatically lifted her skirts out of the way as Colin climbed in beside her. He sat back on the seat and stretched his long legs in the limited space between the bench seats, then reached into his coat and took the house keys from his inner pocket. "Lady Grantham," he called in a singsong voice.

Gillian opened her eyes.

Two heavy brass front door keys dangled from Colin's index finger. "Might I interest you in joining me on an inspection of our property before we begin our honeymoon? Or would you prefer to go on to Shepherdston Hall?"

She beamed at him, and her smile seemed to light up the interior of the coach. "I was hoping you would ask."

Colin grinned his boyishly attractive grin. He rapped on the ceiling and issued directions to the driver. "Take the Post Road to Northamptonshire, by way of Number Twenty-one Park Lane."

"Sir?" the coachman called down from his perch.

"Number Twenty-one Park Lane."

Gillian waved good-bye as the coach pulled away from her parents' town house into Park Lane traffic.

Two and a half blocks up the lane, the coach rolled to a stop in front of the open wrought-iron gates of Number Twenty-one Park Lane. Colin alighted from the coach first, then helped Gillian out.

"Shall I see to your luggage, sir?" the coachman asked.

Colin shook his head. "Wait for us."

Gillian reached for Colin's hand as they walked through the gate, down the steps, then up the brick path and the steps leading to the front door.

Colin paused at the front door and let go of Gillian's hand in order to fish the keys out of his pocket. "Shall we try the keys?" he asked. "Or knock?"

"Mama said there's a temporary staff in residence," Gillian reminded him. "I suppose that means we should knock."

"All right." Colin bent at the knees and swung Gillian up and into his arms. "Go ahead." He stepped close enough to allow Gillian to knock on the front door.

The door opened almost immediately, swinging back on well-oiled hinges to reveal a formally attired butler and a marble entryway.

"Good afternoon," the butler said. "Lord and Lady Grantham?"

"Yes," Gillian answered.

"Please, come in," the butler invited, stepping back to allow them entrance. "And welcome. I'm Britton, and we've been awaiting your arrival."

Colin carried Gillian across the threshold. "Welcome home, Lady Grantham."

Gillian giggled. "Thank you, Lord Grantham. Welcome home to you."

The members of the staff assembled in the front hallway echoed Gillian's words. "Welcome to Herrin House, sir, ma'am."

Colin raised an eyebrow in query as he stared down at Gillian. "Herrin House doesn't have quite the same ring as Plum Cottage, does it?"

"No." Gillian shook her head. "It doesn't. But perhaps that will come in time."

"Along with the special memories," Colin added, in his low, husky burr.

"Along with the special memories," Gillian affirmed.

Special memories. Her soft affirmation was nearly his undoing as desire hit him with the force of a gale wind. He fixed his gaze on Gillian's soft mouth as everything receded except the sight and scent and feel of her in his arms. He wanted very much to kiss her, and his arms trembled with restraint as he fought to keep from pressing her closer as he covered her lips with his own. It was all Colin could do to keep from carrying Gillian upstairs and finding the nearest bedroom so they could begin making a lifetime of special memories.

Gillian looked up at him, and Colin's body tightened in response as she moistened her lips with the tip of her tongue in a self-conscious gesture that sent his blood rushing southward to the part of his anatomy throbbing against the front of his trousers.

He cleared his throat and made a feeble attempt at levity as he struggled to maintain his composure. "And if all else fails, we can always change the name."

The look in Colin's green eyes sent shivers up and down her spine. His arms trembled beneath her, and

Gillian automatically looped her arms around Colin's neck and held on. "What name?"

Colin leaned so close his warm breath caressed her cheeks. "We seem to be causing a bit of a stir among our temporary staff."

Suddenly recalling where she was and why, Gillian blushed and hid her embarrassment by pressing her face against Colin's neck.

The brush of her lips against his neck sent a fresh, sharp jolt of awareness through him. "Shall I put you on your feet, my lady?" he whispered, "or would you like me to carry you on our first tour of our new home?"

"Would you carry me?" she whispered back, "if I didn't want to walk?"

"Indeed, I would, my lady." *Right up to bed.* Once the idea lodged itself in his brain, Colin had trouble forcing it aside.

"Then maybe you had better set me on my feet."

Colin blinked. Was it possible she'd read his mind? He bent and placed Gillian on her feet. "There you go."

"Thank you most kindly, my lord." Gillian smiled a little smile reminiscent of the one Colin had seen on da Vinci's painting of the *Mona Lisa* hanging in the Louvre.

"You are most kindly welcome, my lady."

Gillian noticed movement out of the corner of her eye and realized the staff her mother and father had hired stood waiting patiently for the new lord and lady of the house to remember their presence. She walked over to the butler. "Forgive us for keeping you waiting."

"Of course, my lady," Britton answered. "May I offer felicitations to you and to Lord Grantham on your wedding day on behalf of the staff?"

"Thank you," she replied.

The butler nodded. "With your permission, Lady Grantham, I would like to present the staff."

Gillian nodded, then greeted each member of the staff as Britton introduced them.

There were ten in all. The butler, Britton; the house-keeper, Mrs. Evans; Mrs. Donnelly, the cook; two foot-men, Tanner and Norris; Banning, an upstairs maid; Hill, a downstairs maid; Ridley, a cook's helper; and the scullery maids, Pilcher and Salton.

"We understand that your mother, Lady Davies, hired us as temporary staff," Britton said.

"That is correct," Gillian said.

"Am I given to understand that our positions may become permanent pending your approval?" The butler asked.

Colin gave a slight shake of his head, but Gillian didn't notice.

"Yes," she answered.

He hated to contradict his bride in her first official task as Lady Grantham, but Colin couldn't allow her to retain the staff unless they met his approval. "Pending *our* approval and references and recommendations from trusted staff," Colin added.

Britton bristled. "We all come highly recommended and with references from the Domestic Staffing Service on St. James."

"I'm pleased to hear it," Colin told him. "But Lady Grantham and I require that our staff receive additional security clearances from Mr. Wickham at Bow Street and an unnamed private firm."

Gillian looked askance at her husband.

"Forgive me for treading on your role as mistress of this house, but my connection with the War Office requires that my household staff meet higher standards than most." Colin took hold of Gillian's hand and brushed his lips over her knuckles in a gallant gesture meant to allay his bride's questions as he repeated the reply he and the other Free

Fellows had decided upon when they began their clandestine operations on the government's behalf.

Even the best domestic staffing services fell prey to
liars, thieves, charlatans, confidence men, and agents of
foreign governments. And the War Office had learned long
ago that one of the most effective means foreign and hos-
tile governments used to gain sensitive information was to
provide domestic help to London's elite staffing agencies.
Spies oftentimes masqueraded as footmen, valets, and private secretaries. For what better way for a spy to gather information than to have it handed to him on a silver salver
by the gentleman who employed him?

"I apologize, sir, for my brusque manner," Britton said. "I
wasn't aware of your connection to the War Office."

Colin nodded. "No apology is necessary. My wife's
mother, Lady Davies, was unaware of the additional
requirements—else she would have informed you of it
when she offered you employment here."

"I understand completely, sir," Britton assured him.
"And I don't foresee any difficulties in meeting your additional requirements as my father, my grandfather, and my
grandfather's father served as butler to some of the finest
families in the land."

"Thank you for your understanding," Colin replied.

"Will you be bringing additional staff for whom we
should prepare?" Britton asked. "A gentleman's gentleman, lady's maid, private secretary, or driver?"

Colin looked to Gillian. "I will not, but Lady Grantham
may."

Gillian nodded. "My lady's maid, Nadine Lavery, will
join the household when Lord Grantham and I return from
our honeymoon." She smiled at the butler. "I confess that
my curiosity is beginning to get the best of me. If you
would be so kind as to show us around, Lord Grantham
and I would like to inspect our new home."

Britton bowed. "But, of course, my lady. Follow me."

Colin offered her his elbow. "Shall we?"

Herrin House was a magnificent example of a redbrick Tudor-style town house. The tour of the house started downstairs in the kitchens and the wine cellar, included a brief look at the butler's quarters and pantry, and the housekeeper's apartment and sitting room. Although they didn't explore it, Gillian and Colin paused to survey the small courtyard area connecting the kitchen to the gardens beyond, then moved up to the ground-floor dining room and the first-floor drawing rooms, study, music room, and library. When they concluded their tour of the first floor, Britton led Gillian and Colin up to the second-floor bedrooms, the third-floor nursery, schoolroom, children's bedrooms, and governess's quarters, before concluding with a brief inspection of the servants' quarters and storage attics.

From basement to attics, the house was beautifully appointed with fine furniture, carpets, window hangings, tapestries, and exquisite examples of needlework. The entryway, the staircases, and the drawing-room floors were of white marble. The paneling, trim, mantels, and banisters were made of fine English oak, and the fireplaces in the lower floors were faced with white marble, while the bedroom fireplaces were all faced with exquisitely painted tiles. All the beds—even those in the servant's quarters— were hung with curtains that matched those at the windows, and the library contained floor-to-ceiling bookshelves filled with leather-bound volumes of every description.

Herrin House was clearly the house of an educated gentleman of refined tastes and old money. Its only shortcoming was an overabundance of heavy masculine furniture and the lack of any real feminine or family touches. And those shortcomings could be easily remedied with a few new furnishings and judicious redecorating.

Gillian loved it. And Colin was awed by her father's incredible generosity. They left the attics, where a collection of ancient furniture, trunks of clothing, and wrapped paintings stood sentinel over the lower floors of the house, and retraced their steps past the third-floor nursery and schoolroom, back down to the second-floor suite of rooms that belonged to the lord and lady of the house.

Colin discreetly dismissed the butler as Gillian left his side and entered the sitting room.

The sitting room connected the master's chamber to the lady's chamber on the north side of the suite. The valet's room and the maid's chamber and a series of built-in armoires connected the chambers at the south side.

The spacious sitting room was comfortably furnished with a damask sofa, wing chairs, and a chaise longue that promised a relaxing evening spent reclining before the fire. The sitting room and the lady's chamber were the only truly feminine rooms in the house. The walls of both were papered with a soft, butter-colored silk, and the window dressings and bed curtains were of heavier silk a shade darker than the butter-colored walls. The furniture was painted white and trimmed in gilt. The color scheme created the illusion of sunlight streaming into the room through the mullioned windows. And the polished rectangular mirror hanging above the mantel reflected the light and completed the illusion of sunlight. The sitting room and the bedchamber attached to it were the warmest, most welcoming rooms in the entire house and, other than the library, Gillian's favorite.

She walked to the center of the sitting room and executed a series of graceful pirouettes.

"I take it you're pleased." Colin stood in the doorway, watching, as his bride danced her way around the bedroom.

"More than pleased." She danced over to him. "I'm thrilled. Isn't it the most wonderful house you've ever seen?"

"It is that," he agreed, more than a bit tempted to join his bride in her dance of delight. "I admit to pinching myself more than once to make certain this isn't some kind of dream."

"The house?" she asked.

"The house. The wedding." He smiled at her. "You in that dress."

"Me? A dream? A nightmare, perhaps, but not a dream." She moistened her lips with the tip of her tongue and self-consciously patted several stray tendrils of hair back into place.

"You obviously haven't looked in that mirror." He nodded toward the mirror hanging above the mantel. "Or you would see what I see."

"What do you see?" She knew she shouldn't ask, but she couldn't help it.

"The loveliest bride any man could ever want," Colin said softly.

"I think that's the sweetest thing anyone has ever said to me." Gillian blinked away a sudden rush of tears.

"I meant every word."

"Except the part about wanting me," Gillian said. "You can't tell me that you went to my father's house hoping to find a bride."

"No, I didn't," he answered. "But don't think that means I don't want you."

Gillian blinked at the honest reply he didn't bother to couch in polite, gentlemanly phrases. She saw in that moment that her new husband was exhausted. His green eyes were streaked with red and underscored by dark bruising circles, and she recognized the tired lines bracketing his mouth, and the golden stubble emerging on his cheeks and chin. "It's been a long day already," she said. "And it's only half over. You must be tired. . . ."

"I am tired," Colin said. "But that doesn't change the fact that I want you very much. In every way it's possible for a man to have you."

He wanted her. But she didn't appear to want him.

"It's our wedding night," she replied hesitantly, casting a nervous glance toward the doorway of the lady's bedchamber. "You're legally entitled to take whatever you want."

Colin gritted his teeth. He didn't need any more temptation. The sight of her in that pink confection of a wedding dress was enough to do him in. He was trying to be sensible. And considerate. Didn't she understand the danger of inviting him to share a night in her bed? He had willpower, but he wasn't made of stone. What happened to taking one thing at a time? And not looking too far ahead?

"I thank you for your gracious offer, and I'm quite certain I'm going to regret it in the morning, but I think, perhaps, I've taken enough for one day."

Gillian frowned. "I don't understand."

Colin exhaled. How could he explain without insulting her? He had taken her dowry. Taken a wife. And taken a house. He didn't want to take a lover who didn't want him. Because he wanted her. There was no doubt about that. But there was a great deal of doubt on his part as to whether or not she wanted *him*. Not her husband. Not her bridegroom. Not Lord Grantham. Or the man she knew as Colin Fox. But *him*. Colin McElreath.

He had to know that she wanted him—and him alone— because once he made love to her, there could be no going back. Colin took a deep breath. For the first time in his life, he understood the frenetic society in which he lived. Arranged marriages to barely met strangers were hell. And arranged marriages formed the basis for society as he knew it. A society filled with shallow, cynical, empty people leading shallow, empty lives. Christ! Colin raked his fingers through his hair. When had he become so damned philosophical? What difference would it make if he and Gillian became empty and shallow people populating the ton? He could seduce her. His body ached for release. He could woo her with soft words and equally soft touches, but for what purpose? To get an heir? There were far too many unhappy, unwanted, and unloved heirs in London as it was. Better to wait. Better to protect himself. Better to get to know one another before the deed was done. Before he gave his heart to a woman who might not want it.

"I know it's our wedding night, and I know the law entitles me to take what I want, but I would rather forgo the consummation of our vows until we're better acquainted." Colin said the right words as he met her gaze, but he hoped she would hear otherwise. "If you've no objections?"

Gillian couldn't hide her surprise or her relief. "No, of course not."

Disappointment hit him with the force of a blow, and Colin released the breath he'd been holding and did the finest bit of playacting he'd ever done. "There's no rush." He shrugged his shoulders in a studied show of nonchalance. "We've plenty of time. We're married until death us do part."

Gillian stood on tiptoe, wrapped her arms around his neck, and hugged him. "You're the most understanding man I've ever met."

Her firm breasts pressed against his chest. Colin felt the twin points through the silk of her wedding dress, and his body responded. "I'm not that understanding," Colin murmured, as he leaned down and covered her mouth with his.

Gillian sighed. His kiss was warm and wonderful and welcoming. She closed her eyes and allowed him to work magic with his mouth. She couldn't form coherent thoughts. All she could do was feel. And kissing him made her feel more than she'd ever imagined.

It was impossible to keep her distance. Every instinct she possessed urged her closer, and Gillian obeyed her instincts. She took a step forward and found herself held firmly against his chest as Colin deepened his kiss, tightening his embrace around her waist in a fluid motion that sent her senses spiraling. His kiss was everything she'd ever dreamed about, everything she'd ever hoped for in a kiss. It was soft and gentle and tender and sweet and enticing and hungry and hot and wet and deep and persuasive at once. It coaxed and demanded, asked and expected a like response, and Gillian obliged.

She parted her lips when he asked entrance into the warm recesses of her mouth and shivered with delight at the first tentative, exploratory thrust of his tongue against hers. She met his tongue with her own, returning each stroke, beginning a devastatingly thorough exploration of her own.

Colin bit back a groan of frustration. He promised himself he would wait. Promised himself he wouldn't rush her. He was going to be a considerate lover and allow her to set the pace of their lovemaking—even if it killed him. With that thought in mind, he let his arms fall to his sides and abruptly broke contact with her lips. He drew in several ragged breaths as he leaned his forehead against the top of her head and struggled for control. *Mon Dieu,* but he loved kissing this woman!

"Colin?"

He was gratified to discover that Gillian's breathing was nearly as labored as his own. "Yes?"

"Would you mind very much if we stayed here tonight?"

He groaned.

"I know we aren't going to—" she broke off, searching for the words. "Share a bed . . . but . . . well, even so, we could have a nice dinner and conversation. . . ." She looked up at him. "It won't be much of a wedding night for either one of us if we spend it traveling to Bedfordshire in a coach."

Colin refrained from pointing out the fact that it wouldn't be much of a wedding night either way. "The staff at Shepherdston Hall is expecting us tonight," Colin reminded her. "And I would hate to disrupt their routine for no reason."

"You're right." She looked at him. "It's just that . . ."

"We don't have to spend our whole fortnight at Shepherdston Hall," Colin said. "We can spend a few days and return here, if you'd like. It shouldn't matter whether we spend a fortnight at Shepherdston Hall or only three or four days, so long as we remain in seclusion." He looked her in the eye. "But we need to go there—at least for a few days."

He saw the disappointment in her eyes, and he understood that she was eager to begin making a home for herself at Herrin House. "I suppose so, but . . ."

Colin snorted. Blister it, but he should have realized how tenacious she could be! She was Baron Davies's daughter. She had either inherited the trait or she'd learned it at her father's knee. Either way, she wanted—no, demanded—an explanation. Well, hell, the least he could do was give her one, whether she liked it or not. "Gillian." He said her name softly, clearly enunciating each syllable. "Servants talk."

"And?" She didn't understand the point he was trying to make.

"Tonight is our wedding night, and the fact that we've decided not to consummate our marriage vows might give rise to speculation we could both do without."

"Shepherdston Hall has servants, too," Gillian reminded him.

"Yes, it does." Colin nodded. "But the staff at Shepherdston Hall is entirely trustworthy. We don't know if the same can be said about this one. If we're not going to do what newlyweds normally do, then we're safer not doing it Shepherdston Hall."

Gillian took one last, longing glance around the sitting room. "I didn't think about that," she admitted. "I only thought how nice it would be to spend the night under our own roof."

Colin silently echoed her sentiment. He wasn't looking forward to the journey any more than Gillian was, but everything he'd told her was true. The announcement of his marriage to Gillian Davies had appeared in all the morning papers and would also appear in the evening editions. Their wedding was public knowledge now. Since newlyweds were expected to take some sort of honeymoon and decline social invitations for at least a fortnight, honeymooning at Shepherdston Hall, far away from the prying eyes and gossip of London, was ideal. That was one of the reasons Jarrod had suggested it—that and the fact that Colin hadn't had any place else to take her. If he and Gillian weren't going to be doing what newlyweds normally did on their honeymoon, Colin thought they'd have a better chance of concealing it in the country.

"We might be able to compromise," Colin offered. He wasn't a compromising man by nature, but in the years since they had founded the Free Fellows League, Colin had learned the value of finding the middle ground. "Why don't we have dinner here and then continue our journey to Shepherdston Hall?"

Gillian smiled. "Can we?"

Colin shrugged. "I don't see why not. There should be plenty of light left to travel by. So long as we have an early dinner and are willing to accept whatever Cook has to offer."

"Whatever she has will be wonderful," Gillian said, "because it will be our first meal as husband and wife. And to have it in our new home makes it doubly special." She stared at her husband. "Thank you, Colin."

"You're welcome."

"Not just for the compromise," Gillian said. "Thank you for today. Thank you for marrying me and giving me a second chance."

"Thank *you*," he said sincerely, "for saying yes."

Chapter 20

"There is occasions and causes why and wherefore in all things."
—WILLIAM SHAKESPEARE, 1564–1616
HENRY V

"*Pomfrey promised to send word as soon as* they arrived," Jarrod stood up and began to pace as he briefed the other members of the Free Fellows League in their customary meeting room at White's. "I haven't yet received word."

Griff gave a little half smile. Pomfrey was the butler at Jarrod's country estate. "I doubt they've had time to get to Shepherdston Hall."

"They've had plenty of time," Jarrod contradicted. "It's been hours since the wedding."

"By the by," the Duke of Sussex drawled, "how was the wedding?"

"Quite nice," Griffin said. "I marveled that they were able to accomplish it so quickly without Alyssa's help. Of course, it was a very small wedding. The only witnesses besides Alyssa and me were Lord and Lady Davies, Lord and Lady McElreath and the children, and the rector. But the wedding breakfast was filled to capacity. I'll wager that everyone who received an invitation—" He looked at Sussex and Jarrod. "With two notable exceptions—showed up with a friend or two."

"The announcement appeared in all the papers this morning," Sussex said. "Word got round."

Jarrod concurred. "I ran into a half dozen chaps who wanted details during my morning trot around the Row. I told them I knew nothing more than what I'd read in the papers."

Griff laughed. "So the curious turned out to see for themselves. I vow, I saw people at the breakfast I hadn't seen in years."

That was quite a statement coming from Griff who, since becoming England's newest hero, swore he'd seen and shaken hands with everyone on the island of Great Britain at least once.

"I can't believe Lord McElreath made it," Jarrod said.

"He made it," Griff said. "And he looked quite presentable for a man that foxed."

"Damn." Jarrod scowled. "Did he say or do anything to embarrass Colin?"

Griff hesitated a moment before he shook his head. "Nothing untoward. At least, not publicly. But he and Colin exchanged words."

"Christ!" Jarrod swore. "I was hoping . . ." He looked at Griff. "Apparently, I was hoping for more than Lord McElreath is capable of. I heard he was still at the Hellfire Club at breakfast this morning."

"Winning or losing?" Griff asked.

"He won big until about three A.M., then he began losing steadily. One of his contemporaries finally persuaded him to leave the table before he lost it all."

Griff whistled.

Jarrod's sources of information never ceased to amaze his fellow Free Fellows.

"Would that be the same contemporary who joined you on your morning ride along the Row?" Sussex gave Jarrod an enigmatic smile.

Jarrod didn't answer, but Sussex's victory was short-lived.

"The two ladies St. Germaine attended the breakfast," Griff offered Sussex the bait.

Sussex bit. "Oh?"

Griff nodded.

"Who accompanied them?" Jarrod asked. "Linton? Carville? Nash? Or the Austrian archduke?" He glanced at Sussex.

"It was just the two of them," Griff said. "With the dowager duchess acting as chaperone for Miranda."

Sussex glared at Jarrod. "Why should Miranda's escort matter to you?"

"I've a wager riding on it," Jarrod retorted.

"You what?"

"I've a hefty wager riding on it," Jarrod repeated.

"You wagered on who would be escorting Miranda to Grantham's wedding?" Sussex was appalled.

Jarrod wore the same enigmatic smile Sussex had worn moments earlier. "No, Your Grace," he replied. "I wagered on who would be escorting Lady St. Germaine down the aisle at St. Paul's at the end of the season."

"I'll wager it won't be Linton, Carville, Nash, or an Austrian archduke!" Sussex shot back.

Griff bit the inside of his cheek to keep from laughing outright. "I'll take that wager," he said. "Because I discovered at the wedding breakfast that Miranda has a much more determined admirer. One who announced that he intends to marry her."

Sussex looked stunned.

Even Jarrod took pity on him. "Are you certain?"

Griff nodded. "I have it on excellent authority that this chap means to take Miranda to wife." *Just as soon as he grows up.* But Griff saw no reason to mention that the admirer in question was Colin's brother and only ten years of age.

Jarrod turned and began to pace in the opposite direction. "You don't suppose Colin and his bride ran into trouble on the way to Shepherdston Hall, do you?"

"No," Griff told him. "They got a late start. It took longer for them to distribute their gifts to the members of the wedding party and to the staff than they anticipated." Griff extended his arm to show off the pair of engraved gold cuff links Colin had given him for acting as his best man.

"Very nice," Sussex said. "Dalrymple's Jewelers?"

Griff nodded. "He purchased these for me and a lovely diamond and blue sapphire bracelet for Alyssa when he purchased his bride's betrothal and wedding rings."

Jarrod raised an eyebrow. "He purchased rings?"

"A flawless pink sapphire surrounded by diamonds and a gold band to match," Griff told him.

"There were a number of extraordinary pieces connected to the Grantham viscountancy, if I recall," Sussex said. "What happened to those?"

Griff took a deep breath. "What do you suppose?"

Jarrod uttered a vile curse. "McElreath gambled them away."

"And replaced them with paste while we were still at Knightsguild," Griff added. "But Colin didn't discover it until he went to his parents' town house and asked his mother for the Grantham betrothal rings."

"Bloody hell!" Sussex exploded, banging his fist on the table in a rare display of raw anger. "His father has stripped him of everything."

Jarrod turned and looked at Sussex with new eyes. Sussex hadn't attended the Knightsguild School for Gentleman with them. He hadn't grown up with Colin or been a founding member of the Free Fellows League. Sussex had been an outsider until Colin and Jarrod challenged him to earn a place in the League. Sussex rose to the challenge, and when Griff returned from the Peninsula a hero, he had reluctantly allowed Sussex to join them. Sussex's unexpected defense of Colin surprised him.

"What?" Sussex demanded when Jarrod continued to stare at him.

"I didn't realize you cared," Jarrod answered honestly.

"Why shouldn't I care?" Sussex was stunned. "I'm a Free Fellow and a duke. I've wanted to be one of you since I learned the League existed. I waited years to gain entrèe. Why shouldn't I take exception to the fact that one of my brothers in arms and one of my peers has been stripped of his inheritance by the man charged with the duty of protecting it?" He looked at Jarrod. "Or is that concern reserved only for you and Avon and Grantham because you're original Free Fellows?"

"No," Griff answered. "It is not." He met Sussex's angry gaze. "We are all Free Fellows and brothers in arms. When you became a Free Fellow doesn't matter at all. What matters is that you are one of us. Right, Jarrod?"

"Right," Jarrod agreed.

Sussex stared at Jarrod and then at Griff and back again. "I care more than you think about a great many things, and Colin is one of those things. I admire him," Sussex told them. "I've known far too many peers like Lord McElreath, who drink and gamble and piss away their fortunes and their children's futures. And I know far too many men in Colin's position who weep and wail, bemoaning their bad fortunes whilst begging for loans. But Colin does none of those things. He earns his money."

Jarrod and Griff exchanged glances. "You know about that?"

"I know he doesn't accept any stipends for his work for the War Office. And I also know that the two of you"— he glanced at Griff and Jarrod—"secretly own a prominent investment firm that earns you handsome profits." He waved away their protests. "Don't worry. Your secret is safe with me. I realized Colin was the genius behind it."

"How did you find out?" Jarrod asked. "And how long have you known?"

"We share a banker," Sussex informed Jarrod, "who was eager to assure me that although the investment firm his bank had owned had changed hands, my investments would be entirely safe if I chose to reinvest in the firm at a future date." Sussex smiled. "Of course, he told me this as he handed me a bank draft for the entire amount because the new owners insisted on refunding all existing accounts. When I refused to take his word for it, he confided that the Marquess of Shepherdston and Viscount Abernathy had purchased the majority shares in the firm shortly after they gained their majority. He also confided that he and his good friend, the Earl of Weymouth, owned the minority shares. He told me you insisted on refunding investments because you refused to speculate with a gentleman's capital without permission to do so. Several days later, I received a letter informing me that the firm had changed hands and offering me the opportunity to reinvest."

Griff frowned. "I wonder how many other investors he confided in."

"None," Sussex replied. "He's completely trustworthy. He only confided in me because I threatened to close my accounts in his bank unless he did."

"He believed you?" Griff was surprised. The banker in question had gone to school with Griff's father, was a well-respected member of parliament, and had served as an undersecretary of the Treasury during several governments. Griffin had known Lord Mayhew all his life and knew that he was not a man given to accepting threats from young peers.

Sussex shrugged. "I'm a duke. And a very good customer. Besides, he's my godfather. He knows me well."

"He knows you very well. Well enough to assure me that you were completely trustworthy," Jarrod said.

Sussex's eyes sparkled. "It seems we're sharing sources."

"Yes, it does," Jarrod agreed. "But I suppose that's only natural, since we seem to share a godfather."

Lord Mayhew was a widower. His wife had died at a very young age from complications of a pregnancy, and Mayhew had never remarried. Most people in the ton had forgotten that his late wife was the older sister of the late Marchioness of Shepherdston. Jarrod had been able to purchase the majority shares in Mayhew's investment firm because unless Mayhew remarried and sired a son, Jarrod was his closest male relative and would one day inherit all his holdings.

Sussex was clearly surprised. "I know he has three or four godsons he sees regularly, but I didn't know you were one of them."

"I'm his heir." Jarrod explained the connection.

"He and my father were good friends. Since he was the only man my father trusted to invest his money, he was the perfect choice for my godfather. We have dinner together twice a month when I'm in town—generally on Tuesday evenings."

"We ride together along the Row two mornings a week whenever I'm in London," Jarrod said.

"Make it unanimous," Griff said. "He and my father were best friends at school. We lunch together here at the club two Thursdays a month when I'm in town."

"What about Grantham?" Sussex asked. "Is Colin a godson, too?"

Jarrod shook his head. "No."

"But Colin works with him on investments?" Sussex guessed.

"Not exactly." Jarrod stopped pacing and raked his fingers through his hair.

"Then how?" Sussex wanted to know.

"Colin is damned prickly about the mention of money," Griff said. "Or his lack thereof. He has been ever since we met him. And despite the fact that his father can't gamble worth spit, Colin has a real talent for it. He's a genius when it comes to cards and numbers."

"He was always winning money from us and from the other boys at school. And at university, he did even better. Whenever he'd win a wager, he'd keep half and give the rest to me or to Griff to bank for him," Jarrod continued.

"Colin never wagers more than he can afford and always banks half of it. Jarrod and I were very conscientious about banking his money for him."

"Why didn't he invest it?" Sussex asked. "If he has the talent for making it?"

"He was afraid of losing what he had, and he didn't trust anyone to invest it," Jarrod told him. "And until he reached his majority, there was the additional problem of keeping his father from learning about it. Because Lord McElreath—"

"Would lose it." Sussex finished Jarrod's sentence.

"Yes," Jarrod confirmed. "And Colin needed ready cash to give to his mother to pay creditors and support the family."

Sussex nodded. "I see."

"But it wasn't enough," Griff picked up the conversation. "We suggested he invest some of it, but Colin wouldn't hear of it until we asked Lord Mayhew to explain how he could use some of Colin's cash to make more. We set up a meeting, and Colin agreed to go. And before you know it, he's advising Lord Mayhew and us on investments. We thought it a shame to waste such natural talent, so Lord Mayhew helped us set up a private investment firm where Colin could pursue his Midas touch in anonymity, without fear of having his reputation tainted by the suggestion of his actually working as an investment banker. He invests our money as well as his own, and we pay him commissions. Lord Mayhew kept a minority share of the firm and acts as its head, but Colin makes most of the investment decisions. Unfortunately, this business with the impostor Colin Fox has prevented him from concentrating on his investments as much as he'd like."

"I know he needs to concentrate on increasing his capital more than ever now that he has the additional burdens of Liana's coming out and a wife," Jarrod acknowledged. "He married the girl to protect the League, but I can't help feeling guilty because he doesn't even own a home to which to take her. Her father must have provided a generous dowry. But you know Colin and his prickly pride. He'll never use her money to purchase a house. He'll want to pay for it himself. I don't think he can afford it. Unfortunately, we need him to continue his missions."

"Set your mind at ease on that score, Jarrod, because Colin is going to be fine." Griff grinned. "Viscountess Grantham isn't going to be a financial burden. Her dowry is very generous. And I promise you she will have a suitable roof over her head. Baron Davies gave them one as a wedding gift."

"I can't believe Grantham accepted it," Sussex marveled.

"It would be hard to refuse Number Twenty-one Park Lane, even for someone with Colin's prickly Scots pride."

Jarrod thought for a moment. "Number Twenty-one. That's Lord Herrin's place."

"Was Lord Herrin's place," Griff corrected. "Now it belongs to Lord and Lady Grantham." He grinned at his fellow Free Fellows. "I wouldn't expect word from Pomfrey until tomorrow afternoon at the earliest. I feel certain Colin and his new bride decided to take a look at their wedding gift."

"There's one way to be sure." Jarrod's grin matched Griff's.

"We *are not* paying a call at Twenty-one Park Lane on their wedding night," Griff protested.

"It *is* on the way home," Sussex said thoughtfully.

"And we wouldn't dream of paying a call," Jarrod promised. "But there's no reason we can't drive by to see if it looks occupied."

Griff threw up his hands. "Heaven help us if Colin or my wife hear about this."

Chapter 21

"The bright day is done, and we are for the dark."
—WILLIAM SHAKESPEARE, 1564–1616
ANTONY AND CLEOPATRA

Lord and Lady Grantham had long departed Number Twenty-one Park Lane by the time the other members of the Free Fellows League drove by. Gillian struggled to keep her eyes open as the coach swayed back and forth along the Post Road out of London toward Bedfordshire and Shepherdston Hall.

"Why not give in to it," Colin asked gently, "and sleep?"

Gillian said the first thing that came into her head. "It would be rude for me to sleep while you're awake."

Colin smiled. "Not if I'm keeping watch."

"Are you?" she asked.

"I am if you're going to sleep."

"And if I don't sleep?" She smothered a yawn and asked the question just to hear his answer.

"From the looks of it, I would say sleep is a foregone conclusion," Colin told her. "But if you insist on fighting it, then you keep watch while I slip into the arms of Morpheus."

Gillian came alert, and her eyes sparkled at the suggestion. "What a novel idea! I've never kept watch while someone else slept. Only after—" She broke off in midsentence and covered a yawn with her hand.

"Only after?" he prompted.

"I think I'm sleepy after all." She evaded Colin's question. "Would you mind terribly if I closed my eyes for a bit?"

"Not at all," Colin said. "One of us should try to get some sleep. Go on, close your eyes."

She did as he suggested, and within minutes Gillian was sound asleep.

*The coach rolled through the gates of Shep-*herdston Hall at half past three in the morning.

Colin shifted from his uncomfortable position against the window, then rotated his right shoulder to relieve the tingling pins-and-needles sensation. He turned a bit in the seat and saw that Gillian had opened her eyes. He smiled at her.

The tender look in his green eyes unnerved her. "What is it?" she asked.

Colin reached up and gently rubbed at the pink-and-white indentations on Gillian's cheek. "You have wrinkle marks from my coat on your face."

She frowned. "Your coat?"

"You used my shoulder as a pillow."

"Did I sleep long?"

"A little over three hours," he answered.

"I'm sorry," she apologized. "I only meant to close my eyes for a moment."

"That's all right. You were tired. You needed to sleep."

Gillian stared at her husband. Events of the previous day—her wedding day—came rushing back. "What about you?" The sight of him made her wince. He sat with his shoulders hunched forward, his large body practically folded to fit into the space between the window and the opposite seat. "Did you get any sleep at all?"

"An hour or so, here and there."

His green eyes were bloodshot and full day's growth of blond beard seemed to sparkle on his chin, but he looked roguishly handsome. She hadn't thought it possible for Colin McElreath to look more handsome than he had this morning at the wedding, but he did. Dishevelment suited him.

Gillian suddenly realized that she was entitled to see him this way every morning. She smiled at the intimate thought, and a blush brought more color to her cheeks.

The tiny smile playing about the corners of her mouth intrigued him. "Is something wrong?"

"Oh, no," she murmured, "it's just that . . ." Gillian lowered her gaze to her lap and quickly began to smoothing out the creases in her skirt.

"What?"

"You look so . . . so . . ." Gillian couldn't begin to put her feelings into words.

Colin rubbed his hand over his chin, gauging the growth of his whiskers. "Tired?" he suggested. "Rough?"

Gillian shook her head. *Appealing* was the word that came to mind. And *attractive*. And *manly*. But she couldn't say those things to him. "Different," she finally answered.

"Yes," Colin said, smiling, "I guess the newness has already worn off the marriage. We haven't been married twenty-four hours, and you're already seeing me at my worst."

"If this is your worst," she told him, "then you've nothing about which to worry."

"I beg to differ," Colin replied.

"Oh?"

"We've arrived at our destination, my lady. We have a honeymoon to get through."

Gillian didn't have time to reply. The coach jerked to a stop in front of the steps leading up the entrance door to Shepherdston Hall. Although it was quite late—or early, depending upon your point of view—a butler and two footmen stood with lanterns waiting to greet them.

"Welcome back, Lord Grantham," Pomfrey, the butler, greeted Colin as he descended from the coach. "We've put you and Lady Grantham in the Ivory Suite of the east wing at Lord Shepherdston's request. I took the liberty of removing your clothes from your usual suite into the gentleman's half of the Ivory Suite."

The Ivory Suite in the east wing was directly across the hall from the suite of rooms Colin normally occupied while in residence at Shepherdston Hall. It provided easy access to Colin's customary bedchamber and to the study connected to it, insuring him the privacy he would need to catch up with his work, yet keeping him close to his bride.

"Thank you, Pomfrey," Colin answered as he turned to help Gillian out of the coach. "Gillian, may I present Pomfrey, the butler here at Shepherdston Hall. Pomfrey, Lady Grantham."

Pomfrey bowed low over Gillian's hand and motioned for the footmen to fetch the luggage. "Welcome, Lady Grantham."

"Thank you."

The butler turned to the footmen. "Take the luggage to the Ivory Suite."

"Yes, sir." Two burly footmen began hauling Gillian's trunks off the coach and up the steps.

"Will you be wanting a bath or a bite to eat before you retire, Lady Grantham?" Pomfrey asked.

"No, thank you." She smiled at the butler. "Just a bed."

Colin bit the inside of his cheek to keep from grinning at the expression on Pomfrey's face.

"Very good, ma'am. Follow me." The butler started up the steps.

"Wait!" Colin scooped his bride up in his arms and took the steps two at a time. "Allow me."

❧

*Gillian barely had time to notice her surround-*ings or admire the beauty of the Ivory Suite as Colin whisked her up the stairs and into the suite.

"Here we are, my lady," Colin said as he set her on her feet beside a huge half-tester bed hung with ivory damask curtains.

The bed was turned down in preparation for her, and the small traveling case that contained her nightgown and her personal items had already been deposited in the room. A vase of fresh roses sat on the bedside table. A bottle of very fine vintage French wine rested on a silver tray beside the roses.

"It's lovely," Gillian told him as Colin walked over and closed the outer door to the bedchamber.

"There's a dressing room through there," Colin pointed. "And my bedchamber is beyond. I'll be there if you need anything."

"I won't need anything until morning." She looked a little lost standing beside the bed in the massive room. "Thank you, Colin."

"You're welcome, Gillian."

"Well . . ." He cleared his throat. "I'll say good night then." He turned and walked toward the door that connected the bedchamber to the dressing room.

"Good night."

Colin walked through the connecting door and closed it behind him.

Minutes later, Gillian opened it and walked through the dressing room to the bedroom beyond.

Colin looked up from the writing desk as she walked in.

Gillian stood frozen in the pool of light from the writing lamp on the desk. He had removed his coat and cravat; his waistcoat and his white lawn shirt hung open, exposing a solid wedge of muscle covered by a thick mat of blond hair and the darker circle of one male nipple as he pushed back his chair and rose to his feet in one fluid motion. Gillian didn't realize a man so big could move so gracefully—or that looking at his naked chest could make her shiver and flush with fever at the same time.

"Gillian? Is something wrong?"

She moistened her lips with the tip of her tongue as Colin moved around the desk and walked toward her in his stocking feet.

Colin's heart slammed against the wall of his chest as that unconscious gesture created an insistent throbbing against the front of his suddenly too-tight trousers. He noticed for the first time that she was clutching a filmy white length of fabric to her breasts.

"I . . ." Gillian felt heat course through her body. Her mouth was dry again, and her breathing was rather labored.

"Is there something you wanted?" Colin moved closer.

Gillian sucked in a ragged breath. "My dress," she explained. "I can't reach the buttons."

Colin stared at the bodice of her wedding dress, swallowed hard, and gritted his teeth against the swelling in his trousers. "I don't see any buttons."

"Down the back." Gillian turned around and presented him with her back and the row of buttons that ran from her neckline to just above the small of her back. "I hate to bother you . . ."

Bother him? She was killing him. He ached to kiss her again. And to touch her. Colin wanted to feel her firm breasts in his hands and taste the texture of her smooth skin against his mouth and tongue. He wanted to hold her in his arms and kiss her again and caress her and give her the wedding night both of them deserved to have. He had the urge to touch her—to lift her chin and look her in the eyes and repeat all the promises he'd repeated at their wedding to her and to her family. But this time, he wanted her to know he truly meant them.

". . . but I forgot about the buttons," Gillian continued in the breathy voice that made him want to take her in his arms and shield her from all the hurt in the world. "My lady's maid always helps me with the dresses that button down the back. I chose to wear this one because it matched my betrothal ring." She paused long enough to look down at the ring in question. "But I forgot about the buttons and that Lavery wouldn't be accompanying us on our honeymoon." She knew she was babbling, but Gillian couldn't seem to stop the rush of words. She glanced over her shoulder at Colin and held up the nearly transparent length of fabric. "Do you mind unfastening my dress so I can get ready for bed?"

Her request pleased him more than Colin liked to admit. "I've never acted as lady's maid before," he admitted, fumbling with the first in a long line of tiny pink buttons. "All the women with whom I've shared a pillow have always—" He broke off, abruptly remembering with whom he was sharing intimate details of former encounters.

"I hope you don't mind too much," she said. "Because you're the only one here I feel comfortable enough to ask."

"I don't mind at all," Colin answered, unfastening another tiny button.

"What did the other women do?" Gillian asked without warning.

"Pardon?" Colin unbuttoned another button and stared with longing at the vulnerable spot on the nape of her neck visible through the baby-fine curls covering it. He had the urge to press a kiss there and wondered what she would do if he did.

"You said that all the other women with whom you had shared a pillow had always done something," she refreshed his memory. "But you didn't say what."

"I caught myself in time," he told her. "Before I forgot

my gentlemanly manners and divulged intimate secrets from past rendezvous to my bride." He had unfastened about half the buttons on her dress before he realized her silk wedding dress was boned with whalebone and lined with another slightly heavier weight of pink silk so Gillian didn't need to wear a corset or chemise. He was staring at bare flesh. Colin's heart began to beat a rapid tempo as he stood admiring the indention of her spine, the bend of her tiny waist, and the vulnerable spot on the nape of her neck. Leaning forward ever so slightly, he brushed his lips against her hair. "Gentlemen don't kiss and tell."

"Oh." Gillian sounded disappointed, then covered it. "Of course they don't," she said. "Ladies appreciate that quality in a gentleman."

Colin unbuttoned another two buttons. "Do they?"

"Without question," she answered. "Unless, like me, they're burning with insatiable curiosity."

"You're curious?"

"Insatiably," she admitted.

"I thought you were sleepy," he said.

"I was," she replied. "Until you presented me with that mystery. Now I won't be able to sleep until I have an answer."

That seemed fair enough to Colin, since he doubted he'd be able to sleep knowing she was in the next room lying in bed and wearing that thin silk nightgown.

He unfastened the last of the tiny buttons, freeing her from her wedding dress. The curve of her nicely rounded buttocks was visible through the open back of her dress, and Colin's mouth went dry at the sight of a pair of very brief, very thin silk drawers and a pair of white stockings. He took a deep breath to steady himself before he made the biggest gamble of his life.

"All done." He ran his index finger down the indention of her spine to signal that the buttons were open.

Shivering with reaction at his soft touch, Gillian turned to face him.

Her wedding dress slipped from her shoulders, and Gillian clasped the nightgown to her chest in order to hold the dress in place.

Colin grinned. "There's no reason for you to lose any sleep over my past peccadilloes. I'm willing to satisfy a bit of that insatiable curiosity if you promise never to reveal what I've told you."

"Really?"

"Cross my heart." He crossed his heart.

"So do I," Gillian attempted to follow suit and nearly lost her hold on the bodice of her dress in the process.

"My information isn't free, my lady," he warned. "It will cost you."

"How much?" she asked, willing to meet his demands.

"A good night kiss."

"Just one?"

He shook his head. "No, my lady. A kiss good night for every night we're together for the rest of our married life and—" he drawled.

"And?"

"And a kiss good morning for every morning we're together for the rest of our married life." He dangled the offer like bait before a fish. "And I choose the time and place."

Gillian thought it over. "That's all?"

"If it isn't enough, I could charge you for my services as lady's maid."

"That hardly seems fair," she countered, "since I already pay a lady's maid."

"In London," he reminded her. "Not here."

She looked up at him. "I'm not sure the information is worth that much."

"I am."

"Prove it," she challenged.

"First you must promise to abide by the terms of the agreement."

"I promise." This time she didn't attempt to cross her heart.

"Then it's a bargain." Colin placed his hands on her shoulders and gently turned her around so that she was headed back toward her bedchamber. He bent at the knees and pressed his lips against that vulnerable spot on the nape of her neck. "Good night, Gillian."

He reached for the doorknob, intending to close the connecting door, but she stopped him.

"Please, leave it open." She turned to face him.

"The light from my lamp may keep you awake," he warned.

"I don't mind the light," she told him. "At least I'll know you're there. At least I'll know I'm not alone."

"You're not alone, Gillian, I'm here."

Chapter 22

"What is love? 'Tis not hereafter;
Present mirth hath present laughter;
What's to come is still unsure.
In delay there lies no plenty,
Then come kiss me, sweet and twenty;
Youth's a stuff will not endure."

—WILLIAM SHAKESPEARE, 1564–1616

TWELFTH NIGHT

"*Move over.*"

Gillian opened her eyes and found herself staring at the underside of the ivory damask covering the frame of the half-tester bed. She gave a little squeak of protest and sat up as Colin walked over to the bed and flipped back the covers. "What are you doing?" she demanded, squirming against the feather mattress, fighting to tug her nightgown back down over her hips and legs.

"I'm climbing into bed with my wife," he replied.

Gillian stared up at him. His blond hair was damp, and his face was freshly shaven. A thick white towel was draped over one bare shoulder, and a pair of well-fitted buff breeches, only partially buttoned, rode low on his slim hips. "Why?" The sight of him like that did funny things to her insides.

"To correct my mistake," he answered.

"What mistake?" Gillian ignored his request.

"The one I made when I rang for hot water for a bath and a shave and told Pomfrey I was hungry." He looked down at Gillian still struggling to tug her nearly transparent nightgown down over her legs and smiled. The nightgown revealed as much as it concealed, but Gillian hadn't yet noticed. She had unpinned her hair after she'd left him last night, and now it lay across her pillow in a riot of dark curls. He ached to tangle his fingers in it. "We're supposed to be on our honeymoon, and it might seem a bit suspicious if they had to serve the honeymooners breakfast in bed in two different rooms. It would tend to spoil the romance. Besides, it doesn't take a genius to figure out that we would look more like a happily married couple—a honeymoon couple—if we were sleeping in the same bed." Colin knew his explanation was rather thin. He knew that Jarrod's staff would respect his privacy no matter what. But Colin wanted them to look like a happily married couple, even though they had decided not to consummate the marriage. He had promised not to rush her. And he would keep his word.

After Gillian had retired for the night, Colin had spent what remained of it in the chair beside her bed, watching over her while she slept. Sometime before dawn, he'd realized that he liked keeping watch over her. He liked being her Sir Galahad. If he couldn't take her in his arms and make love to her, he wanted the chance to hold her while she slept. He could live with a chaste marriage as long as he could sleep beside her and protect her and keep her warm just as he had that one night at the Blue Bottle Inn.

Colin glanced at the clock on the mantel. "They brought the hot water for shaving and my bath about fifteen or twenty minutes ago. They should be knocking on the door with breakfast any minute now. Now, close your eyes. This has to look good."

"Why?"

Because he'd meant his vows. Because he wanted to be her husband. Because he spent a great deal of time in a world where nothing was quite what it seemed to be. Because he didn't want his marriage to be a sham. "The Marquess of Shepherdston is one of my oldest and dearest friends. He loaned us his house for our honeymoon, and his staff believes we're here to consummate our marriage. And I would prefer not to disabuse them of the idea."

He took the towel off his shoulder and tossed it on the foot of the bed. "I know you're not an innocent, but don't forget that I behaved like a husband and a gentleman and warned you," Colin told her as he casually unfastened his pants and pushed them down over his slim hips.

Her eyes widened at the sight of him. Gillian opened her mouth to protest, but no words of protest came to mind. All she could think of was how magnificent he was. She had never seen a man completely naked. And never like this. Standing tall and fully erect. Gillian stared. He was beautiful. His wide shoulders tapered into a narrow waist, slim hips, and long strong legs. His chest was covered with curly blond hair that also tapered down into a long, slim line that encircled his navel and pointed to the hard erection jutting from another thatch of curly blond hair. He was big. He was all male. He was completely aroused.

And all mine.

That thought came unbidden. Gillian tried to shut it out, but there was no shutting out the sight of him or the effect it was having on her. She was flushed and hot and damp and swollen in places she couldn't name. And all because he was standing there, looking back at her with that look in his green eyes.

"Is it me? Or haven't you ever seen a naked man before?" Colin asked, genuinely surprised and more than a bit pleased by the awed expression on her face.

"It's both," she whispered.

"But you eloped with a man," he said. "You gave every

sign of knowing what to expect. Of having a certain amount of experience . . ."

"Signs can be deceiving," she reminded him.

Colin frowned. "Were they wrong? Your father and the Bow Street runner?" He raked his fingers through his damp hair. "Is it possible he left you an innocent?"

Gillian shook her head. "They weren't wrong. But it was always dark. I never saw him completely unclothed."

"Bloody hell!" Colin reached for the towel he had tossed aside.

"No, don't!"

Colin halted.

"I like looking at you." She licked her suddenly dry lips.

Colin's erection responded to her words and her gesture by becoming harder and even more prominent. "I'm gratified to hear it," he told her. "That bodes well for our future. But not, I'm afraid, our immediate future. For if I'm not mistaken, we're about to have company." Colin slipped into bed beside her as a knock sounded on the bedroom door. "They're coming to light the fire and deliver breakfast."

Gillian groaned. "How did you know?"

"I heard them coming up the stairs," he answered. "And I smelled the coffee and the chocolate."

Gillian sniffed, but all she could smell was the scent of sandalwood shaving soap and the clean fragrance she'd come to associate with Colin.

The knock sounded again.

"One moment." Colin turned to Gillian. "Do you have a dressing gown?"

"At the foot of the bed," she answered.

Colin leaned forward, grabbed the garment, and frowned. "This won't cover anything."

"It matches my night—" Gillian broke off and looked down at her silk nightgown. "Oh, good heavens!" She looked up at Colin. "Why didn't you say something?"

Colin winked at her. "I was tempted to say something."

He stared down at her long, shapely legs exposed to his view. "But I was equally tempted by the view. I admit to being partial to your long, lovely legs."

"And to think my mother packed this for me to wear."

"Thank heavens for mothers." Colin breathed the prayer. "Yours in particular, for she has excellent taste in night wear and didn't seem particularly worried about you catching cold or suffering a bout of shyness." He gave her his most charmingly boyish grin. "Not to worry. I'll protect you."

"From the maids?" Gillian asked. "I'm sure they've seen ladies in silk nightgowns before."

"The maids probably have," Colin agreed, flipping back the covers and walking around to the other side of the bed. "But the footmen haven't. And I'd like to keep it that way."

"Footmen?"

Colin nodded. "Shepherdston Hall is a male household, and Pomfrey assigns the early morning chores to the footmen to prevent the maids from being underfoot during Lord Shepherdston's and my toilette."

Gillian stared in wonder as he treated her to an exquisite view of his nicely muscled legs and firm buttocks. She thought he was going to answer the door in all his male glory, but Colin climbed into bed. He lay on his side, the bedclothes draped across his hip as he propped himself on his forearm. He had placed himself between Gillian and the outer door and used his body to shield her from view. "Now," he instructed, reaching behind him to pull the covers over her. "Scoot down and cuddle close, and they won't even know you're here."

"Where do you suppose they'll think I've gone?" she asked a bit waspishly.

"Sssh." Her words were muffled and Colin fought to keep from laughing at her show of irritation.

But Gillian wasn't easily muffled. "There are only two beds in this suite, and you're in mine."

"Enter!" Colin called.

The sound of china and silver clattering against a tray sounded on the stairs, then the door opened, and a footman entered. "Good morning, sir. Cook sent your breakfast. Where would you like it?"

Colin motioned toward the small table by the fireplace. "The table will be fine."

The footman carried the tray over to the table and set it down, then bent to light the fire in the fireplace. When he had the fire going, he turned back to Colin. "Shall I pour you a cup of coffee, sir?"

"Yes, thank you," Colin said.

"And chocolate," Gillian whispered from beneath the covers.

"I beg your pardon, sir?" The footman lifted the coffeepot and poured Colin a cup.

"Would you be so kind as to pour a cup of chocolate as well?" Colin asked.

"Of course, sir." The footman lifted the chocolate pot, filled a cup with steaming hot chocolate, and set it beside the cup of coffee. "Do you require anything else, Lord Grantham?"

"No," Colin said. "Nothing—"

"A hot bath!" Gillian hissed, pressing close enough to make herself heard.

Colin felt the twin points of her breasts pressing into his back, felt her slim thighs beneath his, and fought to remember his promise, fought to keep from rolling over and making her his.

"Colin!" she hissed, again.

"And a hot bath," Colin blurted.

"Was your first bath this morning not to your liking, sir?"

Gillian smothered a giggle against his shoulder blade.

If the footman noticed the shaking bedclothes, he was too well schooled to show any signs of it.

"My bath was fine," Colin told him. "But I feel certain that my bride will want a hot bath as soon as she rises."

"Yes, of course, sir." The footman looked at Colin. "We'll begin preparations right away."

"Heat the water," Colin told him. "I'll ring when she's ready for it."

"Yes, sir," the footman said. "Shall I bring you your coffee before it gets cold, sir?"

"No," Colin said. "Thank you."

The footman bowed. "You're welcome, sir, and felicitations to you and to Lady Grantham on the occasion of your nuptials."

"Thank you."

"Very good, sir." The footman turned and left the room.

"Is he gone?" Gillian propped herself on her elbow and peeked out from beneath the coverlet.

"He's gone," Colin confirmed, shifting his weight and rolling from his side to his back. He looked up at her. "Now, where were we?"

"I don't know," she said. "Where were we?"

Colin grinned up at her. "You were telling me you liked looking at me," he reminded her. "And I was about to kiss you good morning."

"Is that where we were?"

"Aye." The one word was a deep, rumbling Scottish burr. She leaned closer.

"If you're willing," he continued in that same deep, rumbling burr.

Gillian was mesmerized by the expression on his face and in his eyes. "Willing to do what, my lord?"

"Willing to let me choose the time and place."

She nodded.

His voice quavered a bit when he met her gaze. "I need to hear you say it, Gillian."

"I'm willing," she said softly.

"Good." Colin rolled Gillian onto her back, then closed

the distance between them, kissing first her lips, then her cheeks and chin and eyelids. He tangled his fingers in her hair and tilted her chin up so that he could kiss the soft spot beneath her ear.

Gillian shivered beneath his touch, tilting her chin even higher to allow him better access to her neck and chest. Colin took full advantage. He used his tongue to trace the flesh visible above the neck of her nightgown. He sat back on his heels, then reached down and untied the neat satin bow at the neck of her white silk nightgown, and worked the tiny pearl buttons loose from their tiny loops. He opened her bodice and spread the sides wide so he could feast on the sight of Gillian's rounded breasts. "You're beautiful," he breathed.

Gillian recognized the look of admiration in Colin's warm green eyes and knew that he meant it.

He leaned forward, cupped one smooth, satiny globe in his hand, and touched his lips to the dark center.

Gillian sucked in a breath at the wonderful sensation his tiny kiss evoked. Desire gripped her. Eager for more, Gillian reached up and threaded her fingers in Colin's thick blond hair and held his head to her breasts. "Again," she ordered.

Colin obeyed, touching and tasting, and gently nipped at the hard bud with his teeth. And then he suckled her, and Gillian thought she might die of the pleasure, as her nerve endings became gloriously alive and sent tiny electrical currents throughout her body, igniting her responses.

"Touch me," he told her. "Please."

"Where?" she whispered. "How?"

Colin took her hand and guided it between their bodies to the place he wanted it most. "Here."

She gripped him, and the feel of his flesh beneath her hand surprised her. He was hard, yet velvety soft, and the contrast intrigued her. She stroked him experimentally. Colin quivered with pleasure and came very close to spilling himself in her hand as Gillian stroked him without shyness but with a tender touch that brought a lump to Colin's throat.

"We must stop." He reached between them and grabbed hold of her wrist to stop the exquisite torture before he spilled himself in her hand.

"Have I done something wrong?"

"Not at all," he groaned. "But I'm incredibly aroused, and I don't want to rob you of your pleasure by reaching satisfaction too soon."

"My pleasure?" Gillian repeated the question as if she didn't understand the concept. "This is the most pleasure I've ever felt."

"Oh, my sweet, someone has been very remiss in your education." Colin's focus automatically shifted from reaching his satisfaction to making certain Gillian found hers. "I've always believed most men are fools when it comes to pleasing their lovers," Colin told her. "And it seems your Colin Fox was no exception. What the bloody hell did he do?"

He meant it as a rhetorical question, but to his surprise, Gillian took a deep breath and answered. "He left me alone at an inn in Scotland. I had never been away from my parents before. I was afraid. So I stood watch at the window."

"When?"

"After he left." She wouldn't say his name. "I watched and waited for his return day after day at the window of the inn where he'd left me. Even after I knew in my heart that he wasn't coming back."

Colin reached over and covered her hand with his. "I'm sorry."

Gillian shrugged her shoulders. "You've no reason to be sorry," she said. "You had nothing to do with it."

"I'm sorry because he hurt you. And I'm sorry he used my name to do it."

"Your name isn't Colin Fox." She spoke the name aloud for the first time in days. And she realized that it was just a name. A name that no longer had the power to hurt her. A name that no longer had the power to tie her insides into knots or to cause her shame or haunt her memories.

Colin chuckled. "You would be surprised at the number of people who only know me as Colin Fox."

"It's a shame I wasn't one of them," Gillian replied jokingly. "I was already Mrs. Colin Fox. We could have forgone the embarrassing interview with my father, the contract negotiations, and the wedding ceremony, and just got on with the honeymoon." Gillian blushed when she recognized the look in his eyes and realized what she'd said. "I . . . um . . ."

"There is that," he said. "But if we had forgone the ceremony, you might have had to forgo the betrothal ring you like so much."

Gillian stared down at her precious pink sapphire. "I would have hated having to forgo this."

"The ring or the lovemaking?" He leaned down and kissed her gently.

"Well," she teased, "until a few minutes ago, I had more reason to appreciate my betrothal ring than I did lovemaking."

Colin shrugged his shoulders and gave her a boyish smile. "I hope we've managed to challenge that point of view." He caressed her breasts, massaging first one and then the other.

"I didn't like it," she murmured so softly Colin couldn't be sure he heard her correctly.

Colin stopped caressing her and leaned closer. "What didn't you like?"

"It," she reiterated. "Lovemaking."

Of all the things she could have said, that was the one thing Colin never expected. "You don't like lovemaking?"

"No."

Colin raised his eyebrow. "Normally, that wouldn't bode well for our marriage," he told her. "But fortunately, we both have a natural aptitude for lovemaking, and your opinion is about to change."

Gillian glanced at him from beneath the cover of her eyelashes. "Is it?"

"Indeed," he promised. "There are women who enjoy lovemaking, my sweet, and you're about to become one of them."

"How can you be so certain?" Gillian asked. "Because I find it hard to believe that any woman could enjoy something so embarrassing and painful and messy."

Colin gave her a tender smile. "Have I done anything this morning that's caused you pain or embarrassment?"

"Not yet," she admitted.

"Oh, ye of little faith," he teased.

"I have faith," Gillian told him, "that the morning is still young."

Colin leaned down and kissed her again.

And his kiss was hot and sweet enough to tempt an angel. But Gillian wasn't an angel, and she didn't need temptation. She pulled Colin down to her until she could press herself against him. She flattened herself against his chest, feeling the heat of his flesh as she deepened the kiss. The twin points of her breasts pressed into him, and Colin groaned.

Encouraged by his response, Gillian allowed her hands to roam over his shoulders and down his back. Colin groaned again. His tongue mated with hers as he showed her what he wanted. Gillian continued her exploration. She moved her hands lower until she reached the tight, smooth skin of his buttocks. His muscles bunched and rippled under her hands as Colin held her tightly, half-lifting her off the bed as he ground his hips into hers and rubbed his throbbing erection against her. He pulled his mouth away from hers and began to trail hot, wet kisses on her face, her neck, her throat, and over to her earlobes. "Didn't you ever get beyond the embarrassment and the pain?" he whispered, before tugging on her earlobe with his teeth.

Gillian shook her head.

"Then I'm doubly sorry he hurt you using my name." Colin brushed his lips against her forehead and then her eyelids in the softest of touches. "Because Colin Fox— whomever he is—is a fool." He looked down at her face. "Was there anything you enjoyed?"

She shook her head once again.

"You eloped with the man, Gillian," Colin reminded her. "You must have like something about him. Something he did . . ."

"He kissed me," She said. "I liked it. And the way he looked at me. And the way he spoke to me before . . ." She buried her face in the crook of Colin's neck. "Afterward . . . after he . . . after the first time we . . . he changed. He didn't kiss me anymore or talk to me. He would just tell me it was time for bed, and I would lie there with my eyes closed, praying he would hurry so it wouldn't hurt anymore." She pulled back so she could look Colin in the eyes. "I was frightened when he left me alone at the inn, but I was also grateful that I didn't have to do it anymore."

Colin breathed a sigh of relief. It wasn't her. It was him. The idiot masquerading as Colin Fox hadn't introduced Gillian to the wonders of the bedchamber, he'd taken her without consideration or preliminaries. "You were an innocent and a romantic," he said. "You like being kissed and held and told you're beautiful." He stopped and looked down at her. "Have I told you you're beautiful?"

Gillian shook her head.

"Because you are," Colin continued. "And you like feeling loved and special. He recognized that and preyed upon it because he enjoys the chase. But once the bugger got what he wanted from you, the excitement of the chase was over for him."

Gillian thought of the night Galahad had slept beside her. "I liked touching," she whispered. "I liked being held at night and knowing I wasn't alone anymore. I know it sounds silly, but I liked sleeping beside someone."

"I'm perfectly willing to share a bed for the purpose of sleeping and touching and kissing and talking." Colin named the things she'd said she liked. It would be sheer torture for him if that's all she allowed him to do, but he would suffer if that's what it took to show her he could be trusted. "And if you get tired of that," he said with a wink, "we can always make love. If you feel so inclined."

She breathed in the familiar sandalwood and soap scent of him, and suddenly Gillian wanted whatever Colin had to offer. "I do."

Colin blinked, then quickly recovered. "I'm delighted to hear it." Colin let go of her wrist, sat back on his heels once again, took her silk nightgown by the hem, and whisked it up around her waist and pushed it up and over her head. "I promise I won't hurt you, Gillian."

Gillian sighed with relief. At last she was naked against him.

Colin turned his attention back to her breasts. He dipped his head and trailed his tongue along the valley between them. He licked at the tiny beads of perspiration. The scent of her perfume teased his nostrils. It was warm, lemony, and all Gillian.

Colin worked his way down the valley, and his tongue seemed to ignite little bonfires wherever he touched her. He tasted the skin above her rib cage, trailed his tongue over her abdomen, circling her navel before dipping his tongue into the indention. And while Colin tasted her with his tongue, he teased her with his fingers. He skimmed his hands over the sensitive flesh covering her hipbones and outer thighs. He felt his way down her body with his hands, finally locating and tracing the deep grooves at the juncture of her thighs with the pads of his thumbs. Easing his way ever closer, Colin massaged the womanly flesh surrounding her mound, then tangled his fingers in the lush, dark curls covering it.

Gillian reacted immediately, squeezing her thighs shut, then opening them ever so slightly to allow him greater access. She couldn't seem to get close enough to him. Her anticipation rose to a fever pitch. She began to quiver and make little moaning sounds of pleasure as he traced the outer edge of her folds with his finger before gently plunging his finger inside. Gillian squirmed, arching her back to bring herself into closer contact with Colin. Colin gritted his teeth. The slick, warm feel and the scent of her were driving him crazy.

The swelling in his groin grew until he was rock hard and near to bursting. He couldn't wait any longer. He had to have her. He had to feel himself inside her, feel her surrounding him, feel them joined together the way husbands and wives were meant to be joined.

Colin withdrew his fingers and placed his hands under Gillian's hips, lifting her slightly as he leaned forward and positioned himself to enter her in one fluid motion. "Gillian?" he offered her the choice, although he seriously doubted whether he could be the gentleman he professed to be and stop, even if she asked him to. "May I?"

"Yes," Gillian answered, instinctively wrapping her legs around his waist. "Now."

She braced herself, expecting pain as Colin surged forward and buried himself inside her. But there was none.

Colin kissed her cheek, then her eyelids, and finally, her mouth. He kissed her gently, tenderly, reverently, and held her as if she were precious and fragile.

Gillian shifted her hips experimentally and bit her bottom lip as the pleasure began to build once again. She lifted her hips again, and Colin understood. He fought to go slowly, fought to maintain control, and his body strained with the effort. Gillian tightened her hold on him. She put her arms around his neck and held on, then locked her legs around his waist once again as he began to move within her.

Gently, slowly at first, then faster.

Gillian followed Colin's lead, matching her movements to his until they developed a rhythm uniquely their own. She kissed him as they moved together—kissed his arms, his shoulders, his neck, his chin, the corner of his mouth. And she trusted him to lead her to that place that seemed just beyond her reach; the place where she became him and he became her, the place where the two of them became one. And then, suddenly, she felt him shiver uncontrollably, heard him shout her name, and Gillian let herself go with him.

The real world seemed to slip away; there was only Colin and the almost unbearable feeling of pleasure spiraling inside her. She called out his name. In wonder. In joy. And in gratitude as he gifted her with an incredibly intense, heart-stoppingly pleasurable release.

Chapter 23

*"'Fondling,' she saith, 'since I have hemm'd thee here
Within the circuit of this ivory pale,
I'll be a park, and thou shalt be my deer;
Feed where thy wilt, on mountain or in dale;
Graze on my lips, and if those hills be dry,
Stray lower, where the pleasant fountains lie.'"*

—WILLIAM SHAKESPEARE, 1564–1616

VENUS AND ADONIS

*G*illian awoke much later to find her head cradled on Colin's shoulder, her hair fanned out across the pillow, and one of her arms resting on his chest. She sighed, then cuddled closer to him and pressed her lips against the side of his chest. "Thank you," she whispered.

"You're welcome," Colin answered in his husky burr as he tightened his arm around her. "I don't seem to be able to resist the young lady who says please and thank you so nicely."

"Then I'll have to be careful not to leave you to your own devices when there are other ladies present," Gillian told him. "For most young ladies know the value of nicely saying please and thank you."

"Believe me, my lady," Colin told her. "I'm happily married and the most trustworthy of men. You are the only lady I cannot resist."

"What of all the other ladies who've shared your pillow?" Gillian teased.

"So, we're back to that again, are we?" Colin chuckled. "I thought you'd forgotten."

Gillian sighed. "You *hoped* I'd forgotten. But you were mistaken. For you see, my lord Grantham, I have a memory like an elephant." She rubbed her fingers through the hair on his chest and began a slow, soothing massage. "I never forget anything."

"If that's the only way in which you resemble an elephant," Colin teased. "I have no complaints."

Gillian turned and propped herself up on her elbow so she could look down at him. "These last few weeks have also given me the hide of an elephant."

"One generally needs the hide of an elephant to survive the viciousness of the ton." Colin smoothed his palm over her from shoulder to thigh and smiled. "But I find no evidence that you've acquired that particular trait." He smoothed his hand back over her from thigh to shoulder. "Though you've done a magnificent job of hiding the wounds."

"I was speaking metaphorically," she said. "And you're avoiding the question."

"Aye," he raised an eyebrow. "My lady has a memory and a vocabulary and . . ."

"And?"

"Kisses to die for."

Gillian tried to not to smile, but she lost the battle. "I'll bet you say that to all the ladies." She emphasized the word *ladies.* "Especially the ones who always do—something—whenever they share your pillow."

"If that was meant to be a subtle reminder, you failed miserably," Colin told her.

"It was meant to be a wifely reminder that you've failed to answer my question."

"That's because a gentleman never kisses and tells."

"You promised information in exchange for good night and good morning kisses," Gillian said. "And you've received your kisses." She leaned down to give him another one as incentive.

"And you received a great deal of information," Colin pointed out. "Haven't we spent a good deal of the morning improving upon your store of sexual knowledge?"

Gillian blushed. "Col . . . in."

"All right," he relented. "I'll tell you what you want to know." He looked her in the eyes. "So, my lady, what is it you want to know?"

"I want to know what all the other women with whom you've shared a pillow always did."

Colin worked hard to keep a straight face. "They always . . ."

"Yes?"

"They wore a wrapper with nothing underneath," he told her. "And they stripped it off the moment I entered the room."

"Is that all?" Gillian couldn't believe he'd teased and tricked her just to tell her that.

Colin laughed. "That's quite a bit when you're a randy young man. I never acted as lady's maid to any of the women with whom I'd shared a pillow because I never had the opportunity. And believe me, my lady, I always appreciated and heartily approved of the gesture—until you presented me with your back and a row of tiny buttons last night."

"I *do* believe you, my lord."

"You do?"

"Who would make up an answer like that?" she retorted. "Of course I do."

Colin hugged her. "I do," he repeated. "I don't think I'll ever tire of hearing you say that."

Gillian laughed. "I would think that in the past two months, I'd said them quite enough. . . ."

Colin lifted a lock of Gillian's hair and began toying with it, tracing the circle of her breast, teasing her. "But not in the context to which I refer," he pointed out.

"No," she agreed, "not in that context." She smiled at him. "I never realized those two words could be so powerful."

"My lady," he drawled. "You have no idea the power those two little words have over me."

Gillian slid her hand down his chest and across the hard ridges of his abdomen, following the arrow of blond hair that led to the tent in the bedclothes. "I think I have some idea," she drawled, as she reached out to take him in hand.

He closed his eyes, bit his bottom lip, and groaned with pleasure. "I have a question for you," he ground out.

"What is that, my lord?" She teased him with the motion she'd learned that he liked best.

"Do you still suffer from insatiable curiosity?"

"Indeed I do," she murmured.

"Are you curious to know what else you can do with that part of my person?"

"I am."

"Then come here." Colin pulled Gillian atop him, kissed her thoroughly, and settled her comfortably upon his throbbing erection.

She awoke to the heavenly smells of chocolate and sandalwood. Gillian stretched like a sated kitten and looked up to find Colin leaning over her. He wore his shirt, trousers, and boots, and he smelled of the sandalwood shaving soap he used. The chocolate aroma came from the cup and saucer he held out to her.

Gillian pushed herself into sitting position.

"The chocolate is hot," he said. "Your bathwater is hot, and your lady's maid is waiting to help you with your bath."

"Is she?" Gillian was all wide-eyed innocence.

"You know better than that, Lady Grantham," Colin told

her, handing her the cup of chocolate. "I believe you've en-gaged me to act as your lady's maid for the duration of this honeymoon. Now, be a good little viscountess and drink your chocolate. When you're done, we'll satisfy a bit more of your insatiable curiosity."

Gillian pretended to pout. "I'll be all clean, and you'll get me all sweaty again."

"I'll do nothing of the sort," Colin told her with a grin. "Because, my lady, the bath I've arranged for you in my bedchamber is big enough for two."

Gillian was speechless. Her mouth formed a perfect *O*, and Colin covered it with his own for a chocolate-flavored kiss. He straightened to his full height and tapped the tip of her nose with his index finger. "Finish your chocolate."

Gillian drained the cup, set it on its saucer, and handed them to him. "All done," she announced.

"Have I told you how much I appreciate your insatiable sense of curiosity?" He set the cup and saucer on the bed-side table, then bent once again and scooped her off the bed and into his arms.

"No," she answered as he carried her from her bed-chamber, through the dressing room, to the big copper bathtub waiting in his bedchamber. "But you will."

She was, Colin discovered, a woman of insatiable cu-riosity and of many talents, but her true talent lay in her ability to make him forget everything except her. As strange as it seemed, Gillian offered him peace in a world gone mad with war. She offered him warmth and laughter and companionship and a promise of a life beyond his im-mediate future. Colin listened to her soft sigh as he sepa-rated her womanly folds with his nimble fingers and guided himself inside her and found refuge in her welcom-ing warmth.

As fanciful as it seemed, Colin believed she had beck-oned him from her window, like a lost princess calling for her prince, and he had somehow heard her. He had found her and answered her call.

Perhaps he had sensed it when he'd seen her standing in the window at the Blue Bottle Inn. Or maybe it had come later when he'd slipped inside her room, held her in his arms, and slept beside her. She offered him a sense of order and serenity he hadn't felt since childhood. And she had given him far more than he would ever be able to repay. It didn't seem possible, but in the space of a few hours, Gillian had become his home.

Gillian laughed softly as Colin shifted his weight and sent waves of water rippling across her body and over the rim of the tub. A few hours ago, she wouldn't have believed it possible, but Gillian found herself sharing a bathtub with a man. In a few short hours, her husband, Colin McElreath, had persuaded her to forget the rules of a lifetime. And she had a great deal of information to add to her increasing store of sexual knowledge. Fortunately, her husband appeared to be an unending source of information and pleasure. How else to explain the fact that she was learning to revel in the passion he taught her?

She picked up a sea sponge he'd placed in the tub and squeezed water over Colin's chest. The water flattened the hair on his chest, revealing a long, jagged scar along his left side that she'd missed in her earlier explorations. The color told her the scar was recent, and its location told her that Colin was lucky to be alive. Gillian traced the slightly raised pink contours with the pads of her fingers. "You've been wounded," she whispered.

"It's nothing," he answered.

"You could have been killed," she said. "How did it happen?"

Colin brushed his lips against her forehead. "I was set upon by a footpad." He told her as much of the truth as he could. "His blade glanced off my ribs."

"What happened to the footpad?" she asked.

"He won't be pulling his blade on anyone else," Colin told her. "Ever again."

"Good," Gillian pronounced, bracing her arms against the side of the bathtub, using it for balance and leverage, as she slid onto his lap and began to tease him. Colin placed his hands on her slim hips and anchored her firmly against him as he licked droplets of water from her breasts. He groaned his pleasure in her ear, and his warm breath made her squirm harder.

"Practicing earlier lessons, my lady?" he asked as she raised herself up as far as she could before sliding slowly down his shaft and wiggling her bottom against him.

"Practice makes perfect, my lord."

"Is perfection your goal?" He groaned his pleasure.

"A worthy goal, is it not?" She leaned forward, splashing water over the rim of the tub as she did so.

"A most worthy goal," he murmured. "I only hope I live long enough for you to attain it."

Gillian widened her eyes, lifted her hips, and slid down his shaft once again. "Is your health in question, my lord?"

"It is indeed, my lady," he told her. "Because you're slowly killing me." Colin looked up at her and then placed his hands on either side of her waist. Before she knew quite how he managed it, Colin lifted her off him, turned her so that she faced the opposite direction, and knelt behind her.

"What are you doing?" she gasped as he molded himself to her buttocks.

"Furthering your store of knowledge," he murmured as he carefully slipped inside her.

Gillian's sharp intake of breath signaled her pleasure as he began to move behind her. In and out and faster and harder until his final thrust sent water cascading over the edge of the tub and across the bedroom floor, and they both collapsed against the rim of the bathtub in an explosion of rampant desire.

"This is the first time I've ever bathed with my lady's maid," Gillian quipped when Colin disengaged himself and helped her to her feet. She stood ankle deep in bathwater as she turned to face him.

"As you've shown such an affinity for it," Colin retorted, "I can promise you it won't be the last."

"Lavery is in for a surprise," Gillian teased.

"Not if she's French," Colin replied with a wink.

"Oh?" Gillian arched an eyebrow in a very good imitation of the gesture Colin used.

"I've spent a great deal of time in France over the years," Colin said, reaching for a length of toweling. "The French are far more adventurous in the bedchamber than are the English."

"Is that so?" she asked a bit more sharply than she intended.

Colin grinned as the green-eyed monster of jealousy settled on Gillian's shoulder. "A man can learn a lot from a French lady's maid. I added a great deal of information to my already impressive store of knowledge in some of the finest houses in Paris." He smiled as he trailed the towel over her sensitive flesh from her belly button to the triangle of dark curls between her thighs.

Gillian shivered beneath his erotic touch. "Well, I, for one, have always felt that good solid English girls make the best lady's maids."

"They're adequate," Colin agreed. "Some are even exceptional, but most lack the true adventurous and playful nature of a French lady's maid." Colin caressed her with his finger as he pretended to ponder her words more closely. "And none, I think you will find, will ever be as adventurous or playful or knowledgeable as the lady's maid you have currently engaged." He lowered his voice until his words seemed to rumble in his chest, becoming a husky, seductive growl. "Or as trustworthy or as loyal."

Gillian held her breath in anticipation. "No?"

"No," he replied.

"Then, I see no reason to change," she told him. "For I am more than satisfied with the lady's maid I've currently engaged."

"Then, I've no need of references?" He teased her with the towel, retracing the path his fingers had taken with the soft cloth.

"No," she managed, her breath ragged with need. "For I have great need of you."

"Now?" he asked.

"And for a great many years to come," she pronounced with a sigh as he lavished her aching center with attention.

Chapter 24

"Let me take you a button-hole lower."
—William Shakespeare, 1564–1616
Love's Labour's Lost

*G*illian entered her bedchamber to find her lady's maid had laid out an evening gown and undergarments for her to wear.

"I thought we'd dress for dinner and give the staff a chance to get a look at my bride."

Gillian turned to find Colin lounging in the doorway. He was already dressed in evening clothes. "You were hiding me from the staff this morning," Gillian quipped. "Things have changed beyond recognition in the passing of a day."

"You weren't dressed to meet the staff this morning," Colin reminded her. "And I wasn't hiding you." He winked. "I was shielding you."

"And tonight, you wish to show me off," she concluded.

"I've kept you in bed all day." Colin leered at her.

Gillian batted her eyelashes at him. "Not all day," she said. "I did spend a pleasant hour or so in the bath."

"And now that you're all clean, I thought you might enjoy a chance to sit down to dinner." He walked up behind her, encircled her waist with his arm, and pulled her back against him.

"Isn't it a bit early for dinner?" she asked.

Colin buried his nose in her hair and breathed in her
perfume. "We're keeping country hours," he reminded her.
"And I'm hungry. We haven't eaten more than a bite or two
all day. I need sustenance in order to keep up with a wife
suffering from insatiable curiosity." He tugged on her earlobe with his teeth. "And we might as well give the staff
something to do."

"Rather than just something to talk about." Gillian
turned to face him, and then reached up and put her arms
around his neck.

Colin chuckled. "A woman of wit. I like that in a wife."

"A man who appreciates it," she countered. "I like that
in a husband."

"Then we're fortunate we've made such a good
match." Colin's voice was low and husky and trembling
with emotion.

"In bed and out of it."

"Don't tempt me," he warned. "I'm trying to be considerate, and you're perilously close to ending up back in bed."

"I intend to end up back in it," she informed him. "As
soon after dinner as can politely be arranged."

"You," he said, punctuating the pronoun with a kiss,
"have probably had enough lovemaking for one day."

"Can one ever have enough lovemaking?" she asked.

"Oh, Gillian . . ." Colin hugged her close. "Remember
you said that, my sweet. Because once the soreness sets in,
you're bound to feel differently in the morning."

"Will you?" she challenged.

Colin shook his head. "It doesn't usually work that way
for men. Chances are I'm going to want to start each morning making love to you for the rest of my life."

"Then I hope you live to be ninety," she said.

Colin laughed. "If there's any hope of that happening,
I'll need food. And quickly." He let go of her, then walked
over to the bed and picked up her delicate undergarments.
"And since you cannot go down to dinner wearing that," he

nodded toward her silk wrapper, "we'd better get you dressed."

"I'll need a corset," Gillian told him.

Colin frowned. She hadn't needed a corset with her other gowns. "Can't you go without it?"

"I'd be delighted to," she informed him. "But I don't think you'll be pleased with the results."

"Why don't we try it and see?" Colin suggested, doing his best to avoid testing his newly acquired lady's maid skills by having to lace Gillian into a corset.

Colin slipped her chemise over her head and followed it with her gown, then buttoned her into it.

But when Gillian turned to face him, he realized why she needed a corset. His heart caught in his throat as his blood rushed to his nether regions and began a steady throbbing against the front of his trousers. "Why didn't you warn me?"

"I thought I did."

The squared bodice of this particular gown was cut lower than her wedding dress had been—too low to offer any support for her lush bosom or any coverage. Anyone looking down at her could see from bosom to belly button with very little effort. "Where do you keep your corsets?"

"There should be one in the smaller trunk."

Colin returned moments later, gripping one in his large hand.

Gillian waited while he unbuttoned her, then stepped out of her evening dress.

"Over or under your chemise?" he asked.

"That depends on whether you prefer indentions from the boning of the corset on my flesh or wrinkle marks from my chemise," she informed him.

"Which is more comfortable for you?" he asked.

"No corset is more comfortable for me," she taunted.

"That's out of the question with this dress," he told her. "So, over or under? Which is it?"

"Under," she answered perversely, simply because he'd have to touch her bare flesh to lace her in.

He whisked her chemise back over her head, and Gillian smiled at the reflection in the mirror as she watched Colin tackle the corset and its laces with similar speed. He retrieved her chemise and dress and fitted both into place before he began buttoning the long row of buttons on the back of her evening dress. "Are you certain you've never done this before?" she asked.

"Quite certain," he said, fumbling with the last button. "I'm a man," he said, by way of explanation. "And we're generally more interested in the undressing part of the job." He looked up and met her gaze in their reflection. "But I'm very observant and something of a prodigy when it comes to performing difficult tasks like lacing corsets and buttoning a hundred tiny buttons."

"You chose this dress," Gillian reminded him, smoothing the skirts of the blue silk gown. "You could have chosen one that didn't require a corset or one that fastened in the front or one with fewer buttons."

"None of them fasten in the front," Colin informed her.

"What?" Gillian was taken aback. "I have dozens of dresses that fasten in the front."

"You should have had your lady's maid in London pack one or two," Colin suggested. "For the sake of variety." He smiled down at his wife. "I'm not a patient man by nature, and I can't guarantee the safety of your buttons much longer."

His comment surprised her. He claimed he wasn't by nature a patient man, and yet he had shown her nothing but patience and understanding from the beginning.

He was everything she could ever want in a husband and an exceptional lady's maid. Gillian smiled at the thought. "If you rip them off, you'll have to sew them back on."

Colin looked horrified by the suggestion.

"That *is* one of the responsibilities of a lady's maid," she said.

"Remind me to increase Lavery's salary when we return to London," Colin said.

"Why?" Gillian asked. "Because she's French?"

"Because I can't promise I'll be nearly as patient with these damned buttons when I don't have to sew them back on." He took a deep breath, then slowly expelled it. "And if all your dresses are like this one, Lavery is going to be sewing on a lot of them."

Gillian retrieved the small leather jewel case from her trunk, then opened it, selected a pair of earrings crowned with light blue topaz stones, and fastened them in her earlobes. When she'd finished, she turned to Colin. "Your turn."

He gave her a wicked grin. "I don't wear earrings, my lady."

She cocked her head and studied his face. "Perhaps you should," she speculated. "A gold hoop or an emerald stud to match your eyes would give you a rakish, piratical look."

"I'll take it under advisement." He offered her his elbow. "But for now, I'll take you in to dinner."

"What about my hair?" Gillian asked. "I generally wear it up at dinner."

"You're on your honeymoon. Dinner in the country is fairly informal. You look beautiful. I prefer your hair down. And my skills as a lady's maid, though considerable, do not extend to hairdressing," Colin told her. "Shall we go?"

"All right." Gillian placed her hand in the crook of Colin's arm and allowed him to lead her down the stairs to dinner.

"So," he said when they reached the landing and started down toward the dining room, "the first day of our honeymoon is almost over." Colin looked over at Gillian, waggled his eyebrows, and leered at her. "What shall we do tomorrow?"

Gillian burst out laughing. "I don't know," she answered. "Did you have anything special in mind?"

Colin rolled his eyes and pretended to ponder the situation. "Our honeymoon could turn deadly dull if we continue in the same vein," he deadpanned. "So I thought we should find some way to amuse ourselves. . . ."

"I agree," she joined in the teasing. "What do you suggest?"

"Shepherdston keeps a fine stable. We could go riding."

Gillian shook her head. "Not unless it's in a coach or carriage. I don't ride."

Colin frowned. "At all?"

She shook her head. "My father never kept horses. And I never learned how to ride."

"What do you do for exercise," he asked, "if you don't ride?"

"I walk."

"Walk?" Colin shuddered in pretended disgust. "God invented horses and carriages so we wouldn't have to walk."

Gillian stuck her tongue out at him. "I like to walk. For miles and miles." She looked up at him. "We could go for a walk. There must be somewhere to walk on an estate the size of this one."

"Indeed there is, my lady," Colin told her. "Shepherdston Hall has a huge garden with a labyrinth and a pond and a pavilion and a parkland beyond."

"A pond?" Gillian's eyes lit up.

"An ornamental fish pond," Colin elaborated. "Too shallow for bathing but just right for wading."

"And sailing boats . . ." she added.

"And sailing boats," he confirmed.

"Do you have any boats we could sail?"

Colin glanced over to see if she was teasing him, but Gillian was completely serious about sailing boats on the pond and eagerly looking forward to it.

She smiled up at him. "I love sailing boats. When I was a little girl, my father and I would take our toy boats—"

"Your father has toy boats?" Colin couldn't imagine that the Baron Davies he'd met and with whom he'd negotiated would bother with the likes of toy boats—or with little girls. But he knew the man had a soft spot for his wife and daughter and could be quite sentimental on occasion, so perhaps toy boats weren't completely out of the question.

"My father loves boats," Gillian told him. "And ships. He owns a fleet of them. Beautiful sailing vessels that navigate the oceans of the world and dock in all sorts of exotic ports of call, bringing back silks and satins and cotton from Egypt and all sorts of spices—even tea and coffee."

"I thought Lord Davies was a silk merchant."

"Silk was the primary article of trade when he first began, but over the past few years, trade negotiations and troubles with China and Japan have caused him to expand his store of goods," she explained.

Colin grinned. "Has he by any chance expanded his store of goods to include French brandy and other hard-to-get items of contraband? Items for which there is a great demand and a great deal of profit?"

Gillian was indignant. "Papa would never risk his patent by engaging in smuggling contraband. His title means too much to him, and he's proud to have attained it legally."

Her answer surprised him. Almost everyone engaged in shipping did a bit of smuggling. It seemed unlikely that a man of Baron Davies's wealth and means would refuse to take part in the profiteering. "There is a great deal of profit to be made."

"Papa doesn't need to smuggle. He stocked up on those items years ago, in anticipation of a war. He had warehouses full of French brandy and bolts of damask and lace he bought before the war. Because we cannot sell contraband items to the public, we still have an ample supply to meet our private demand."

"You have a private demand for contraband items?"

Gillian's eyes sparkled. "You might say we have a royal patent as official and *legal* suppliers of French brandy and other hard-to-come-by items. And that while serving in his capacity as a royal patent holder, my father was elevated in status from Mr. Davies to Baron Davies."

"You know a great deal about your father's business," Colin complimented her.

"I should," she said. "I am my father's only child and the heiress to everything he's worked so hard to build. Until I reached the age of ten and three, I spent nearly every waking hour at the warehouse and on the docks learning the business. And every Tuesday and Thursday afternoons, if the weather was good, Papa and I would take our toy boats to the Serpentine in the park and sail them."

"What happened when you reached the age of ten and three?" Colin asked, as they entered the dining room.

Gillian blushed. "I blossomed into a young lady," she said. "And my father thought it was too dangerous for me to roam the warehouses and the docks. Everything changed. There were no more Tuesday and Thursday afternoons at the park. From then on, I was educated by a governess at home, where I learned the ladylike arts of needlework and the piano, watercolors, languages, and how to run a household."

"Sounds deadly dull by comparison," Colin commented.

Gillian laughed. "It was. And although we didn't sail them on the Serpentine anymore, Papa and I continued to design and build toy boats. And he brought home the ships' manifests for me to inventory so I could keep up with the business and my higher mathematical skills."

"You enjoy mathematics?"

"I love it," she told him. "I love puzzles and ciphers, and

I'm something of a prodigy when it comes to cards and accounts and balances." She used the same turn of phrase he'd used earlier. "Unfortunately, playing cards and the pianoforte and balancing household accounts is a young lady's only true opportunity to use her higher mathematics."

"Except for designing and building toy boats . . ." he reminded her.

"Yes," she said. "Except for that. You should see my collection. I know every ship in Papa's fleet, along with their trade routes, cargo, and usual ports of call. At one time, I knew all the captains and first mates, but the fleet has grown since I roamed the docks and now I only know their names. I have models of all of them from the first one to the latest one. There are twenty-four of them, and they're all ladies or princesses." Gillian smiled, remembering. "We take turns naming them. Papa and Mama name the ladies, and I name the princesses. There are twelve of each." She glanced over her shoulder at Colin as he pulled out her chair and seated her at the dining table. "I apologize for babbling, but I haven't—"

"Had the opportunity to sail boats on a fish pond in years," he guessed.

"You did say Shepherdston Hall has a pond perfect for it," she reminded him, her blue eyes sparkling with mischief.

"Yes, I did," Colin agreed.

"And you did say that our honeymoon could turn deadly dull if we continued in the same vein for the remainder of it," Gillian continued.

The footman pouring the wine into their glasses coughed to keep from snickering.

Colin glared at him, then turned to Gillian and acknowledged her comment with a nod of his head.

"And you were looking for something else to do."

"Aye."

"And since I don't ride and you don't walk, sailing

boats on the pond would be a perfectly wonderful way to spend the day tomorrow."

The look of disappointment on his face was priceless. Gillian had to work to keep from smiling.

"Is that what you want to do tomorrow?" Colin asked.

Gillian couldn't risk talking for fear of giggling. She bit her bottom lip, stared at her plate, and answered with a nod.

Colin lifted his hand and signaled Pomfrey, who stood at the far corner of the dining room, supervising the service of the meal.

"Sir?" Pomfrey appeared at Colin's side almost instantly. "Is something amiss with your dinner?"

"No, Pomfrey, the meal and the service are excellent." Colin paused for a moment. "Lady Grantham and I were discussing our schedule for tomorrow, and we were wondering if there are any toy boats on the premises?"

"Boats, sir?" Pomfrey was confused.

"Yes, Pomfrey, sailing boats." Colin was beginning to lose a bit of his usual good humor. "The kind Lord Shepherdston sailed on the pond in the garden when he was in still in short breeches."

"I vaguely remember Lord Shepherdston having toy sailboats," Pomfrey told him. "But I never remember him sailing them on the pond." He looked at Colin. "There was never anyone with whom he could sail them." He thought for a moment. "If the boats are still here, they would be in the nursery or the schoolroom or perhaps the attics. I'll go up there myself, after dinner, and check."

"Thank you, Pomfrey," Colin replied. "Lady Grantham and I are most appreciative."

"What shall I do with them if I discover their whereabouts, sir?" the butler asked.

Colin looked to Gillian for the answer.

"Please have someone bring them up to the Ivory Suite," Gillian instructed. "And leave them outside the outer door in the corridor." She met Colin's questioning gaze and smiled her most brilliant smile. "And Pomfrey, there's no need for you to hunt them tonight. Tomorrow will be quite soon enough, for Lord Grantham and I will be otherwise engaged until afternoon."

Chapter 25

"I am not in the roll of common men."
—WILLIAM SHAKESPEARE, 1564–1616
KING HENRY IV, POINT 1

"What's this?" The Duke of Sussex looked up from the morning newspaper as Jarrod, Marquess of Shepherdston, walked into their customary private room at White's and tossed a stack of deciphered messages on the table in front of him.

"Trouble," Jarrod answered succinctly.

Griff set his cup of coffee aside, picked up several messages, and began to read. "Where did you get these?"

"From a French agent operating between Edinburgh and Paris," Jarrod told them. "Our agent lifted these from his person and replaced them with duplicates."

"Risky move," Sussex said.

Jarrod smiled. "She's very good at what she does."

Sussex nodded in complete understanding.

"Colin recruited her," Jarrod continued. "And we provided enough of the original code to make the messages appear authentic as long as our Frenchman didn't look too closely at the placement of some of the codes. And our agent made certain he had more important things on his mind."

Griff closed his eyes and gritted his teeth. He didn't like

using prostitutes as agents, no matter how patriotic or how good they were. It troubled him to know that in addition to bartering their bodies to earn a living, these women were bartering their lives for snippets of information. But if the work the female agents did prevented one British soldier from losing his life to a French sword, saber, rifle, pistol, or cannon, Griff deemed the work worthwhile and was grateful to them for doing it. Griff opened his eyes and finished reading the deciphered messages and passed them on to Sussex. "You're right," he said, looking over at Jarrod. "This can't be good."

"But what does it mean?" Sussex wondered aloud.

"It means we bloody well sent Colin into the viper's den!" Jarrod snapped. "We married him into a family of bloody traitors!"

"We didn't marry him into anything," Sussex protested. "He did that himself."

"Colin allowed the baron to blackmail him into marrying his disgraced daughter, and he did it in order to protect the League," Jarrod reminded them. "And we let him walk into Davies's trap." Jarrod raked his fingers through his hair, then got up and began to pace the length of the room. "I knew what it was, and I sent him into the viper's nest. Alone."

"Spilled milk." Griff shook his head. "Besides, we don't know that the baron is a traitor." He held up his hand when Jarrod would have protested. "It may look bad, but things aren't always what they appear to be. And it's possible that Baron Davies could be as ignorant of these"— he gestured toward the stack of papers—"as Colin is."

"You think the fact that Baron Davies and his Bow Street runner pursued our Colin under the guise of pursuing Colin Fox is a coincidence?" Jarrod demanded.

"You know better than that." Griff made a circling motion with his finger. "Pace the other way, Jarrod. You're wearing out the carpet on that side."

Jarrod complied.

Griff resumed his argument. "I don't believe in coincidence any more than you or Daniel." He nodded toward the Duke of Sussex. "I'm just saying that it's possible that something bigger is going on. Something we're not seeing."

The use of his Christian name took Sussex by surprise. It was the first time in nearly two years that Griff had addressed the duke by anything other than his title or his style. It might not mean much to Jarrod or to Griff—in fact, neither one of them seemed to notice—but Sussex noticed, and for him it meant he'd finally been granted complete acceptance into the Free Fellows League by its founding members.

"I agree with Griff," Sussex replied. "And with you, Jarrod. This isn't a coincidence any more than having the impostor use Colin's alias was a coincidence, but like Griff, I believe it's possible that the baron is unaware of what's going on around him."

"These messages tell us the baron's fleet of ships is ferrying French agents all over the globe, and you want me to believe he's unaware of it?" Jarrod was astounded by his fellow Free Fellows' willingness to accept the baron's innocence.

"We expect you to believe it's possible," Griff said. "Because it is."

"It's unlikely," Jarrod insisted.

"I don't think so." Sussex looked Jarrod in the eye. "How aware are you of what takes place in your London home or your country estate? Are you aware of the power struggles within your staffs? Can you say for certain that every man in your employ is completely trustworthy? Do you know where they are every hour of the day? Can you be certain that they earn the salary you pay them?" He paused. "Because I know that I cannot," Sussex told him. "I trust my butlers and housekeepers to know and not trouble me overmuch with the details of running the households.

But, if the truth is known, I have no idea if what they tell me is the entire truth or only a portion of it. And I suspect the same is true with Lord Davies. But in his case, the situation is magnified tenfold because his estates are ships at sea, hundreds, even thousands of miles beyond his control."

Griff nodded. "All it takes is one dishonest or desperate sea captain."

"Point taken," Jarrod acknowledged.

"There is no doubt that the business with the impostor Colin Fox and this information that Davies's ships are being used by the French as a means of transportation for its agents is connected," Griff said.

"What we need to discover is how," Sussex concluded.

"What we need is to warn Colin that his father-in-law is under suspicion and find out how much he knows about the situation."

"Interrupt his honeymoon?" Griff asked.

"It's going to be interrupted anyway," Jarrod said. "He's scheduled to make a clandestine trip to France at the end of this week."

Sussex winced. "He isn't going to like that."

Jarrod shrugged his shoulders. "There's no one else to send. I can't leave and go to France, and neither can you or Griff." He thought for a moment, then brought up the subject the Free Fellows League had been dancing around since Sussex had joined them. "We need more Free Fellows."

The other two Free Fellows nodded.

"We're in agreement about that," Griff said. "We've known it since we decided to work through the War Office." He looked at Jarrod. "And you and Colin recognized the problem and used Daniel while I was away at war on the Peninsula."

"And now that you *and* Colin are married, we need more unmarried Free Fellows. The question is who? And how do we decide?" Jarrod turned to Sussex. "Any suggestions?"

Sussex took his time before answering. "The problem, as I see it, isn't finding young men to recruit. There are plenty of young bucks willing to join us. The problem is finding the right match. The candidates need to be like us. Of a similar ages and backgrounds. They need to be men who won't draw attention to themselves or make anyone stop and wonder why they are suddenly in our company." He looked from Jarrod to Griff. "And I think that whomever we select as candidates should go through an apprenticeship similar to mine."

Griff frowned mightily. Sussex had earned his place in the Free Fellows League by pursuing Griff's bride while Griff was away at war. His mission was to test Alyssa's fidelity and protect her from less honorable would-be suitors. "You want to find someone to pursue Colin's bride?"

"No," Sussex shook his head. "But we need someone to help us keep an eye on her while Colin is away. Our candidates will have to prove themselves worthy of the honor of being a member of the Free Fellows League, as I had to prove myself worthy. If the new Lady Grantham and her family are involved in traitorous activities, the impostor Colin Fox may still be on the scene." He looked at Jarrod. "And that could be dangerous for our Colin."

Jarrod nodded. "We're not forgetting that someone hired an assassin to kill him."

"Exactly," Sussex said.

"Have we any League candidates?" Griff asked.

"Well," Sussex took a deep breath, "there's my cousin, Manners. . . ."

Jarrod groaned. "Not Jonathan. He whined incessantly."

"Have you seen him lately?" Sussex asked.

"No, thank God."

Sussex chuckled at Jarrod's quick reply. "He's almost as tall as I am. He doesn't whine anymore, and he finally inherited a title."

Griff arched an eyebrow.

"Paternal uncle," Sussex explained. "No relation to me. But Manners is now the Earl of Barclay, and the title came with property and a healthy income."

"But, Manners . . ." Jarrod hadn't yet gotten past his distaste for the chubby whiner who had occupied the cot next to his in the dormitory of Knightsguild. "He was under my feet every time I turned around back at Knightsguild."

"He's wanted to be a Free Fellow since the day you formed the League," Sussex argued. "He's entirely trustworthy, and he worships you, Shepherdston."

"What?"

"You're his hero," Sussex confided. "When we were growing up, all he talked about was how much he wanted to be like you."

Jarrod glanced over at Griff. "What do you think?"

"He's kept our secrets for nearly twenty years," Griff said.

"He told Sussex every move we made," Jarrod protested.

"I was the only person he told," Daniel said. "And he only told me because we were all we had. I was his only friend and he was my only friend. And we both wanted to be a part of the Free Fellows League more than anything."

"All right," Jarrod gave in. "We'll give him a try, but if he whines or complains, he's out." He looked at Griff. "How about you? Any candidates?"

Griff took another sip from his coffee cup. "I've had my eye on the new Marquess of Courtland."

"Alex Courtland?" Sussex asked.

Griff nodded. "He's a year or two younger than we are, but I've been impressed by what I've seen so far."

"He was a year behind me at Eton," Sussex said.

"If I'm not mistaken, he danced with Colin's bride at Lady Harralson's the other night," Jarrod added. "Handled himself very well. Made a favorable impression on me and on Colin."

"We'll take a vote," Jarrod said. "Shall we approach Courtland and Barclay?"

"Yea." All three of them raised their hands.

"And Colin?" Jarrod asked. "Yea or nay?"

Griff and Sussex turned to Jarrod. "Send for him."

Chapter 26

"He is the half part of a blessed man,
Left to be finished by such a she;
And she a fair divided excellence,
Whose fullness of perfection lies in him."
—WILLIAM SHAKESPEARE, 1564–1616
KING JOHN

The toy sailboats sat outside the outer door to the Ivory Suite for two days before Colin and Gillian decided to put them to use. It rained all day the first day and part of the second. But the sun came out from behind the clouds on the afternoon of the second day, and the honeymoon couple emerged from their bed in an effort to prevent their honeymoon from becoming a deadly dull affair.

Gillian picked up her bonnet and gloves as Colin buttoned her into a simple pale green muslin gown. She hummed a happy little tune and swayed to and fro while he struggled with the buttons. "Hurry."

"Hold still," he said. "Or I won't be responsible for what happens to your buttons."

Gillian stared at the toy sailboats resting on the table. "Do you think they'll still float?"

"I'm sure of it," Colin said. He and Gillian hadn't left their bedroom in two days, but Pomfrey had sent word that he'd located two toy sailboats in the attic and would leave them outside the suite as soon as he'd cleaned the decades of grime from them.

Colin had retrieved the two boats after he and Gillian had climbed out of bed following a leisurely morning of lovemaking and a hot bath. The two boats—one red and one blue—were as clean as Pomfrey could make them, and Colin had no doubt that they would float.

He leaned forward and placed a kiss on his favorite spot at the nape of Gillian's neck. "All done."

Gillian pulled on her gloves and preceded Colin out the door, the red sailboat cradled safely in her arms. Colin followed close behind with the blue sailboat.

They exited the house through the back door and made their way across the garden around the labyrinth to the fishpond. Gillian ran toward the pond, and Colin gave chase. He caught up with her as she reached the water's edge and gave her a quick kiss before they prepared their boats for launching.

"Shall we race?" she suggested.

"What shall we wager?" he asked.

"Wager?"

"What's the point of racing if there's nothing to win?" he asked.

"Papa and I used to race to prove who was the better sailor," Gillian told him.

"I suppose that's reason enough," Colin agreed. "But not nearly as much fun as the wager I had in mind."

"What did you have in mind?" Gillian's palms were damp inside her gloves as she smoothed nonexistent wrinkles from her muslin skirts.

Colin untied the ribbons of her bonnet, moved it aside, then whispered in her ear. "Deal?"

His words sent shivers of anticipation up and down her spine, and Gillian was tempted to lose, just to see how creative Colin could be, but she was made of sterner, more competitive stuff. And if she won, she got to choose.

She stuck out her hand. "Deal."

Colin ignored her hand. "I prefer to kiss on it."

Gillian reached up and locked her arms around his neck. "So do I."

"Ready. Set. Go!" Colin called out as he and Gillian launched their boats from the side of the pond, then raced downstream following their course as they headed toward the finish line. Gillian raced ahead of him, and Colin watched as a gust of wind lifted her skirts and blew them back around her legs, displaying the outline of her long, slim thighs.

"I won!" she shouted, plopping down on the bank, stripping off her gloves and bonnet and hiking up her skirts so she could roll down her silk stockings and wade into the pool to retrieve her boat.

"I'll get it," Colin offered. He was wearing tall boots, and although they weren't completely weatherproofed, his boots would keep him from getting wet.

But Gillian was already splashing across the pond to get her boat.

Colin's breath caught in his throat at the sight of her.

She waded to the edge of the pond, handed her boat to Colin, then waded back for his blue one. Her dark, curly hair was loose and hanging down her back. Her arms and feet were bare and exposed to the afternoon sun, and her skirts soaked from hem to hip. She looked a mess, and yet Colin thought he'd never seen her look so beautiful in bed or out of it.

As he reached out a hand to help her out of the pond, Colin realized that somewhere between London and Shepherdston Hall, sometime between his wedding and the third day of his honeymoon, he'd fallen in love with his wife.

They raced the boats three more times, and Gillian beat

him twice more. Colin laughed as she proclaimed victory once again. He had given serious consideration to losing on purpose, but that hadn't been necessary; Gillian had beaten him fair and square. The only race he'd won had been the one where the sails on Gillian's boat had come loose, causing the boat to capsize.

Normally, he hated losing, but he was honored to lose to his wife and happy to find that her winning had made her so happy. Colin swept her up into his arms.

"I won," she crowed once again. "I beat you three out of four times."

"Yes, you did," he answered agreeably.

"So," she looked up at him. "I get to claim the prize."

"Your wish is my command."

"I choose the labyrinth." Gillian reached up and framed Colin's face between her hands. "Now."

Colin shrugged. "Let's hope it's the gardeners' day off."

❧

Colin and Gillian were enjoying the second course of dinner when Pomfrey quietly entered the carpeted dining room, leaned over Colin's shoulder, and spoke in a low voice.

"I apologize for interrupting your dinner, Lord Grantham, but the military dispatches have arrived from London. Several are marked urgent, including a note from the master."

"Thank you, Pomfrey. I'll attend to them right away."

Pomfrey bowed. "Very good, sir."

"Did the dispatch rider return?"

"No, sir." Pomfrey glanced at Gillian, then back at Colin. Colin nodded, and Pomfrey elaborated. "He's having his supper in the kitchen, and we've made room for him in the servants' wing."

"Is he expected to return tonight?"

"He didn't mention it," Pomfrey answered. "And the dispatches are sealed."

Colin toyed with the stem of his wineglass. Sealed dispatches usually contained enciphered messages—messages that had been deciphered and required action by Colin or messages that required Colin's help to decipher them. And the fact that Jarrod had sent him the dispatches while he was on his honeymoon meant they were important.

Colin exhaled. Although he hadn't yet seen or read the dispatches, he was willing to bet that he was about to resume the mission that Baron Davies and his Bow Street investigator had interrupted. He exhaled. "Please have a pot of coffee sent to the study," Colin said.

"Yes, sir." Pomfrey turned on his heel and left the dining room as quietly as he'd entered.

"Colin?" Gillian reached over and placed her hand on his. The butler had spoken so softly that she hadn't been able to hear his side of the conversation. But she had heard Colin's side, and she recognized the look of concern on his face. "Is something wrong?"

He looked across the table at Gillian. Her cheeks and nose were sunburned, and he knew that other parts of her anatomy were also sporting a new pink color. "The world is about to intrude on our honeymoon."

Gillian sighed. "We knew it couldn't last forever."

That was true. But he'd thought it would last the week. He thought he'd be granted that much. Four days wasn't enough. Four days wasn't nearly enough. "I thought it would last a sennight," Colin told her. "At least." But he was scheduled for France at the end of the week, and Colin had no choice but to attend to the mission.

He finished his dinner and pushed his plate aside. "Excuse me, my sweet, but Pomfrey tells me urgent messages to which I must attend have arrived from London."

"Is there anything I can do to help?" she asked, as he stood up and walked around to her side of the table.

"I won't know until I re—" He'd almost told her that he had dispatches to read. "See what work Jarrod sent up from London."

"Jarrod?"

"The Marquess of Shepherdston. We share several business interests."

Gillian pretended to understand, though Colin offered no further explanation. "Oh."

He leaned down and brushed his lips against her hair. "I may be quite late coming to bed," he said. "You've had a hard day winning sailboat races and collecting the bounty for it. No need for you to wait up."

"You've had an equally hard day losing sailboat races and distributing the bounty." She smiled at the memory of the hours they'd spent in the labyrinth after the toy sailboat races. I'll wait up for you no matter how late it is."

> G,
>   *Sorry to interrupt your holiday, my friend, but duty calls in London. Your schedule is fixed, and we require your presence as soon as possible.*
>   *As ever,*
>   *M*

The message, written in code, was addressed to G, which stood for Galahad, and signed by M, which stood for Merlin, Jarrod's code name.

It was Colin's summons back to London and had been accompanied by a stack of coded messages marked urgent. He stared at the stack of messages he'd spent the better part of the evening deciphering. They had been opened and resealed with Merlin's seal, so Colin knew that they had been opened and read in London, but Jarrod made it policy not to send the deciphered messages, only the originals. These originals had come from one of the French agents operating in Edinburgh. Colin pulled out his most recent copy of the French deciphering table. The messages were written in a form of numeric code. His deciphering table saved a tremendous amount of time in the deciphering process because it showed the numbers and their alphabetic equivalent in current use. But the French had begun changing the code in recent months, rearranging numbers to make code breaking more difficult. Colin had studied Conradus and been taught by George Scovell and Colquhoun Grant, and he knew that anyone with a full command of the French language and the knowledge that *e* was the most commonly used letter in the French language, or that words ending in double letters most frequently ended in *ee,* or that *et* which meant *and* was the most common word in the French language, or that a single letter on its own was an *a, y,* or a consonant with an apostrophe could begin to decipher the messages without too much trouble.

No, the problem with these messages wasn't breaking the code but believing the message. Bloody hell and damnation! They were wrong. They had to be. Anything else was unthinkable.

But the source of the information contained in these messages was impeccable. He knew the agent. He'd recruited her. And she'd never been wrong before. But there was always a first time, and this appeared to be it. Because, according to these, his father-in-law, the baron, Lord Davies, was in league with the French. Davies's ships transported French agents and government officials to ports of call in England, Scotland, Ireland, Wales, the major port cities of Europe, the Caribbean, and the Americas. According to these, everything that had happened since that night in Edinburgh had been part of an elaborate ruse to draw the real Colin Fox into the baron's trap.

Everything. Gillian's elopement and abandonment in Edinburgh. The baron's investigation and the hiring of the

Bow Street runner. All of it was a ruse to force the real Colin Fox into declaring his true identity.

And it had worked like a charm. Not only had the real Colin Fox declared his identity, but he'd married the baron's daughter. According to these, the baron had used his daughter as bait. And Colin had walked into the trap with his eyes wide open.

It couldn't be true. And yet . . .

I'll do whatever's necessary to secure you as husband for my daughter, because your position doesn't allow for scandal any more than hers does. The baron's words came back to haunt him. Time and time again. Had he? Had the baron done more than simply blackmail him? Had he engineered the whole scheme? Colin didn't want to believe it, and yet he knew that while the messages intercepted from the French might not be entirely true, a great deal of what they contained was.

But what was truth? And what were lies? Was it coincidence that the ship that had taken him from Paris to Edinburgh had been one of Davies's ships? Was it coincidence that he had first seen Gillian at the Blue Bottle Inn? Or that a husband who happened to go by the name of Colin Fox had abandoned her there? Was it a coincidence that the trail the Bow Street runner followed had led straight to the War Office and the secret Free Fellows League?

What was the truth? And what was all a part of an elaborate scheme to catch a spy? And was Gillian part of it?

Colin pushed aside his cup of coffee and reached into the top desk drawer for a bottle of whisky and a glass. He poured himself a glass of whisky, downed it, and poured another. He sipped his whisky as he pulled another message from the stack of papers, this one detailing the routes of Davies's ships. Colin studied the routes and realized that those particular ships had docked in ports that coincided with his most recent travels. But he was unable to come up with any other clues that might lead him to discover the identity of the impostor Colin Fox.

He finished his whisky, then pulled out the urgent messages Jarrod had sent Colin to decipher.

Gillian was as good as her word. She waited up for him through the long hours of the night and into the wee hours of the morning. When the casement clock downstairs struck the hour of three and Colin had still not come to bed, she decided to investigate.

She found him asleep in the study, his head cradled upon his arms on a stack of papers. A cup and saucer that had contained coffee and a bottle of Scots whisky and a glass had been pushed out of the way to the far corner of the desk.

Gillian walked over to the desk and placed her hand on his shoulder. "Colin?"

Colin awoke with a start and shot to his feet, sending papers scattering across his desk and onto the floor. A gold seal suspended from a thick gold chain rolled off the desk and landed on the carpet beneath a sheet of paper under Colin's chair.

Gillian dropped to her knees and began picking up the loose papers at her feet.

"Leave it!" Colin ordered.

But it was too late. Gillian had already gathered a handful of papers and begun straightening them. She looked down at the papers covered in cipher. "What is this? Some kind of puzzle?" she asked, looking up at Colin.

He groaned and reached for the papers.

She handed them to him, then bent once again to retrieve the single page beneath his chair. She pulled the sheet of paper from beneath Colin's chair, then reached for the gold seal on the chain and picked it up, too. "Can't lose the Grantham seal," she teased, as she pushed herself up from her knees. "You'll need it for your correspondence."

"It's not th—" Colin could have bitten his tongue out.

"Whose is it?" She asked as her curiosity got the better of her and she turned it over to study the indention. "Shepherdston's?" No, not Shepherdston's. She'd never seen the Shepherdston seal, but she'd seen this one. It was engraved with the impression of a mounted knight, and she'd seen it once before in a puddle of hardened green wax.

Gillian glanced from the seal she held in her hand to the cube of bright green sealing wax sitting on Colin's desk. "Galahad."

Chapter 27

❦

"*Forward, I pray, since we have come so far,*
And be it moon, or sun, or what you please.
And if you please to call it a rush-candle,
Henceforth I vow it shall be so for me."

—WILLIAM SHAKESPEARE, 1564–1616
THE TAMING OF THE SHREW

"*What did you call me?*" Colin asked.

Gillian supposed that someone else might be intimidated by his tone of voice and the furrow in his forehead, but he didn't intimidate her. "Galahad," she answered, pulling herself up to her full height and looking him in the eye. "I called you Galahad because that's who you are. You're Sir Galahad."

"Sir Galahad?" Colin arched an eyebrow and pretended innocence. "Like the knight in the Arthurian legends?"

"Yes," she replied, "just like the knight in the Arthurian legend. Sir Galahad, whose purity and virtue allowed him to see the Holy Grail."

Colin laughed, showing all of his perfect white teeth. "You have obviously mistaken me for someone else, my lady."

Gillian firmed her lips into a thin, disapproving line. "A situation with which you seem to be increasingly familiar. I mistake you for Galahad. My father and his Bow Street detective mistake you for Colin Fox. Yet your name is Colin McElreath, Viscount Grantham. Or is it?"

Her words stung. But her disapproval stung even more, and Colin responded in kind. "You know my name, Lady Grantham," Colin told her. "You share it. Along with my pillow."

She'd also shared a pillow with Galahad. It had been a chaste pillow, but he had shared it with her. Gillian thought of that night Galahad had slept beside her. Remembered that she'd been thinking of Galahad when she'd told Colin about the time she'd spent at the Blue Bottle Inn. "I liked touching," she'd whispered. "I liked being held at night and knowing I wasn't alone anymore. I know it sounds silly, but I liked sleeping beside someone." And he had been the one to hold her.

Now, Gillian understood why she'd felt so comfortable in Colin's company from the very beginning. Why he'd seemed so familiar. It was his scent. It had clung to the pillowslip and the bedclothes of her bed at the Blue Bottle the morning after he'd spent the night there. And she had remembered and recognized the warm, welcoming scent of the sandalwood soap he wore. She had trusted Colin from the moment she'd met him and all because she had fallen in love with Galahad and Galahad had proven himself to be trustworthy.

"I shared a pillow with Galahad, too," she said, softly reminding him of that night. "In Scotland."

Gillian realized she had given him ammunition with which to hurt her the moment she'd opened the door to old wounds her first honeymoon had left. She prayed he cared enough about her to live up to his reputation as Sir Galahad and protect her, rather than hurt her.

"Did you?" he asked.

Tears burned her eyes as she breathed a prayer of thanks. "You know I did," she replied, holding the seal close to her heart. "You were there."

"I've never been to Gretna Green." He tried to bluff once again, but she wasn't having any of it.

"Nice try, my lord," she informed him, her heart in her eyes as she looked up at him. "But you know as well as I do that Gretna Green can't compare to the Blue Bottle Inn in Edinburgh."

Colin raked his fingers through his hair. "What do you know about the Blue Bottle Inn in Edinburgh?"

"I know that it's no place for a lady." She took a step closer to him. "A man who called himself Galahad told me that."

"What were doing there?" he asked.

"Trying to find my way home to you." She put her arms around his neck. "When were you going to tell me that I've been there all along?"

Her words sent a rush of desire coursing through him. He had been waiting all of his life to find someone who understood how he felt. And Gillian had just put his feelings into words.

Colin held her close. There was no rhyme or reason to it. He'd simply looked up, seen her standing at the window, and had wanted her. He hadn't even seen her clearly, but he'd recognized a kindred spirit when he saw one. She stood waiting at the window. Colin had wanted her to be waiting for him. "Oh, hell, Gillian, you were never supposed to know." He placed his hands on either side of her hips and lifted her, without warning, onto the top of the desk.

It was an effective way of distracting her.

"When were you going to tell me that I've been there all along?"

Those words registered in recesses of his brain as Colin skimmed her nightgown up over her legs and bunched it around her waist. Reaching down, Colin freed himself from his breeches, then lifted her hips and guided himself into her welcoming warmth.

Gillian cried out his name as he entered her. She lifted her legs and locked her thighs high around his waist.

Colin closed his eyes, threw back his head, and bit his bottom lip as he sheathed himself fully inside her warmth. His entire body shook with the effort of holding back the tide of pleasure he knew would come. Colin lost his battle to maintain control as her movement forced him deeper inside her. He began to move his hips in a rhythm as old as time.

Gillian matched him thrust for thrust as she followed the primitive cadence of their pounding hearts. She clung to him, reveling in the weight and feel of him as he filled her again and again, giving everything he had to give.

She closed her eyes and allowed tears of joy to seep from behind her lashes and run down her face.

Colin was her Galahad. He was the man of her dreams. He always had been. He was the man who'd set her free and won her heart.

Gillian gave herself up to the emotions swirling inside her, gave voice to the passion with the small moans that escaped her at each wonderful thrust. She tightened her muscles around him, holding on as the exquisite pleasure peaked, then muffled her scream against his shoulder.

"Gillian." Colin felt her tremors surrounding him and called out her name. As he collapsed atop her, completely spent, completely satisfied, Colin brushed his lips against her cheek and buried his face in her curly brown hair.

Tasting the saltiness of her tears, Colin lifted his head and looked down at her beautiful face. Her blue eyes were wide open and dark with passion. Her lips were plump, swollen from his kisses, and the stubble on his jaw had abraded the soft skin of her face.

A lump caught in his throat. He wanted to say something profound, something beautiful, something to explain the way he felt.

He wanted to say something that would make her open her heart and declare her feelings for him.

But Sir Galahad couldn't say anything at all.

He could only feel.

I love you.

❧

"Colin?" Gillian smoothed her nightgown down over her legs and slid off the desk. "This is yours, isn't it?" She opened her fist and offered him the seal.

Colin took it from her and slipped the chain over his head and around his neck.

"It looks as if it belongs there," she said.

He glanced down at the seal lying half-concealed by the hair on his chest. "It does."

"So," she drawled. "We've only been married four days, and you're already keeping secrets from me."

Colin pursed his lips in thought. "Only the secrets that predate our wedding."

"Your appearance in my life as Sir Galahad definitely predated our wedding."

Colin exhaled, then closed his eyes and hung his head. "Yes, it did. And so did the only other secrets I'm keeping."

Gillian retrieved the sheet of paper that had slipped out of her grasp and landed on the desktop as they made love. "Secrets that have something to do with these messages." She glanced down at the paper and frowned as she studied it more closely. "And the trade routes of several of my father's ships."

Colin opened his eyes and met her gaze, willing her to understand that as a man of honor, he could not reveal the secrets of a lifetime, even to her.

Gillian took a deep breath. The innkeeper's wife's description of Galahad came rushing back. *The smuggler.* "May I ask you a question?"

"I won't promise I can answer it," Colin told her. "But I'll try."

"All right," she agreed. "Did you follow me to Edinburgh?"

"No. I arrived in Edinburgh after you did, but I was there on business that had nothing to do with you. I saw you for the first time standing at the window," he answered her truthfully.

"You were the one in the alley."

He nodded.

"But you never worked for my father, and you weren't hired to follow Colin Fox or to find me and bring me home?"

Colin shook his head. "I'd never met your father until the day before you and I married. And I only learned about the man you knew as Colin Fox the afternoon before I met with your father and the Bow Street runner."

"Then why?"

"I was on my way back to the Blue Bottle the night I was set upon by the footpad I told you about. Circumstances prevented me from reaching my room by way of the front door. I had to find another way, so I climbed up on the roof of the laundry in the close and used the ledge to make my way to my window." He looked at Gillian. "My room was just down from yours. I reached it only to find it occupied by characters looking to do me more harm. I knew I was bleeding from my wound and too weak to retrace my path, so I slipped inside your room to escape them."

"How did you know I was alone?" Gillian asked.

"I didn't," he told her. "I knew you'd been left alone because I heard the innkeeper and his wife discussing your situation, but I didn't know you were alone until I climbed in your bedroom window and saw you curled up in bed all by yourself." He took another deep breath before resuming his explanation. "You weren't supposed to know I was there," he said. "I intended to be long gone before you awoke."

"But I surprised you."

"Aye." The one word was riddled with emotion. "In every way."

Tears rolled down her cheeks. "You knew I was afraid. You held me through the night and paid my way home. You saved me, Colin."

"No more than you saved me, Gillian."

"When you danced with me at Lady Harralson's, you knew who I was and what I'd done." Gillian looked down at her lap and began pleating little folds into the paper on her lap.

"No," Colin told her. "I had no idea who you were until I met with your father. All I knew was that I felt guilty for leaving you behind when you asked me to take you with me." Colin shrugged his shoulders. "I couldn't take you with me, but I didn't like the idea of leaving you behind and at the mercy of the innkeeper and his wife. I did what I could."

She drew a shaky breath and tackled the question uppermost in her mind. "Are you planning to use my father's ships to smuggle French contraband?"

"No," he answered honestly.

"Then what's this about?" She waved the pleated paper on which the Davies shipping schedules and trade routes were written beneath his nose.

"We think that someone else is using your father's ships for that purpose."

"*We?*"

Colin groaned. He considered it a sign of just how dangerous she was for his peace of mind and how comfortable he had become in Gillian's presence, that he, who never blundered or fell prey to foolish slips of the tongue where the Free Fellows were concerned, had made several in front of Gillian. He had fallen asleep over a stack of coded messages. At the rate he was going, Colin would be lucky if she didn't know all of his intimate secrets by morning.

He took a deep breath, then exhaled and decided to tell her as much of the truth as possible.

"He lied, didn't he?" Gillian asked before he had a chance to answer her. "He lied about being an agent for our government and working against the French. He lied about all of it." She looked at Colin. "He used your name because you are everything he wanted to be, but was not. Our meeting. Our wedding. All of it was arranged, wasn't it? Even before we met. We were like marionettes, and he has been pulling the strings. Please, tell me the truth. Because none of this is coincidence."

"No, not coincidence, Gilly, my love." He lowered his voice to that husky Scottish burr that always sent shivers of awareness up and down her spine. "Fate. It was fate. Because we belong together." He stared into her eyes. "And everything I've told you is the truth. Or as much of it as I can safely divulge. I work with the government in the War Office. These messages were intercepted from French agents and sent to me because my new father-in-law's—your father's—name is occurring far too frequently for comfort."

"Does your work for the government involve smuggling?" she asked.

"It has upon occasion," he admitted. "And it's also involved the apprehension of smugglers. Why do you ask?"

"The innkeeper's wife at the Blue Bottle called you 'the smuggler.' "

"I'm delighted to hear it," he said. "Mistress Douglas has reason to suspect that I am a smuggler, and I prefer that she and her husband continue to think it."

"I have reason to suspect you're a smuggler as well," Gillian reminded him.

"Do you believe me when I tell you that I don't intend to use your father's ships for that purpose or for any purpose?"

Gillian stared into Colin's eyes and read the truth in them, then lowered her gaze and studied the pattern in the carpet.

"Gillian? Do you?" He held his breath as he waited for her answer, for it had suddenly become more important than the air he breathed.

"Yes," she whispered, praying that her faith in him wouldn't be betrayed simply because she wanted so badly to believe him.

Colin reached out and tilted her chin up so he could see her expression. "Are you certain?"

She nodded. "And I can prove it."

He managed a tender smile. "You don't have to prove anything to me."

"Maybe not," she allowed, "but if you intend to help Papa instead of harm him, you need to know that the information on this sheet of paper and the letters on some of the cryptographical puzzles are wrong."

"What?"

Gillian pointed to the trade route Colin had deciphered. "This is wrong. *The Lady Dee* has a port of call in the Firth of Forth in Edinburgh, but *The Diamond Princess* doesn't sail those waters. She sails from the Mediterranean to the southern coast of Africa. *The Pearl Princess* sails the Orient, and *The Lady Royal* sails the Caribbean and has a port of call in Port Royal." She looked at Colin. "This schedule, or whatever it is, has them sailing the wrong routes and calling at the wrong ports. None of Papa's ships are sailing in Calais or any other French ports."

"You're certain?"

"Of course, I'm certain," Gillian told him. "We named them that way. Each of our ships is named for the trade route it sails. It's our company's practice. The Dee is a river in Scotland, so *The Lady Dee* sails to Scottish ports. Diamonds come from Africa, so *The Diamond Princess* plies her trade in ports of call in Africa. Pearls come from the Orient, and Port Royal is in the Caribbean Sea, and so forth."

"All twenty-four ships are named in this manner?"

"Yes. It began as a game," she said. "When I was little, it was a way of teaching me geography as well as Papa's business, and we've continued it because we could tell the trade routes of all the ships at a glance, just by knowing their names."

"Who knows about this?"

"Papa and Mama and me," Gillian answered. "And I suppose it's possible that one or two of the most senior clerks and the older captains might know of it." She thought for a moment. "It isn't something we trumpet, but it isn't something we hide, either."

"So, it's possible that a clerk or a sea captain or first mate with less experience would be unaware of the specific way the ships are named."

"Of course, it's possible," Gillian said. "Obviously, whoever compiled this got it wrong."

"Would the captains of these ships sail the wrong routes if they were ordered to do so?"

"It has to be possible," she allowed. "If these ships were where this says they were, then all of them except *The Lady Dee* are in the wrong waters. I think that would depend primarily on two things: who's captaining the vessel and whether they're heading home or heading out."

Colin frowned, not fully understanding the point she was making.

Gillian elaborated. "These are merchant ships, Colin. Cargo space is dear because every bit of space that isn't used for the crew and the food stores is used for cargo. The more cargo, the more money to be earned from it. Ships leaving London have empty cargo holds. They could put into the wrong port and take on cargo or passengers fairly easily, but a ship coming into London from a trip abroad is filled to the gills with cargo and a crew eager to reach home. A detour to another port would be hard to explain to the crew and to those of us who await the ship." She studied the paper. "In this case, three of the four ships are way off course. There's no reason for ships bound for the Mediterranean, the Caribbean, or the Orient to sail north to Scotland. Even the crew had to question that."

"That would depend on whether the crew is in on the scheme or not," Colin guessed. "And on who authorized the change in the trade route." He turned to Gillian. "Who is responsible for doing that?"

"Papa."

"And if the good baron isn't available?"

"Me," she replied. "Or Papa's designated scheduling clerk."

Colin looked his wife in the eye. "Do you think it likely that your father might be unaware of his ships' whereabouts?"

She shook her head.

"Gillian, I've seen *The Lady Dee* docked in the Firth of Forth."

"That's where she belongs," Gillian reminded him.

"Yes, I know," he replied. "But I sailed from Marseilles on her. And I saw *The Diamond Princess* docked there less than a fortnight later."

Gillian was so worried about her father and his wayward ships that she didn't think to inquire about why Colin had been in Marseilles. "Something is wrong," she concluded. "Papa didn't authorize that. I'm sure of it."

"So am I," Colin agreed. "We need to return to London as soon as possible."

"What about those?" Gillian gestured toward the pile of enciphered messages. She studied Colin's deciphering. "That should be an *a* and that should be a *y* and those two should be an *l* and an *r*."

Colin shuffled through the papers Gillian had retrieved and stacked until he located the deciphering table. He studied it for a moment before he turned to Gillian. "Not according to the table."

"The table is wrong," she insisted. "Look at the grouping

of numbers here," she pointed to the passage in question. "And here. The message doesn't make sense unless you change this to an *l*. What does the table say?" she demanded.

Colin read it, then turned to her. "You're right. The table is different. They must be changing it."

Gillian picked up another page of enciphered messages and quickly began deciphering it.

"How do you do that?" Colin was amazed. He was good at deciphering, and the Duke of Sussex was even better, but he doubted that either one of them could decipher as quickly as Gillian could and without Conradus or a deciphering table to help her.

"I like puzzles," she reminded him. "And this is just a matter of recognizing the numerical patterns and figuring it out."

Colin grinned at her. "If I swear you to secrecy and promise to make it worth your while, would you consider spending an hour or so before we depart for London working for the government deciphering codes?"

"On one condition."

"What's that, my lady?"

"That you repeat what you did to me this afternoon in the labyrinth."

Colin's grin grew even broader. "So, you liked being kissed in your secret places?" he teased.

"Oh, yes!" Gillian blushed to admit it, but it was quite the most wickedly exciting and incredibly satisfying kiss she had ever had. And she was eager to experience more of the same.

"It's a deal, my lady," Colin told her. "When and where?"

She straightened to her full height and looked him in the eyes. "In the coach. On the way to London." She gave him a wicked smile. "I'll dress accordingly."

Chapter 28

"They say best men are molded out of faults,
And for the most, become much more the better
For being a little bad."

—WILLIAM SHAKESPEARE, 1564–1616

MEASURE FOR MEASURE

They departed Shepherdston Hall for London at dawn, and the journey was by far the most pleasant trip Gillian and Colin had ever made. The hours flew by as the carriage rumbled along the Post Road covering the distance between country and city, and the lovers inside the carriage occupied themselves with the covering and uncovering of each other.

They arrived at the outskirts of the city flushed with color and pleasantly sated. And as they put their clothing to rights and lingered over sweet kisses, Colin took Gillian's hand in his and looked her in the eye. "I need . . . I want . . ."

"That's a start," she taunted him.

Colin took a deep breath and tried again. "About last night . . ."

Gillian arched an elegant eyebrow in anticipation. "Yes?"

Colin frowned. "I owe you an apology, my lady, for the way I took you without preamble on the desktop like a—"

Gillian placed two fingers against his lips to stop the unnecessary words. "I don't recall any need for an apology.

In fact, I found the situation quite to my liking—and quite satisfying."

He kissed her fingers and bowed his head, and Gillian took pity on him and made his task so much easier. "When do you leave?"

"How did you know?" He looked up at her in surprise. The messages she'd spent part of the night helping him decipher had said nothing about his mission, only that he was needed in London.

She drew a shaky breath and managed a slow, wistful smile. "Your kisses taste of good-bye."

Colin closed his eyes for a moment, then opened them again. "I have to go," he told her. "There's no one else. Whoever made those unauthorized changes to the shipping routes went to a great deal of trouble to arrange it. The moment your father becomes aware that his ships have been used for nefarious purposes, the game is over. And desperation is dangerous. Your father has spent a lifetime building his business. I won't allow anyone to endanger it."

A sudden rush of tears clogged her throat, and it was all Gillian could to do nod her head without crying.

"I don't anticipate a long absence," he said softly, "but there is always the chance that . . ." Colin couldn't stem the feeling of urgency he felt or stop the sense of foreboding that something was about to happen. Something for which he needed to prepare. "That I'll be delayed or . . ." He knew the success or failure of the mission depended upon him and that it was possible he wouldn't return, but Colin looked at Gillian and swore otherwise. "I'm coming back, Gillian. I promise."

"Don't make promises you cannot keep," she warned him, reaching up to trace the outline of the scar on his chest through the fabric of his waistcoat and shirt. "There are footpads with daggers on every corner."

"Daggers I can handle," Colin joked. "It's the pistols I worry about."

She blanched.

"It was a joke," he rushed to reassure her.

"Don't joke about things like that," she ordered. "Not to me."

"All right," he agreed, turning her hand so he could press his lips against her palm, then close her fingers around the kiss to hold it. "I won't be accompanying you to Herrin House," he said at last. "You'll have to go without me."

Gillian slowly expelled the breath she hadn't realized she was holding.

"I do have a favor to ask," he continued.

"Anything."

"My sister, Liana, is in her first season."

"I know."

"She needs help," he said. "Someone other than Maman. Someone younger, who can help her with the latest fashions and things . . ."

He was putting things to rights, making certain his family would be taken care of, should something happen to him.

"I'll be honored to help," Gillian told him.

"She has no jewelry," Colin told her. "She'll need help with that."

"I'll take care of it."

"And if you can find the time," he added. "I'm sure Malcolm and Gregory would enjoy learning how to sail toy sailboats." He smiled at her. "I'm told that Tuesday and Thursday afternoons on the Serpentine are the best times."

"Are you planning to be away that long?" she asked. "Or are you trying to tell me that you aren't coming home?" The coach turned into the drive at Number Twenty-one Park Lane.

"I hope to be home to help you," he said at last. "But if things should not work out the way we've planned . . . Avon or Shepherdston will contact you. If you need anything—anything at all—go to them."

"I'll wait for you, Colin McElreath."

"Gillian . . ."

"I'll be watching and waiting for your return."

The coach rolled to a stop, but Gillian made no move to exit. Colin continued to hold her hand as the footmen unloaded her trunks. "I suppose you'll be needing your French lady's maid once again."

"I suppose," she replied glumly.

"Hey," he lifted her chin with the tip of his index finger. "No more tears. I'm not abandoning you. I'm coming home. As soon as possible. And when I do, Lavery will get a raise in salary and a few days off."

She closed her eyes.

"Gillian . . ." He tried once again. "Gillian, I'm Sir Galahad. Galahad always returns."

"You had better," she warned, her blue eyes flashing. "Because I'll be waiting and I . . ."

He waited for her to say it, waited for her to give him an opening.

She looked up at him, recognized the tender look in his green eyes and thought for a moment that he might be on the verge of telling her how he felt.

"I look horrible in black."

When the Free Fellows League met at White's in their usual room, all four of them were present for the first time since Colin's wedding.

"Sorry to call you back from your honeymoon," Jarrod apologized.

"We were planning to return to London early, anyway," Colin said.

"*We?*" Sussex couldn't resist teasing him a bit about the way things had changed.

Colin took the good-natured teasing in stride. "Gillian is eager to get to work putting Herrin House to rights."

"How is it?" Jarrod asked. "In good shape?"

"I like it just as it is," Colin told them. "Old Herrin had excellent taste. But it's definitely a man's home. The feminine touches are few and far between." He made a face. "There's going be a lot of fabric swatches and decorating involved."

"If she's anything like Lyss," Griff said, "she'll want to get started on that right away." He looked at Colin. "Do you think she would mind a little help on the project? Shopping for fabrics or something . . ." There was a hint of desperation in Griff's voice. "I've been so busy, and Alyssa had been bored almost to tears. She hates the endless rounds of morning calls and at homes. And Miranda's been no help," Griff complained. "She's as bored with the ton as Alyssa is."

Colin took pity on his friend. "Send 'em around to visit," he told him. "But, please, wait until I've left for France."

Jarrod cleared his throat. "Excuse me while you compare notes on your states of domestic bliss, but we've work to do before you leave." He looked at Colin. "Welcome back. Did you get a chance to decipher any of the messages? And what do you think of Baron Davies's involvement with the French?"

Colin reached for the dispatch pouch, then slid it across the table to Jarrod. "Finished."

"All of them?"

Colin nodded. "Every last one of them."

Jarrod reached inside and pulled out the documents, taking note of the information they contained, but also noticing the changes in the cipher code. "This is remarkable work."

All of the messages had been deciphered. All except one. Jarrod glanced at it, recognized the code for Galahad, and read it. He arched an eyebrow in query at the content of the simple code. Unless the French agent who had written these had changed radically since the last time Jarrod read his messages, something was amiss. But Jarrod didn't comment on it; he simply passed the documents on to Griff, who read them and passed them on to Sussex.

"Yes, it is," Colin agreed. "And you can thank the object of my domestic bliss for doing it when next you see her."

Griff bit the inside of his cheek to keep from smiling at Colin's reply.

"You allowed your wife access to deciphered messages?" Jarrod's voice rose in direct proportion to his growing sense of alarm.

"I allowed my wife to *decipher* them." Colin looked around at the other Free Fellows, daring them to object. "She's a hell of a lot faster at it than I am."

"She knew the French codes?" Sussex was equally concerned.

Colin shook his head. "She knew the French codes were wrong. Or rather, she knew that the copies of the French deciphering table we have in our possession were out of date."

Jarrod narrowed his gaze at his best friend. "And how did she come by this information, unless she's in league with French?"

"In league with the French!" Colin shot up from the table, nearly upending it in the process.

Jarrod glared at him. "Yes, in league with the French. Didn't you read any of these messages, Colin? Or were you too busy tumbling—"

"That's enough!" Griff joined the fray, moving to stand between Colin and Jarrod to keep the two hotheaded friends from coming to blows.

"What Jarrod is trying to say—" Sussex began.

"I know what Jarrod is trying to say!" Colin snapped. "He's trying to tell me that my wife and her family are French spies."

"Exactly," Jarrod said. "Only you're too bloody besotted with her to see it."

"What I see," Colin enunciated clearly, "is that someone else is using Lord Davies and his daughter and me for their own purposes." He shot Jarrod a nasty look. "If Gillian's a French spy, I'm bloody King George!"

"Then how did she know about the codes?" Sussex asked in a level, reasonable tone of voice.

"She didn't know they *were* codes," Colin replied. "Until I told her." He held up his hand when Jarrod would have interrupted. "Yes, Jarrod, I told her they were codes. But only after she told me there were errors in my answers to my numerical puzzles."

"Good lord!" Sussex breathed.

"Gillian is something of a prodigy with numbers," Colin told them with no small amount of pride. "She's a genius at mathematics, and she knows almost as much about Lord Davies's imports and shipping as he does." He reached for the stack of messages until he found the one Gillian had pleated. "She's the one who explained that this information is wrong. And that the French have made changes to their deciphering tables. She has the ability to look at groups of numbers and see the patterns." Colin looked at his fellow Free Fellows and began relaying what he'd learned from Gillian.

"Good lord!" Sussex exclaimed once again when Colin had finished. "If we relay this information to Davies—and we must—we're liable to push this traitor—whomever he is—into a very desperate corner."

Jarrod nodded. "If what you suspect is true—" He turned to Colin and held out his hand in apology and friendship. "Your bride and her father are—"

"Targets," Griff concluded.

Colin nodded his head. "I know." He leaned close. "I think she was a target all along."

"I don't follow," Griff said.

"What if her elopement was a kidnapping in disguise?"

Colin looked at his friends and colleagues. "What better way to gain control of twenty-four merchant ships than to gain control of the owner of them?"

"And what better way to do that than to gain control of a member of the owner's family?" Griff added, as complete understanding dawned.

"Unless—" This time, Sussex played devil's advocate. "I'm not saying I believe it," he explained. "Only that it's still possible that the baron arranged everything to trap you."

Colin agreed. "Except that the baron knew nothing about the Blue Bottle Inn, and neither did his investigator. Gillian never said a thing. She kept her meeting with Galahad a secret. The Bow Street runner and Gillian's parents believe she spent two days in an inn at Gretna Green."

"The Bow Street runner could easily check that," Jarrod said.

"He did," Colin told him. "That's where he learned about the other two wives."

"So, the runner and Lord Davies could have arranged everything and pinned it on you."

Colin shook his head.

"Why not?" Jarrod demanded.

"Colin Fox had been to Gretna Green, but I never have."

"What?" Sussex was surprised. "You've never been to Gretna Green?"

"I'm a Free Fellow," Colin said. "I had no reason to go there and have always avoided the place like the plague." He looked at the others. "If I had chosen to fight Baron Davies's blackmail, I could have proven I wasn't the man Gillian married." He shrugged his shoulders. "Hell, Gillian could have proven it."

"And if you weren't in Gretna Green with Gillian, someone else was. Someone who then took her to Edinburgh and abandoned her, probably for a king's ransom—"

"A king's ransom of ships," Colin said.

"But if there was a request for ransom, I haven't heard anything about it," Jarrod said.

"They tried," Colin said. "But there was nothing to ransom because I, or rather Galahad, gave Gillian the money to go home. Galahad paid the bill at the inn, hired a coach and driver, and paid the innkeepers handsomely to forget she had been there. Gillian was home by the time the ransom note arrived."

"Bloody hell!" Jarrod exploded. "I think you're right."

"Who is the impostor?" Griff asked.

"I don't know," Colin said. "I suspect he may be a clerk in Lord Davies's firm. And I intend to find out."

"If you go to France now," Sussex pointed out, "and leave your wife alone at Herrin House, she could be in danger."

"I'm not going to France." He looked at Jarrod.

But Jarrod had something else on his mind. "A clerk," he said. "A clerk . . ." He snapped his fingers. "Bloody hell. A clerk." Jarrod turned to Griff and Sussex. "Remember the meeting after Colin's wedding?"

They nodded.

"Remember when I told you about my trot around the Row when so many curious chaps approached me wanting information about the wedding and the wedding breakfast?"

"Yes," Griff said.

"One of the men who approached me was a clerk," Jarrod said. "I didn't think anything of it at the time, but now it seems strange that a clerk, who had never approached me before, would approach me and request personal information about a friend. Especially, a friend's wedding."

"Did you recognize him?" Colin asked.

"He clerked for Mayhew for a while," Jarrod answered. "I used to see him there, but he left months ago, and when I asked Mayhew what had happened to him, he said the ambitious young man had resigned to accept a more lucrative offer from—"

"Davies Silk and Linen Importers," the others answered in unison.

"What color were his eyes?" Colin demanded.

"Damnation, Colin! How the hell should I know what color his eyes were?" Jarrod snapped.

"How about a name?" Sussex said.

Jarrod snapped his fingers again. "Something with an aitch. Harper, Hooper . . ." He looked up. "Holder. I remember the name plaque on his desk. J. Holder."

"I remember Holder," Griff said.

"So do I," Colin added. "And the son of a bitch has a rather extraordinary pair of blue eyes." He headed for the door, but the others stopped him.

"This requires brains, Colin," Griff said. "Not brawn. If we're going to catch a fox, we need a good plan and a sturdy trap. Exercise a bit of patience now, and we'll get him. Tear off like a hothead, and he'll get wind of it and go to ground."

The four Free Fellows looked at one another and agreed.

"We know where to start," Colin said. "But we're going to need help."

"Not to worry," Jarrod told him. "We've already selected two candidates we mean to approach."

"Who?" Colin demanded.

"Daniel's cousin, Barclay," Griff told him.

"I don't know Barclay," Colin said.

"Sure you do," Jarrod interrupted. "He's that damned whiner, Jonathan Manners. Most recently, the Earl of Barclay."

Colin nodded. "Manners is a good man. He used to whine, but he's grown up. And he is completely trustworthy." He looked at Jarrod. "Who's the other?"

"Courtland."

"I've only met him once or twice," Colin said. "But I liked what I saw."

"Our opinions exactly." Jarrod nodded in satisfaction.

"Will they help?" Colin asked.

"Manners will, without a doubt," Daniel told him. "As for Courtland . . ." He shrugged his shoulders.

"See what you can do," he said to Sussex. "You're in charge of recruiting. But do it fast, because I don't intend to go all the way to France to set this trap."

"You won't have to," Jarrod promised, grinning at Colin. "Oh, and for your information, you missed one."

"One what?"

"Message to be deciphered. It's in the dispatch pouch, and it's addressed to you. In code." He reached over, lifted the pouch from the table, and tossed it to Colin.

Colin opened it, retrieved the message, and read:

Galahad,
Go wherever your quest takes you. Do what needs be done. But come home only to me.
Hurry. I'll be waiting with open arms. Je t'aime.
Your lady fair,
Gillian

Jarrod winked at him. "You *were* right, my friend. The lady certainly knows how to cipher."

Chapter 29

"One for all, or all for one, we gage."
—William Shakespeare, 1564–1616
The Rape of Lucrece

The Free Fellows League prepared to spring the trap on the elusive impostor Colin Fox two days hence. Colin, Viscount Grantham, wanted to spring it immediately, but the planning took a bit of care and Baron Davies's cooperation, as well as the assistance of the two new candidates for admission into the Free Fellows League.

Part of the plan called for Colin to leave on his trip as planned and to leave his bride at home at Herrin House. Another part of the plan called for cooperation of a different sort.

It called for Alyssa, Duchess of Avon, and Miranda, Marchioness of St. Germaine, to pay a call on the new Viscountess Grantham.

Their mission was to convince Lady Grantham that her husband had asked them to help her get Herrin House in order. They were to focus her attention on decorating her house, to keep her out of trouble and out of danger. For Colin was very much afraid that his wife might decide to take matters into her own hands and approach her father, thereby alerting the fox they meant to trap.

Alyssa did as her husband asked and invited her close friend, Miranda, to accompany her as she paid a call on Lady Grantham on the second morning after Colin's departure.

"What's this all about?" Miranda asked as she and Alyssa drove from Alyssa's town house to Number Twenty-one Park Lane.

"We're paying a welcome call on Lady Grantham," Alyssa answered.

Miranda chuckled. "I think that's obvious. The question is why, Alyssa? In case you've forgotten, Grantham and his bride are still on their honeymoon. They won't be receiving guests." She blushed. "And we shouldn't be calling."

"Nonsense." Alyssa brushed away Miranda's concern. "She'll see us." She turned to her best friend. "She can't refuse a duchess."

Miranda rolled her eyes. "Being Duchess of Avon has finally gone to your head, Alyssa. I think I liked it better when you were Viscountess Abernathy."

Alyssa laughed. "That's because you outranked me then, and we had to do all the things you wanted to do."

"True," Miranda admitted. "But this . . ."

Alyssa leaned closer to her friend. "Colin's away, and Griffin asked me to drop in on Gillian to make certain she's all right."

Miranda had learned not to ask too many questions when Alyssa mentioned Griffin or his friends' names in the same sentence. There was something amiss with the four of them—Griffin, Jarrod, Colin, and Daniel—and Miranda knew that although Alyssa was privy to most of what went on, her lips were sealed. The Duchess of Avon would never betray her husband's confidences. "Why didn't you say so in the first place?"

"Say what?"

"That you're on a mission for Griffin," Miranda told her.

"I didn't know if you'd understand," Alyssa admitted. "But Colin has to be away, and he's worried about leaving his bride at home by herself, and well, you know how good he and Jarrod were to me when Griffin was on the Peninsula. You remember how they dropped by Abernathy Manor to see me every chance they got."

"I remember." She and Sussex had stopped by to see Alyssa every chance they had gotten, too. But both for very different reasons.

"I'm just returning the favor," Alyssa said, gathering her basket of housewarming gifts as the coach turned into the drive at Number Twenty-one.

Alyssa rang the bell. "The Duchess of Avon and the Marchioness of St. Germaine to see Lady Grantham," she announced when the door opened.

"Come in, Your Grace." The butler took the cards Alyssa proffered, then stepped back and led them upstairs to the drawing room. "Lady St. Germaine. If you will wait here, I'll inform Lady Grantham that you've arrived."

The butler backed out of the drawing room and disappeared up the stairs. Alyssa and Miranda took the opportunity to look around.

"I wonder what's taking so long," Miranda said, when long minutes had passed and the butler failed to reappear.

"I hope she's all right," Alyssa said. "Colin would never forgive us if anything happened to her while he's away."

"Madame is indisposed, Your Grace."

The French lady's maid bobbed a curtsy as Alyssa and Miranda turned at the sound of her voice and found her standing in the drawing room.

"Indisposed?" Miranda repeated.

"Yes, Your Grace."

"I'm not Her Grace," Miranda corrected, nodding toward Alyssa. "She is."

"But of course," the maid replied smoothly. "Please forgive me for not recognizing you, Lady . . ."

"St. Germaine," Miranda replied, paying close attention to the maid. "You're Lavery, aren't you?"

"Yes, madame."

"Then you should know me. You were with my cousin, Baron Chemsford's, household, were you not?"

"Yes, madame." The maid widened her extraordinary blue eyes and bobbed another, deeper, more respectful curtsy.

"And before that," Miranda continued, narrowing her gaze, "you were with the Viscount Wensley's household."

"You have a good eye, if I may say so, Lady St. Germaine. And a good memory. As you say, I have been fortunate to be employed by the baron and the viscount as well as Lady Grantham."

"Whom we have come to see," Alyssa reminded her. "Now, if you would be so kind as to show us the way."

"Madame cannot see you," the maid insisted. "She is indisposed."

Alyssa lifted her chin a notch higher and used the voice her mother always used on difficult servants. "She will see us. We have a message from her husband for her ears only. And I'm quite certain she would be very distraught if we were to leave without delivering it. Now, either take us to Gillian, or get out of the way so that we might find her on our own."

The maid stepped back, then turned and led the way to the master suite.

"You do that very well," Miranda leaned forward to whisper when the obstinate Lavery opened the door to the suite, then turned on her heel and left.

"I should," Alyssa answered. "I had my mother do it to me often enough."

Alyssa and Miranda crossed the yellow sitting room and knocked on the door of the closest bedroom. There was no answer. "Gillian?"

"In here," she called from the doorway of the other bedroom. She was dressed in a loose-fitting morning gown, and her hair was fashioned into a neat chignon, but it was obvious that the maid hadn't lied. Lady Grantham was deathly pale and in distress and not up to having visitors.

Alyssa set the basket of gifts on the nearest table and rushed forward.

Gillian attempted a curtsy at the sight of the duchess, but Alyssa stopped her. "Bother that!" She looked at Gillian. "Your maid told us you were indisposed and weren't receiving callers, but we had to see for ourselves. Now, get back into bed before you fall down. We'll only stay a few minutes." She stood on Gillian's left, and Miranda stood on Gillian's right, and together, they walked her back to the huge master bed.

"Is there anything we can do?" Miranda offered as they helped Gillian back into bed.

Gillian blushed.

Alyssa raised an eyebrow in query. "Pardon me for being forward, but is it possible that you're . . ." She paused and cleared her throat. "With child?"

Gillian shook her head. "Quite the opposite. My monthly has started with a vengeance." She blushed. "Thank goodness Colin isn't here. I would hate for him to see me like this."

Alyssa chuckled. "It is a bother, but you would be amazed at how sympathetic, thoughtful, and inventive husbands can be at this time of the month." She frowned. "Are you in a great deal of pain?"

Gillian nodded. "It's been late before, but never this uncomfortable."

"I have just the thing," Alyssa told her. "Miranda will stay with you while I run home and get my potions." She smiled at Gillian. "Don't worry. I'm very good. I'll have you feeling better in no time."

"Please," Gillian said. "Don't bother."

"It's no bother," Alyssa assured her. "I'm happy to do it. We're just down the lane. Practically neighbors." She started for the door. "I'll only be gone a few minutes if the little dragon doesn't try to stop me again."

Gillian started to protest, but Alyssa was already heading out the door.

"Let her do it," Miranda advised. "You'll feel better, and Alyssa will be thrilled that she was able to do something for someone besides pay social calls."

"Thank you." Gillian managed a smile.

"I'm Miranda St. Germaine, by the way," Miranda told her. "We met at your wedding breakfast, but we didn't have an opportunity to speak."

"I'm sorry."

"Oh, posh!" Miranda waved her apology aside. "You had better things to think of on your wedding day than meeting me. Besides, we have plenty of time to become friends. Alyssa likes you. And if Alyssa likes you, I like you. I was her maid of honor. And she was thrilled that she got to be yours." Miranda made a face. "And although I would have been honored to do it, thanks for not asking me. I've earned a reputation as the ton's perpetual bridesmaid, and I'd just as soon let someone else have the title and the gossip that goes with it."

Gillian laughed.

"Speaking of which . . ." Miranda took a deep breath. "You needn't worry about the ton crucifying your reputation anymore. That's one of the benefits of having Alyssa and Griff as friends. They're the Duke and Duchess of Avon, and no one wants to upset them. And it doesn't hurt to have their parents on your side, either."

"Or you, I suspect," Gillian offered, thoroughly at ease with Miranda.

Miranda shrugged. "That's one of the benefits of being a marchioness in my own right. Nobody knows what to make of me, so they generally leave me alone and let me do what I want." She met Gillian's gaze. "Perhaps this isn't the time or place to mention it, because I'm probably stepping in where I don't belong, but you did receive references when you hired your lady's maid, Lavery, didn't you?"

"Yes," Gillian said, "she came with glowing references from the Lady Exeter, Lady Barfield, and Lady Chemsford."

Miranda frowned. "Are you certain she gave you references from Lady Chemsford?"

"Yes. She came to work for me shortly after she left Lady Chemsford's service. She came highly recommended, and I've had no complaint with her service." Lavery's skills couldn't compare with a certain viscount's, but Lady Miranda didn't need to know about that. "Why?"

"She was dismissed from Lady Chemsford's service for forging her references from her former households—including Lady Barfield's and Lady Exeter's. She was dismissed from both of those households without references." Miranda shrugged her shoulders. "But as long as she's working out well and you're happy with her, that's all that matters. Skilled lady's maids are difficult to come by and even harder to keep. So it's good that Lavery has been given another chance."

"I didn't intend to give her another chance," Gillian answered honestly, "because I didn't know she needed one, but I am a firm believer in granting them." She smiled.

"You're very fortunate to have Lord Grantham," Miranda told her.

"I know."

"And I think he's equally fortunate to have you."

"I'm back," Alyssa announced, making her way into the room before busying herself with her bag of potions. "Your butler is bringing up a pot of strong tea and a tray of cakes to go with this . . ." She waved a bottle at Gillian. "And then we'll fix you right up."

Alyssa was as good as her word. When the tea arrived, she filled a teacup half full of her potion, topped it off with tea, and then handed it to Gillian.

Gillian drank it down, and soon her discomfort vanished.

Alyssa and Miranda spent the afternoon entertaining her, and the master bedroom reverberated with the sound of laughter.

"Will you come back soon?" Gillian asked when Alyssa stood and announced that she had to get home to Griffin.

Alyssa nodded. "We'll be back to check on you tomorrow and to bring you the remedy for the headache you're going to have."

Gillian was puzzled. "How do you know I'm going to have a headache tomorrow?"

"After an afternoon spent imbibing tea laced with mead and Scots whisky." Alyssa laughed. "How could you not?"

Miranda groaned. "We're all going to need the remedy tomorrow."

"How did it go?" Griff asked, as soon as Alyssa and Miranda walked through the door.

"She was indisposed," Alyssa told him. "But we saw her anyway."

Miranda laughed. "That lady's maid didn't stand a chance against the Duchess of Avon."

"Is she all right?"

Alyssa nodded matter-of-factly. "Her monthly arrived with a vengeance."

Miranda blushed bright red. Almost as red as Griffin.

He coughed. "I'm not so sure that Lady Grantham would appreciate your confiding such personal information, my love." He gave her a rueful look. "I'm not certain I want to have such personal knowledge."

"You don't," Alyssa told him. "But Colin will." She looked at her husband. "Especially when he learns he's not going to be a father right away."

Griff nodded. Although Colin had accepted full responsibility when he married her, there was no doubt that this would be welcome news. For now he knew that when he

did become a father, there would be no doubting the pater-
nity. "That *will* be welcome news, given the circumstances."

Alyssa turned to Miranda. "Did you tell her about her
lady's maid?"

Miranda nodded. "I told her that her maid had been dismissed from Lord Chemsford's, Lord Barfield's, and the
Earl of Exeter's households."

Griff froze at the sound of the three peers whose wayward daughters had eloped to Scotland. "What is this about
her maid?" he asked. "Tell me everything."

Miranda related everything she could remember, and
when she finished, Griffin asked, "Do you think the maid
suspected you knew anything?"

"Of course she suspected," Alyssa answered. "She was
a perfect gorgon to Miranda. They recognized each other
on sight."

Griff crossed the drawing room in several long strides
and rang for the butler and the footmen. "Send someone
through the back garden to alert Manners and Shepherdston. Hurry. It's time to put the plan into action."

"What plan?" Alyssa demanded.

"I'll tell you later." Griff grabbed the tall hat and over-
coat his butler handed him, kissed his wife, and hurried out
the door.

Chapter 30

"Saint George, that swing'd the dragon, and e'er since
Sits on his horse back at mine hostess' door."

—WILLIAM SHAKESPEARE, 1564–1616

KING JOHN

*G*illian looked up from the book she was reading as Lavery entered the bedchamber.

"Did you have a pleasant afternoon, madame?" Lavery asked, straightening the bed Gillian had left.

"Yes, I did," Gillian answered. "Very much. Thank you."

"Then you didn't mind receiving visitors after all?"

There was an edge to Lavery's voice that made the hair on the back of Gillian's neck stand on end. "No," she answered cautiously.

"Then you won't mind receiving one more."

"What are you doing here?" Gillian recognized the voice from the past. She pushed out of the wing chair and stood up to face him.

He smiled at Gillian, then began moving closer. "What? No kiss for your long-lost husband? No greeting? No words of love?"

Gillian raised her chin a bit higher. "You are not Colin Fox. And you are not my husband. I may not know your true name, but I know what you are," she told him. "The only thing I have to say to you is get out of my house." She glared at Lavery, who moved to stand by his side. "And if you engineered this reunion by letting him in, you go with him."

"Gillian, Gillian," he taunted. "That's no way to talk to my sister."

"Your *sister?*"

"Joel Lavery, at your service." He gave her a mocking bow. "But my English friends call me Joel Holder." He chuckled. "You, of course, know me as Colin Fox, a name I chose from the myriad payment vouchers that crossed my desk during my brief tenure as a clerk at Scofield's Haberdashery. I thought it apropos as I was, so to speak, a fox in the henhouse." He chuckled once again. "A very rich henhouse. And you were such a pleasant little hen." He shrugged. "I'm afraid my sister doesn't take orders from you. She takes her orders from our beloved Emperor Napoleon and me." He grinned at Gillian, allowing her to see, for the first time, the pistol he held in his hand. "And so, Lady Grantham, do you." He jerked Gillian up against him and shoved the barrel of the pistol against her ribs.

"What do you think you're doing?"

"I'm taking you back to Scotland, where you'll stay until my sister and I receive our ransom." He tried pulling her along behind him, but Gillian lifted her feet off the floor. He dragged her as far as the stairs. "Walk, my lady," he ordered. "Or I'll shoot you where you sit."

"Then shoot me and be done with it," Gillian told him, "because I'm not leaving this house." She had promised Colin she'd be waiting, and that was a promise she intended to keep. "I made the mistake of going to Scotland with you one time, and I refuse to go back."

Holder pulled the hammer on the pistol and prepared to fire.

"No!" his sister shouted. "She's no good to us dead. Think of the money and the ships. We must have the ships."

Holder eased his thumb off the hammer. "Did you take care of the staff?" he asked his sister.

She nodded. "They are all *indisposed.*" She looked at

Gillian as she emphasized the word. "From the medicinal I slipped into the ale at the noon meal."

"And the butler?"

"He met with an iron in the butler's pantry." She smiled. "He won't bother us."

"Can we make our way out the front door?"

She nodded. "The coach is waiting out front."

"Good-bye, Sister," Holder said, "I'll meet you in Scotland. Come, Gillian, let us away." He cuffed Gillian on the side of her head with the pistol and half-dragged, half-carried her out to the waiting coach. He snatched open the door of the coach and shoved her inside.

"Go! Go! Go!" came the shout from within as soon as the door slammed.

The driver obeyed, whipping the horses into a gallop as the coach pulled away from the sidewalk and raced south.

"Gillian, my love, are you all right?" Colin scooped her into his arms and cradled her next to his heart.

Gillian recognized his voice, smelled his sandalwood soap, and knew she was safe. She opened her eyes, saw her husband, and began to cry. "I thought you were gone," she sobbed. "I thought you'd gone back to Scotland or France or wherever it was you had to go."

"I told you I'd be back." He looked down into her shining eyes. "Galahad always returns. And I kept my promise."

"So did I," Gillian told him. "I promised I'd be waiting for you, and I was."

"And I was never more glad to be home with you than in this moment," Colin told her. "I thought I had lost you, Gillian." He hugged her closer. "Dear God, how I love you!"

"And I love you, my Sir Galahad."

⟍

"Wait!" Holder shouted as he watched the coach tear away. "Wait! You left me!"

"Indeed, they did," the Marquess of Shepherdston commented, dryly. "For they have a honeymoon to finish. And three's a crowd on a honeymoon."

Holder turned to find himself surrounded by men brandishing shiny pistols. "Shepherdston."

"At your service."

"And so am I," the Duke of Sussex said, pointing his own weapon at Holder. "Drop the pistol!"

Holder hesitated.

"Drop it or turn it on yourself," the Earl of Barclay declared. "I don't care which. But do it now or die."

Holder dropped his weapon. "My sister—"

"Is already in the Marquess of Courtland's custody." Shepherdston informed him, waving the all-clear signal as Courtland led Lavery out of Herrin House and into the custody of Mr. Wickham, the Bow Street runner.

Joel Holder, escorted by the triumphant members of the Free Fellows League, joined his sister on her journey to the Brixton Gaol.

Epilogue

"This word, 'love,' which graybeards call divine."
—WILLIAM SHAKESPEARE, 1564–1616
KING HENRY THE SIXTH, Part IV

"*Y*our father was right," Colin said as he cradled his wife against his heart. "Herrin House is no Plum Cottage."

"It's wonderful," she said, glancing around the modest cottage. The plum trees were blooming, and the fragrance wafted through the bedroom window. "I can't believe you brought me here," she said, "when you could have driven me around the block and taken me right back home."

"And waste a perfectly good opportunity to kidnap you? And make memories in Plum Cottage?" He chuckled. "Not bloody likely."

"*He* was taking me back to Scotland." Gillian shivered at the memory.

"He wouldn't have gotten very far," Colin told her. "Griff was driving and I was the coachman."

"How did you know who he was or when he would come?" Gillian asked.

"We set a trap and waited to see who would walk into it." He kissed the bump on the side of her head. "We suspected it had to be a clerk in your father's firm, so we alerted Lord Davies and Wickham, the Bow Street runner, and told them of our suspicions. We learned that Holder was one of three clerks recently employed by your father, and that he had clerked at other firms that handled vouchers in the name of Colin Fox—my alias," Colin explained. "Lord Davies pretended to discover the irregularities in the shipping routes and called a meeting of all the clerks with access to the shipping orders and manifests after he signed them. Holder proved quite adept at forging Lord Davies' signature and reassigning the trade routes. Because he'd only been employed by Davies Silk and Linen Importers a short time, he wasn't aware of the significance of the names of the ships. He simply sent the ships with the cargo Bonaparte required to French ports."

"Didn't anyone question the change in the routes?" Gillian asked.

Colin nodded. "Several senior captains and members of the crews. Unfortunately, Holder was in a position to intercept the captains' written inquiries. He replied to their queries with letters informing the captains that the state of war between England and France and the very real fear of spies and piracy dictated immediate changes in trade routes and constant rotation of the crews, and then forged your father's signature to the documents."

"Good heavens!" Gillian blanched. "He could have gained complete control of the shipping line."

"He very nearly did," Colin said. "No one would have suspected a thing if his hubris hadn't gotten the better of him."

"I don't understand." Gillian frowned.

"He loves France and worships Bonaparte, but he craved a way of life he couldn't have. He had been born into a family that had served aristocrats for generations. But Holder didn't want to serve. He wanted power. And he found a way to get it by supporting Bonaparte's rise to power. Bonaparte promised to reward his service and his loyalty once the war was won with an English dukedom and all the lands, money, and power that accompany the title. Unfortunately for Holder, war is expensive and he needed to find another way to help Bonaparte finance it, so he and his sister devised a scheme to marry English money. But his position as a French agent necessitated that he work as a clerk and no gentleman member of the ton would allow a clerk to marry his daughter. He . . ."

"Eloped with foolish young ladies like me with more money than sense . . ."

"Overstepped his bounds when he began courting ladies who should have been beyond his reach. All of his victims were daughters, wards, and widows of newly elevated and minor peers. He targeted ladies at the bottom or on the fringe of society. Ladies who had means, but who would generally be ignored by the ton." Colin managed a smile.

"I can't believe I was so gullible."

Colin brushed her lips in a tender kiss. "Holder was very good at what he did. He offered you romance and adventure and became what you wanted him to be. If you had wanted a scholar, he'd have been an Oxford don. If you had wanted a pirate, he'd have been the captain of a pirate ship. He was a confidence man who fooled a great many people. You made a mistake in trusting him, but he made a far greater one when he tempted fate by using my alias." Colin kissed her again. "You were fated to be mine. Holder was a fool to leave you alone at the Blue Bottle Inn where I could find you. I promise I won't make that mistake. I'll never leave you alone."

"You said there were three clerks," Gillian whispered between kisses. "How did you know which one masqueraded as Colin Fox?"

"Holder was the only clerk with extraordinary blue eyes," Colin told her. "He couldn't hide his eyes and everyone remembered them. Once we began asking the right questions and piecing the puzzle together, it was simply a matter of deduction." Colin squeezed his eyes shut. "The game was up as soon as your father called the meeting. Whoever needed the ships knew he would have to find another way to get them. Since Holder had tried to be rid of me once before, I let it be known that the real Colin Fox was on his trail. There I miscalculated. I thought he'd try to make his escape on one of your father's ships, so I led him away from you and your parents and waited for him at the docks. I knew you were protected, because Griff and I had Bow Street post guards around Herrin House. I was sure he would come after me." Colin tenderly pressed his lips against the bump on Gillian's head once again. "But he went for you and ransom money instead. I'm sorry, my love."

"You didn't know about Lavery," Gillian reminded him.

"No," he agreed. "I didn't know about Lavery."

"I'm certainly glad we didn't raise her salary," Gillian said.

"Me, too," Colin agreed. "And I can promise you there'll be no more French lady's maids in our household. Especially if they have brothers who elope with the daughters of the house, then hold them for ransom or blackmail their fathers."

"It wasn't about me at all," Gillian said. "It was about money."

"It was about helping Napoleon win the war," Colin explained. "Everything they earned from blackmail and kidnapping went to finance French spies."

Gillian shook her head. "I can't believe I was foolish enough to think I was in love with him." She leaned down and kissed her husband, her Galahad. "I didn't know what it was until I met you."

"If you hadn't eloped with him, he would have kidnapped you, my love. The result would have been the same. He needed your father's ships."

"I could have made it a trifle more difficult," she protested.

"And then you might have risked changing fate." Colin kissed her thoroughly. "And you and I were fated to be together."

"For all the good it does you." She gave him a rueful smile. "In my present condition."

Colin laughed. "You'd be surprised how at how inventive and creative I can be."

"The only thing that surprises me about you is how much you love me."

"How could I not," he asked, "when all you've ever done is love me in return? I got your gift, my lady fair." He reached beneath the pillow and pulled out Gillian's cipher.

"And I got yours, my love." She rolled over and propped herself on her elbow so she could look down at him.

Colin quirked an eyebrow at her. "And what was that?"

"A second chance."

Turn the page for a preview of

HARDLY A HUSBAND

The third novel in Rebecca Hagan Lee's
Free Fellows League series

"When a woman wants a man and lusts after him, the lover need not bother to conjure up opportunities, for she will find more in an hour than we men could think of in a century."

—Pierre de Bourdeille, Abbé de Brantôme, c. 1530–1614

LONDON, 1813
Early spring

*J*arrod, fifth *Marquess* of *Shepherdston*, looked up from the stack of deciphered messages he was reading as his butler, Henderson, entered the study of his Park Lane town house.

"I beg pardon for disturbing your work, sir, but you have a visitor."

Jarrod glanced at the clock on the mantel and lifted an eyebrow in query. "Who would be calling at this hour?" It was nearly four o'clock in the morning, and although the hour was still early by the ton's standards, it was much too late to be paying a social call.

"I'm afraid I cannot tell you, sir," Henderson answered.

"Why not?" Jarrod demanded.

Henderson met his employer's disapproving gaze without flinching. "The young female wouldn't give her name."

"What young female?"

"The one dripping water upon the drawing room rug, sir," Henderson replied. "I would not have allowed the forward creature entrance," he explained, "but she insisted you were expecting her. Are we expecting a visitor this evening, sir?"

Jarrod frowned. "No, we are not."

"Shall I send her packing, sir?"

"In this weather?" Jarrod sighed, then raked his fingers through his hair. He collected his ciphers from the surface of the desk and locked them in the top drawer. "No, send her in."

Henderson raised an eyebrow, but he didn't voice his opinion on the unusual turn of events. Unattended females did not pay calls on gentlemen and most certainly did not turn up on unsuspecting gentlemen's doorsteps.

Jarrod walked over to the drinks table, poured himself a glass of whisky, then walked over and stoked the fire.

Henderson opened the study door and announced the visitor. "The female, my lord."

Jarrod pursed his lips, then turned to face his visitor. The figure in the hooded back cape was tall and slim, and from the looks of it, soaked to the skin. "Good evening. Won't you come in and warm yourself by the fire?"

She walked over to the fireplace. Steam rose from the fabric of her cape as she neared it. "Thank you, my lord."

Her voice was soft, deeply provocative, and hauntingly familiar. Jarrod took a sip of his drink, then remembered his manners and frowned. "Would like something to eat? Drink?"

She gave him a mysterious smile. "I'm not a woman of the street," she said. "Yet."

"Pardon me," he said. "But I'm at a disadvantage."

"That's unlikely," she told him, flipping back her hood to reveal her face and her hair. "I've never known you to be at a disadvantage, Jays."

"Sarah," he breathed her name. "What the devil are you

doing here? Alone? At this hour?" Jarrod couldn't stop staring at her. Her plump lips were tinged with blue from the cold, and her long red hair was wet and plastered to her head, but she was as lovely as he remembered.

"You're a hard man to catch, Jays." Sarah Eckersley stared up at him. "I came the only time I thought I might find you at home. Alone." She left the fireplace and moved closer to him. "You are alone, aren't you, Jays?" Sarah reached up, removed the glass of whisky from his hand, and took a sip from the same place his lips had touched.

Jarrod narrowed his gaze at her. "Except for the twenty or so employees in this household and you, I am quite alone."

Sarah took another sip of his whisky, then handed it back to him. "I don't think our presence makes much difference," she said. "I think you're always quite alone."

"Oh?" Jarrod arched an elegant eyebrow. "Have you come all the way from Helford Green to discuss my solitary state of affairs?"

"No." She shook her head. "I've come all the way from Helford Green for lessons."

"Lessons?" He was puzzled. "In what?"

"Seduction."

Jarrod choked on a mouthful of whisky and set the glass aside. "Sarah, be serious," he began as soon as he'd recovered well enough to speak.

"I'm very serious," she told him. "I need to learn the art of seduction, and I came to the most seductive man I know for lessons."

"Lessons for what purpose?" Jarrod didn't know whether to be insulted or flattered. Flattered that Sarah found him seductive or insulted because she thought he would agree to give her lessons on the subject.

"I have no dowry to offer a man," she said. "All I have is my body." Sarah reached up and unfastened her cape, then let it fall to the floor. "I need to learn how to use it."

Jarrod caught his breath. Sarah Eckersley, the rector's

daughter from Helford Green, had come to him wearing nothing more than a white lawn nightgown beneath her cape. And he had never seen anything more lovely. He leaned closer until his lips were only inches away from hers. "Forgive me if I'm reading this the wrong way, but are you here because you're in the market for a husband?"

Sarah tossed her hair over her shoulder, then reached up and put her arms around his neck. "I'm here for lessons, Jays." She focused her gaze on his lips. "You can start by teaching me to kiss."

"I'll kiss you," he said, because he was too damned lily-livered to resist. "But I'm not going to marry you."

"I don't expect you to marry me," Sarah told him.

"Why not?" he asked, slightly affronted.

"Because," she breathed against his lips, "you're a very seductive man, and I have no doubt that you'll be an excellent lover, but you're hardly what one would want in a husband."

Barely a Bride

by
Rebecca Hagan Lee

The noblemen of the Free Fellows League have vowed
to "avoid the inevitable leg-shackling to a female for as
long as possible." But when Viscount Abernathy is
called off to war, he must obey his father's
wishes that he marry—and fast.

Two years later, Abernathy returns from battle scarred
and weary, hoping to love the wife he hardly knows.
Now he must try to win his wife's heart by
wooing the bride he left behind.

0-425-19124-9

**Available wherever books are sold or
to order call 1-800-788-6262**

BERKLEY SENSATION
COMING IN MAY 2004

Kinsman's Oath
by Susan Krinard
In a future world, two telepaths meet and quickly
realize they have nothing in common—except the love
they share for each other.

0-425-19655-0

Fade to Red
by Linda Castillo
When Lindsey Metcalf's sister is kidnapped, she enlists
the help of Michael Striker, a cop who plays by his
own rules. And soon they are both drawn into a
seductive and inescapable trap.

0-425-19657-7

A Lady of Distinction
by Deborah Simmons
Lady Juliet Cavendish is an accomplished Egyptian
scholar, but when Morgan Beauchamp appears, she
finds she'd rather study him.

0-425-19656-9

Charming the Shrew
by Laurin Wittig
A sharp-tongued beauty meets her match in a man
who vows to tame her with the power of his love.

0-425-19527-9